AFTERGLOW

Afterglow

ARIA WYATT

HeartEyes Press

HERE IS MY WISH FOR YOU:

When the winds of change batter your foundation, and clouds
darken your sky, may you find your calm in the storm.
May you feel whole—even when your world is torn in two—and
know that it isn't your fault. Understand it won't be like this
forever.
Grow toward the light that shines in darkness and latch on to the
silver linings. One day you'll find peace in the chaos.
And if your parents find love again, let every blended family
bridge the canyons carved.

This book is dedicated to the children of divorce.
Cheers to your resilience, tenacious spirits, and capacity for love and acceptance.

SOLANA

MOOD MUSIC: "HEAD ABOVE WATER" BY AVRIL LAVIGNE

You *know* you're pissed when you can smell your anger. When your brain short-circuits, sending out flares and smoke signals in a cerebral mayday of sorts. Since right now isn't the time—or place—to lose my shit, I attempt some calming breaths. Sometime between my second and third inhalations, it occurs to me that something's actually burning.

Fantastic.

I drop my phone and make a beeline from the back lawn to my abandoned post in the Busy Bean Café's kitchen.

A wall of heat slams me when I yank the oven door open. Stuffing my hand in a mitt, I snatch the tray of cookies I've burned and plop the sheet on a nearby counter. I shove my spatula beneath one, praying for a small miracle. Yeah, nope. The charred remnants taunt me as I shake my head at the time and ingredients I wasted.

While I was busy arguing with Burlington University's financial aid department, I completely forgot to set the oven timer. I have some experience working as a barista in my former campus's coffee shop, but my baking skills are limited to heating pie in a microwave. Namely, the kind with a timer that beeps every few minutes to remind you when something's done. I have no business operating industrial ovens—or *any* appliances—that aren't equipped with a "Hey, are you still with me?" feature. But at least the smoke detectors didn't go off.

Yet.

I crank the exhaust fan to its highest setting and rub my temples. God, I wish this shitstorm of a day would end.

I knew it would be a rough one when I woke up anxious. That's never a good sign because it sets the tone for my day, no matter how hard I try to redirect. Sleep is supposed to be restorative, but as the anniversary of my parents' deaths approaches, my nights have been anything but. The nightmares are intense. Not only am I exhausted, but I'm tired of washing my sweat-drenched sheets each day. Factor in my recent money snags, and I'm a regular ray of sunshine.

My best friend and coworker, Will Barnes, saunters into the back. He sniffs the air and points to the oven's digital panel. "Hey, Sunny, this numbered gadget here is called a timer."

I roll my eyes. "Thanks, Sherlock."

"Maybe try using it next time?" He gestures to the cookies I ruined. "That's a sacrilege."

"It's not like I *tried* to burn them, okay?" Muttering to myself, I scrape the carcasses into a nearby trash can.

"What's up with you?" Will's warm, chocolatey gaze searches my face. "You were thirty minutes late this morning, when you're always early to everything. You've been off your game all day. Even Zara noticed when she stopped in earlier."

Zara Rossi gave me a job at the Busy Bean after I forfeited a full scholarship to my dream college two weeks before the start of fall semester. When I'd left my hometown to attend school in New York City, I hoped it would be a permanent move, but the Big Apple was a bit too chaotic with everything going on in my head. So here I am, back in Colebury, Vermont, taking online classes and burning cookies like a champ. Hopefully, I'll get my shit together these next few months so I can return to New York in the spring. Sans scholarship, of course.

"I'm having a bad day."

"Well, duh." Will clamps a hand on my wrist, halting my carcass scraping. "You're good. I think you got it all."

"No, there's definitely still some on here." I fixate on a patch of burned dough, rubbing the utensil over the cookie sheet like someone will drown a puppy if I don't remove every crumb.

He snatches my spatula. "Sunny, look at me."

"What?"

He waits until our eyes meet. "You tell me."

"I'm all right." I force a smile. "Slept like shit, that's all. Oh, yeah, and the financial aid office lost my file, so Moo U disenrolled me from my online courses for lack of payment."

His eyes widen. "Shit. That sucks. Did you get it straightened out?"

"Yeah, but now I want to punch something."

He takes a step back. "What *else* is bothering you?"

"I'm fine."

"You sure? I can stand here all day." He points to the kitchen door. "Or at least until the next customer walks in."

Will has been my friend since kindergarten. He's not buying my feigned normalcy act. He never does, so I'm really not sure why I keep trying to fake it. One thing's for damn sure—either I come clean, or he'll make good on his words and bug the hell out of me all day. William Henry Barnes does persistence like no other.

"I'm waiting," he sing-songs with an impatient foot tap.

My chest deflates with the world's heaviest sigh. "Okay, fine. I had a panic attack before work this morning, and I still haven't been able to shake it."

He raises a dark brow. "Another? That's four this week."

"This seems to be my new normal. Anyway, that's why I was late."

"Was it another random one this time, or did something trigger you?"

See, that's the thing about panic attacks. You don't get to decide when they happen. I'm adept at avoiding my triggers, but the attacks which come out of nowhere are the bane of my existence.

I squeeze my eyes shut. "I had to take a detour on my way to work because of a downed tree. The cop redirected me down the section of highway I always avoid. I was fine until I drove past the site of the accident and saw the little wooden cross someone stuck by the side of the road. Then everything just kinda hit me. I had to pull over until it passed."

Change is a surefire way to spike my anxiety. When plans change, like this morning's detour, I lose control of the situation. Losing control freaks me out—almost as much as the unknown and the constant barrage of what-ifs that plague me. It's like I'm always waiting for that other shoe to drop. Or, in this case, a tree.

Just six weeks ahead of the fifteenth anniversary, passing the accident site cut deeper than it would've on a normal day.

Shuddering, I blink back tears and try to force myself back to the present. Unfortunately, despite years of my shrink's best efforts, I've yet to master the techniques of mindfulness.

Will wraps his arms around me. "I'm sorry, Sunny."

"Thanks. You'd think after fifteen years, I could coexist with my memories like a normal human being." I pull from his hug and reach for the spatula he confiscated. "I need to get back to work."

Will holds the utensil behind his back. "No, you need a change of scenery. How about you work the counter and do the barista thing for the rest of the day? I'll take over back here until the muffins are done. Then I'll join you out front, and we'll tag-team it." He hands me a yellow apron with the café's logo embroidered on the front. "Put this on."

"Thanks. I did tell Zara coffee was more my thing. Everyone

knows I'm a shitty baker." I tie the apron strings behind me. "Why would she stick me in the back?"

Zara owns this establishment with her best friend, Audrey Shipley. The Busy Bean is their creative brainchild, and I'm grateful to be employed here. Too bad I've only been on the job two days, and my scattered brain has already cost them in wasted inventory.

"The plan *is* for you to be out front." Will gestures to the kitchen. "This is part of your orientation. Zara and Audrey want everyone well-versed in all aspects of the place. Especially for times like these when Hot Roddy is out sick."

Will has a nickname for everyone and a *huge* crush on Roderick Waites, the Busy Bean's full-time baker. I haven't met him yet, but Will deemed him *sexy as fuck*. We have similar taste in men, so I trust his assessment.

"Does he know you call him Hot Roddy?"

"Fuck no. I have more game than that."

I snort. "*That's* debatable."

He wags his brows. "I mean, while I'd love to take him for a spin—"

"Too bad he's taken." I chuckle and flick his earlobe. "And I'm pretty sure Kieran would kick your ass if you tried to put the moves on his man."

Will gives a wistful sigh. "Kieran can captain my Shipley too."

Roderick's boyfriend, Kieran Shipley, is a former Busy Bean employee who still picks up the occasional shift to help out when the café is short-staffed. He's here today, and we'll likely have him for a few more shifts until Roderick gets over his stomach bug.

My best friend has nicknamed the pair "Kierderick," elevating their swoon status to his upper echelon of gay couple relationship goals.

I poke Will's chest. "How about we get back to business before you start air-humping the appliances. And can we *please* skip the orientation?"

"Nope. Think about it, Sunny. If someone calls out, or shows up late, the rest of us kinda have a clue and can jump in where we're needed." Something beeps, drawing his focus to the other oven. "Oh good, they're done." He withdraws a tray of muffins and places it on a cooling rack.

"I get it, but I'm not in the right headspace for figuring out how to bake."

"I know. That's why I'm telling you to go out front." He glances at the bumblebee clock on the wall. "Hurry up. Our afternoon rush is about to start. I just have to finish up with these muffins. They're supposed to get a lemon glaze drizzled over the top."

I raise a brow at him. "Wow. So, your desire to linger in the kitchen has nothing to do with getting a better view of Kieran?" He flushes and gives me the double middle finger, so I snort. "Yeah, that's what I thought."

Kieran is Audrey's cousin by marriage, so he'll always be part of the Bean's extended family. He's also a stellar artist, which is one of the many reasons Will is enamored with him. Yes, Kieran is gorgeous and has a heart of gold, but the Shipley grump quotient can be a bit high for me.

After growing up under my half-brother's roof, my tolerance for *any* level of surliness is virtually nonexistent. Cody is fifteen years older than me, and we barely speak.

"I know you skipped lunch, but have you eaten *anything* since breakfast?" Will asks, looking me over.

"No, I'm good."

"Tough titties. Gigi stopped by earlier with a delivery of her Dark Horse Mochaccino cupcakes, and you're having one. You clearly need a pick-me-up."

"I'm fine, Will."

"Bullshit. Now, get your ass out front."

Knowing better than to argue with my stubborn bestie, I give him a thumbs-up and head for the front counter.

I should probably familiarize myself with the array of delicious pastries, muffins, cookies, and cupcakes on display in the glass cases. Instead, I stare through a leaded-glass window at the Winooski River. I've always loved walking along the section of riverbank by the old mill. The expanse of neatly mown grass with clumps of planted flowers is the perfect place for a picnic. Maybe I'll head down by the river during my break for some running water-induced Zen. I could use a little of that today.

My head jerks toward the parking lot when a silver truck squeals to a halt in front of the door. Despite the windshield's glare, I can tell the driver is on his phone, flailing his arms and slapping the steering wheel.

Will appears at my side, distracting me with a decadent chocolate creation. "This is the Busy Bean's signature cupcake. Wait until you taste it." He grins and sets the plate in front of me, waving his hand with a flourish. "Trust me, it's fucking life-changing."

"Oh yeah?" Will shares my enthusiasm for all things chocolate, so—like with his views on men—I trust his opinion.

"Not only is it infused with espresso, but the mocha frosting is to die for. See that gem on top?" He points. "Chocolate-covered espresso bean."

I stuff a huge chunk in my mouth and moan as the flavor coats my tongue. "Wow."

"Told you."

The door opens, and a few customers file in. We get to work filling their orders, moving around one another like we've worked together for years instead of days. Every so often, I wrap a napkin around my cupcake and sneak a bite because I can't help myself.

Will brushes past me, shaking his head as he peeks outside. "Ugh. That dude's a moody fuck," he mutters under his breath. "Maybe we'll get lucky, and he won't come inside. What a waste."

I turn my attention back to the pickup that has been idling for close to ten minutes now. "Why? Is he hot?"

He fans himself with a stack of napkins. "Wait until you hear his Irish brogue. Did I mention he's a lumberjack?"

I flush and grip the zinc countertop. "A hot Irish lumberjack? Sign me up."

"Well, maybe not a lumberjack exactly, but he works with wood."

"When you say, 'works with wood,' do you mean how *you* work with wood, or do you mean like a legit carpenter?"

Will barks a laugh. "He builds shit, Sunny. With wood and tools. *Jesus.* Not everything I say has a sexual connotation."

"Yeah, okay." I jut my chin toward the window. "So, who is he? Someone we know from high school?"

"Nope. He's in his thirties." He pours himself a cup of coffee. "His name is Declan something. Even though he's a regular, I really don't know much about him. Mr. O'Sexy McFuck hasn't said two words to me."

"I don't know of any Irishmen in Colebury." Since my dad taught in the Colebury school district, and Cody and I went to school here, I know most of the guys in town. Some of them *far* better than I'd like to. Shuddering, I steal a sip of coffee from Will's cup. "Declan, huh? How long has he been in the area?"

"Dunno. Like I said, he doesn't talk to me, so I haven't quizzed him for his demographics."

I smile at the next batch of customers entering the café and watch the pickup for a moment. The driver is *still* yelling on his phone. "Well, somebody needs to tell Lumberjack Declan to stop driving like a dick and polluting the pristine Vermont air. Who knows? Maybe it'll be me."

Will snorts. "Good luck. He'll bite your head off."

"C'mon, Big Willy Barnes, you know me better than that." I elbow him in the ribs. "I bite first."

DECLAN

MOOD MUSING: DON'T ASK

My ex-wife has the blood of the Devil running through her veins. I clench my phone tighter, fighting off the urge to run it over with my truck. "For fuck's sake, you can't keep doin' this to me, Darcy. I rearranged all my jobs so I could see him today."

"Your schedule isn't my problem."

"My *schedule* keeps the child support flowin' in your direction, so a little courtesy would be grand."

"Liam doesn't want to see you."

"That's a crock of shite. Put him on the phone."

"He had a long day at school, so he's . . . napping."

I grit my teeth. "Funny, I just heard him runnin' through the house."

She sighs. "Oh, well . . . maybe he's up now."

"If he doesn't wanna see his dad, let *him* tell me."

The evil witch has nothing to say to that because she knows damn well my boy loves our visits. He tells me how much he looks forward to *Liam and Daddy time* on Mondays, Wednesdays, and Sundays—the measly twelve hours a week we get to spend together. We have our routine, and I enjoy it as much as he does.

Our first stop is always the Busy Bean Café for chocolate milk and a jam doughnut. Then, weather permitting, we do some type of outdoor activity. My four-year-old's energy level never ceases to amaze me. After he wears himself out, I make him a quick meal, and we spend the rest of our time in my woodworking shop. Liam loves to use sandpaper on the pieces of scrap wood I save for him.

Today is Thursday. Darcy asked me to reschedule yesterday's visitation for today. I desperately want to see my son, so I made it happen. Then she has the nerve to cancel on me ten minutes before she's supposed to drop him off?

"Put Liam on the phone," I growl, seconds away from losing it.

Darcy hangs up.

"Son of a bitch." I heave my phone out the window and knock my forehead on the steering wheel a few times.

Moira, my Irish wolfhound, whines and licks my face, her tail thumping on the passenger seat. I ruffle her fur. "She won't let me see him again, girlie. It's fuckin' killin' me."

She sniffs my neck, tickling my ear, then rests her paw on my thigh. The small gesture comforts me, serving as a good reminder that Moira's the only female I need in my life. I turn to face her, dodging a lick to my nose. "I know, you're waitin' for your croissant."

And there goes the tail again.

Much to my veterinarian's dismay, I have a bad habit of giving Moira people food, but it's hard to resist those soulful puppy eyes. *What Dr. Penley Brooks doesn't know won't hurt him.* Right? Then again, my friend has the uncanny ability to read me, so I'm sure he'll figure out I'm still spoiling my dog. Of course, Zara once let it slip that Pen buys muffins for his lab mix, Doggy, so he's really one to talk about canine overindulgence. *Do as I say and not as I do.*

Moira whines as if she can sense my guilt. One of these days,

I'll stop buying her pastries. Today is not that day. I climb from my truck with a sigh. "Gimme a minute, girlie."

Stooping to retrieve my phone, I scowl at the cracked screen. I really need to get ahold of my temper, but Darcy pushes me to my limits. It's not enough that she got the house and everything in it. I pay a hell of a lot of money to not see my boy more often. Yeah, it's my fault, but that doesn't make it any easier.

I yank open the bakery's front door and march inside. The Busy Bean is part of my daily routine and serves as a convenient midpoint between my cabin in the woods and the farmhouse a few towns over where Darcy resides with her second husband. I live for our thrice-weekly car park child exchange.

I arrived during the afternoon rush, so I make my way to the end of the line weaving through the café. While I wait, I take in the décor—familiar yet surprising. The Busy Bean is truly a mecca of artistry and quirky details, and there's always something new to discover.

As a woodworker, I love the eclectic medley of mismatched antique furniture. The upholstery itself is a testament to Audrey and Zara's vivid personalities. I've noticed how the regulars always gravitate toward the same seating, Liam and myself included.

When we aren't seated at the counter, Liam likes the oak bench with zebra-print cushions. Meanwhile, I'm drawn to the chair I refinished for them a few months ago—a cushy giraffe-print armchair with ornate carvings on the maple legs.

I admire the finish on the wide pine floorboards and wooden beams painted black to look like chalkboards. Zara likes to decorate them with various cartoons and snarky sayings. I spot the Irish blessing she scrawled in white chalk for my benefit, pleased to see it's still there. "May you be in heaven half an hour before the Devil knows you're dead." Last week, she made me tell her a bunch of blessings and limericks until she found a saying she liked. She's a witty one, that Zara. She picked that particular blessing because she loved the idea of telling Satan to fuck off. I'd have to agree.

As an outsider in a small town in Vermont, it's easy to feel isolated, but Zara, Audrey, and their families have always welcomed me. Even Roderick and I have become friendly.

The Busy Bean reminds me of my father's pub in Galway, where I had my first drink and started my love affair with Irish whiskey. I've traded booze for hot cider, but I crave the inviting pub vibe of this bakery. There are plenty of bars in town—like the place right across the car park—but I don't dare set foot in one. This is the closest I'll allow myself.

"Hi, what can I get started for you?"

I spin toward the lilting female voice and frown. I come here just about every day and I've never seen this woman. She's a pretty little thing who comes up to my shoulder. A black T-shirt peeks from beneath the bright yellow apron that covers her breasts. She's cinched the tie around her waist, showcasing her hourglass figure.

"Hello?" She props both hands on her hips. "Would you like to order something?"

My gaze snaps to her face and locks on to a set of eyes the exact shade of golden amber as whiskey. With tanned skin, and thick, honey-blonde hair, I'd swear I walked into a distillery. My throat tightens, and the hairs on the back of my neck stand on end as I try to find the words to answer.

Her mouth starts to move again, drawing my focus to her lips. Full and pink, like a wild Irish rose. "I brewed a fresh pot of coffee and the drink of the day is a dirty apple chai." She licks those plush lips and adds, "With apples from the Shipley orchards, of course."

My stomach twists into a knot as I glance at the section of countertop that looks like a bar. I'd give my left arm for a pint of Guinness. And I'd give both arms for some whiskey. Desperate to derail that train of thought, I force my gaze to the display of artisanal honey from some of the local apiaries. Funny how the warm amber color also reminds me of whiskey, making my mouth water.

Then again, maybe it's blondie who's got me salivating. Whiskey be damned, I'd sell my soul to the Devil for a taste of her.

She clears her throat and waits to speak until my gaze flicks back to her face. "Shall we try this again?" She raises a brow, her lips tipping into a smirk. "How. Can. I. Help. You?"

Kieran Shipley, Roderick's partner who fills in on rare occasions, strides out front with a tray full of muffins and sets them on the counter. He jerks his chin at the new girl. "Put these in the case." She nods and follows suit as Kieran turns to me with a smirk. "Here for the croissant Moira shouldn't be having?"

"Roderick tell you about that?" I rub my jaw. "Or did Penley pop in here to tell you to cut me off?"

He chuckles. "Nah, it was Roddy. Believe it or not, he's working on a recipe for Moira- friendly pretzels."

"I'll be his best customer." I clear my throat. "How're you gettin' on, Kieran?"

He pulls a croissant from the display and places it in a paper bag. "Keeping busy. You?"

"Nothin' ever changes, bud. How much do I owe you?"

He smiles and holds out the bag. "This one's on me. Give Moira my love."

"Will do. Thanks." I peek at blondie, who's currently giving me the side-eye.

Christ, those eyes . . .

I've never seen anything like them. Despite the furrow of her brow, everything about this girl oozes warmth and honey. Sunshine and whiskey. I haven't so much as looked at a woman since Darcy fucked me over, but I can't seem to tear my gaze off this one.

SOLANA

MOOD MUSIC: "I'LL BE THERE FOR YOU" BY THE REMBRANDTS

What the actual fuck just happened?

That was easily the most bizarre encounter I've ever had with a man. I stare after the retreating truck, running my hands up and down my goose-bumped arms.

Kieran chuckles from beside me. "I see you've met Declan."

"Uh, if by *meeting* Declan, you mean, he eye-fucked me while buying a pastry for some woman, then yeah."

He shakes his head. "Moira's not—"

"Kieran, you have a phone call," Will announces from the back room. "It's Roddy," he adds with a grin.

Smiling, Kieran retrieves the empty muffin tray and heads to the back without another word.

I guess the Declan conversation's over.

As if reading my mind, chatterbox Will makes his way behind the counter to prove me wrong. "Declan's hot, right?"

Hot? The man's face was nothing short of breathtaking. And his eyes . . . storm cloud gray. I swear, I heard thunder rumble in the distance. Or maybe it was my heartbeat? Doesn't matter. No one's ever looked at me that way—like he wanted to drape me over the counter and feast on me.

Declan was a picture of rugged, lumbersexual hotness. I ache to tangle my hands in his dark auburn hair, brush back the pieces falling over his forehead. His resonant Irish brogue sizzled along my nerve endings like lightning. Factor in his sexy, scruff-covered jawline—in that place beyond stubble, but not quite beard—and a height of well over six feet, and I was rendered to a pool of lust. Celtic knotwork tattoos peeked from beneath a plain white T-shirt that conformed to his muscles, and *damn* . . .

"Understatement of the year." I chug some cool water to calm my senses, wishing I had spare panties to change into. "But Declan O'Sexy McFuck has a roving eye. He's probably a cheater."

I have zero tolerance for cheating. Back in May, I broke up with my boyfriend for that very reason. Turns out, Chris was tired of waiting for me to give it up, so he screwed one of my roommates instead. Nothing like coming home from a Calculus final to discover the scene. There I was, relieved to be done with solving differential equations, while Chris differentiated Jessica's legs apart.

Will cocks his head to the side. "What do you mean?"

"Never mind." I turn my attention to the espresso machine. I force a swallow and blink back tears. *Let it go.*

"I hate when you say that." He searches my face. "You're thinking about Chris again, aren't you?"

"No." I stare at my feet. In truth, Chris did me a favor. At least I found out what kind of person he was before I lost my virginity. "Okay, maybe a little."

Will sighs. "Sunny, you need to forget about his dumb ass."

"I know. It just hurts sometimes."

He squeezes my shoulder. "I have some news that'll cheer you up."

"I'm listening."

"Riv's coming home this weekend for a visit."

River Washington is the intelligent friend who rounds out our trio of smart, funny, and sweet. Will is the funnyman, and I'm the sweet one. Supposedly.

She's a few years older than us, but her mom ran the youth chorus program Will and I joined in second grade. We met River during one of our many rehearsals and hit it off immediately. Nowadays, we look forward to reunions with our favorite busy med student who seldom comes home from Boston on weekends.

"But the semester just started."

His lips curve into a sheepish smirk. "She wants to make sure you're all right."

River is the quintessential mother hen who wants to become a psychiatrist like her dad. I'm her favorite pet project.

"William Henry Barnes, did you tell River I've been having more panic attacks?"

He prances back toward the kitchen. "I think I hear the oven timer beeping."

"Answer me, William."

"Don't wanna burn the cookies again," he says over his shoulder. "Too much sacrilege for a Thursday."

DECLAN

MOOD MUSINGS: IF SHERLOCK CAN DO IT...

"So, who is she?" I clutch the phone, interrogating my best friend and business partner, Ethan Wilde.

"Dunno, dude. Alec never mentioned a new girl starting at Zara's place. And like I told you, I haven't seen her yet."

Ethan bartends at the Gin Mill on weekends, saving up the extra cash he earns for our joint business venture, the development of an eco-friendly tiny house resort. Aside from the inheritance I've stashed, all my extra money is diverted into Darcy's account. I have no problem paying child support, but it would be nice to see my boy more often.

"Damn." I lean against the workbench in our shop in defeat. "I hoped you'd know her."

"Do you want me to ask Zara's brothers? Or I can grab some coffee on my break to see if I recognize her?"

"Nah, don't. Last thing I need's people wonderin' why I'm askin' questions. I'll figure it out on my own," I mutter, digging my boot into a pile of sawdust.

"How was your visit with Liam?"

I clench my jaw. "Darcy fuckin' canceled."

"Again?"

"Yep. She called just as I pulled into the lot at the Busy Bean. Said Liam didn't wanna see me."

"That's bullshit. You can't let her get away with that."

"I know."

"I mean it, Dec. It's happened one too many times."

"What choice do I have?"

Moira makes her way over and leans against my legs. I pat the top of her head and rub her velvety ears between my fingertips.

"Take her ass to court."

I squeeze my eyes shut. "And lose my visitation rights permanently?"

"Don't jump to the worst-case scenario. Look at Penley Brooks —he got joint custody of his kid. Happy endings happen, man. You just need to put in the work."

"Pen and I have entirely different circumstances. He has an amicable relationship with his ex and he never lost custody to begin with."

"Right, but what I'm saying is, you could have that kind of co-parenting situation."

I snort. "Are we talking about the same Darcy?"

"Stop giving her power—she's not the governor of Vermont."

"Don't underestimate her, Eth. She's a paralegal, for fuck's sake. She knows every judge in the county and then some. After what happened, I'm lucky to get what I have."

"Look, you fucked up. But you're getting help. Anyone who knows you, can see how hard you're trying. Besides, you're a damn good father. Even Darcy knows that."

"Funny. None of that matters since she married that other dick."

"It could be worse. At least she's not shacking up with some asshole who beats them. I've seen Bridges around Liam and it's obvious he cares for the little guy."

"Don't you see it, Eth? She's tryin' to replace me."

"Dec, stop. Even if Liam *does* like his stepfather, that doesn't mean he'll stop loving you. You're his dad—he idolizes you, bro."

"What happens when he realizes I'm not worth idolizing?"

"Not gonna happen. You know better than to make the same mistake twice."

I stare at the Celtic phoenix tattoo I had done when I finished detox in Montpelier. It's on the inside of my left wrist so I can never reach for a whiskey bottle—or a flask—without being reminded I'd gone down in flames. And just like a phoenix, I rose from the ashes a better man. Yet every time Darcy keeps Liam from me, it's like she's hanging me on a cross to die.

I rub my palms, massaging away the ache from the imaginary nails. "Then how come she's still crucifyin' me for the one I made?"

"Wish I had an answer for you, Dec." Ethan's phone beeps while he speaks. "Shit, I gotta go. My mom's calling back with measurements for a shed she wants built. Later." He hangs up.

Sliding the phone in my pocket, I turn to Moira. "Wanna go for a ride?"

Her tail thumps on the floor of my shop, sending a cloud of sawdust airborne.

After a quick sweep and change of clothes, Moira and I pile into my truck. "Where to?" I ask like she's really going to answer. I'm sure the amount of time I spend talking to my dog makes me a fool, but aside from Ethan, she's the only one who keeps me company most days. "I'm thinkin' we should pop by the market for food. That work for you?" Moira barks her reply. "Good. I'm hungry too."

Twenty minutes later, I ease into a parking spot beside a beat-up, yellow Ford Mustang. "Sit tight, girlie. I'll be out in a minute." I roll down Moira's window. She whines and licks her chops, tail thumping like always.

I shake my head at the junker beside me with the underin-flated tires. Don't people take care of their vehicles around here? My gaze lands on a sun decal in the back window.

Where have I seen this car before?

SOLANA

MOOD MUSIC: "DRUMMING SONG" BY FLORENCE + THE MACHINE

The cashier eyes my groceries with amusement but doesn't say anything. Toaster pastries, sugary cereal, and a pint of Ben & Jerry's Karamel Sutra Core ice cream are just what the doctor ordered for tonight's episode of eat my feelings. While my selection is far from nutritious, after a day like today, I don't give two shits what Edna, the judgmental cashier, thinks.

I hand over a twenty and watch her try to figure out how much change to give me. "Eight dollars and seventy-two cents," I say, before she can even finish typing the numbers.

"Excuse me?"

"That's how much change I get back."

She widens her eyes. "You did the math in your head?"

"Always do." I tap my temples. "I'm a numbers girl."

"You should go to school for math."

"I am." I pocket my change and smile. "Have a nice night."

"You too, hon."

I head outside, plopping the groceries on my passenger seat. An enormous gray dog barks from behind the wheel of the truck parked beside me. I peer at its scruffy face and smile. "Hello to you too. Hopefully, your owner is hooking you up with some tasty treats."

Something over my shoulder catches the dog's attention. It thumps its tail and prances like a show horse. I spin around and lock eyes with the man I haven't stopped thinking about all day.

Declan.

Had I not been distracted by his dog, maybe I would've recognized the silver truck. Then, I would've hightailed it out of here before he came outside. But nope, Clueless Solana strikes again.

He holds up a bag. "Got enough treats for six o' her." The dog barks and whines as she jumps up and down, bonking her head on the ceiling. "Jaysus, Mary, and Joseph, Moira. Settle down before you knock yourself arseways."

Moira's not his wife. I glance at his left hand. No ring. Maybe he isn't married. I don't know the guy, and he seems like a bit of a dick, so I'm not entirely sure why that relieves me.

His stormy gaze finds mine once more. "Hello again. Twice in a day. What're the odds?"

"Technically we never exchanged hellos the first time."

He stares at me with the same intensity as in the café earlier, but deeper and more primal. If eye-fuckery was an Olympic sport, this dude would win the gold. My heart picks up speed when he holds out his hand. "Let's change that, shall we? I'm Declan."

I reach for him on instinct, and his warm palm engulfs mine. "I'm Solana, but everyone calls me Sunny or Sunny-D because my last name's Delgado."

"Solana is a beautiful name."

And it sounds divine coming from you.

I focus on his pillowy lips, wondering how they'd feel pressed to mine. Or all over my naked body.

"It's Spanish for sunshine. My mom picked the name since she was from Spain," I blurt, forcing myself to breathe. "And thanks."

"Nice to *technically* meet you," he murmurs, still holding on to my hand. The strength in his grip sends a flare of heat to my lower belly.

I peer up at his face. "Likewise."

"Although most people aren't concerned with technicalities when it comes to me."

"Well, *I'm* not like most people, Declan."

"Good to know." His eyes darken to smoldering charcoal, and he strokes his thumb over my knuckles.

Everything inside me catches fire.

It always amazes me how much you can learn in a moment. From a single glance, to a few words and a lingering touch, I know all there is to know about this man. What I don't know is *why* he has this effect on me. One thing's for damn sure, though. It's only a matter of time before my virginity packs her bags and I land in his bed.

Moira barks, and he releases my hand. "Your tires need air."

I glance down at them. "Thanks, I just got this piece of crap last week."

"They didn't fill 'em when you bought it?"

"Apparently not," I mutter, embarrassed by the shit box I picked up in Montpelier. I needed a cheap ride—looks like I got my wish.

"It's dangerous drivin' around like that. In all honesty, you could use a whole new set of tires."

"Why? They said these ones are good for sixty-thousand miles."

Declan leans down and touches my back tire, placing his thumbnail in one of the grooves. "See this? You don't have shit for tread, which is even more dangerous than not inflatin' them."

"Guess I'm one big accident waiting to happen." My stomach bottoms out as painful memories surface, but I shove them back down.

Some unnamed emotion flashes across his face. He clears his throat. "Just get 'em looked at, will you?"

"Okay."

Moira whines, so he pats her head. "You gonna let me in,

girlie?" She does a circle on the seat, her tail hitting his face. "I guess that's my answer."

I laugh. "You're taking too long with her treats."

"Nah, she's always like this." He pushes Moira to the side so he can sit, then closes his door. "Very excitable."

Like me.

"Well, I won't keep you any longer." I tuck a strand of hair behind my ear. "It was nice to meet you, Declan. I'm sure I'll see you around."

He sweeps his gaze over my body, making me flush. "You will." My nipples tighten at the dark promise in his tone. "Good night, Solana."

He watches as I make my way around the Mustang and plop into the driver's seat. I shove my key in the ignition with shaking hands. Except, when I turn it, nothing happens.

I bang on the dashboard a few times and try again. Nothing. Not even a click.

"Fuck."

Declan hops out of his truck, addressing me through my open passenger window. "You all right?"

"It won't start."

"What happens when you turn the key?" He walks around the front, stopping outside my door.

"Absolutely nothing."

"It's probably your battery. Pop the hood so I can look." I reach down and pull the lever. He lifts the hood and peers beneath it, shaking his head. "I can try to give you a jump start, but the battery's completely corroded. Acid's spillin' all over the place." He peers through the windshield at me. "Lemme guess, nobody checked that for you?"

"Nope." No one ever checks anything for me. Then again, I never ask for anyone's assistance. I refuse to play the helpless maiden part—or be a burden—and I'll walk before I ask Cody for anything. Too bad my vehicle didn't get the memo. "I only bought this car because it's yellow."

Declan raises a brow. "You didn't look at the engine *at all*?"

"Listen, engines aren't really my thing. All I know is it's a 1976 Mustang." I rub a hand over my face. "Outside of driving, my car skills are limited to refilling my gas tank and the wiper fluid reservoir."

He closes the hood and walks over to me, resting a hand on my roof. "Marker Motors is probably still open. I'll drive you over there to buy a new battery."

"I shouldn't go places with strangers."

He gives me a squinty glare. "We're not strangers anymore, Solana. And I'm not leavin' you alone in the dark with a disabled vehicle. So, either we go get a battery or I'll drive you home. Your choice."

I could wind up in a ditch somewhere, but my instincts tell me that won't happen. I glance at the security cameras outside the grocery store. Besides, if he *does* kidnap me, the cops will find my car here and have plenty of video footage to use. Declan's a regular at the Busy Bean, so Will could identify him. Since he's nice to dogs and his concern for me seems genuine, I decide to go for it.

I grab my purse and climb from the vehicle after closing the windows. "Battery, it is." Chewing my lip, I look up at his face. "Are you sure you don't mind?"

"Wouldn't offer if I minded." He points to his truck, so I follow him around the front. "You good with a tongue bath?"

Wait, what? I stop short and blink a few times. "Excuse me?"

"Jaysus." He claps a hand to his forehead. "Moira. She'll probably lick you to death." His cheeks and neck flush deep crimson as I burst out laughing. He pinches the bridge of his nose. "Sorry. Didn't realize how that sounded 'til it came out."

"It's fine." I pat his arm and giggle. "After a day like today, I needed a laugh."

He opens his passenger door for me. Before I can climb in, he stops me with a hand on my shoulder. "Didn't mean to make you uncomfortable."

"You didn't." I settle and fasten my seatbelt.

I'll gladly take him up on any offers that involve his tongue. I flush at the thought and press my knees together.

His stormy gaze burns into me. "I'm a gentleman, Solana."

"Yeah, I picked up on that with your whole safe vehicle speech and the fact that you aren't leaving me in the dark." Although, I'd be hard-pressed to find another *gentleman* who looks at me the way he does. I can't explain it, but his attention makes me feel like a goddess.

"So, you *were* listenin'? Most people tune me out when I get on my soapbox."

"I already told you . . . I'm not like most people."

Declan stares at me, the truck's interior light casting an eerie glow on his face. His eyes dart to my lips and linger, so I give them a slow, deliberate lick. His gaze snaps back to mine, paralyzing me with its intensity.

"Solana, you . . ."

"Yes?" It comes out breathless, but *damn*, I love how he says my name.

His throat moves on a swallow. Instead of answering, he closes his eyes. Then the door.

Declan makes his way around the front and slides into the driver's seat. He starts his truck, flipping the radio on. "She crowdin' you?"

"Who? This tiny pup?" I scratch Moira's head. "What's the deal? Your parents wouldn't let you have a horse?"

"You'd be right. I grew up in the city."

"What city?"

"Galway."

"Where's that?"

"Western coast of Ireland." He starts the truck.

"What's it like there?"

He eases from the parking lot, making a left onto the main road. "The city's lively. Pubs and restaurants everywhere. The rest of it's very green. Like Vermont."

"Do you have a lot of forests there too?"

"Some, but not like these ones. Ireland has a lotta farm country. Picture miles and miles of fields separated by rock walls and dotted with sheep."

"How'd you end up here?"

"Long story."

I point to my watch. "I've got time."

"My best mate's from Colebury. We both attended uni in Dublin. He invited me to come here for a visit one year, and I never went back."

"What did you study?"

"Architecture."

My brows shoot upward. "Wow, that's awesome. Is that what you do for a living?"

"Yes and no."

"Thanks for that incredibly ambiguous answer."

He searches my face for a moment before speaking. "Got a woodworkin' business with my best bud, Ethan. We also do some tree removal, mainly so we can use the wood in our shop. We build furniture to sell and do repairs and refinishing." He flicks on his turn signal. "But our newest venture involves the design and construction of tiny houses."

"Why tiny houses? Do you live in one?"

"No, I have a cabin in the woods." He points to Moira. "Besides, she'd need one of her own."

"So, why tiny houses?" I repeat, noticing how he skirted my question the first time.

He raises a brow. "You ask a lotta questions, Solana."

"We Vermonters call it conversation. You should try it sometime."

6

DECLAN

MOOD MUSINGS: TALK ABOUT A HEAD-SCRATCHER.

I don't know what to make of this woman. She's an intriguing cocktail of naivety and wisdom. Innocence and seduction. A sweet indulgence I'd sell my soul to sample.

I've never felt an attraction like this. It's almost impossible to breathe, cramped in the cab of my truck with her. What the hell has gotten into me? Ethan is the player who sleeps with a different chick each night. I haven't touched a woman in four years. Not since Darcy. Nor do I intend to. But damn, I want to do more than touch Solana Delgado. What I wouldn't give to strip her naked and fuck her on my workbench. We'd have wood chips and sawdust in our hair, but she'd be too busy screaming my name to worry about it.

My cock hardens with the thought, pressing against the material of my jeans. I clench the steering wheel. No, I can't sleep with her. She doesn't need to deal with my baggage. No one does. Besides, I can hardly *speak* to the woman, let alone have the wherewithal to fuck her.

And she's right. Conversation *is* a two-way street, and I haven't initiated a damn word. Then again, it's also been years since I've talked to a woman, so it stands to reason I wouldn't know where to start.

"Why haven't I seen you before today?" It's the best I can come up with.

She smiles. "I grew up around here, but I just moved back from New York City last month. I started at the Busy Bean on Tuesday."

"What were you doin' in New York?" This one comes out more like an accusation, which wasn't my intent.

"College." She chews that plush bottom lip again and stares out the window. "But I still have two more years. I'm taking online courses this semester."

"For graduate school?"

"No, my bachelor's in math. Primarily accounting and financial analyst stuff. Most people probably find accounting boring, but that's my jam. I love the practicality of it."

She seems too mature to be working on an undergraduate degree. I would've sworn she was at the post-doctorate level.

I must be making a face because she cocks her head to the side and gives me the squinty eye. "What?"

"Nothin'. Just thought you were older."

"I'm only twenty-one. I mean, I'll be twenty-two next month, but people always assume I'm older." She raises a brow. "How old are *you*, Mr. Declan?"

"Thirty-four." I gather my wits. "You seem mature for twenty-one."

Solana strokes Moira's head and gives a wistful sigh. "I guess I was forced to grow up faster than most."

"And why's that?" I'm asking questions now. Conversation stuff. This is good.

She stares out the window. "My parents died when I was seven. My older brother raised me and he's not the coddling type."

"I'm sorry." I reach for her hand but quickly pull back. I'm afraid if I *start* touching this woman, I'll never stop, and that's a rabbit hole I can't afford to go down. "That must've been hard for you."

"Yeah, I really miss them. What about you? What are your parents like?"

"My dad owns a pub called Kings of Connacht in Galway. He's your typical rowdy Irishman. I never knew my ma because she surrendered me at birth."

Why am I telling her all this? I never talk about my ma—I barely mentioned her to Darcy and I was married to the woman for fuck's sake. What is it about this chick that has me spilling my guts? Why is she so goddamn easy to talk to?

"What do you mean, 'surrendered' you?"

"Story for another time, Solana."

"Do you see your dad often?"

I shake my head. "Haven't seen him in almost six years."

"You sound like that makes you really sad."

"It does." I meet her gaze. "But I've got reasons for keepin' my distance."

I clamp my jaw shut before I tell her my life's story. She doesn't need to know how broken I am. How I'd give anything to run back to Ireland and drown my pain with a bottle of whiskey. How Eamon O'Shaughnessy has never met his grandson because Darcy thinks my dad is the reason I started drinking. She's wrong, but it doesn't matter.

We pull up outside Marker Motors and I turn off my truck. "You wanna come inside?" I glance at Moira draped across her lap. "Or keep this one company?"

"I'd hate to move her. Besides, I don't know anything about car parts." She reaches in her purse and pulls out a twenty. "Here's money for my battery."

"Be right back." I stuff the cash in my pocket with a chuckle. I don't have the heart to tell her a decent battery costs close to a hundred dollars.

Moira rolls belly-up and nuzzles into Solana's lap. For the first time in the four years I've had her, she seems unfazed that I'm leaving her behind. "Don't miss me too much, girlie."

Solana giggles. "Don't worry, she won't."

I head inside and greet Colin Murphy, one of the guys who works the counter when Mr. Marker isn't around. "Colin, how're you gettin' on?"

"Doing great, Declan. How can I help you?"

"I need a battery for a 1976 Ford Mustang."

His eyes widen. "When did you get one of those?"

"Belongs to a friend."

He nods and pulls up some listings on his computer. "Lemme check in the back." He disappears through a door.

I scroll through pictures of Liam on my phone, smiling at his chubby cheeks. God, I miss that boy. He's a happy-go-lucky kid, full of energy and always giggling. His little smile lights up even my darkest days.

He'd love Solana's sunny spirit.

The thought comes out of nowhere, and I nearly drop my phone. No *way* am I going there. Darcy would lose her mind if I ever brought a woman around our son. Besides, not only do I have more baggage than the Dublin Airport, but Solana is too young. I force the idea from my brain.

However, regardless of Darcy's—or anyone else's—hypothetical lack of approval, I'm not about to let a young woman be stranded in a car park at night.

Colin reenters the room with a grimace. "I've got bad news and good news."

"Gimme the bad first."

"The bad news is I don't have the battery in stock. But the good news is I can order one and have it here tomorrow."

"Let's do it."

"Midgrade or premium?"

"Get me the best battery they make." I frown. *Why'd I say that?* Solana doesn't need a premium battery.

"It'll cost you around one hundred and thirty bucks." Colin looks up at me. "That cool?"

I hand over my credit card. "As long as it's here tomorrow, I don't care about the cost. Also, can you please give me a quote for all-season tires?"

Hopefully, I can talk Solana into getting new ones. I shouldn't care about her tread depth, but I do. It's not that she's special—everyone should have safe tires.

"For the same vehicle?" Colin asks.

"Yep. Preferably ones with a good warranty."

"Sure, what size?"

"Damn, I forgot to look. I'll have to get back to you."

"That's fine." He hands over a business card. "Email me, or call the shop, and I'll take care of it tomorrow." He tears off the receipt and gives it to me. "I'll call you when the battery's here."

"Sounds good." I wave and head outside, frowning at the heavy bass beat that reaches my ears. Solana's cranked the music in my truck.

I climb into the driver's seat. "A deaf guard dog's no use to me, you know."

"Sorry. I couldn't help myself." She quickly turns it down. "Who sings this? His voice is *amazing*."

"Dermot Kennedy. He's from Dublin."

"What's this song called?" She cranks the volume once more and closes her eyes, savoring Kennedy's throaty, soulful rasp.

"Power Over Me."

The hairs on the back of my neck rise. Kennedy's lyrics describe the Solana Delgado effect better than if I'd written them myself.

I've only known her a matter of hours, but she steals my breath with no effort at all. Swaying in her seat as she hums, her long, honey-blonde hair cascading over her shoulders, she's warmer than sunshine and more tempting than whiskey. I haven't even noticed a woman in four years, but right now, she's all I see.

I grip my steering wheel to keep from touching her. All I can do is stare as the song winds down.

She opens her eyes. "What?"

"Huh?"

"Why're you looking at me like that?"

"I, uh . . . I'm . . ." I clear my throat. "You're beautiful." *Fuck.*

Widened whiskey eyes peer back at me as the blush creeps up her neck and cheeks. "Thank you."

I nod and point to the store. "He had to order your battery, so I'll take you home. Do you need anything from your car?"

"I bought ice cream. If it weren't Ben & Jerry's, I'd say screw it."

My cock throbs at the way she bites her lip. I want to draw the plush flesh between my teeth and give her a nip. Then lick and kiss every fucking inch of her.

I clear my throat again and start the engine. "Okay." She's worried about ice cream melting in her car when I'm ready to melt into a pool of lust right beside her.

"I mean, it's Karamel Sutra Core," she says, like it's the Holy Grail of ice creams. "Have you ever tried it?"

"Nope."

"Seriously?" She points to a gas station up ahead. "Pull in there, please."

"Why?" For a moment I wonder if she's bailing on me because I've reverted to one-word answers. I pull into the lot and turn off the truck.

"Well, for one, I'd like to buy you some gas for carting me around."

I wave her off. "Not happening."

"Fine. I need spoons."

"For what?"

"You're trying the ice cream, silly." Solana hops out and bounds into the store.

I can't help but notice the way her cutoff jean shorts mold to her arse. I quickly look away because I don't want to gawk. But

I'm a fucker for curves, so, in a matter of seconds, I'm swiveling my head back in her direction. *God, that arse.* My palms twitch at the thought of taking her over my knee. I imagine caressing the skin of her bottom, rosy from my spanks, while she writhes and moans in my lap. Groaning, I squeeze my eyes shut.

When did that become my fantasy? I shift in my seat and look over at Moira. "I'm so fucked, girlie."

Solana returns with a huge smile on her face. "All right, now we're ready. You're in for a treat."

I'm already getting one. We ride to her car in relative silence because I'm afraid if I speak, I'll tell her the things I want to do to her body.

Solana listens to the music, softly humming. Moira's tail thumps against my thigh.

I park beside the Mustang once more and wait as she gathers her belongings. She climbs back inside and pats Moira's head.

"Where to?" I ask.

"Do you know where the Maple Haven Inn is?"

"Is that the big yellow one on the river?"

"Yes."

"You live at a bed and breakfast?"

She shrugs. "For now. My decision to move back was last minute, and I'm only staying in the area for a semester, so it was easier than signing a lease. Besides, my best friend's family owns Maple Haven."

Fifteen minutes and four Dermot Kennedy songs later, we pull up outside the inn. The place has a farmhouse feel, with a huge wrap-around porch.

Solana smiles and unbuckles her seatbelt. "C'mon. Let's sit on the porch. Otherwise, I have a feeling Moira will try to steal a taste."

"It's late. I should get going." I need to place some distance between us before I do something I regret.

She smiles. "You gonna turn into a pumpkin?"

"Got work to do."

"No, you don't. You just said it's late." She tugs my sleeve. "Come sit with me. You're trying this ice cream. The flavor is life changing." I open my mouth to protest, but she presses a finger to my lips. "I won't take no for an answer."

Well, fuck. So much for an escape plan. I cut the engine and nudge my dog. "I'll be back in a bit, girlie."

I follow Solana, and we settle on the porch steps, her leg mere inches from mine.

I rub the back of my neck. "So, tell me, what's so special about this flavor?" I figure if I keep the conversation flowing, maybe I can distract myself. Maybe *not* act the part of horny teenager.

She hands me a spoon. "Make sure you dip into the caramel core."

I manage a jerky nod and taste test the dessert. "Wow."

"Right?" She stuffs a spoonful in her mouth. Her eyes flutter closed in delight. *I* want to be the reason her eyes flutter and her toes curl. "How do you like it?"

Hard and fast. I clear my throat. "It's good."

"Good?" She chuckles and nudges me. "C'mon, you can do better than *that*. Good is a weak adjective."

"Delicious." The ice cream is a decadent surprise. Just like her.

"That's more like it." Solana digs her spoon in, then stops mid scoop and peers up at me with those soulful eyes. Right now, the color's more amber than golden. Darker than Jameson, like wildflower honey or maple syrup. "Thanks for looking out for me tonight. I'm not used to that. From anyone."

"My pleasure, Solana."

She sets the ice cream carton on the porch behind us. "You can take the rest home. I should get to bed. I've got to do a quiz tomorrow morning before I head to the Busy Bean."

"Goodnig—" Before I can finish the word, she grabs both sides of my face and kisses me.

7

SOLANA

MOOD MUSIC: "THE CLIMB" BY MILEY CYRUS

"Wait a minute." Will yanks me into the storage pantry at the Busy Bean, closing the door behind us. "You did *what*?"

"You heard me."

Excitement flares in his eyes as he rubs his hands together with glee. "Like *really* kissed him?"

"I kissed him on the lips if that's what you're asking."

"Holy fuck, Sunny." He bops me on the nose. "You're a little floozy."

I snort. "Yeah, okay." That's our standing joke. Will is the promiscuity to my innocence. I hate that he sleeps around, but at least he's smart about it. Meanwhile, despite my raging libido, I've never touched a penis or seen one in the flesh. "It was a sweet kiss. There wasn't any tongue or anything."

"Wait, he didn't kiss you back?"

"No. I'm pretty sure I startled him." I flush and look away. "Honestly, I shocked myself. I don't know what came over me."

Will raises a brow. "Uh, maybe the fact that he's sexy as fuck? Honestly, you should drop the virginal shit and get laid. You don't need a white dress to have some fun."

"Never claimed I was waiting for marriage."

"Then what *are* you waiting for?"

"Excuse me, but you didn't grow up under Cody's roof. You think it was easy for me to date with *him* breathing down my neck?"

"That's what your slutty college years were for."

"Tried that, remember?"

"Ugh. Chris is stupid. Tell me more about your Irishman."

"He's not *my* Irishman."

"Yet." Will wags his brows. "Because if *I* liked women, and one as beautiful as you kissed *me* without warning, it would be a game changer. I saw the way he looked at you when he came into the café yesterday. Whether you realize it or not, that man wants you." He gyrates his hips. "And not to mention . . . he gives off big dick energy."

I frown, shaking my head. "He was actually really nice to me."

Will barks a laugh. "Your innocence is so cute sometimes."

"No, really. He wasn't a dick at all."

"I'm not calling *him* a dick. I'm saying . . ." He holds up his hands as measurement.

"*Oh* . . ." I flush. "Yeah, well, clearly I don't know much about those."

He snorts. "You think?"

I ignore his remark. "So, anyway, I grabbed his face and kissed him. Then I ran inside like a scared puppy. He sat on the porch for a good three minutes before leaving."

"Doing what?"

"Just sitting there. Like I said, I think he was stunned."

"That's epic. You're a goddess."

"Yeah, but you know that's not me. I don't even talk to hot boys, let alone kiss them."

"Sunny, Chris was a boy. Declan O'Sexy McFuck is a *man*." Will shimmies his hips. "And a big, burly, hot one at that."

I nod. "He's even hotter up close. He smells good too." I press my fingertips to my lips in memory. "And he has really soft lips."

He grins. "You'd better watch out before you fall victim to the legend of the Busy Bean barista."

"I'm sorry, *what?*"

"We've lost just about every barista who's worked here."

"That sounds ominous."

"It's not." He flutters his lashes. "They fall in *love* and move on to bigger and better things. That's what happened with Murphy, Charli, Mason, and my homegirl Sasha-sash Natasha, just to name a few. Me thinks there's an invisible Cupid lounging in one of the armchairs out front."

I roll my eyes. "Well, I won't have to worry about that because I'm only here for a semester anyway."

"Never say never," he croons, rolling the r like a French chef.

"Oh yeah? Tell me, if everyone's destined for love, why are *you* still here?"

"Pfft. You won't see me catching feelings. I'm immune to that shit." He waves a dismissive hand. "Anyhoo, back to your story. What else happened with McFuck?"

I quickly fill him in on the rest of the details of my Declan encounter last night, starting from the grocery store.

Will holds up a hand when I get to Marker Motors. "Wait, how much did you give him for a car battery?"

"Twenty dollars. Why?"

"Dude, they're like a hundred bucks. He didn't ask for more money?"

"No. All he said was the guy had to order it." I clap a hand to my forehead. "I'm such a dumbass."

"You seriously thought you could get a car battery for twenty dollars?"

"Uh, excuse me, but since when did you become a car parts expert?"

"I'm not an expert, but I know how much a battery costs."

"How come *you* didn't tell me my tires are underinflated? Or point out the lack of tread?"

He shrugs. "Didn't notice. With all the shit my dad piled on my plate, looking at cars isn't exactly high on my list of priorities."

"Good point."

When Will isn't at the Bean, he works alongside his father at their family's title search company, Barnes Abstract. He *hates* it. An artist at heart, he'd much rather be creating abstract illustrations. Or *any* art, for that matter. At this point, he'd probably settle for Play-Doh and macaroni sculptures.

I feel bad for him when he talks about what a curmudgeon Mr. Barnes can be. I swear, the man reminds me so much of Cody. Will and I often sit around and bitch about our crotchety father figures. Then there's our bestie, River, a girl who's lucky enough to be blessed with the world's greatest dad.

I glance at Will. "Yeah, so, River's dad gave me a ride to work today."

"Wait, your car's still at Kwik Mart?"

"Yeah. I realized after Declan left last night that I never got his number or anything. Hopefully, he'll reach out. Unless my kiss turned him off."

"I highly fucking doubt that one, Sunny. I'll meet you out front." He exits our pantry hideaway.

I make a pit stop at the restroom before heading back to work. Passing through the kitchen door, I stop in my tracks. Lo and behold, Declan's seated on a stool at the coffee bar. He looks up from his menu and a shiver of awareness courses down my spine.

His gaze locks on to me, tracking my every move as I help the few customers waiting by the register. My heart hammers against my ribs. I try to breathe, but the heat in his eyes makes it damn near impossible.

The green and black flannel over his white T-shirt and jeans exudes rugged lumbersexual hotness. My hands twitch to peel off his clothes so I can discover what muscled promise land lies beneath.

"I tried to help him, but he said he'd wait for you," Will whispers as he passes me carrying a buttered bagel.

"Oh." My palms start to sweat, and a flock of hummingbirds zings through my stomach as I approach Declan. "Good morning. What can I get started for you?"

His stormy eyes capture mine. "Do you have anything with a caramel core?"

I release one of those nervous girly laughs at his mention of our shared ice cream. "Here I expected you to say something like, bangers and mash or corned beef and cabbage."

He raises a brow. "If you want a leprechaun, I'll give it to you, Solana Delgado. But that'll cost you a pretty penny, now."

"Speaking of pennies, I owe you money. My friend schooled me on car parts this morning. Don't pretend you got that battery for twenty dollars. Let me know what it was, and I'll give you the difference."

"Not sure what you're talkin' about." He keeps a straight face, but then the corners of his eyes crinkle.

"Looks like the Irish really *do* have smiling eyes."

"Do you wanna run down the list of stereotypes?" His gaze darkens to charcoal. "I'd say, 'Kiss me, I'm Irish,' but you already did that, didn't you?"

Oh my God.

"About that." Heat floods my face. "I, uh . . . well, I—"

He rests his elbows on the counter and leans in close. "I'll take a hot cider and an apple turnover."

I blink, surprised and relieved by his gear shift, then quickly jump into action. "Coming right up." I force a few deep breaths and pour him some cider, then choose the turnover with the most icing, and set the treats in front of him. "Here you go, Mr. O'Shaughnessy."

His name rolls off the tongue nicely. I wonder what else—

"Thanks. How was your quiz?"

I raise a brow. "I'm surprised you remember."

He doesn't answer, just stares through me again. I'm willing to bet he's thinking about our kiss. Aka, that time my libido went rogue.

"I got a one hundred on my quiz," I eek out, shaking off my embarrassment.

"Well done." He sips his cider. "I need your car keys."

"For what?"

"Well, the battery isn't gonna put itself in. And last I checked, tires don't inflate themselves."

"Oh, right. I was going to ask Will later."

"Ask me what?" Will chirps, appearing at my side. He thinks he was being stealthy over there, rearranging cookies, but I'm on to him. Nosy fool has been eavesdropping the whole time.

"To put air in my tires."

Will glances between Declan and me and smirks. "Yeah, I'm not sure I know how to do that."

Liar.

"Hi, I'm Will Barnes." He sticks out his hand to Declan, who shakes it.

"Good to meet you, Will. I'm Declan O'Shaughnessy." He tilts his head to the side. "Are you related to Solana?"

"No, but we've been best friends since kindergarten." Will grips the edge of the counter and leans in close. "Hurt her and I'll slaughter you."

I slap his arm. "Jesus Christ, William! What the hell's the matter with you?"

"What? It needs to be said." He points to Declan. "Don't worry, I tell *all* her suitors the same thing."

Fucking shoot me now.

Declan chuckles and rubs his jaw. "I'll keep that in mind." He glances at Will. "So, I'm guessing your family owns the inn?"

Determined to salvage my pride, I push pass the awkwardness and speak, "No, that's our other best friend. River is a med student in Boston, but she's coming home for a visit tomorrow."

"Tonight, actually," Will corrects me with a smile. "Surprise!"

"All the more reason to make sure your car's working." Declan holds out a hand.

I clasp his palm and give it a tentative shake. "Thought we did this part already?"

His lips curve into a smirk. "Wasn't lookin' for a handshake, Solana. Give me your keys."

Oh, right. Where is my brain today? "Hang on, they're in my purse in the back." I quickly rush to the kitchen, retrieving the set of keys with my giant sun keychain.

When I return, Declan's laughing at something Will said. Knowing Will's humor, I'm not surprised Declan finds him funny. What shocks me, is how his deep laughter makes my insides flutter. Since when does a laugh turn me on? Then again, I've been fluttering since I laid eyes on him.

He watches my approach and smiles when I hand over the keys. Will grabs a dish tub to clear one of the tables, so we're alone once more.

"You still haven't told me what I owe you for the battery."

"Don't worry about it."

"I *am* worried about it."

His smile steals my breath. "You worry too much, Solana."

"If you only knew the half of it."

DECLAN

MOOD MUSINGS: WHO KNEW I LOVED PINK?

Christ, she's beautiful when she blushes.

I swear, I can still taste her lips from last night. Strawberry lip gloss mixed with the chocolate and caramel ice cream. I'll never be able to eat any of those again without thinking about Solana.

I still can't believe she kissed me. It's a damn good thing I was so stunned, or I would've pulled her onto my lap and kissed her senseless. Then draped her over my shoulder and carried her back to my truck. Instead of me tossing and turning alone all night, we would've been tangled in my sheets, making love until sunrise.

I clench my jaw and stare out the window at the riverbank. I've always been a fucker for the drink, but in the past twenty-four hours, my alcohol cravings have all but vanished. Since my mid-teens, not a day has gone by without them. While I haven't had a drop of liquor in four years, the desire to drink is a constant, gnawing ache. Some days I crave whiskey more than I want to breathe. And others, it's a ghost on the periphery, waiting to grab me by the throat. There are times when the cravings whisper through my head. On the hard days, they're a dull roar. And when Darcy keeps Liam away from me, the whiskey screams my name like a banshee.

The moment I laid eyes on Solana Delgado yesterday afternoon, something inside me settled. I can't explain it, but it's almost like she's taken the place of the alcohol.

It isn't right. I shouldn't hunger for a young woman I barely know. I shouldn't ache to taste, touch, and consume her. I need to stay the fuck away from Solana, but God, I *crave* her.

"Are you all right?" She touches my arm.

I turn my head to face her. "Yeah, why?"

"You have a tortured look on your face right now."

"I'm grand. Just thinkin' too hard." I stand abruptly and plop a ten-dollar bill on the counter. "Be back later." She eyes my uneaten turnover and blinks a few times, but simply nods instead of answering. Pocketing her keys, I head outside. My phone rings on the way to my truck.

"Hello?"

"Hi, Daddy."

I slide into the driver's seat. "Hey buddy, is everything all right? You don't usually call me in the middle of the day."

Liam sniffs. "I miss you."

"I miss you too." I force a cheery tone when I want to curl into a ball and cry. "You know I love you to the coast of Ireland and back, right?"

"Yeah, but I don't get to see you enough."

"I know, buddy. Where are you right now?"

"At Grammy's. I had a tummy ache, so she picked me up from school. I asked if I could call you and she said yes."

My former mother-in-law is one of the few people who thinks it's important for Liam to have a relationship with me. Too bad Darcy turned out like her father.

"Why does your tummy hurt?"

"Because I'm sad."

"What's makin' you sad?"

"Mommy said you can't come to my birthday party when I'm five." A sob crackles through the phone.

His birthday's in a little over six weeks. I already knew I wasn't invited to his party because Darcy made it clear when she planned it. The wench is so hung up on denying me, she doesn't see how much it hurts our son. I tried to explain, but she's stubborn as hell. Once she's got something in her head, she'll dig her heels in—no matter who suffers.

"Don't cry, buddy. I promise we'll do something extra special for your birthday."

"But I want you *there*, Daddy."

My eyes water. "I know. And I want to be there too. But I can't."

"How come?"

What can I say? Because I made a terrible mistake, and your ma doesn't trust me? Because four years ago, I was too drunk to realize the consequences of my actions? What do I say to my little boy when I'm the real reason for his tears?

"Can I talk to Grammy for a moment?"

"Okay." He sniffles. "Grammy, Daddy wants to talk to you."

"Hello?"

"Hi, Ginny."

"How are you, Declan?"

"I was all right until I heard him cryin'."

"He's been weepy since I picked him up. The school nurse thinks it's an emotional thing—not an actual stomach issue. He doesn't have a fever and he's eating fine."

"Do you think it would be okay if I popped over for a bit?"

"I don't know . . . Darcy will be here to pick him up at noon."

I glance at my watch. "It's only ten thirty. Can I please just stay for a few minutes to give my boy a hug?"

"I think that should be okay. As long as you leave before she gets here so I don't have to hear about it."

"Thanks, Gin. You're the best. I'll be there in ten minutes."

Goodbyes always hurt more when they happen before you're ready. That's how I feel *every* time I hug Liam goodbye. Right now, kneeling on his grandmother's porch, is no exception.

"Daddy, please don't go," he sobs, clinging to my neck.

"I have to get back to work."

His little lip quivers. "You *always* work."

"I know, but that's what Mommies and Daddies need to do. One day, when you get older, you'll have to work too. I know it's hard to say goodbye, but I'll see you Sunday. That's two sleeps from today."

He sniffs and rubs his nose on my shoulder, smearing snot on my flannel. "Okay."

"I love you to Ireland and back." Ruffling his thick, red hair, I brush it away from his face.

"I love you to the moon and stars, Daddy."

I kiss his chubby cheek. "I love you *beyond* the sun, the moon, and the stars."

"Is that a lot?" he asks.

"Yeah, baby, it's a lot." I give him one more squeeze. "You be good for Grammy now."

"He's always a good boy for me." Ginny smiles and takes him by the hand. "How about a cookie? I made the chocolate chunk ones you like."

Liam's gray eyes light up. "Yes, please."

I stand, turning my gaze to Ginny. "Thanks for lettin' me pop over, Gin. I truly appreciate it."

She smiles and hugs me. "I know you do. Take care of yourself, Declan."

"You too." I stoop to kiss the top of Liam's head. "See you Sunday, buddy."

"Bye, Daddy. I love you."

"Love you beyond." I force a smile and hop inside my truck, clenching my jaw as I start the engine.

The tears fall freely from the moment I watch Liam's little wave in my rearview mirror, to when I park outside Marker Motors. I wipe my face with the bottom of my T-shirt and chug some water before heading inside. I'm sure I look like hell from crying, but I don't have time to worry about it.

Colin motions to the counter. "Hey, Declan. I've got your battery right here."

"Thanks again for your help."

"Anytime. Did you take a look at the quote I sent you?"

"Yeah, go ahead and order the tires."

"You want me to bill you when they come in?"

"Nah, I'm here. I'll just pay for them now." I hand him my credit card, shocking us both.

I hadn't planned to buy the tires—I just wanted to show Solana the quote and talk her into getting them. But here I am, purchasing tires on a whim for a woman I literally just met. One who's too young—and too sweet—to be involved with a man like me. I scrub a hand over my face and sigh.

What the fuck am I doing?

"Sounds good. I'll call you when they're in. Probably early next week." He grins. "So, who're they for?"

"Like I said last night, a friend."

"Wilde mentioned something about a little blonde who caught your eye . . . Is it the same chick who was in your truck last night?"

"Don't worry about it." I march out of the shop in a huff.

Grand. It's only a matter of time before that tidbit starts circulating. Fucking small towns.

Better yet, fucking Ethan with his stupid mouth. I should've known better than to say anything. Colin is his cousin.

I crank the music and head for the grocery store. Dermot Kennedy is singing "Glory," and once again, Solana comes to mind.

It's those eyes. I can't get them out of my head.

9

SOLANA

Will is on break, so I'm alone, which freaks me out a little. On the plus side, nothing needs baking, so at least I can't fuck up too badly. The bell on the café's door jingles. The hairs on my neck prickle and I don't have to look up to know it's Declan. My heartrate instantly lurches into overdrive.

I toss my cleaning rag into a bucket, then take a few breaths before turning. "Hey, you're back."

"I am." He sets my keys on the counter. "I cleaned up the battery acid in your engine and installed the new one. I filled your wiper fluid too."

Something's different. His voice is gravelly, and his face is set in stone.

"Thank you." I peer up at him, but he doesn't look me in the eyes.

"You shouldn't let any of your fluids get low," he grumbles. "It's not good for the car.

"All right, I'll keep that in mind. Thank you." I touch his arm, and he finally meets my gaze with puffy, red-rimmed eyes. He was only gone a few hours, but it looks like he pulled an all-nighter. "You okay?"

"Yep."

"I appreciate your help, Declan."

He nods. "Your tires are properly inflated too. But the tread's still shit."

"I'll look into getting new ones after I get a few paychecks."

"I already ordered them."

"*What?*"

He shrugs. "Winter's coming."

I fight off the urge to make a "Game of Thrones" joke and walk around the counter to him. "For one, I can't afford tires right now. Also, it's only *September.*"

"Are we not in the Northeast?" He rubs the back of his neck. "Realistically, we've only got another ten weeks or so until it snows."

"That gives me ten weeks to save for tires." I do some quick math in my head. If I tuck aside thirty or forty bucks from each check, I should be able to swing it. Of course, I have no clue how much tires cost. If a battery is close to a hundred, my guess is five times that. "Hopefully, I'll have enough by Thanksgiving."

His charcoal gaze burns into me. "Already taken care of."

"Declan, while I truly appreciate your help, I don't feel comfortable owing you money."

If there's one thing I hate more than feeling helpless, it's being indebted to another person. Cody never let me forget a single thing he did for me and I'm tired of always being the burden.

"Consider it a gift then."

"Hold up. You did *not* buy me tires. That's insane. You don't even know me," I whisper, rubbing at my goose bumped arms.

"I know you well enough to know tires land on the bottom of your list." His clipped tone makes me jump. "I know you'd rather put yourself in danger than ask for help. That you're so desperate to assert your independence, you purchased a car that has *no business* bein' on the road!"

My jaw drops open. Blinking rapidly, I take a step back.

"Sorry." Declan rakes a hand through his hair and sighs. "Didn't mean to get sharp with you. I've had a shit day." He steps closer and softens his tone. "Please accept the tires as a gift. I hate the idea of *anyone* being stranded or skidding off the road during a snowstorm. I'll feel better knowin' you're safe out there. Especially with the influx of foamies and all the leaf-peepers that'll turn up in a few weeks."

Ever since the Giltmaker Brewery's Goldenpour started winning awards, Colebury has been a hotspot for craft beer fanatics—or foamies, as we call them. Factor in the fall foliage lovers, and the area becomes a bona fide tourist hub. With our newly hopping bar scene, cases of drunken driving are on the rise.

He touches my shoulder. "Just tryin' to look out for you, Solana."

It's interesting—my only living family member doesn't care about my safety, so why should Declan?

"Thanks. I'm, uh, not used to someone doing that."

"I know." The corners of his lips twitch, but he doesn't smile. Then he turns and walks out the door.

I stare after him, flummoxed as fuck and equally grateful.

<hr>

After my shift, Will drives me over to the grocery store to retrieve my Mustang which has *no business being on the road*. As one does with their bestie, I fill him in on every detail of my bizarre Declan encounter.

He glances at me. "Told you he's moody. His ex-wife probably pissed him off."

"Hold up." I grab his wrist. "Why is this the *first* time I'm hearing about an ex-wife?"

The bastard has the balls to look sheepish. "Didn't seem relevant before."

"Didn't seem relevant? Are you kidding me? What *else* do you know, William?"

"He has an adorable little boy—"

"Wait, he has a *kid*?" I squeeze his wrist tighter. "Why wouldn't you tell me he's someone's *father*?"

He smirks. "Didn't seem relevant."

"I can't believe you."

"Oh, c'mon, Sunny. It's not like I expected O'Sexy to develop a sudden odd fascination with you."

I release him and cross my arms. "I'm not interesting?"

"That's not what I mean, and you know it." Will shakes his head. "Look, the guy shows up almost every day. Sometimes he has his son with him, other times he's alone. Either way, he's not friendly. Today was the first time he and I had a conversation outside of me taking his order." He rakes a hand through his dark waves. "Like I said, I didn't expect him to run out and buy you new tires, which is equal parts creepy and sweet, by the way."

"Yeah, I was thinking the same thing. The guy doesn't even know me. Why the hell would he drop a couple hundred bucks for my car? Lord knows Cody would never do that."

"You're looking at like five hundred bucks."

"That's insane. I'm paying him back whether he likes it or not."

"Yeah, I don't blame you. I know you hate feeling like a charity case."

I rub at my arms. "Yup."

He gestures between us. "I'm not purposely withholding information. We just didn't have much time to chat with how busy it was today."

I sigh. "I'm sorry. I get it. What *else* do you know about Declan?"

"Not a whole lot. I mean, he's always quiet. I've only seen him smile when he's with his kid. I once overheard Zara telling Audrey his ex-wife seems like a super-bitch, but that's really it."

"Are we absolutely *sure* he's single?" The last thing I need to do is bark up some married man's tree.

"Yeah. I asked Zara this morning."

I grab his arm again. "You told her I'm flirting with a customer?"

He laughs. "No. I acted like I wanted to know for myself. Since I'm the established flirt and all."

"What did she say?"

"Well, after squashing my hopes and dreams by making it clear he's not gay, she said he hasn't been with anyone since his divorce."

"When did that happen?"

"Four years ago."

"Damn. That's a long time to be single. I wonder what transpired."

"Dunno, but I get the feeling the ex-wife doesn't let him see his kid as much as he'd like."

"What makes you say that?"

"She picked the boy up early last week, and I thought McFuck was going to lose his shit."

"Huh. That seems kinda cruel. What's her story? Is she a customer at the Bean?"

"Nope. None of us have actually talked to her because they do the kid exchange outside."

"Is there anything *else* I should know?"

"Zara said he has a lot of shit to deal with."

"Like what?"

"She didn't elaborate. But at least you have the weekend to mull things over."

That was part of my arrangement with Zara when I started. I wanted to make sure I had time for schoolwork, so she gave me Saturdays, Sundays, and Tuesdays off.

"What time will River be home? And dare I ask what she has in store for us?"

He laughs. "Eight. She wants to go to the Gin Mill."

"That'll have to be a 'you and her' thing, since I don't drink, remember?"

Will bats his lashes at me. "We were kinda hoping you'd be our designated driver."

"You know I'll always drive, but I'm not going to babysit you two."

"I promise we'll behave."

I snort. "Yeah, okay. I've heard *that* before."

10

DECLAN

MOOD MUSINGS: HE WOULDN'T… OH, BUT HE DID.

Tonight's AA meeting at the church was the usual, with me quietly listening to everyone else. Despite my sponsor's attempts, I never share anything with the group. I'm not one to be open about my feelings, but the sense of community makes me feel accepted—even if it's only a few nights a week. It's comforting to know I'm not the only alcoholic in Colebury.

My friend May Shipley was there like always. She's a sweetheart, so I enjoy chatting with her and her partner, Zara's brother, Alec Rossi. Alec owns the Gin Mill and is part-owner of the Speakeasy Tap Room. Years ago, I made him promise to never serve me a drink if I turned up in one of his bars. He's kept the vow, but recently introduced me to some of his delicious nonalcoholic brews inspired by May. I enjoy them at home because parking my arse on a barstool is asking for trouble.

Seeing people who have it a lot worse than I do puts my issues into perspective. I admire those who've had slipups but keep getting back on the wagon. Fortunately, I haven't been there. I haven't swallowed a drop of alcohol since I hit rock bottom four years ago. The ability to see my son hinges on my sobriety, which is one hell of a motivator.

I slide into my truck and glance at my phone. Two missed calls and a text from Darcy. I unlock the screen.

Darcy:Who the hell do you think you are, showing up at my mother's house?

A snarl rips from my chest. Who do I think I am? Liam's father, for fuck's sake. She makes it sound like I'm some pedophile off the streets. Or a deadbeat who doesn't support them.

My phone rings. I narrow my eyes on the screen, expecting to see Darcy's name, but it's Ethan.

"What?" I bark the greeting, still pissed at him too.

"Well, hello to you, too, sweetheart."

"You're on my shit list." I close my eyes and lean my head against the headrest.

"What the hell did *I* do?"

"Talk to Colin Murphy recently?"

"Yeah, he called me this morning. Said you were at the shop last night with a little blonde in your truck."

"And what did *you* say?"

"I asked who she was. I'm confused, is asking questions suddenly a crime?"

"No." I sigh and rub my temples. "He made it sound like you told him about her. I thought you were flappin' your trap."

"You thought wrong, dick." Ethan chuckles. "Always jumping to conclusions. Who's the blonde? The girl from the Busy Bean?"

"Don't worry about it."

"You realize when you say that I automatically know what's up?" He laughs. "You're so predictable, Dec. How was your meeting, by the way?"

"Good." I glance at the time. "Aren't you workin' tonight?"

"Yeah. You should stop by the Gin Mill on your way home."

"And do what? A jig on top o' the bar?"

"I didn't say you have to come *in*. Text when you get here. I have something to give you."

"Like what?"

"You'll see." He hangs up.

Ethan and I don't exchange gifts, so I'm baffled. Unless he finally fixed Liam's bike chain.

I head over to the Gin Mill and scan the car park. The place is packed. I spot Ethan's Jeep and pull in behind it before texting him.

He saunters outside a few minutes later, grinning from ear to ear. I wonder how many phone numbers he's scored during his shift—or more accurately—who he plans to fuck tonight.

Ethan's got the dreamboat bit going for him, tall and blond with royal blue eyes. At the same time, the bastard plays his bad boy cards just as effectively with tattoos, the body of an MMA fighter, and a motorcycle. He's got no shortage of women to take to bed.

I hop out of my truck and jut my chin at him. "What're you grinnin' about?"

"Lotsa pretty ladies in there, Dec."

"You say that every weekend."

"They're especially gorgeous tonight."

I roll my eyes. "Why'd you tell me to come here?"

"I fixed Liam's bike chain. It's greasy, so watch out." He hands me a bag. "Also, I have something for you to do together." He pulls an envelope out of his glovebox and hands it over. "I thought the little guy might enjoy this."

It's a bunch of tickets to next Sunday's hockey game at Moo U.

"Thanks, man. He'll love it." I glance at the game time printed on the ticket. "I usually have to return Liam by two or three. I dunno if Darcy will let me—"

"I already cleared it with her."

"How'd you manage that?"

Ethan loops an arm over my shoulder. "I'm coming too."

"That's great, thank you." I point to the tickets. "But why'd you get five?"

"Well, I thought you could invite Pen and Henry." He grins. "That is, as long as you don't mind me being the fifth wheel in your little single-dad bromance."

I chuckle. "We're more like a two-member support group."

Penley Brooks and I connected during my many visits to the Colebury Vet Clinic with Moira. His son is a few years older than Liam, but the boys get along great. We try to get them together as much as possible. With his good-natured attitude—and damn near infectious positivity—Pen is a valued confidante and sounding board. Lord knows he's listened to many of my Darcy tirades. It's nice to have someone in my corner who understands the challenges of single fatherhood, and I appreciate that Ethan isn't jealous of our bond.

One thing's for sure—Liam will be over the moon if Pen and Henry can join us at the game.

I hug Ethan. "Thanks. You're the fuckin' best."

"My pleasure, Dec. After the shit she pulled with canceling your visit, I wanted to help out."

Ethan's older sister is one of Darcy's best friends, so she's always had a soft spot for him. He's also the most persuasive fucker I've ever met.

"I really apprec—" A flash of yellow snags my attention. My gaze darts over Ethan's shoulder to the bar's entrance. The outside lights bathe a trio of exiting bargoers in a soft golden glow.

Solana.

She's wearing a long yellow dress with a denim jacket. Her hair hangs loose around her shoulders, cascading down her back. She's walking arm-in-arm with Will from the Busy Bean and an attractive black woman, who I assume is their friend River.

They're headed for a red Honda Civic in the corner of the car park. Both friends are singing, but the scowl on Solana's face tells me she's not amused.

Ethan spins around, following my line of sight. "It's her, isn't it? The one from the Busy Bean?"

"Yeah." I duck behind his Jeep. I'm too raw from my meeting to be close to her right now. Then again, I shouldn't go near her *at all*.

"Had a feeling." He rubs his jaw. "That's another reason I told you to come here. They've been at the bar for a while. She fit the description you gave me. She's only twenty-one. You're thirty-four. Do the math."

"Already did. I dunno what's wrong with me, Eth, but I'm drawn to her."

"Well, she's gorgeous, and it's been years since you got laid. I say, go for it."

"Nope. There're a million reasons I'm *not* goin' there."

"Oh, c'mon, Dec. A little pussy never hurt anyone. You need to get some action before you fucking implode. Your life's dull, bro. And *nothing* shines brighter than an orgasm."

"Last time I went down that road, I wound up with a wife who didn't love me and a kid I don't see." While I don't regret Liam in any way, my life took a turn for the worse after meeting Darcy. I squeeze my eyes shut and change the subject. "They drunk?"

"Just her two friends. Your girl is their DD." He chuckles. "She's pissed though. Been trying to get the other two to leave for an hour. Who's the dude?"

"He works with her at the Busy Bean."

"He's hilarious. But the other girl," he stares at River's arse for a moment, "*Damn*, she's hot."

"She's studying to be a doctor." Not that her career choice has anything to do with her sex appeal, but Ethan is a fucker for intelligent women.

"Oh, really?" He grins and clicks his tongue. "Good to know. I think I need a checkup." Before I can stop him, the bastard whistles.

SOLANA

MOOD MUSIC: "GOING UNDER" BY EVANESCENCE

Great. I finally got my friends to leave the Gin Mill and now we're stalling again.

I glare across the lot in the direction of the ear-splitting whistle. It's coming from the bartender River spent the last three hours ogling. Evan or something. He's gorgeous, and he drips of sin and sex—two traits right up River's alley.

He beckons her over with a curved finger and a panty-melting, come-hither stare.

She flashes her sultriest smile. "Be right back, guys."

"Nope. I'm coming with you."

She waves me off. "Not necessary."

River struts toward the bartender and I follow, struggling to match my stride to hers. It's times like these when I'd kill for her dancer's physique and height. Not to mention her innate gracefulness. As my little legs are double-timing to catch up, I can't help but feel a bit awkward by comparison.

"Slow down, Riv. He could be a serial killer for all we know."

River laughs. "Pretty sure Alec does background checks."

"That doesn't mean anything. People are good at hiding shit. Maybe he hasn't gotten caught yet?"

"Hey, wait for me." Will follows us across the lot, belting out Whitney Houston's "I Wanna Dance with Somebody."

"Hello, again," River croons, stopping in front of the bartender. "I don't think I got your full name."

What she really means is she's too drunk to remember it, but—even under the influence—River has always possessed a smooth-talking sophistication.

"Ethan Wilde." He holds out his hand.

She clasps his palm. "Nice to officially meet you, Ethan *Wilde*." She sweeps her gaze over him. "I'm River Washington. This is my girl, Solana Delgado." She points to Will. "And Whitney Houston over here is our bestie, Will Barnes."

"Nice to meet you." Ethan points to the opposite side of the Jeep he's standing near. "This is my buddy, Declan O'Shaughnessy."

Oh my God.

I swivel my head to the side as Declan steps into view. My heart stops when I meet his stormy gaze.

Hands in his pockets, he slowly approaches, pausing a couple of feet away. The air between us crackles as he watches me like we're the only two people in the lot. "How're you gettin' on? Tires still inflated?"

Will swats River's arm. "Riv. This is O'Sexy McFuck, the hot Irishman Sunny told you about."

Declan tenses.

I squeeze my eyes shut, ready to crawl beneath a rock and die. Drunk Will has a habit of blurting out shit that could make a hooker blush. "William, I may murder you before this night is over." I wave an arm at Declan. "Also, that's *his* nickname for you, not mine."

"Don't pretend you disagree," Will scoffs. "Did you *not* refer to him as pure, lumbersexual hotness?"

Fuck.

Ethan chuckles. "Lumbersexual? Never heard that one."

"It basically means he's hot in an outdoorsy way. You know, the flannel-wearing, wood-chopping type. Sunny likes his big muscles and—"

I clamp a hand over Will's mouth. "Okay, so, we're gonna head out now." I grit my teeth. "Before someone gets their ass kicked."

While I can't even *look* at Declan, I feel his gaze burning into me. Will bites my finger, so I release him with a death glare.

Ethan points to my friends with a hearty laugh. "Looks like you have your hands full."

"You mean with my drunk friends who broke their promise to behave if I agreed to go to a bar with them tonight?" I clench my jaw. "Yeah, you could say that."

I don't drink. I don't understand the appeal of paying money to consume empty calories, act stupid, and make bad decisions.

Like getting behind the wheel and killing innocent people like my parents.

"Oh, c'mon, Sunny." River wraps an arm around me. "Lighten up."

Now she sounds like Cody, which *really* strikes a nerve. If there was an award for dismissal, my brother would hold first place.

I point to Will's Honda. "You two need to get in the car before I leave your asses here."

"Sunny, relax," Will says.

No. I'm done with people telling me to *relax*, and I've been on the receiving end of far too many *just calm downs*.

I lost my calm when I watched my parents die. I'll never forget how helpless I felt, strapped in the backseat of their minivan, pinned against the metal door and bleeding from the shards of glass that sliced me. How my mother screamed when she realized Dad had died on impact. And how when her screams stopped before the ambulance arrived, I knew I'd lost her too.

My ears start to ring and my scalp prickles. My heart races and my lungs stop working. Knowing it's too late to stop the panic train from plowing into me, I clutch my chest as my vision blurs with tears.

12

DECLAN

Solana stumbles backward, white as a ghost and gasping for breath.

Will grips her shoulders. "Just breathe, Sunny. You're okay."

She doesn't seem to hear him. Her eyes dart around the car park and her entire body trembles as tears roll down her cheeks in torrents.

River grabs Will's arm. "We need to get her home."

Ethan steps forward. "Not happening. Neither of you are good to drive. Where're the keys to that Honda?"

"Sunny has them." Will reaches into Solana's jacket pocket and retrieves the keys. Ethan holds out his hand. Will hesitates, but eventually drops them into his palm.

Ethan pats his Jeep. "Either I'll drive you two home after my shift."

River stiffens her spine. "What about Solana?"

I point to my truck. "She's comin' with me."

She shakes her head. "I don't think that's a good idea. She needs her friends right now. Besides, she's not in any position to make decisions for herself."

"There's nothin' to decide. Solana needs to go home and that's where I'll take her."

Will touches River's shoulder. "He drove her home the other night, remember?"

"Yeah, but she wasn't in the middle of a panic attack then."

"Why're we wastin' time discussin' this? Solana, do you want me to give you a ride home?"

She manages a jerky nod.

"That answers that." I guide her to my truck with a gentle hand on her elbow. She settles in my passenger seat and mops at her face.

I snatch the wad of napkins I keep in my glove box for Liam messes and hand them to her. "Dry your eyes. I'll be right back."

"Thanks," she whispers, blowing her nose.

I head over to her friends. "Why's she upset?"

River narrows her eyes, propping her hands on her hips. "I don't think it's any of your business."

Ethan touches her arm. "Declan's only trying to help her. Just tell him why she's panicking in case she flips out during the drive."

River exchanges a look with Will.

He speaks first. "The panic attacks are a regular thing for Sunny. They've been getting worse, which is why she moved back to the area this semester. We're approaching the fifteenth anniversary of her parents' deaths."

"What happened to them?" I ask.

"They were killed by a drunk driver on Sunny's seventh birthday," River answers.

"Jesus Christ," Ethan sputters. "*On* her birthday?"

She nods.

I stare at my truck, unable to speak through my shock. Solana rests her head against the window. I can't see her tears from here, but her shaking shoulders tell me she's still crying.

Will stares at his feet. "Yeah, so it was a dick move for us to ask her to be our DD so we could get drunk tonight. Obviously, the whole situation triggered her."

River glares at him. "Maybe it had something to do with you embarrassing her in front of *him*."

My voice finds me again. "I'm takin' her home now."

I stalk over to my truck and hop inside. I glance at Solana as I start the engine. Curled into herself, she leans against the door, sobs wracking her petite frame.

I know I should say something to help calm her, but what? What does one do in these circumstances?

Instead of talking, I turn on the radio. Dermot Kennedy's "Lost" fills the cab, and once again, the fucker is singing the soundtrack to my life.

No matter how badly I want Solana, I'm a gentleman first. I'll make sure she gets home safely. After that, I need to pull back. I can't bring my baggage into this poor woman's life—she has enough of her own to worry about. Besides, she's moving back to New York in the spring.

And while I'd sell my soul to have her close to me, I've got a million reasons to keep my distance. If Solana ever knew *my* history, I have no doubt she'd hate me.

SOLANA

MOOD MUSIC: "WALK ME HOME" BY P!NK

It's raining. Both from my tears and the drops spattering Declan's windshield as we drive toward Maple Haven.

He glances at me. "I won't ask if you're all right because I know you're not. But if you wanna talk about it, I'm here."

"Thanks. It's just—" He flicks on his blinker and I realize he's about to turn onto *that* highway. "Pull over." I gasp and clutch my throat. "Please."

He jerks the truck to a stop on the shoulder and throws it in park. "What's wrong? You gonna be sick?"

"No." I point. "Can't go down that road."

"It happened on this highway?"

I'm moderately surprised he knows what I'm talking about, but then again, I'm sure bigmouth Will gave him the scoop.

"Yes. About two miles ahead."

"Then I'll take us a different way."

He reaches for the shift, but I stop him. "Can we please just sit here for a while?"

"We'll stay for as long as you need." He turns off the ignition, dropping his keys in the console.

"I always hoped it would get easier, but it hasn't."

"Taking this particular route?"

"No, I mean everything. The anxiety has gotten so bad, I can't focus. That's why I left my dream college and moved back home for the fall semester."

"What happens when the semester ends?"

"Hopefully, I'll try New York again." I shake my head bitterly. "But this time it'll cost me a fortune since I forfeited my scholarship."

He raises his brows. "Why'd you do that?"

"Everything went down the tubes in May. For starters, I walked in on my boyfriend in bed with my roommate."

"*Jaysus.*"

"Yeah, so I moved out of our apartment and stayed with a different friend through the summer. But as the fall semester loomed closer, the grief and anxiety got to be too much. It's been fifteen years since I lost my parents, but it feels like yesterday. If anything, the milestone hurts more."

"Some wounds never close." He clenches his jaw and stares out the windshield. "And others ache for a lifetime."

"I'll be twenty-two at the end of next month. I haven't celebrated a birthday since the accident."

He nods. "Makes sense. It's hard to celebrate through our grief."

"Yeah, and I was in the car when my parents died, which pretty much ruined my birthday for the rest of eternity."

"My God . . ." He snatches my hand. "I'm so sorry."

"Thanks. It was raining just like tonight. We were leaving the bowling alley after my party. I remember whining about my stomachache from eating too many cupcakes. The other driver's headlights blinded my father. By the time Dad realized the car was going to hit us, it was too late. He jerked the wheel to the right. Instead of colliding head-on, the impact crushed the driver's side, killing him instantly. I was on the passenger side, behind Mom. She died before the ambulances arrived. The other driver was wasted. He went to jail for a few years." I clench my jaw. "They let him out in March, and the piece of shit got his second DWI in May."

Declan squeezes my hand. "Solana, I wish I had words for you."

I interlace my fingers with his. "Words can't heal me. Nothing can."

We sit in silence, with him holding my hand. The only sounds are the rain and our breathing. His presence steadies me like a beacon in the fog, his warmth guiding me to shore. Anchored by his strong grip, I relax against the seat as calm washes over me.

After a few minutes, I turn to face him. "I don't drink, and I never go to bars. I only agreed to go to the Gin Mill so I could make sure my friends got home safely."

"They feel bad about askin' you to come out."

"No, it's my fault. I knew it was a shitty plan, but I let Will convince me. I suck at boundaries. Add that to my list of failures."

"You should see my list."

"Does yours include the inability to cope?" I shake my head and stare out the window. "My parents would be so disappointed. Especially my mother."

"Why do you say that?"

"From what I can remember from childhood, Mom was a fiercely determined woman. Sadly, I don't have the infamous Rosita Delgado spine. She'd be furious if she knew I crumbled instead of busting through obstacles."

"I've seen people crumble from a lot less." Declan squeezes my hand. "You don't give yourself enough credit. You're still pursuin' your degree."

"I know, but I should've been able to handle New York."

"Big cities aren't for everyone."

"Yeah, but small towns suck sometimes."

"Yep, I agree with that one. Some days, I'd give anything to move back to Ireland. My son, Liam, is the only reason I stay."

"How old is he?"

"He'll be five on October thirtieth."

"Seriously? That's *my* birthday."

"Wow, what're the odds?" He brushes his thumb over my knuckles. "His birth was the best day of my life. I'm sorry the date brings you pain."

"Maybe I'll try to think about Liam this year as a distraction. What's he like?"

Declan's eyes soften. "He's perfect. Sweet, funny, rambunctious—everything a little boy should be."

Since he hasn't technically told me he's divorced, and I don't want him to think I knowingly hold hands with married men, I release my grip. "You and your wife are blessed to have him."

He stiffens, his eyes going cold. "*Ex*-wife. We've been divorced four years."

"Oh, sorry."

"Nothin' to be sorry about."

I change the subject. "Is there anything you *like* about Colebury?"

He nods. "Sure. Outside of people meddlin', there's something peaceful about Vermont. I've got a private lake on my property, which is my sanctuary. Ethan's here too."

"Is he your best friend?"

"Yeah, and my business partner. We do the woodworking gig, but we're also buildin' a bunch of eco-friendly tiny houses to offer as lodging. Ethan owns a stretch of riverfront land in Kingsbury."

While I'm familiar with the quaint hamlet that's twenty minutes east of Colebury, I've never visited that section of the Winooski. I've heard it's woodsy and secluded—the perfect place for a sanctuary.

"Wait, so, do you mean like a tiny house bed and breakfast?"

"Probably more like a motor lodge, though we do have plans to offer some food once we're established." He smiles. "Instead of renting a room, guests can choose from the dozen or so houses. Some will be rustic, like log cabins. Others will have a more modern feel. We even have one themed like a farmhouse. I love it because while I enjoy workin' with my hands, this gives me a chance to use my architecture degree."

"That sounds so freaking cool. It's very Vermonty."

Declan chuckles. "That's what Ethan always says. Originally, we planned to make them identical, but I spend a lotta time at the Busy Bean—damn near every day—and I love the array of antique furniture there. Since foamies come in all varieties, we figured we'd mix things up a bit with the structural design. Zara and Audrey were honored when I mentioned Busy Bean was the inspiration."

"I bet. You and Ethan remind me of them."

He raises a brow. "How so?"

"Well, aside from the best friend and business partner aspect, Ethan seems friendly like Audrey."

The corners of his lips twitch. "And *I'm* not?"

"Not exactly, no. Don't take this the wrong way, but you and Zara share the prickly vibe."

His rich, hearty laugh fills the cab. "Prickly? That's a new one."

"She's gotten much better, though."

He laughs harder. "But I'm still a dick?"

I shake my head. "While that was my first impression, I've since decided you're not a dick. *At all.* I truly appreciate you being there for me tonight."

His laughter fades, and he reaches for my hand again, squeezing it tightly. "It's my pleasure, Solana."

"You barely know me, yet you've been so kind—looking out for me for no reason. I'm not used to that. The men in my life haven't been the rocks I needed. Sometimes, I just want someone to listen and *be* there. You did that for me tonight and you don't even know me."

He watches me from across the darkened truck. "I know you well enough to know you don't see what others see, Solana."

"What do you mean?"

"Everyone crumbles. You forget how many times you've put

yourself back together. That's the beauty of being broken. The cracks and chasms run deep, but each time you rise and dust yourself off, you stand a little taller and shine brighter."

"I don't shine, Declan."

"Just because you can't see it, doesn't mean it isn't real." He shakes his head. "Even in darkness, you've got a glow about you. Your ma was on to somethin' when she named you Solana."

SOLANA

MOOD MUSIC: "NEVER LET ME GO" BY FLORENCE + THE MACHINE

Headlights from a passing car illuminate Declan's face for a fleeting moment. His gaze burns into me, watchful and intense. I wonder how he'd react if I kissed him again, and not just a peck on the lips this time.

"It's gettin' late now." His brogue rumbles along my nerve endings, igniting them. "Let's get you home."

He starts the engine and pulls away from the shoulder, heading down a different road to avoid the accident site. While he doesn't let go of my hand, neither of us speaks until we pull up outside Maple Haven.

I point to the inn. "I need to use the rear entrance so I don't wake any guests. There's a deck that overlooks the river. My room is on the upper level, just inside."

"I've got an umbrella. I'll walk you to the door."

"It's all right. You don't have to."

"I insist." His tone brooks no refusal. "I'm a gentleman, Solana. Wait in the truck until I come for you." He releases my hand and hops out, retrieving an umbrella from behind his seat.

"Damn, it's really pourin'." He opens it and hurries around the front to my door, holding the umbrella over me while I exit.

With a gentle hand on the small of my back, he leads me toward the deck and gestures for me to go upstairs ahead of him. *Next-level chivalry right here.*

We stop outside the main door, and I rummage in my purse for my keys. His warm presence so close behind me sends a shiver of awareness down my spine, hardening my nipples.

I locate the keyring and turn to face him. "Declan, thank you."

He adjusts his umbrella so the drops from the gutter don't hit me. "My pleasure, Solana."

God, I love how he says my name. I ache to hear him moan it. I stare up at his face, illuminated by the flickering porch light. Pieces of his russet hair fall over his forehead. Charcoal eyes watch me from beneath a fringe of dark lashes. With his sculpted jawline and perfect nose, I've never seen such a thoughtful, beautiful man.

"I appreciate everything you've done for me." My gaze drifts to his mouth. "Especially *this*." I stand on my tippiest of tiptoes and press a soft kiss to his lips.

A groan rumbles deep in his chest, sending a flare of heat to my core. "Solana . . ."

This is one of those defining moments in life. The kind you look back on one day and applaud your own boldness. In a move that's completely out of character, I kiss him deeper, teasing the seam of his lips with my tongue.

Declan chucks the umbrella over the railing and seizes my waist. "Fuck the bloody reasons." The growl leaves his lips as they crash down over mine, hard and possessive.

My back collides with the door. He spears his fingers into my hair, deepening our kiss. With his other hand clamped on my hip, he leans his full weight into me. His erection makes itself known, pressing into my belly. Arousal pools between my thighs at the thought of him moving inside me.

Declan's lips claim me like he's starved for my taste. His

tongue surges into my mouth, tangling with mine. He groans and rolls his hips, kissing me harder than the storm raging from the heavens. Raindrops pelt us, saturating our clothes, but he doesn't stop.

Moaning, I clutch his shoulders and hook one of my legs around him. He grips my thigh, yanking me closer. The delicious friction against my lady bits ignites me. I roll my hips in rhythm with his, beckoning him to take this further.

He suddenly pulls back. Gasping, he drags both hands through his sopping wet hair. "We should stop before I lose my fuckin' mind."

"We can't stop." I'm breathing just as hard, drenched in every sense of the word. "I need you to help me lose *my* mind."

Declan sweeps his lust-filled gaze over my body. "You don't know the kinds of thoughts you got runnin' through my head."

"Thought you were a gentleman?"

"Oh, I am." His gaze darkens as he once again backs me to the door, caging me between his arms. He lowers his lips to my ear. "If I weren't a gentleman, I'd fuck you right here, right now. Up against this door in the pourin' rain."

I gasp at the tidal wave of lust his words unleash. "Maybe I want you to."

"You'd better be careful, now." His heated whisper gusts the shell of my ear, the rasp of his stubble teasing my neck. "Don't poke a sleepin' bear." He steps back, tilting my chin up to look at him. "'Cause I'll make you scream so loud, your neighbors will know my name." After a quick kiss to my forehead, he bounds down the steps without another word.

I sag against the door, clutching my chest.

Declan O'Shaughnessy came at me like a fucking hurricane, and so help me God, I need his storm.

15

DECLAN

MOOD MUSINGS: CRAVINGS NEVER DIE. THEY SIMPLY CHANGE FORM.

I'm so close. I clench my hand tighter, roughly stroking as images of Solana torment me. I've never wanted a woman so badly. It's all-consuming. Her scent, her taste, the way she rubbed against me when we kissed. Her leg wrapped around me, my hands in her hair.

A low groan rips from my throat, and a few more strokes take me over the edge. *"Fuck."* My cock throbs and pulses, the cold shower washing my release down the drain. Leaning my forehead against the cool tile, I squeeze my eyes shut and try to breathe.

I've had zero desire since Darcy. In fact, I wouldn't know I had a dick if I didn't need to piss through it. I haven't jerked off in close to a year. Maybe two? This is now the second time I've done it in the past eight hours. Last night, after a hellish, blue-balled ride home, I jumped into the shower and rubbed one out while moaning Solana's name. My sleep, if you can call it that, consisted of tossing and turning through a series of vivid erotic dreams. I awoke with the biggest morning wood of my life. So, here I am, before I've even had a sip of coffee, palming my cock in the shower. Again. If I continue this trajectory, I'll rub the skin right off.

I see Solana every time I close my eyes. My insides heat when I think about how close I came to shoving that yellow dress up around her waist and fucking her until neither one of us could stand.

My cock twitches, ready for another round with Rosie Palm and her five sisters, but I've got things to do today. I don't have time to stand here fantasizing about a much younger woman. One who's equal parts sweet and sultry. Naïve, yet jaded. I allow the cold water to flow through my hair and down my back, hoping to bring my lust to a simmer—or maybe just a rolling boil—instead of the inferno I've got going on.

But it doesn't work.

I knew I was a goner the first time Solana looked at my lips like she wanted to taste them. But when her hand slid to the back of my neck, pulling me closer, I lost control. Her moans awakened something inside me I never knew existed. For the first time in my life, I've found something I crave more than whiskey.

During our ride to breakfast at the Colebury Diner, I filled Ethan in on everything that went down with Solana last night. Except for the kiss. *That* is my private morsel to savor.

He drums his fingers on our table. "I've never seen that happen before."

"You mean the panic attack?"

"Yeah, it was like a switch flipped inside her. The poor girl was terrified."

I swallow a sip of coffee and nod. "She said it happens a lot. She left college in New York and moved back to Colebury because of it. I still can't believe she was in the car when her parents died. I can't fathom what she saw."

"And heard. And *felt*. It gives me chills to think about." Ethan shakes his head. "It's a good thing you stopped by. She seems at ease with you."

"True, but she probably wouldn't have panicked if Will hadn't teased her about me. Solana clearly didn't appreciate him runnin' his mouth. How was she at the bar?"

"Fine, at first. She seemed annoyed when Will started to sing loudly. She *really* got pissed when they gave her shit about leaving. I guess they'd agreed on a time beforehand, but River was dragging her feet." He flashes a wolfish grin. "*I* certainly didn't mind the view."

"I bet you didn't." I snort, stabbing a bite of omelet. "What was River's deal? She didn't seem thrilled with the idea of Solana ridin' with me."

"She called herself a mama hen. After we dropped her off, Will told me she's got good reason to be protective of Solana."

"Like what?"

"He didn't say." Ethan stares at me over the top of his mug, his blue gaze narrowed on my face. The color's particularly piercing this morning. "You haven't so much as looked at a chick in years, but you seem preoccupied with this one. What's the deal?"

I shrug. "Don't worry about it."

"Do you like her?"

"I *said*, don't—"

"Yeah, yeah. I heard you." He waves a dismissive hand. "Did you happen to mention your situation?"

"She knows about Liam and that I'm divorced." I drag my fork through a glob of ketchup and sigh. "But I left out all the other shit."

"Probably a good idea. How'd she react to hearing you're a father?"

"Didn't seem to faze her. I'll know more on Monday when she meets Liam at the Busy Bean."

"You gonna pursue this?"

I've been asking myself that same question since last night. When I learned a drunk driver killed Solana's parents, I swore to keep my distance. The last thing she needs is an alcoholic in her life. The thought of her knowing my past twists my stomach into knots. I haven't felt so disgusted with my addiction since I lost Darcy's trust.

But when Solana held on to my hand like I was the only force tethering her to the planet, I knew I couldn't stay away. That kiss, with those soft, decadent lips, destroyed my defenses. Some primitive part of me craves being the man she turns to when life gets rough. Yeah, I want to fuck her senseless, but I also want to be the one who calms and steadies her.

Ethan waves a hand in front of my face. "Earth to Declan. Do you read me?"

I rub my temples. "You ask a lotta fuckin' questions."

"Relax, Dec. I'm not trying to be all up in your shit. I just wanna see you happy for once. You deserve it."

I shake my head. "I deserve a lotta things, Eth. Happiness isn't one of them."

16

SOLANA

Someone's knocking.

I roll to my side, shielding my eyes from the sunlight streaming through my window. It's ten o'clock. I haven't slept this late on a Saturday in years. I'm sure last night's self-induced orgasm—courtesy of my long-neglected vibrator—is the culprit. I've always had the libido of a teenage boy, but I never did anything about it because Cody wouldn't let me date. I turned to self-love, honing my vibrator skills at a young age. Even during my darkest days, the glow of pleasure made me feel alive. The orgasms gave me something to look forward to in my hollow existence.

I'll never forget my brother's words when he found my toys and threw them in the trash. *Fifteen-year-old girls shouldn't be touching themselves. You're a pig. Mama would be disgusted with you.* That was when I started to hate him.

But things got worse.

I moved out at sixteen, cutting ties after he failed to protect me from one of his friend's advances. The only time I ever went to him for help, Cody called me an attention-seeking drama queen

79

and turned the blame on to me. Apparently, it's not okay to walk around your own house in a skirt. God forbid a grown man can't keep his hands to himself. After the incident, I stayed with River until I went away to college.

There's another knock at my door, followed by River's muffled voice. "You awake?"

"Well, I am *now*." I march across the room and yank the door open. "What's up?"

River pushes her way inside and plops onto my bed. "I'm sorry Will and I got carried away last night."

Closing the door, I settle beside her. "It's fine."

"No, it's not, Sunny. The only reason I came home this weekend was to make sure you're okay, but instead, I got drunk and acted like an asshole. Will and I feel like shit."

"I could've said no."

Her espresso-colored eyes meet mine. "Except, you wouldn't because you'd want to make sure we got home safely. Instead, we got wasted and let you ride home with a stranger."

"Declan's not a stranger."

"I don't know him, so in my book, he is." Her assessing gaze sweeps over me. "What happened last night?"

"Nothing."

"Bullshit. *I'm* the one who's hungover, yet you would've slept another two hours if I didn't wake you."

"Yeah, thanks for fucking up the best sleep I've had in ages."

"You're avoiding my question." Her full lips curve into a smirk. "But nice try."

I roll my eyes. "I already have a psychiatrist, thank you very much."

She snorts. "You gonna tell my dad about O'Sexy McFuck?"

"Absolutely not."

"Then start talking."

I can't stop the Cheshire cat grin from spreading across my face.

River's eyes bulge, and she grips my chin. "Oh. My. God. Did you *fuck* McFuck?"

"Of course not. I only kissed him."

"Spill it. I want every detail."

"It was mind-blowing. He was so . . . I want . . ." My eyes flutter closed at the memory. "River, he's . . ." I open my eyes. "I don't have words."

"You'd better find them, sister." She grins and clicks her tongue. "Because Mama Hen needs to know."

After a few breaths, I fill her in on everything that happened. I spare no detail because I know she'll pry until she gets them anyway.

"*Damn*, girl. Look at you, taking charge of the situation." She squeezes my knee. "But my favorite part of your story is, *I'll make you scream so loud your neighbors will know my name.*"

Her mock Irish brogue makes me chuckle. "I know, right? His voice is hella sexy."

"Yeah, I agree, he's hot as fuck. But you're vulnerable right now, so you need to be careful. Hear me out for a minute." She straightens, and her tone grows serious. "Sunny, I know I'm busy with school and all, but I'll *always* make time for you. I don't care what time of day or night it is, if you need to talk, call me. This semester, I'm going to try to make it up here for a visit at least once a month."

I shake my head. "No. You need to focus on school."

"And I *will*, but I need to be here for you."

"School comes first, Riv."

"Girl, you know damn well I won't sit back and watch you suffer. You're my ride or die, so I'm gonna ride out the storm with you." She pokes my ribs. "And guess what? I won't let you isolate yourself again. That's another reason you're going to see more of me."

River has firsthand knowledge about my tendency to retreat within my shell when life gets too overwhelming. She's the one who finally cracked me after the incident with Cody's friend.

"Don't worry. I'm not at the retreat and shelter-in-place phase yet."

"Yeah, but I'm not gonna let down my guard. I hate that you're having so many panic attacks. I wish I could do something to make them go away. Although his bossiness isn't my thing, I'm glad you have McFuck hanging around to distract you." She tugs a lock of my hair. "However, instead of worrying about *my* studies, you really should focus on making sure he doesn't disrupt *your* schoolwork."

"School comes first," I repeat, giving her a nudge. "He won't change that for me. It's hard to explain, but I feel safe with Declan. As much as he turns me on, he calms me. He didn't try to fix me, he just *listened.* He held my hand like I mattered to him, like he truly cared I was hurting. Honestly, just having him there made me feel better. And Mother of God, *that kiss . . .*"

"You know what this means, right?" A slow grin crosses her features. "Say sayonara to your hymen."

17

DECLAN

MOOD MUSINGS: DEEP BREATHS DON'T DO SHIT.

The car park at the Busy Bean is packed this morning. I'm parked beside Solana's Mustang, drumming on my steering wheel while I wait for Darcy to drop off Liam. Since school started, our visits switched from morning to afternoon. Last night, however, Darcy called to tell me she was keeping Liam home from school because of an asthma flare-up. Normally, she wouldn't let me have him on a sick day. I wonder what's different this time.

We always do the child exchange outside. My ex-wife has never even set foot inside the Bean, which is just as well. I don't need her tarnishing my happy place. Besides, Zara would probably have a hard time hiding her distaste—totally my fault, since I've confided in her over the years. And while I've never been on the receiving end of the Rossi glare, I've seen it happen, and it's downright scary. Last thing I need is Darcy knowing I'm running my mouth about her.

I glance at the dashboard clock. She's late, of course. But if *I* had the audacity to bring Liam home late, I'd never hear the end of it. Swear to God, if she cancels on me again, after I rescheduled today's jobs, I'm going to lose my shit and drive over there.

Finally, her black Mercedes pulls into the lot. She eases into the newly empty spot beside me and turns off the car. She makes her way around to the rear passenger side but doesn't open Liam's door yet.

I hop out of my truck. "Hello."

"Hi." She hands me Liam's inhaler. "His asthma is really bothering him today. I nebulized him at midnight. I almost called you to cancel, but my boss and I have a meeting in Burlington, and my mother's not available to watch him."

"I can handle it."

She waves a finger at me. "Don't let him run around all crazy, and *don't* give him any milk. He can have more albuterol in an hour if he needs it."

"We'll hang low. Does he have a fever or anything?"

"No." Darcy twists her thick, red hair into a bun. "He's just congested. I think it's the change of seasons. He gets like this every fall."

"He seemed fine yesterday."

Her green eyes narrow on my face. "Or maybe *you* weren't paying close enough attention."

I clench my jaw. "Don't start, Darcy."

"Well, it's true. Anyway, I'll be gone all day, so I need you to keep him until after six."

Good thing I cleared my schedule.

"What happened to your other half? I thought he only worked until three?"

Darcy usually enjoys rubbing it in my face that Bridges is the one who gets Liam off the school bus each day—something I'd love to be able to do.

"He's got things to do today. Besides, Liam isn't his responsibility. Declan, if you can't handle this, I'll call Kelly."

Ethan's sister is Darcy's backup babysitter.

"I'm capable of takin' care of him."

She rolls her eyes. "That's debatable. Anyway, Liam's teacher told me he's not where he should be for a kid starting kindergarten."

"How so?"

"He should be able to recognize and write most of the alphabet, but he only knows a few letters. Clearly, your visits are taking a toll on his schoolwork."

I'm seeing red, and it has nothing to do with her hair. "Excuse me?"

"You're a distraction."

"I'm his *father*," I growl, balling my hands into fists.

"Don't remind me. Anyway, if you can find time in your busy schedule, he needs to practice his letters."

Darcy opens the back door and unbuckles Liam, while I force a calm I don't feel. We'll practice his letters all day long. I'll make damn sure I'm not to blame for his schoolwork suffering.

"Hi, Daddy." Liam flings himself into my arms. He's got on jeans and a blue polo. To my surprise, he's wearing the work boots I got him to match mine.

I squeeze him tightly and reach for the Spiderman backpack Darcy hands me. "Hey, buddy."

"I don't feel good, so Mommy said I don't have to go to school."

"That's right, but we're still gonna practice those letters."

He pouts. "Letters are boring."

"School's important, bud." I release him and point to Darcy. "Say goodbye to your ma, now. Then we'll get you your doughnut, and Moira her croissant."

"Where's Moira?" he asks, peering into my truck.

"She's home. We'll see her in a bit."

Darcy kisses both of his chubby cheeks, then hugs him like he's going off to war. "I love you, sweetheart."

"Love you too, Mommy."

She stands and turns to me. "I don't want him hanging out in your shop, breathing in all the sawdust. He really needs to rest today, Declan. Don't lose his inhaler. Oh, and don't forget to give him lunch and dinner."

"Got it." I clench my jaw, biting back a snarky comment about starving him after I let him run with the wolves and perform Satanic rituals.

I take Liam's hand, guiding him toward the café, while Darcy hops into her car and leaves.

The bell on the door jingles as we walk in. Solana's alone behind the counter, cleaning the espresso machine. She looks up and smiles. "Good morning, gentlemen."

My cock twitches at her word choice. I still haven't recovered from our kiss, but Liam's with me, so now is not the time for lustful thoughts. "Good morning, Solana."

Her face softens when she looks at Liam, which happens *every* time a woman sees him. Not to brag, but with his gray eyes and thick, red hair and freckles, my son is beyond adorable. Add in his chubby cheeks and sweet nature, and most females are goners.

"Good morning, Liam," she sing-songs, placing her hands on her hips. She's wearing jeans and a black V-neck, with the yellow apron over top. She's divided her hair into two braids, one draped over each shoulder.

"How does she know my name, Daddy?"

I squeeze his shoulder. "Solana Delgado is a friend of mine. Now, mind your manners and say hello."

He gives her a bashful smile. "Hello."

"What can I get for you?"

"Chocolate milk, please."

I shake my head. "Not today, bud. Your ma said no milk with your asthma. Too much phlegm, remember?"

Solana glances at me. "Can he have apple juice, instead?"

"That's perfect." I nudge Liam toward the display case. "Go ahead and pick your doughnut. I see they have chocolate today."

He giggles. "Daddy, you *know* what kind I like."

With all the family turmoil he's dealt with, it's not surprising Liam's a kid who loves his routine. In fact, he clings to his normal like a security blanket. Roderick has tried on multiple occasions to broaden his pastry horizons, but he *always* chooses the same kind.

"Thought maybe you'd try something other than a jam one," I say with a chuckle.

Solana smiles at him. "My absolute favorite are the jelly doughnuts." She lowers her voice to a stage-whisper. "Sometimes, I have two of them."

His eyebrows pop upward. "Jelly doughnuts are my favoritest ones too."

"Then you have great taste, Mr. Liam."

He pouts. "But Daddy only ever lets me have *one*."

"Your Daddy is a smart man. You wouldn't want a tummy ache, right?"

He shakes his head. "No. I don't like tummy aches."

Solana crinkles her nose. "Me neither. They're no fun. Go ahead and pick out the best doughnut." She winks and points to the display. "I think the one in the back has extra jelly inside."

Liam flashes a grin. He recently lost his first tooth, so his smile's even cuter than before. When he called to gush about the tooth fairy visiting, I shared the tales my father would tell me about Anna Bogle, the young leprechaun girl who collects children's teeth in exchange for a gold coin. The story enthralled him, so I had Dad mail me some old Irish coins. I stuck them in a green envelope and gave it to Liam at our next visit, telling him Anna Bogle had left him something at my cabin. His little face lit up with wonder.

It's those moments with Liam I cherish more than anything— watching him learn and discover and imagine. His ma gets to be a constant presence in his life while I'm limited to mere hours. I miss out on so much, so I do my best to make those hours count. I pack our visits with stories and fun, always striving to create positive memories. I try to give him little morsels of me to hang on to, like breadcrumbs in a forest of Darcy.

He points. "I want that one, please."

"Coming right up." Solana meets my gaze, her whiskey eyes

stealing my breath as always. Her glossy pink lips look like a dew-covered Irish rose. "And for you?"

Everything inside me tightens. I can't answer. I can't even breathe. Seeing her, so fresh-faced and beautiful, sweetly interacting with my son, does something to my chest.

She gives me a knowing smile. "How about a mug of hot cider and an apple turnover?"

I nod.

Liam nudges me. "Daddy, use your words."

18

___

SOLANA

___

Good Lord, these O'Shaughnessy men.

With his cheeks and stormy eyes, Liam has me head over heels in a matter of minutes. My uterus and ovaries join hands and sway, singing songs about babies and motherhood.

Declan's wearing jeans and a black Henley, with the first two buttons undone. The material stretches across his muscled chest and shoulders. He's shoved his sleeves to his elbows, giving me a nice view of his tattoos and corded forearms. His russet hair is still damp from his shower, and God *damn,* he smells divine.

He guides Liam to the end of the counter. They settle while I plate the food and pour their drinks.

Declan watches my every move, his gaze like a secret caress. No one has ever looked at me the way this man does. *I'll make you scream so loud your neighbors will know my name.* I can still feel his hands on me—possessive and intense. I can still taste his minty lips and feel the rasp of his stubble on my face. Nothing compares to that kiss, and I'd give anything for an encore.

I set Liam's plate and juice glass in front of him. "All right, we have one jelly doughnut and an apple juice for Mr. Liam." I place

89

Declan's plate and mug on the counter. "And for the *gentleman,* we have Shipley hot cider and an apple turnover." I give him a sweet smile and add, "I gave you the one with the most icing."

Declan's gaze flares with heat. The corners of his lips twitch, but he doesn't smile.

"Daddy, say thank you."

He flushes and clears his throat. "Sorry. Where're my manners? Thank you, Solana."

"You're welcome. Please let me know if you need anything."

Another customer walks in, so I make my way over. While pouring the woman's coffee, I hear bits and pieces of Liam and Declan's conversation.

"She's really nice," Liam says, around a bite of doughnut. "I like her name."

"It means sunshine." Declan wipes some jelly off Liam's chin. "Her ma picked it."

"Who picked *my* name?"

"Your ma and I agreed on it."

Liam tilts his head to the side. "How come you don't do that anymore?"

Declan furrows his brow and bites into his turnover. "I'm not sure what you mean, bud," he says after chewing for a moment.

"You and Mommy don't agree. You're always mad at each other. How come?"

Declan sighs. "I'm not mad at your ma."

"She's mad at you. I heard her telling Grammy on the phone after you came to see me there. Why is Mommy mad?"

I can't help but wonder about Liam's mother and why she'd let a little boy worry about this kind of shit.

Declan sips his cider and takes a few deep breaths. It doesn't take a genius to see the poor guy's struggling to come up with an answer. "That's a question for your ma."

Liam's lip quivers. "I'm sad you can't come to my birthday party."

"Me too, bud."

"But *why*, Daddy?"

Deciding Declan needs a little help—and Liam could use a distraction—I approach them once more. "How're you two doing? Everything tasty?"

"Delicious, thank you." Declan flashes me a grateful look and digs out a pen, scrawling the letter A on a napkin. "Liam, when you're finished eating, I want you to practice."

He pouts. "I don't wanna work on my letters."

"You need to."

"But it's—"

"No buts. This is important. If you don't do your schoolwork, Henry and his dad won't be able to join us at the hockey game."

Ah, parental leverage. I remember Cody's bargaining days. Although, he was usually more than willing to dump me at a friend's house, so he didn't have to deal with me.

Liam sighs and takes the pen, tearing the napkin as he drags it along. "See? I can't do it without paper." He crosses his arms.

Declan scrubs a hand over his face.

"Hold on, I have something that might work." I head for the back room, grabbing a few dry-erase markers and one of the white boards we use to write the drink specials. I return to the front, holding the board out to Declan. "He can use this."

I set the markers in front of Liam. "I found some colorful markers for you to use. Check out that blue—it matches your shirt."

"Thanks, Solana." He reaches for the blue marker and uncaps it, carefully making a wobbly A on the board.

"That's an awesome A," I gush, admiring his work. "Can you think of a word that starts with A?"

"Apple."

"Wow, you're super smart. I have an idea. How about you see how many letters you can write while I make coffee for those customers?"

"Okay." Liam turns his attention to the board. "I bet I can make seven."

"Let's see what you've got. Ready . . . set . . . go!"

I grin at Declan and turn to leave.

He snags my wrist. "Thank you." The sincerity in his gaze could melt a glacier.

After about fifteen minutes of hustling behind the counter, I raise a brow at Declan. He gives me a thumbs-up.

"Solana, come look," Liam says.

I flit over, dramatically wiping my forehead. "Whew. That was a lotta coffee. How'd you make out?"

Liam holds up the board. "I got all the way to Z."

"That's fantastic."

He grins. "Z is for zebra. They have stripes."

"That's right, bud. Your letters look great. I'm proud of you." Declan squeezes Liam's shoulders, pressing a kiss to his temple.

My ovaries release another sixteen eggs.

"Thanks, Daddy." He stiffens. "Uh-oh, I think I need to go potty."

"Go ahead. Make sure you flush and put the seat down." Declan touches his arm. "And don't forget to wash your hands."

"Okay. Be right back." Liam jogs to the restroom.

Declan watches him close the door, then turns to me. "I can't tell you how much I appreciate your help before. His ma said the teacher informed her he's fallin' behind in school."

I point to Liam's letters. "These look great to me. He *just* started kindergarten, so I wouldn't get too stressed over it."

He clenches his jaw so hard, his nostrils flare. "Except, she insists *I'm* the reason."

"Wait, she's blaming you for him struggling?"

"Yep. Apparently, my visits disrupt his schedule. She called me a distraction."

I curl my lip. "Wow. It sounds like she isn't playing fair."

"That's puttin' it nicely. Anyway, I need to keep on him about practicing. Trouble is, he gives me a hard time." He points to the colored markers. "This was great. Thank you."

"I'm happy to help, Declan. He's adorable, by the way."

"Thank you." His gaze softens. "Isn't he, though?"

"Like seriously cute." I motion to his face. "He has your stormy eyes."

He raises a brow. "Stormy?"

"Fits the persona," I explain with a chuckle, then gesture toward the bathroom. "How come Liam's not in school today?"

"His asthma's actin' up." He hands me a napkin and pen. "Write down your number."

"My phone number?"

"No, your social security. I'm stealin' your identity."

I laugh. "You can have it. You don't wanna be me."

"Likewise." He glances at the bathroom door as Liam comes out, wiping his wet hands on his pants. "Write it, Solana."

I scrawl my number and fold the napkin in half, exhilarated by the prospect of seeing more of him. I slide it across the counter. "Is this official spy business?"

He stuffs the napkin in his pocket. "Your tires are in. We need to schedule a time to put them on."

"Ah, that's right." I nod, secretly disappointed he's not asking me out. Then again, why would he? I'm a teenybopper compared to his adultness. "When's good for you?"

He pats his pocket. "We'll talk."

DECLAN

MOOD MUSINGS: MY SELF-CONTROL IS PRECARIOUS AT BEST.

Liam is draped across my lap on the couch, his little snore whistling in rhythm with the rise and fall of his chest. He zonked out five minutes into the movie he picked, and for whatever reason, I'm still watching.

I stare at Solana's contact info in my phone. I saved her number the moment we left the Busy Bean. Part of me wants to call her just so I can thank her again for helping with Liam's letters.

After five minutes trying to convince myself not to, I tap on her name to send a text.

Declan: Hello, Ms. Delgado.

Her reply is instantaneous.

Solana: Who's this?

Declan: The "stormy" one.

Solana: Hi. How's Liam feeling?

Declan: He's napping now, but I can't stop watching the talking snowman.

Solana: Olaf is the best.

Declan: Yeah, he's funny. What time do you start work tomorrow?

Solana: Actually, I have the day off.

The excited flutter in my belly surprises me. All day, I tried telling myself I only wanted her number to take care of the tires, but that's a crock of shite. My cock twitches in agreement.

Declan: What's on your agenda?

Solana: Nada.

Declan: Meet me at Marker Motors at nine. My buddy Jude said he can squeeze you in between two of his paint jobs, but it may take a while. I figure we can grab food while we wait. Does that work for you?

Jude Nickel is a mechanic friend of mine who I met through May Shipley. He does body work at Marker's. Tires aren't usually on his list, but since he's the one who answered the phone when I called, he offered his help. Jude's a great guy all around and a wizard when it comes to cars.

Solana: Yes, tomorrow works. Also, I went to the bank on my lunch today. I'm paying you back for the tires.

Declan: No.

Solana: Too bad. You're getting five hundred bucks from me whether you like it or not.

Why can't she accept a gift? Has no one ever done something kind for her?

Declan: Stop being stubborn. It's nonnegotiable.

Solana: I'll keep the money under one condition.

Declan: Reread my previous text.

Solana: You're bossy.

I chuckle because she's right. But now I'm curious.

Declan: And what is your condition?

Solana: Too bad—you missed your chance. Now I'm not telling.

Declan: Please?

Solana: Reread MY previous text. (And the ones before it.)

20

SOLANA

MOOD MUSIC: "SECRET" BY MAROON 5

Palms sweating, I pull into the lot at Marker Motors. Declan's already here. My stomach flip-flops when he steps out of his truck. He's got on jeans and a white T-shirt, and with his muscles and tattoos, the simple attire couldn't be sexier.

I turn off my ignition and climb from the Mustang. "Howdy."

"Morning." He holds out his hand. "Gimme your keys." I plop them into his palm. Declan opens the passenger door to his truck. "Get in."

"Bossy much?" I chirp, sliding into the seat.

He stands in the open doorway, blocking out the sun. He waits until I've clicked my seatbelt to speak. "For the record, *Solana*," he pins me with his gaze, "it took tremendous effort not to show up at your door last night."

"Too bad you didn't."

His eyes darken to charcoal. He licks his lips, and the ache between my legs intensifies. "Like I told you before, don't poke a sleepin' bear." He slowly closes the door, stalking into the shop.

The man has some serious pent-up sexual frustration. I wonder if it comes anywhere close to mine. My nipples prick the inside of my bra as my lower belly heats and tightens. I've never had such an intense physical response to a man, which is part of why I held on to my V-card for so long. That, and Chris was the only person with whom sex could've been feasible, but the idea never felt right with him. Right now, squirming in Declan's truck, I'm glad I held off.

He returns after a few minutes and hops into the driver's seat. "Ready?"

I nod and press my knees together. "Where're we going?"

He starts the truck. "Montpelier."

"Why?"

"I need to go to the hobby shop," he explains, pulling onto the highway.

"I love that store. I like making jewelry with beads. I haven't done it in a while, but maybe I'll pick up something today. So, tell me, what are *your* hobbies?"

"Outdoorsy stuff."

I snort. "That clarifies it, thank you."

He chuckles and glances over at me. "Hiking, fishing, and boating, to name a few."

"Shouldn't you be hitting up a sporting goods store, instead?"

"This isn't for me. I've gotta pick up paint for Liam's birdhouse."

"Oh, cool. Did you two build it?"

He nods. "Yeah, on Sunday. We designed it together, but I did the saw work and glued the pieces. Liam did all his own sanding."

"Are you going to hang it on your porch, assuming you have one?"

"I've got a lovely porch, but no. It's a gift for his ma's birthday. Hers is a few days before Liam's."

"Why would you make her a gift if she's bitchy to you?"

"Well, no matter what happened between us, she'll always be his ma. As the first woman in his life, it's important to me that he respects her. When he grows up, I want him to respect *all* women, even if they don't show him the same decency."

"I love that idea."

He nods. "Liam was the best gift she ever gave me. Part of my job as his father is to teach him right from wrong. It goes beyond making sure he behaves—it's about preparin' him to be a good man. They say kindness starts at home, so if that means I need to indirectly acknowledge my ex-wife's birthday, then so be it. Same goes for Christmas and Mother's Day. I always make sure he's got something to give her."

"Does she do the same for you?"

"No." He meets my gaze. "Like I said, it's about *giving* respect, even when we don't receive it. *Even* if the other person's goal is to make your life a living hell."

I shake my head. "You're a better man than me."

"Well, I can't expect him to follow through if I don't lead by example."

"You have this whole parenting thing all figured out."

"Not really, but I'm working on it. I also helped him build the birdhouse because I want Liam to know I have his back. I need him to *know* if he needs me, I'm gonna be there. Whether it's for help, advice, or money—it doesn't matter—I'll do anything for him. So, when he came to me and said he wanted to make somethin' special for his ma, it gave me a chance to prove my words aren't empty."

"You're a good father, Declan."

"Thank you. Doing right by Liam is my number one goal in life. I said I'd help him make him the best damn birdhouse there is —and I don't make promises I can't keep—so that's what we're doin'." He chuckles. "But he wasn't happy with my lacquer color choices, so I told him I'd pick up paint."

"I'm really moved by this. His mother will love the gift. You've nailed that *be the bigger person* thing."

He snorts. "Maybe not."

"Why? What do you mean?"

A grin overtakes his face. "She *hates* birds."

"Seriously?" I laugh and nudge him. "You built a birdhouse for a woman who hates birds?"

"Yep. For the record, the birdhouse was Liam's idea." He glances at me. "But I *may* have been extra enthusiastic about it, secretly hoping a bunch of crows land on the thing and squawk at all hours of the night."

I laugh. "I'll start a list. First, we need neon sparkly paint. Then, some super-addictive crow bait."

"That's why I designed a feeding tray for the house." His rich laughter fills the cab. "I already bought the birdseed."

———

Declan eating an omelet is one of the sexiest things I've ever witnessed. The Celtic knotwork tattoos going up his arms are gorgeous. *He's* gorgeous. The way the muscles in his forearm flex when he uses his knife has me wishing I stashed some spare panties in my purse.

"I love your tattoos," I blurt.

"Thanks." He holds out his arms. "They're a work in progress. These are just the visible ones. I've got more."

Why does that make me want to peel off his clothes in the middle of a diner in Montpelier?

"Let me see the one on your wrist." I clasp his hand and tug him closer, giggling when I realize what the intricate ink is. "You even got a bird tattoo to piss her off?"

"No, this one was for me. It's a phoenix. I like the symbolism. Do you have any tattoos?"

I nod. "I have an elaborate sun on my lower back."

His pupils dilate slightly. "Nice."

"Will designed it for me. Maybe I'll show it to you some time."

He clenches his jaw, his gaze burning into me. His shoulders rise and fall with each breath as lust pours off him in waves, sending a flare of heat to my core. "Solana . . ."

"Yeah, yeah, I know. Sleeping bear and whatnot." I flutter my lashes and reach across the table. "Here're my thoughts on that." In a move that shocks me, I press my finger in the center of his chest and flash my sultriest smile. "Poke."

He flags our waitress over. "Check, please."

DECLAN

MOOD MUSINGS: DOPAMINE HAS NOTHING ON THIS.

I've never been this turned on. Not even when I used to sneak a fuck with one of my university professors during her office hours.

I stare straight ahead, my gaze fixed on the highway. I don't dare look at Solana. All she'd have to do is bite that luscious lower lip of hers, and I'd pull over and fuck her on the side of the road. We're almost at Maple Haven. I would've brought her to my place, except Ethan's there, installing a new electrical outlet in my kitchen.

We stop outside the inn, but I don't turn off my truck just yet. I won't make any false assumptions—I need her to invite me inside.

"Are you forgetting something?" she asks with a giggle.

"Like what?"

"We never stopped to get my car. You sped right past the place."

"I didn't forget. We can do that later."

"What are we doing right now?" She twists her body to face me.

"That's up to you."

"Well, you drove us here, so I'm assuming you have something in mind?"

We stare at each other, the air crackling between us. Her gaze flickers from my eyes to my lips, then back again. I don't know whether it's her stubbornness or if she's suddenly bashful, but I can tell she doesn't want to make the first move. I'll die if I don't taste her kiss, so I lean in. Her lips part and her eyes flutter closed.

I brush my mouth over hers, a mere second of contact, then slowly pull back. "Like I said, it's up to you."

With shaky hands, she turns off the ignition and unclicks our seatbelts. "Come inside."

"You sure?" My voice is gruff, thick with desire. I meet her gaze, watching and waiting. While I may be somewhat domineering in the bedroom, I won't pressure a woman into anything. Ever. Right now, I'm so turned on, I can't even think, so I need her to be crystal clear about what she wants. If it's sex, I'll give it to her, but I won't take unless *she's* ready to give. "Answer me, Solana."

"Yes." Her consent is the sexiest sound that has ever reached my ears. She opens her door and steps out onto the gravel driveway. "You coming?"

I shove my door open and jump out of the truck, nearly tripping on myself. I follow her down the path to the inn's back deck and we climb the steps in silence. Images of our rainstorm kiss flood my memory, making my cock throb. I glance at the door I'd pressed her up against and consider reenacting the scene, but it's broad daylight now. The other guests may not appreciate that.

Solana grips the doorknob, still trembling.

I stop her with a hand on her shoulder. "Are you sure you want me to come in?"

SOLANA

MOOD MUSIC: "PUT YOUR HANDS ON ME" BY JOSS STONE

I don't consider myself a flirt, or any sort of temptress, but my body hums with a newfound awareness of my sexuality.

I peer at Declan over my shoulder. "Yes, I want you to come insi—"

He snags my waist, hauling my back to his chest. "Was hopin' you'd say that."

Judging by his erratic breathing and the size of the erection pressing against me, his control is slipping. His desire makes me feel sexy—not dirty or slutty. I want to test his limits while exploring mine. More than that, I want to snap his control.

I wiggle my butt, relishing his rough exhale. "I'm in the mood to poke you again."

"You're doin' a bloody good job of it, honey." His brogue thickens when he's aroused, and it's hot as fuck. He brushes his lips over my ear. "And guess what . . . this bear's all done sleepin'."

Oh my God.

He releases me, and I lead him inside the inn. We pause in the dimly lit hallway while I fish for my keys in my purse.

Hands trembling, I locate them and unlock the door to my room.

"Welcome to my humble abode." I usher us inside and turn to face him, closing the door as I speak, "It's not much, but—"

His lips crash down over mine. He spears his hands into my hair and guides me across the room. The backs of my knees meet the edge of my mattress. I clutch at his chest, fisting the material of his T-shirt. He groans and nudges me onto my bed, breaking the kiss to pull off his shirt and kick his shoes off.

Declan stands over me, and I lose my breath at the sight of him shirtless. Holy fuck, the body on this man is carved from granite —all smooth, hard lines.

Both arms have full-sleeve Celtic knotwork, with the phoenix on his left inner wrist. The inkless skin of his chest is covered in a smattering of dark brown hair that trails down his washboard abs. My gaze follows until it disappears beneath his waistband. The mirror behind my door reflects the elaborate Celtic dragon on his back. The colorful tattoo is easily the most exquisite ink I've ever laid eyes on. The creature's wings span Declan's shoulder blades, and its body covers the length of his spine.

"Wow."

"Like what you see?"

"The dragon is amazing."

"Thanks." He brushes the hair back from my face and smiles. "I'm hopin' to catch a glimpse of that sun you were tellin' me about."

I remove my T-shirt and toss it on the rocking chair beside my bed that doubles as a nightstand. His gaze settles on my lacy white bra, pupils dilating. Rising and shifting to my knees, I slowly turn to give him a view of my lower back.

He traces his fingertips over the tattoo. "This is beautiful."

"Thank you."

He skates his hands over my shoulders, dragging my bra straps with them. "I want this off." Instead of unhooking it, he yanks it to my waist.

I clutch my breasts and stare over my shoulder at him. *"Jesus."*

He flashes a wicked grin. "Weren't expectin' that, huh?"

"No."

"Your expectations won't do you any good with me." He trails his thumb down my backbone. "Now, turn around."

Arousal floods my panties at his bossy tone. I slowly turn to face him, with my hands still covering my breasts.

He points to my pillow. "Lie back." He waits until I settle, then prowls up the bed to me, nudging my legs apart. He kneels between them and points. "Gimme your hands."

I lower them, exposing my breasts. My nipples harden with the cool air from my ceiling fan. His reverent gaze makes them even harder.

"So sexy." Declan seizes my wrists with one hand and pins them over my head. He feathers his fingertips across my breasts. I gasp when he grazes my nipples. My position of vulnerability heightens each sensation, making my back arch off the bed. He smiles and massages circles with his thumb. "You like that?"

"God, yes."

He lowers his mouth to a nipple, sucking it between his lips. His tongue flutters on the hardened peak. I moan and struggle against his hold, desperate to knot my fingers in his hair and pull his head closer.

Declan tightens his grip. "I'm not lettin' go 'til I've had my fill of your gorgeous tits." He meets my gaze. "But say the word, and I'll stop, Solana."

"I don't want you to stop."

"Good." He gives my nipple a hard suck, dragging his tongue back and forth over the peak. He switches breasts, giving me a repeat performance on the other side. The gasping moans leaving my lips should make me shy, but they don't.

Not even a little.

Declan releases my hands and trails his fingertips to my waistband, searching my face as his touch travels lower. "You good?"

My hips jerk with his touch. "Yes."

He takes off my shoes, then pops the button on my jeans and lowers the zipper, shoving them over my hips. He moves aside so I can kick them off, then settles once more, kissing his way down my belly. No one's ever gone down on me, so I'm equal parts nervous and excited. Declan is a mix of gruff and tender, domineering in a way that tells me he likes getting what he wants in bed.

I hope my body lives up to his expectations. I ache to satisfy him and take care of his needs. More than that, I want to keep him coming back for more. I clench my fingers in his hair, making him groan. The primal sound stokes my body even hotter.

He toys with the waistband of my panties, then slides a hand inside to tease my clit in slow circles. Before I can get used to the rhythm, he grips the panties and tears them down the center.

"Oh, my *God.*"

He slowly shakes his head. "Not God. Just Declan." He stares up at me, his eyes smoldering with lust as he pushes the cotton material aside. "And I'm gonna lick every fuckin' inch of you, honey." He slides his hands beneath me, palming the cheeks of my ass. "Put your legs over my shoulders."

He kisses the inside of each trembling thigh and works his way inward. A wanton moan spills from my lips with the first swipe of his tongue through my drenched entrance. He groans, spearing his tongue inside me, again and again.

I've mastered the art of silent moaning, courtesy of my years of self-loving. Right now, I couldn't stop my moans if I tried—and with Declan's groans, and the clench of his fingers on my ass—I don't care who hears me.

Warm wetness surrounds my clit. My hips jerk when he swirls and flicks his tongue over the bundle of nerves.

"*Declan.*"

"Say it, honey." He ramps up the intensity. "Let me hear you."

"Oh . . . yes." I tug on his hair. "Just like that. Don't stop." I writhe in his grasp, bucking my hips against his tongue. My thighs and stomach muscles tighten. My back arches off the bed. My body clenches, hovering at the edge.

He groans and gives me a hard suck.

Everything releases, sending me flying. "Yes. Oh, God, *Declan*." I wail his name, digging my nails into his scalp. No self-induced orgasm compares to this blinding pinnacle of ecstasy.

"That's right, honey. Let me fuckin' hear you," he growls, picking up the pace. He doesn't stop until after he wrings another orgasm from my quaking body.

"*Declan*." I push at his shoulders. "No more. It's too much."

He rears up like a stallion, seizing my mouth in a plundering kiss. His tongue tastes of a heady mixture of mint and salty sweetness. I never imagined I'd find it erotic to taste myself on a man's mouth, but here I am, hungrily stroking my tongue against his.

He grinds his hips, rubbing his massive jean-covered length against the sensitive flesh between my thighs. The friction makes me come a third time. I moan his name and clamp my legs around him. "I need you."

He reaches between us, yanking his jeans open before swiftly kicking them off. His hard cock juts against the gray boxer briefs he's wearing, with a small circle of moisture at the tip. I've never seen a penis in real life, let alone felt one thrusting inside me. And from what I can tell, Declan is huge.

He snatches a condom from his jeans pocket and tugs his boxers down.

Holy fuck.

A shiver of trepidation courses down my spine, watching him roll the rubber on. My vibrator doesn't come anywhere close to what he's packing.

He settles on top of me and presses my trembling legs farther apart. Chest heaving, he pins my hands at my shoulders.

"Declan, I . . . uh . . . I—" Swallowing, I meet his gaze. "I need to tell you something."

His eyes glitter with savage lust. "We can talk later. Right now, I'm gonna fuck you through this bed."

With the weight and heat of his body on top of me, and how the broad head of his cock nudges my entrance, we're so close to fucking, I can taste it. And I'm ready. I *need* to feel him thrusting inside me.

My subconscious tells me it might be wise to mention how I've never been fucked, period—let alone through a bed.

"This is my first time," I blurt out.

He freezes, and I sense my little announcement was ill-timed. "First time for what?"

I take a deep breath. "I'm a virgin."

I know it's a mistake the moment the words leave my lips. The heat in his gaze plummets. He blinks a few times, then jumps back like I dumped a bucket of ice water over his head.

He grips my chin. "*What?*"

Since the first two times didn't register, I reword my response, "I've never had sex before."

"*Jaysus*, Solana." He runs both hands over his face. "You're just tellin' me this *now*?"

"I still want to," I whisper, reaching for him. "But I just wanted you to know ahead of time."

Shaking his head, he squeezes his eyes shut. "No, I can't do this." He removes the condom, tosses it in the trash, and yanks on his boxers and jeans.

I sit up, utterly bewildered. "Wait, what are you doing?"

He retrieves his shirt and shrugs it on. Then roughly laces his boots. "I have to go. I'm sorry, Solana."

I scramble to the edge of the bed, knotting my hands in my hair. "You're leaving?" My voice is shrill with panic. Tears blur my vision. "I don't understand."

Declan doesn't even look at me as he leaves.

Heavy footfalls on the steps and the squeal of retreating tires confirm his departure. The sound is a knife to my chest.

Unable to think or breathe, I burrow beneath my comforter and curl into a ball. Mortified tears soak into my pillowcase. I offered myself to him, allowing him to touch and kiss my body in ways no one has ever done, and he walked out on me. What a fool I was to trust him.

This humiliation is far worse than when Cody found my sex toys and called me filthy. This even surpasses when I told him his best friend, Phil—a man I trusted—had tried to force himself on me. I shudder on a sob and curl deeper into myself.

Forget Cody not believing in me, his shaming and disgust, or any forcible touching endured from Phil, I've *never* felt dirtier than I do right now.

My scalp prickles, and my ears buzz. I gasp, but my lungs refuse to cooperate. I claw at my bedsheets as the stifling panic suffocates me.

DECLAN

MOOD MUSINGS: I SHOULD REALLY START ASKING QUESTIONS. BEFORE I NEED ANSWERS.

Ethan slaps the back of my head. "Seriously, Dec. What the fuck were you thinking?" He yanks open my glove box and helps himself to a piece of gum. He shoves it in his mouth and stares across the truck at me, loudly chewing while he shakes his head. "Go ahead. I'll wait for your dumbass explanation."

Twenty minutes ago, I picked him up so he could help me retrieve Solana's car from Marker Motors. I filled him in on what happened, hoping for some advice. Clearly, that quest was misguided.

He cracks his gum. "Still waiting, jackass."

I narrow my eyes at him. "You gonna sit there and insult me, or actually fuckin' listen?"

Ethan cups his ears. "I'm listening, bro. Now tell me what possessed you to walk out on her like that?"

"Didja miss the part with me tellin' you she's a *virgin*?"

I still can't wrap my head around it. When Solana said it was her first time, I thought she meant her first orgasm or her first time being with an older man or something. *Not* that she was a virgin.

After she repeated herself, it still took a moment for her words to register. I seriously thought I was hallucinating. I knew *what* she was saying, but I wanted her so fucking badly, I didn't want to believe her. But then, taking in her widened gaze and trembling thighs, it all hit me, and I panicked.

I should've given her an explanation, but my gut told me to distance myself. With the taste of her sweet body on my lips and tongue, her moans filling my head, and the burn of the lust in my veins, I was in no condition to be someone's first.

Ethan shakes his head. "No, I got the virgin part loud and clear. So, she's never fucked anyone before." He shrugs and flicks his gum wrapper at my windshield. "What's the big deal?"

"You don't get it, Eth."

"No shit. That's why I'm asking."

I sigh heavily. "I didn't wanna hurt her."

"Would you have stopped if she told you to?"

"Of course. What the hell kind of question is that?"

"I'm just trying to get into your head. You want this woman more than you ever wanted Darcy or any of the chicks in college. But when the time came, you tucked your tail and took off."

"I haven't touched a woman in four fuckin' years."

Ethan rolls his eyes. "Which is why you *need* to get laid."

"Solana's a virgin. She needs a man to make love to her."

"Am I missing something?"

I pull into the lot outside Marker's. "Look at my life. It's a shitshow."

"Your dick works, right?"

"A drunk driver killed her parents. I'm an *alcoholic.*"

"Recovered alcoholic," he corrects me, squeezing my shoulder.

"No, it's not past-tense, Eth. I fight that battle every day. I'm recover*ing*, but I'll never be recov*ered.*"

"Listen to me. You haven't had a drop of whiskey in four years. That's something to be proud of."

"But look at what happened to get me here."

"You can't change the past. You can either run from it or learn from it. You, my friend, did the latter."

I snort. "Here we go again with the motivational shite."

"Uh, you should think about listening, dick. I know my shit. Anyway, what I'm saying is this. As your best friend, I *hate* how you discredit your progress. You don't see what I see. How far you've come and what you've accomplished during your recover*ing*." He jabs a finger in my chest. "You're a good man and a damn good father. You work hard and treat people with respect. Open your eyes, bro. You own a home. You're in business with the coolest motherfucker in Colebury, and we're making bank. Not to mention, our tiny house resort is gonna blow the lodging industry out of the water. You have a lot to offer this girl."

"Liam is my number one priority. Darcy would never allow me to bring him around a woman, and she'd flip her shit if she knew Solana's age."

My ex-wife just turned thirty-seven. Our age difference always bothered her when we were married. I can almost hear her ranting about my poor judgment for involving myself with a woman so young.

"Age ain't nothin' but a number."

I rub at my temples. "I can't give her a relationship or any sense of normalcy."

"Who says she wants that?"

"I know she does."

He raises a brow. "Did you ask her?"

"No."

"Then you *don't* know." He shimmies his hips. "Besides . . . there's nothing wrong with a relationship based on sex."

"There *is* when she's a virgin and you can't trust yourself not to fuck her senseless. She's too sweet for that." I shake my head and clench the steering wheel. "And she's been through more trauma than a young woman should ever have to face. Bottom line, Solana is only in town for the semester. She needs to focus on her degree—not me. I have no business touchin' her."

"Okay, then keep your distance."

"That's the plan. *After* I return her car."

I park the Mustang outside Maple Haven and turn off the ignition. Ethan pulls up beside me in my truck.

He hops out, ready to switch seats, and points to Solana's keys in my hand. "Don't forget to return those."

I hold them out to him. "Can you please run them up to her?"

"C'mon, Dec. You're not a coward. Own up to your actions. *You* should bring the keys to her. And gee, I dunno, maybe give the poor woman an explanation for why you ran out?"

I clench my jaw. "She won't care about my explanation—she was crying before I even left the room."

He shrugs. "Okay, then don't explain. Let her wonder about your reasons and think something's wrong with her. I have an idea—why don't you just throw the keys at her feet, pat her on the head, and make her feel extra worthless?"

I narrow my eyes at him. "I wanna hit you sometimes."

"Think about it. You're a grown man. Act like one."

"What if she wants to talk?"

"Is that a serious question?" Ethan pinches the bridge of his nose. "You fucking *talk* to her."

I point to my truck. "I mean, are you good with sittin' here awhile?"

He slides into the passenger seat and pulls out his phone. "Take your time. I don't have shit to do today." He grins. "Except maybe watch a little porn in your truck."

Shaking my head, I trudge around the back of the inn and climb the steps with leaden limbs. My hands shake when I knock on Solana's window. She doesn't answer. Not that I expected her to.

Opening the porch door, I enter the inn's darkened hallway and jiggle the doorknob to her room.

It's unlocked.

Maybe it's because I grew up over a bar, but I'm a firm believer in always locking one's doors. Besides, for a small town, Colebury has seen its share of criminal activity in the recent past. I'm annoyed Solana would leave herself vulnerable. What happens if someone comes after her?

I'll fucking kill them, that's what.

Regardless, her door *is* unlocked, and I'm still holding her keys. While I know I shouldn't let myself in uninvited, leaving them out in the walkway isn't an option. I figure I'll just put them on her dresser and then head out to look for her. Hopefully, some creep didn't yank her into his big white van.

I push the door open and step inside, inhaling deeply. Her soft vanilla scent fills my nose. My cock twitches, and I can almost taste the honey between her thighs. "Solana?"

To my surprise, she's here. Although she's hiding—in the form of a large lump in the center of her bed—but at least now I know she's not tied up in someone's trunk. I stand in the doorway, wondering when I became such a worrier. I wait for her to say something.

She doesn't.

The rhythmic rise and fall of the blankets she's burrowed beneath tells me she's breathing, but I'm not sure if she's asleep or ignoring me.

"Here're your keys." I set them on the dresser and walk to her bedside. "Your tires are good to go. I left the warranty paperwork in your glovebox. After you've driven for about fifty to one hundred miles, you need to bring the car back in so they can re-torque the wheels. It's important because if the lug nuts are too tight, you risk warpin' your rotors. If they're too loose, the wheel could fall off while you're drivin'." I tap the lump of blankets. "Jude said you don't need an appointment for that, so make sure you do it. You also need to have the tires rotated regularly. Since you don't do a lotta drivin', at every other oil change will suffice."

I rub at my jaw, unsure why I feel the need to give her a lesson on tires right now, but the stuff I'm telling her is necessary to keep her safe.

"Tire rotation is essential for proper tread wear, so please don't forget. I know you just bought the thing, but you were overdue for an oil change. They took care of that for you. Changin' your oil is important, Solana. Pay attention to the sticker on your windshield." I take a breath. "Or maybe I'll just call to remind you."

"Thanks." Her muffled voice relieves me. A little hand appears from beneath the covers. She points to a bag that hangs from a hook on the wall. "The money's in an envelope in my purse."

"I don't want your money."

"It's *your* money. Now take the five hundred bucks and leave."

I swallow tightly. "Look, it's not that I don't want you—"

The lump of blankets shudders. "Please just go."

Her bitter whisper cracks my heart down the center. "Solana, look at me."

"No."

I settle on her bed with a sigh. "My actions had nothin' to do with you. You're—"

She sits up in a flurry of blankets and pillows. "Who the hell do you think you are?" Fury flashes in her swollen, reddened gaze as tears stream down her cheeks. "You don't get to barge in here and act all patronizing like you didn't mindfuck me."

"I'm sorry." My gaze drifts to her thin, white tank top, lingering on her hardened nipples. She's not wearing a bra, and despite her anger, she's got my mouth watering again.

She catches me looking and grabs the sheet, pulling it up around her breasts. She points to her face. "Eyes up here, asshole."

"Look, Solana, I didn't mean to upset you when I left."

"Upset me?" she shrieks. "No, you *humiliated* me. I gave

myself to you, and you rejected me with zero explanation. You acted like you thought my virginity made me weak or defective."

I grip her shoulders. "That's enough."

"Well, it's true. You made me feel *dirty*." She sneers, her eyes narrowed into slits. "Then you ran out of here like I'm some rookie whore who didn't give you your money's worth."

Before I realize what I'm doing, I lunge on top of her and pin her to the bed, my nose touching hers. "I said, *enough*. I mean it, Solana." Her name leaves my lips on a low growl. "I never wanna hear you sayin' that about yourself again."

"Then close your ears," she curls her lip, "or, how about not making me feel that way in the first place?"

"You think I don't want you?"

"Oh, I *know* you wanted me. I'm not so inexperienced that I don't know what an erection means. But then you left without having the balls to explain yourself. Why? Because my lack of experience turned you off? News flash, not everyone knows the Kama Sutra by heart."

I blink a few times and stare at her face. She's serious. She truly thinks I don't want her because she's a virgin. I release her shoulders and sit back on my heels. She needs some space, and I could use a moment to gather my wits.

"Nothing about you turns me off. Solana, I want you more than I've ever wanted *anyone*, but you're a virgin."

"I think we've established that." She cocks her head to the side. "From what I understand, there are plenty of men eager to add the cherry-popping notch to their belt, so why is my virginity such a deal-breaker for you? Would you rather I give you a call once the deed's done?"

"What're you talkin' about?"

"Would it make you happier if I let someone else deflower me? You know, hit up the bars on college night and bring home some random dude to screw? I'm sure I could find someone who's willing."

My blood boils at the very thought of another man touching her. "Absolutely not."

"Then I suggest you get over it. Believe me, I've thought this through. I think I made it quite clear I want you. *And* I gave you my consent more than once, so what's the problem?"

"Solana, listen to me." I stroke her cheek, wiping the tears away. "I left earlier because I haven't even looked at a woman in four bloody years. I was afraid I wouldn't be gentle enough with you." She rolls her eyes, so I grip her chin, forcing her gaze to mine. "Do you hear me? I'm tellin' you I was scared, okay? I was afraid to hurt you. I didn't want to make love—I wanted to fuck you hard and dirty. And that's no way to go about losin' your virginity."

"You should have just told me what you were feeling instead of running out on me." Her voice breaks, and she gives a few rapid blinks. "That was a dick move. And for the record, I'm not afraid of you."

I slowly shake my head and brush my thumb over her lush lips, then release her chin. "I didn't think you were, but that doesn't make it right."

"So that's it? I'm so broken and inexperienced you think I can't handle you?" She crosses her arms. "I'm not fragile, Declan. You'd be surprised what I'm capable of."

"I'm *not* saying you can't handle me. I'm saying you don't want *me* to be your first. I can't give you what you need. I'm no good for you, love. You deserve better."

"No, I deserve to be the one who determines what's in my best interest. *I'll* worry about my wants and needs, who's good for me, and what I'm ready for." Her nostrils flare. "This might be a foreign concept for a bossy bastard like yourself, but you don't make decisions for me. Period."

"I'm not making decisions for you. I'm tryin' to do the right thing."

"Here's a start." She waves her finger in front of my face. "Trust my judgment. Don't undermine me or treat me like a goddamn child. I've had opportunities to have sex, but I chose not to." She grabs both sides of my face. "Guess what? If I *didn't* want to sleep with you, I wouldn't have kissed you that night with the ice cream. I wouldn't have kissed you a second time outside my door in the rain. And I wouldn't have invited you in here to—" She squeezes her eyes shut and takes a few breaths. "Look, I've never *allowed* someone to touch me, but I wanted your touch the moment I saw you."

"What do you mean by that?"

"Uh, are you even listening?"

The hairs on the back of my neck stand on end. "I'm talking about how you said the part about being touched. Did someone touch you without your permission?"

She tenses and snatches her hands away, wrapping her arms around herself in a hug. For a fleeting moment, panic flares in her gaze. But then, just as quickly, she stiffens her spine, and her poker face kicks in. It all happens in a matter of seconds, but it doesn't take a detective to know my question struck a nerve.

"While I appreciate your help with my car, I need you to accept the money. If my virginity is too big a burden, I sure as hell don't want you buying tires for me."

The abrupt change of subject tells me I need to do some digging, but now's not the time.

I rub at my temples. "Solana, for the last fuckin' time, love. You're *not* paying for the tires."

SOLANA

MOOD MUSIC: "COLLIDE" BY HOWIE DAY

"It seems we're at an impasse, Mr. O'Shaughnessy."

I'm angry, but I should still be livid. Right? After today's shit-show, Declan's presence alone *should've* triggered another panic attack. But other than when I nearly slipped about the Phil incident, I'm feeling . . . calm.

It doesn't make any sense. With each passing moment, a piece of my anger fades into the background like some creepy mirage that was never there in the first place. Maybe my softening has something to do with his safe car speech—or maybe I'm just an idiot—but either way, my mood has improved since his arrival.

"No, it's not an impasse, Solana. It's a done deal. Like I said, it's not up for discussion."

I lean in close. "You're making decisions for me again."

He crosses his arms over his chest and glowers. "No, I'm not. I'm just tellin' you the way it's gonna be."

"You're extremely bossy. You know that, right?"

"You've said it multiple times, so yeah, I'm aware." He juts his chin at me. "Are *you* aware of your stubbornness?"

I lift my shoulders in a weak shrug.

He shakes his head. "I just don't understand why you're bein' so difficult about the damn tires. Is ensuring your safety a crime?"

"No."

"Then what's your issue?"

"I hate being a charity case."

"I don't think of you as a charity case, so I'm not treatin' you like one." He rubs at the back of his neck. "But if you feel that way, I must be doing something wrong. Look, I'm sorry. Hurtin' your pride is not my goal. If it makes you feel better, I'll let you give me a quarter of the cost."

"No. Let me pay half." I pad across the room to my purse and pull some money from the envelope. "Here's two hundred and fifty." I stop in front of him. "Please take it."

He grimaces when I place the bills in his hand, but then he folds and stuffs them into his pocket. "You happy now?"

"Yes, actually. I feel much better about the whole thing."

"Good." Declan stares up at me. "I'm sorry about today. The last thing I wanna do is hurt you."

I wave a dismissive hand. "It's fine."

"I need you to understand something." He pats the bed. "Sit."

I plop beside him.

"Solana, you're young, kind, smart, and incredibly beautiful. In my *opinion*, you deserve someone who can give you the world."

I snort. "Yeah, okay."

"No, I mean it." He touches my cheek. "Hear me out. Any man would be lucky to have you. While I'd sell my soul to be him, I'm not that man. I've got more baggage than you can imagine. Suffice it to say, my ex-wife gets off on making my life a livin' hell. She limits my visits with Liam, and it fuckin' kills me. That boy is my everything. I won't risk losin' him."

"I'm not trying to come between you and your son. I'd never do that."

"See, the thing is, you wouldn't have to *try*. His ma would find out your age and rip me apart. Darcy already questions my judgment."

"You make it sound like I'm fifteen. I'm a grown-ass woman."

"I know, but I married an extremely irrational one. My gut's tellin' me I should stay away from you, but I can't." He cups my cheek. "I can't explain the force of my attraction to you, but I won't pretend it's not there. I want you, Solana. Desperately."

"I want you too."

"I'm not claiming to know exactly what you're lookin' for, but I do know this." His gaze burns into me. "I can't give you what you need. A normal relationship with me isn't possible. I've already done the marriage and kid thing and failed at it. I'm not willing to make the same mistake again. I can't give you anything conventional."

"Who said I—"

He holds a finger to my lips. "Let me finish. If you want sex, I'll give it to you. As much and as often as you want. But that's all I'm good for."

I shake my head. "You've already proven that's not true."

"Listen, I've done a lot I'm not proud of. My life isn't a row of perfect houses with two-car garages. I don't do white picket fences. My reality is a rusted-out boxcar that ran off the tracks." He brushes his thumb over my bottom lip. "Say what you like, but you deserve much better than that."

"Declan, I need *you* to understand something. My life has never been contained by a picket fence. I'm full of barbed wire and splinters, and I haven't felt at home since my parents died. I'm broken in every sense of the word."

"You're not broken."

"You don't know the half of it—I'm broken beyond repair. I shattered fifteen years ago, and I've lost hope of ever putting myself back together. I'm not sure who you think you're looking at, but I'm just a shell of a girl with some serious daddy issues."

He snorts. "You don't have daddy issues."

"Oh, but I do. My brother's version of parenting was detached at best. I've *never* had someone to turn to. Someone to look up to. Someone who cared about my safety. There were no hugs, no words of encouragement. I didn't have a home filled with warmth and security."

I clench my jaw, fighting back the tears I know are coming. "Forget any semblance of emotional support—other than food, shelter, and basic requirements, he gave me nothing. I'm not kidding when I tell you he was like an ornery old man in a nursing home, angry because his pudding didn't have enough tapioca in it." I thump my chest. "*I* was the pudding factory's tapioca girl. The scapegoat for his every frustration. He never even tried to hide the fact that he resented me. And as far as my anxiety goes, forget it. There was no reassurance or understanding —just nine years of dismissal. 'Get over it, Sunny. Let it go. You're ridiculous. You're a pig. You—' "

"He berated you?"

I squeeze my eyes shut. "Declan, you have no idea."

He rests his hand on my knee. "I'm sorry."

"I'm not telling you this so you can feel bad for me. I just want you to understand where I'm coming from." I meet his gaze with ferocity. "I'm only in town for a few months, so if sex is all you can offer, then I'll take it." A tear rolls down my cheek, so I quickly wipe it away. "Because I'm really fucking lonely, and that closeness is more than anyone's given me in fifteen years. So, yeah, I'd say I have daddy issues."

Declan pulls me into a hug and kisses the top of my head. "As long as you don't call me Daddy during sex, I'm okay with your supposed issues."

I wrap my arms around him and bury my face in his chest. I listen to his heartbeat as my tears soak into his T-shirt.

"Solana, you're livin' proof there's true beauty in being broken. Every piece of you shines like the sun, reflecting a light you can't see." He tightens his embrace and gently strokes my back. "I'd give you the moon and stars if I could."

"Just hold me," I whisper. "That's all I need."

After a few minutes, his warmth and steady breathing slow my tears. I look up at him with a small smile. "Thank you."

"My pleasure, honey."

"Wait, how'd you get my car here?"

"Ethan rode over with me." He points to the window. "He's sittin' out in my truck."

"Oh my God, he's been waiting this whole time?"

He chuckles. "Oh, trust me, he'll live."

"I didn't mean to keep you." I chew my lip. "I'm sorry."

Declan captures my face in his hands. "No more apologizin' today. I'm glad we cleared the air between us."

"Me too. Will I see you at the Busy Bean tomorrow?"

He nods. "I'll pop by after I pick Liam up from school. He looks forward to his jam doughnut, and that's something we always do together. Besides, he eats enough carrots with his ma."

"Can't wait to see him."

He smiles, the corners of his eyes crinkling like always. "He asked me about you last night."

"Really?"

"His exact words were, 'Daddy, why do you get stars in your eyes when you look at Solana? How come you don't know what to say to her?' "

My heartbeat kicks up a notch with my breath. "How'd you respond?"

"I told him stars shine brighter in darkness."

"Do they?"

"Yep. And the sun is the brightest star of all." He takes my lips in a slow, tender kiss. "Have a good night, Solana."

25

DECLAN

MOOD MUSINGS: JUST GO AHEAD AND NOMINATE ME FOR "FATHER OF THE YEAR." NOT.

I glance over my shoulder at Liam strapped in his car seat. "I know you think letters are boring, but it's important to learn them. What if you want to be a writer one day?"

He shakes his head. "I don't wanna write. I wanna build things like you, Daddy."

"You may not realize this, but I do a lot of writing with my job. Uncle Ethan needs to be able to read my measurements. We can't build furniture, fix cabinets, or design our tiny houses unless we can read what I've written."

"I know." Liam sighs and crosses his arms over his chest. "But why does our last name have to be so hard? Mrs. Parker said I need to write the whole thing. It's not fair. David Fay is really good at his name."

"Just so you know, O'Shaughnessy is an awesome last name. I bet David Fay *wishes* he had our name." Despite feeling his pain over writing our lengthy surname, I make the statement with gusto. Mainly because I'd love for him to take pride in our Irish heritage. One day, I hope to bring him to Ireland to meet my dad. "Also, we have a pair of lions on our coat of arms."

"What's a coat of arms?"

"It's like a family symbol. I'll show you a picture when we get to the Bean."

"It's not that I don't like our name, Daddy. It's just really hard to write." He meets my gaze in the rearview mirror. "Mommy said I can change it to Bridges when I get older."

"Like hell!" I slam on the brakes, startling us both, then quickly pull over before someone rear ends us. "There will be none of that. Your name is Liam Joseph O'Shaughnessy."

"But Bridges only has seven letters instead of twelve. If I change it, Mommy and I can match."

I slam my fist on the steering wheel. "*He* is *not* your father! I won't have you takin' his name. Not now. Not *ever*!" My roar echoes through the truck.

Big, fat tears roll down Liam's cheeks, followed by a whimper.

"Liam." I squeeze my eyes shut and try to catch my breath. "Look, I'm sorry I yelled. It hurt my feelings when you said that, and I overreacted." I reach for his hand, but he turns away from me and leans against the door. "I'm so sorry, buddy."

"I wanna go home."

Tears burn in my eyes as I meet his little gray glower. "I'm sorry I yelled. Please forgive me. Let's go get your doughnut."

He wipes his eyes. "I don't want a doughnut."

"Okay, that's fine. But we need to pick up Moira's croissant. Solana said she'd set one aside for her."

He perks up. "Solana will be there?"

"Yeah, bud. That's her job."

"Maybe I *will* have a doughnut. Can I please have chocolate milk today?" His lip quivers when he looks up at me.

I brush the tears off his cheeks. "Of course. Tell you what, just for today, we'll get you a big milk with extra chocolate and I'll even let you have *two* jam doughnuts if it makes you happy."

Am I buying his forgiveness with sugar? Yes. Do I care about my methods right now? No. As long as he stops crying, I'll let him eat whatever he wants. Although, I should probably add some new tactics to my mea culpa arsenal before I give the kid cavities or high blood sugar. Darcy would love that.

Liam shakes his head. "No, Solana said that would give me a tummy ache. I'll only have one."

"And *that's* why you're the smartest boy in the world."

"Why?"

"Because you listen to the advice of wise women."

While the yellow Mustang is parked in the lot, telling me she's working, Solana is nowhere to be seen. Her absence sends me into a momentary panic. The last thing I need today is to disappoint Liam after I told him she'd be here.

"How come I don't see Solana?"

"Maybe she's on her break." I scout the café, praying that's the case.

Then, Solana appears from the back room, and all is well with the world. At least that's how it feels when Liam's eyes light up at her approach. Her honey-blonde hair is tied in a ponytail, which sways as she walks. Much like her hips. My cock gives me a thumbs-up. *Not now, you eager feck.*

"Hi, Solana." Liam's voice cuts into my imaginary conversation with my anatomy. "We were worried you weren't here."

"Why hello there, Liam." She grins and makes her way over to the counter. "Of course, I'm here. I had to check on something for Roddy. Don't worry, I saved a jelly doughnut for you." She points to me. "You in the mood for another turnover, or can I interest you in something else?"

Yeah, you. I clear my throat. "I'd love a turnover, thank you." She smiles, and it soothes me better than a spoonful of honey does a sore throat. "How're you doin' today?"

"Not bad." Her whiskey eyes search my face, no doubt seeing the evidence of my meltdown in the truck. "How about you?"

I rub the back of my neck. "Had a rough day, but I'm better now."

"Glad to hear it. Are you thirsty?"

"Yes. I'll have tea with honey, please."

I'm the rare Irish person who's not a tea drinker. Never have been. Back home, whenever I refused a cup of tea—which may as well be Ireland's national drink—people would ask if I was feeling well. Maybe it's because I grew up over a bar, but I've always gravitated toward coffee, usually with a splash of whiskey. In fact, I don't even want tea right now, so I'm not sure why I ordered it. Then again, it's not like I can ask for a cup of honey.

Solana points to the chalkboard on the wall. "What kind?"

"The sweet kind. Wildflower or whatever."

She furrows her brow. "No, I mean which *tea*?"

"Right. Uh, I dunno, how about green?"

"Yeah, you look like you could use some Zen. I'll be right over with it."

I nod instead of answering. I know I'm not that easy to read. Why is she so intuitive? How can she pick up on my mood with a single glance when Darcy claimed I was too stoic?

"I need to go potty," Liam announces.

"You know what to do." I pay for our stuff and head to the end of the counter to wait for him where we usually sit.

Solana approaches with my tea and an assortment of artisanal honeys. "These are some of the lavender and wild berry infusions we get from Hunnie, our supplier. I brought you a sampler."

She has no idea which direction my thoughts are traveling, so I lean in close. "Thanks, but I wanna sample you again."

She flushes a soft pink, and I fight off the urge to kiss her. "We'll discuss that later. But first, I want to know why you're upset."

I sigh. "On our way over here, I lost my temper and yelled at Liam. He talked about changing his surname to his stepfather's because it's easier to spell than O'Shaughnessy. He didn't mean anything by it, but I took it the wrong way. Then he informed me his ma told him he could change it to match hers when he's older. She's basically encouraging it."

Solana curls her lip. "That's fucked up."

"Right. Anyway, I lost my cool. I didn't mean to scare him, you know? It's just—"

"You think she's trying to replace you?"

"Exactly. She'd love nothin' more than to get rid of me. I tried to apologize, but Liam wasn't havin' it. He cried and told me he wanted to go home. Then *I* cried. It's funny, I wasn't a crier until I became a dad."

"That's understandable. Children have a way of touching people's hearts."

I nod. "The only reason he's smilin' is because I told him we were gonna see you."

"Aw, he's so sweet."

I sip my as-yet-unhoneyed green tea and meet her gaze. "Quite honestly, Solana, you're one of the only reasons I've smiled today too."

Liam approaches and settles on the stool beside me.

I grip his wrists to check his hands. "Did you wash?"

"Yup."

"With soap?"

He nods and picks up his doughnut. He takes a colossal bite, and the jam's smeared on his chin in seconds.

"Tasty?" Solana asks with a grin.

"Mm-hmm." He swallows the bite. "Thank you."

"You're welcome." She hands him a napkin. "How was school today?"

He shrugs and wipes his mouth. "Okay. But Mrs. Parker made me feel dumb."

Tensing, I set down my cup. "Wait a minute, you didn't tell me that."

"I was *gonna* tell you, but then you yelled at me. That's why I don't like writing our name. I tried to spell it and couldn't. Mrs. Parker said I don't try hard enough."

"That's a crock of shite," I mutter, squeezing six different kinds of honey into my tea. The Busy Bean has certainly broadened my honey horizons—before moving to Vermont, I never knew there were so many varieties of the sticky, sweet goodness. "Mrs. Parker doesn't know what she's talkin' about." Furious the old bat would make my child feel stupid, I stir like spoons are going out of style. "Complete and utter shite."

"You keep saying bad words, Daddy."

"Sorry. I really need to work on that, don't I?"

"Uh-huh."

I pat his back. "I'll help you practice today so we can show Mrs. Parker she's wrong."

"Great idea." Solana touches Liam's hand. "Practice is really important because practice makes—"

"I know, I know." He crosses his arms over his chest and pouts. "Practice makes perfect."

She shakes her head. "That's not what I was going to say."

"Liam, what did I tell you about interruptin' people? Please apologize to Solana."

His lip quivers. "I'm sorry."

She smiles. "It's okay, kiddo. What I was going to say, is practice makes *progress*."

Liam lifts an eyebrow. It's a move from Darcy's playbook, but it's cute on him. "Progress?"

"Yes, progress." She ruffles his hair. "You see, no one's perfect. It's not possible. If you're always trying to be perfect, you'll spend a lot of time feeling disappointed or sad. Kinda like you do now, right?"

He nods. "I'm sad Mrs. Parker thinks I'm dumb."

She squeezes his hand. "Well, you're *not* dumb. You're human. We all struggle sometimes, Liam. It's okay to not be perfect. It's okay to be human. That's why I say practice makes progress because as long as you're trying to *be* better and *do* better, everything will turn out okay. Look at me." Liam meets her gaze, and Solana smiles. "Do the best you can. If you try something and can't do it, try again. Always keep trying and never give up. Because one day, you'll make yourself really proud."

"I want to make Mommy and Daddy proud too."

"Well, I don't know your mommy, but I consider your daddy my friend, so I'll let you in on a little secret. You ready?"

"Uh-huh." Liam nods eagerly and leans in to listen.

"Your Daddy is *already* very proud of you. He loves you and thinks you're doing a great job with your letters. You don't have to be perfect for him—all he wants is to see you happy and healthy. So just keep trying to do better. Your *progress* will make him even prouder." She straightens and flashes me a smile. "Am I right?"

"One hundred percent." My voice is thick, barely over a whisper. Roderick must be chopping onions in the back because my eyes are burning and tearing up again. I swear, I'm not a crier. "Thank you. He needed someone to lift him up today."

"I know." Solana's gaze softens, the pools of golden amber touching my soul. "You both did."

I look away because her face is getting blurry now. I clench my jaw to keep a tear from spilling over. She saves me a shred of dignity and pretends not to notice.

Instead, she turns back to Liam. "So, what do you think, Mr. O'Shaughnessy? Do you want me to go grab the whiteboard and markers so you can work on your last name?"

"Yes, please." He bounces on his stool as Solana disappears into the back room. "Daddy, wait until you see how good I can make our name."

I pull him into a hug and bury my nose in his hair. "I love you." A tear lands on top of his head. I blink a few times and pull myself together. "Let me show you that coat of arms."

I release him and snag my phone to search for an image.

Liam touches my hand. "Daddy, I'm sorry I hurt your feelings. I'll never change my name."

"You can be whomever you wanna be. I'll love you no matter what your name is." I tip his chin up and bop his nose. "As long as you promise to always be kind. Remember what I told you my dad used to say when I was growin' up?"

"Yes. Pop-Pop said we should be kind to the Earth, to animals, to ourselves, and to others. Did I get all of them?"

Hearing my son's little voice recite my father's words makes my damn eyes burn again. What I wouldn't give for them to have a relationship.

"Yep, you got them. He also used to say, 'Treat others the way you want to be treated.' That means, you say you're sorry when you hurt someone. You learn from your mistakes and try to do better. You lift people up when they're down. Encourage them when they feel like quittin'. Include them when they feel left out. That's what it means to be kind, Liam. Kindness is all I ask of you."

He nods in understanding. Then straightens like a lightbulb went off in his head. He purses his lips while his little mind processes the epiphany. "So, what Pop-Pop and you really mean, is we should all be like Solana?"

"Yeah." I smile and hug him tightly. "Be just like Solana."

SOLANA

MOOD MUSIC: "NICE & SLOW" BY USHER

It's seven o'clock when my phone finally buzzes with the text I've been waiting for.

Declan: Come over.

My fingers fumble the letters as I type.

Solana: You sure?

Declan: Yes!

It was nearly five before he and Liam left the Busy Bean this afternoon. He planned to take him out for pizza, and then back to his mother.

Declan was quick to squash the idea when I suggested we reschedule our evening together because he still seemed upset. He scrawled his address on a napkin so fast, I'd swear it was a lightning strike.

After my shift, I hurried home to shower, shave my legs, and put on a couple coats of mascara. I tossed some toiletries and a change of clothes into an overnight bag, which I'm bringing even though I don't know if Declan will ask me to stay. While I despise making assumptions, I really hate feeling underprepared. My plan is to leave it in my car, so I don't *seem* too presumptuous.

I give myself a quick once-over in the mirror, pleased with the outfit I've chosen for my virginity-ending booty call—dark jeans, ballet flats, and a plum-colored V-neck sweater. Will always tells me the color brings out my eyes, and since Declan seems to enjoy looking into them, I figured it was a solid choice.

I snap a selfie to commemorate my outfit for tonight's milestone and send it to Will and River with the caption: Hasta la vista, virginity.

I should be somewhat apprehensive, right? I'm *a little* nervous, but those nerves aren't what I'm used to feeling in circumstances like these. Tonight's jitters manifest themselves as an excited flutter in my lower belly—not the panic that surfaced every time Chris suggested we have sex.

The thing is, even though I've only known him a matter of days, I trust Declan. I feel closer to him than I ever felt with Chris, and we dated for six months.

Declan's apology and behavior after yesterday's misunderstanding prove him a high caliber of man. When he returned my car, he probably didn't think I was listening to his safety dissertation, but I was. Then he made me feel better about the whole situation by allowing my monetary contribution. He didn't simply listen, he actually *heard* me when I talked about not wanting to feel like a charity case.

Even though the situation still has me miffed and embarrassed, his explanation for why he walked out when he learned I'm a virgin made perfect sense. I appreciate that he didn't want to hurt me—physically or emotionally. While Declan insists all he can give me is sex, he's already given so much more.

I'm used to crying alone. Since I'm leaving in January, I know I can't get used to it, but it felt so good to have a warm chest to lean on and strong arms to encircle me. A steady heartbeat against my ear, instead of the echo of my pulse in my head.

I know he'll take things slowly and be gentle for my first time, and maybe that's why I'm not as nervous as I thought I'd be. Although, I can't say the idea of being fucked hard and dirty *doesn't* appeal to me.

Declan's log cabin is huge. Deep in the woods, situated on a private lake with a view of the mountains, he's got his own slice of tranquility. It's dusk. Light spills from the windows, illuminating the plants and shrubbery outside. His meticulously stacked woodpile looms near a large shed, similar in design to the cabin. At the far side of the shed stands another massive structure, which I'm assuming is his workshop. Maybe I'll ask him to show me his tools and some of the furniture he's built. Although, right now, I've got only one *tool* in mind.

My footsteps crunch on the gravel path as I head for his front door. He must've heard my car pull up because he's leaning against the open doorway looking sexy as hell in jeans and a black T-shirt.

"Hello, Solana. Have any trouble findin' the place?" His rich brogue rumbles down my spine as always.

"No, your directions were perfect." I climb the steps and stop in front of him, peering into the cabin. "Where's Moira? I expected a tongue bath."

His low chuckle hardens my nipples. "Oh, you're gonna get a tongue bath, honey." He sweeps his gaze over me. "But I'll be the one givin' it to you."

My breath rushes out of me, and my panties graduate from damp to wet. I've been here for all of thirty seconds, and I'm ready to strip naked on his front porch.

"I'll keep that in mind." I gesture to the dog bowl on his porch. "No, really. Where's Moira?"

"Ethan's got her for the night. I don't want us to have any interruptions."

27

___

SOLANA

___

"Are you ready for this?" Declan interlaces our fingers and lifts my hand to his lips, pressing a kiss to each knuckle while I take in my surroundings.

His bedroom dominates the cabin's upper floor. I had to cling to the railing when we climbed the stairs because my legs wobbled like jelly. His private space is more refined than I imagined for a man so rugged. Several framed prints of the Irish countryside adorn the wall near his dresser. There's a sleek, hammered steel compass on another wall, alongside a watercolor painting of the Cliffs of Moher.

We're seated on the edge of his king-sized bed. His luxurious navy-blue comforter feels like he splurged on a thread count that's out of my league. Dark shades cover his windows, but the moon shines through a pair of skylights over his bed, casting a soft glow over the furniture. On the far side of his room, is an ornately carved wooden spiral staircase that leads to—

"What're you thinking?"

I meet his stormy gaze. "Just taking in the scenery."

"Like what you see?"

"Your home is lovely."

"Thanks." He kisses my hand again. "But you still didn't answer me, Solana."

"About what?"

He pats his bed. "Bein' ready for this."

"I'm ready." And I truly am—even though my palms are sweating, my breathing is erratic, and the butterflies in my stomach are going haywire.

He searches my face. "You sure?"

"Yes." I rummage in my purse. "I stopped at the pharmacy for condoms and—"

He points to his nightstand drawer. "I have everything we need."

"I figured, but I didn't want to assume." My hands tremble, so I shove them beneath my thighs to still them.

Declan frowns. "Are you nervous?"

"Yes, but not because of you."

"Tell me what's on your mind."

"Um . . . well, let's see . . . I have no idea how to please a man. I've never touched a penis. I hadn't even *seen* one in the flesh before yesterday, and that was for, like, all of a millisecond."

"Wait, you've never seen one? At all?"

"That's what I just said." I narrow my eyes. "Why does it matter?"

"It doesn't. I just figured I'd need to explain that we do things differently across the pond. Certain customs, commonplace for men in the States, are actually pretty rare in Ireland." He flushes and clears his throat. "But since you've no frame of reference to begin with, let's just . . . uh . . . forget I brought it up."

It takes a moment for what he's saying to register. And the hint of shame in his tone is something we'll need to revisit. "I think every part of you is perfect."

He touches my cheek instead of answering.

"Anyway, I want to do more than just lie there, but I don't know *what* I'm supposed to do. I probably should've asked someone or watched porn before I came over." I look away. "I dunno, I guess . . ."

"You guess what?"

"I'm worried about disappointing you." I shyly meet his gaze. "I don't want you to think I'm a shitty lay."

"First of all, you need to relax." He runs his fingers through my hair. "Trust that I'll take care of everything."

I know he will, but I want to make sure his needs are met. I'm not sure how I'll accomplish that when I've only ever attended to my own.

"Second, porn is hardly a good representation of real-life sex." He shakes his head. "And while asking people about it would've been a better option, everyone's first time is different. Many women don't enjoy it at all, so it's unlikely I'll be able to get you to come. Please don't worry about disappointin' me. Trust me, you won't. Instead, I want you to focus on what *you* feel. Do you think you can do that for me?"

"Oh, I know how to get myself off. I've had *tons* of orgasms with my vibrator—"

Shit. I clamp my mouth shut as my face and ears heat. My fingernails are suddenly the most fascinating thing I've seen all day. This rose gold nail polish is nothing short of epic.

He tips my chin up. "Tell me more."

"Not happening."

"Why?" He brushes his thumb over my lower lip. "What happened to that boldness I've seen from you?"

My brother calling me a filthy pig when he caught me touching myself, led me to believe all men would find my self-gratification methods trashy.

Of course, Declan is *nothing* like my brother. Outside of yesterday's misunderstanding, he's never made me feel dirty or ashamed. But that doesn't mean I'm not worried about his opinion.

"I don't want you to think less of me."

He blinks. "Think less of you for givin' yourself pleasure?"

I nod.

"Solana, that's one of the craziest statements you've ever made." He grips both sides of my face. "The image of you writhin' on that little bed while you touch yourself, is the sexiest thing my mind has ever conjured. A woman takin' control of her body—her pleasure—is beautiful, *especially* when that woman is you." He licks his lips. "And tomorrow, you're gonna show me how you do it."

"Uh, *nope*." I give a vigorous shake of my head to make him release my face. "There's no way in hell I'd let you watch."

Yet, deep inside, there's a voice telling me I want him to. Deeper still, is the part of me that needs him to.

"Got news for you, honey," he kisses my neck, "you *will*."

I love the way his brogue thickens when he's turned on, and how the dominance in his tone makes my heart race.

"Tomorrow, you're gonna let me watch you bring yourself to orgasm. Then I'll take over and we'll see who does it better." He licks the shell of my ear. The scrape of his stubble and the warm wetness of his tongue steal my breath. "And I promise to win that little contest again and again." His words, uttered in a husky whisper, send tingles down my spine because I *know* he'll make them a reality.

And with that oath, he burns off some of the fog of shame that's clung to me for all these years. My nerves dissipate, leaving behind a woman who is confident in her sexuality. A woman who feels beautiful and empowered instead of dirty.

"We'll see," I whisper.

"Lemme give you some incentive. I haven't stopped thinkin' about you since the moment I first saw you. You were so beautiful that day in the café, I couldn't speak." He nudges me to lie back on his bed and waits until my head rests on his pillow to continue, "And after you kissed me in the rain the other night, I needed a cold shower. And now that I've tasted the honey between your thighs, I'm damn near obsessed with you, Solana." He grips my chin. "So, I don't want you feelin' embarrassed about a fuckin' thing with me. Especially not when it has to do with that perfect body of yours. You hear me?"

"Yes."

"Listen, you're the first woman I've touched in four years. I'm out of practice, so I don't want to disappoint *you*, either. More than that, I don't wanna hurt you. I know you think I'm bossy, but you're in control here. I'll stop in a heartbeat if you ask me to."

"I know."

"Let me make love to you, honey." He brushes the hair back from my face. "I wanna get closer to that light that glows from within you. Maybe I can keep a bit of sunshine for myself."

I grip his face and pull his lips to mine. His kiss unravels what's left of my worry. I'm ready for this. For Declan—in whatever capacity he'll give himself to me—for as long as I can have him.

He breaks the kiss. "Undress for me."

Emboldened by his desire, I sit up and lift my sweater over my head. I toss it aside and unfasten my jeans, sliding them over my hips. I kick them off and lean back on my elbows.

His gaze darkens, traveling the length of my body. "Keep goin'."

"I will . . . after you take off your shirt."

He whips off the T-shirt and heaves it across the room, then turns to face me again. When I don't move, he lifts an expectant brow.

I toy with one of my bra straps. "Actually, I want your pants off before I remove this."

"We can do that." His jeans are gone in an instant, landing near his crumpled shirt. "Now, let me see those luscious tits of yours."

"You, sir, have a *filthy* mouth."

"I'm just gettin' started. Wait until your panties come off."

Flushing, I playfully slap his arm. "*Declan.*"

"That's right, honey. You'll say my name a lot louder when my tongue's teasin' your pussy."

His words ignite something inside me, some wanton part of myself I've kept locked in a tower of my shame. Well, fuck that shit. Castles are meant to crumble—it's time for that kingdom to fall. I rise onto my knees and remove my bra like a queen hanging up the final piece of her armor.

I toss the pink lace garment in the pile with Declan's clothes, then cup my breasts. "You want these?"

"Damn right, I do."

I rub my thumbs in circles over my nipples. "Come and get them."

"Solana . . ." The dark warning in his tone makes my inner muscles clench. "Honey, I'm tryin' so hard."

I scoot a little closer. "Trying to do what?"

"Not get carried away."

"Maybe I need that from you." I slide my matching panties off and fling them. I trail my fingertips down my abdomen to my center and meet his gaze. I swipe a knuckle through the wetness gathering there. "You want this?"

"More than I wanna fuckin' breathe."

"Then take it."

He lunges, knocking me backward, and covers my lips with his own. Tongue surging into my mouth, Declan's kiss steals my sanity. His calloused hands are everywhere at once. He cups my breasts and strokes the nipples while we roll around on his bed. His big, solid body moves on top of me, the thick length of him pressed against the juncture of my thighs. All that separates us is a layer of cotton—a barrier I want gone.

I grip his waistband. "Take these off."

"Not yet," he groans the words, kissing his way to my breasts.

He sucks each nipple like a favored treat before moving lower. I know what delicious ecstasy is to come, so my thighs fall open for him. Declan seizes the invitation and grips my hips, yanking my body to his mouth.

He stares up at me, lips hovering inches away from my center. "I want you to watch me lick you." He drags his tongue up and down, teasing my body's entrance before plunging inside.

My eyes flutter closed. "Declan, that feels so good."

"Watch me." My gaze snaps to his face with his erotic command. "Don't take your eyes off me. Not for a second." He flattens his tongue and rubs it on my clit.

I clutch his shoulders. "*Declan.*"

"Watch, Solana." He flickers his tongue on the sensitive nub a few times before switching back to long, decadent licks.

"Oh, God . . ." I knot my fingers in his hair and tug, urging him on.

"I fuckin' love the taste of you." He groans, pressing open-mouthed kisses everywhere his lips reach. "Mmm . . . sweeter than honey and more addictive than whiskey."

"Declan, please . . ." I thrust my hips toward his marauding tongue like I'll die if he stops.

"Watch me, baby."

My gaze finds his silky, russet brown hair, haphazardly tousled from the clench of my fingers. His long, dark eyelashes that fan his cheeks with every blink. I love the feel of his pillowy lips with all their softness, and how they're at odds with his hard jaw and the coating of red-brown stubble pricking my inner thighs. I can't see his urgent tongue, but I *feel* it from my scalp to my toes. And when he looks up at me with those swirling pools of molten charcoal, something inside me irrevocably shifts.

With his gaze pinned to mine, Declan clenches his fingers on my ass. And he keeps licking and rubbing and flicking his tongue on my clit until I fucking lose it.

"Oh, fuck . . . *Declan.*" My release curls my toes with its intensity. Before I can come down from the orgasm, he lifts me off the bed. Panting, I cling to him. "What're you doing?"

He carries me across the room and sets me on his dresser so we're eye-to-eye. He peers deep into mine. "Change of scenery."

"We're doing it *up here*?"

He sheds his boxers and rolls on a condom. "Honey, I plan to fuck you on every surface my cabin has to offer, but here's where we're gonna start."

I gasp when his lips find my neck. "Shouldn't my first time be in a bed?"

"Maybe." He sucks my earlobe, then gives it a nibble. "But if I *didn't* get you away from that bed, I would've fucked you into the mattress. And we can't have that happenin' just yet." He retrieves a bottle of lube from his nightstand drawer, squeezing some onto his palm as he approaches. "I figure I'll have a better chance of controllin' myself over here."

"Oh." It's all I can muster as a flare of lust incinerates me.

My thighs tremble as I watch him coat his thick length with lube. *This is it. It's happening.*

I'm ready for sex. For him. His body, and everything he has to offer. I'm so fucking thankful I didn't waste this milestone on Chris.

He nudges my thighs farther apart and grips his cock, lining himself up. "Solana, look at me." I meet his gaze. "Are you sure you want this?"

"Yes, Declan."

"*My God.* The way you say my name destroys me." He brushes his lips over mine in a soft, tender kiss. "I'll go slow but say the word and we'll stop. Understand?"

"Yes."

He kisses me again and eases forward, his cock stretching me to the brink of pain. My eyes water as I gasp and cry out against his lips.

"God, Solana, you're so fuckin' tight."

I cling to his shoulders as my body accepts him, inch by rock-hard inch. Pleasure hovers on the periphery, but right now all I can focus on is the sensation of being filled. It nearly overwhelms me, but Declan helps me acclimate. I squeeze my eyes shut and dig my nails into his skin as he slides deeper.

"Ungh. . ." The groan comes from his chest once he's fully seated inside me. It's a reward to finally witness some of his pleasure. The idea that *my* body is making him feel good, is a heady concept—one that pleases me to the depths of my soul.

He doesn't move for a moment, no doubt watching my response or waiting for his cue to stop. But I'm not going to stop him. Not now, not ever.

After years of emptiness, I want this fullness more than I imagined I would. I want *him* more than I expected to.

When I'd envisioned losing my virginity, I wasn't prepared for the emotional end of the spectrum. Yes, our bodies are joined, but I didn't expect to feel this connected to someone. It's almost like he's become a part of me. I don't know how people have one-night stands. Declan's only been inside me for a minute and I can't fathom anyone else taking his place. Ever. My chest tightens with the thought.

"You all right?"

"Mm-hmm." I can't open my eyes yet because I'm afraid he won't be there for me to hold on to when I do.

He rocks his hips slightly. "This okay?"

I nod.

"I don't wanna hurt you, love, so you need to tell me," he whispers, touching my cheek.

My eyes flutter open. "I'm okay, just move slowly."

He nods and starts to move. His controlled, rhythmic rocking feels amazing, so my body starts to relax around him. He palms my breasts, stroking and caressing them while he moves. I arch into his touch and moan.

He presses on my thighs. "Open a little wider for me."

I spread my legs even more as Declan changes his pace to a slow grind. His cock rubs my G-spot in ways my little vibrator never could.

I cling to him tighter. "Oh my God."

"Feel good?" His questions are getting choppier as we go along.

"Yes." I flex my hips to meet him, taking him deeper inside.

"Oh, *fuck*," he says through a clenched jaw.

He clutches my hips and moves a little faster. Then he slows, nearly pulling out, before easing back in. He does it a few times, and each time my body is almost free of him, the ache to pull him closer rises like a cresting wave.

His lips brush my ear. "Watch." I meet his gaze, and he points to where we join. "Watch me fill you."

Seeing the thick length of him slide into me like we belong this way, breaks through the remaining rocks in my tower, turning them to dust. I've never felt so alive. So free. So cherished. This man, with all his gruffness and domineering ways, makes me feel things I didn't think were possible. And I know I'll never get enough of him.

He pulls back slowly, then surges forward with another loud groan. "You feel so good."

I feel him in my chest. While it's his most powerful thrust yet, it's nowhere near his full potential. The wanton goddess inside me wants him to get there. I need him closer. I need his body on top of mine. I need more.

I cup his jaw. "Declan, I want to move to the bed."

"Okay." He hooks his arms under my thighs and lifts, hustling across the room. He lowers us to his bed and settles on top of me. Lining himself up, he fills me, hitting home in one hard thrust.

"Oh!"

"Wrap your legs around me."

The position's angle and friction provide *exactly* what was missing on the dresser. The heavy weight of him, with all those glorious muscles, anchors me to this moment. I savor each sensation from his warm, gasping breaths at my neck, to the scrape of his stubble on my skin. His slow, deep thrusts and the way he's fisting the sheets on either side of my head. The power in his movements, the clench of his thighs and butt as he delivers each thrust. And I *love* how he's rubbing against my clit and G-spot at the same time—something I could never quite accomplish during my solo sessions.

"Oh, *Declan*." I arch into him and moan.

"I love hearin' you, baby." He lifts his head and searches my face. "Does it feel good?"

"So good." It comes out on a wail, but I can't help it. I grip his back tightly as each thrust takes me higher.

And higher.

My orgasm builds within, strengthening and gaining traction as he moves.

"Solana, come for me, honey."

Declan buries his face at my neck and whispers my name over and over again like a prayer. Like he needs this closeness—our beautiful, primitive connection—as much as I do. Each raspy invocation tickles my skin as he worships my body. And every deep, rolling thrust is a devotion that lifts me out of the darkness.

I tighten my legs and slide my grip to his ass, pulling him closer. "Please don't stop."

The moans leaving my lips mix with his feral grunts and groans. My hips meet his thrusts faster and harder until I release, wailing his name. None of my countless alone-time orgasms come close.

Nothing compares to this.

Declan becomes a machine. He chases his climax, using my body the way he's craved, showing just how much restraint he exercised before. His pounding thrusts take me over the edge a second time. His entire body tenses, coiling like a spring.

Then he finally snaps.

"*Fuck.*" The veins in his neck stand out as he slams into me. Once. Twice. Three times. "*Solana . . .*" He keeps moving, riding the waves of his orgasm, before collapsing on top of me after a few more thrusts.

We're both gasping and covered in sweat. My legs are still wrapped around him. Everything trembles and quakes, throbbing and pulsing with the aftershocks of my release. I couldn't speak if I wanted to. Declan clings to me, his chest and shoulders heaving, cock still inside me. I can't explain the tears filling my eyes, or the clawing ache that settles in my heart at the thought of losing him in January.

After a few minutes, he rests his forehead against mine. "You all right?"

"Yes," I whisper, blinking the tears away. "Are you?"

"No."

Panic grips my chest. "What's wrong?" My insecurities rear their heads and tears gather once more, blurring my vision.

He cups my face and stares deep into my eyes. The affection in his gaze is plain as day. "Nothing's wrong. You're perfect. I swear to God, Solana, I'll never, *ever* get enough of you."

His words, and the reverence in his tone, join with the awestruck expression on his face, telling my insecurities to fuck off.

My breath rushes out of me in relief. "Then, why'd you say you're not okay?"

"Because I just found my new addiction."

28

DECLAN

Solana wrecked me.

She's got me so twisted up inside, I don't know how to move forward.

Both of us are panting. She's still wrapped around my body, her pussy gripping my cock. I brush a finger over her kiss-swollen lips and stare into her eyes. They're darker now. Amber with flecks of gold. The moonlight streaming from overhead casts a silvery glow on her cheekbones, pink from the scrape of my stubble. All at once, she's gold and silver and rose. Honeyed whiskey and sunshine. She's so sweet and sultry and radiant, it hurts.

I've never slept with a virgin—not even when I was one—so I didn't anticipate the fallout of taking Solana's virginity. The heady responsibility I shouldered when she allowed me places no one else has ever been. By gifting me her body and trust, she awakened something dangerous inside me—a primal, possessive instinct that makes me want to pound my chest and roar.

I'd stupidly thought having sex would soothe the burn of my desire. Instead, I want to fuck her until I'm all she knows.

Me. My name. My cock.

Because now that I've had a taste of heaven, I'll be damned if I'll go back to hell.

She didn't read into my addiction comment, which works for me. Everyone thinks I'm just a drunk, so it's refreshing to meet a woman who doesn't know that side. A woman who sees me for who I am—not the man I was. While I hate not being honest with her, I can't bear the idea of Solana turning her back on me for my mistakes. With her eyes so full of need, looking up at me like I'm her hero, I'd sell my soul to the Devil to be the man she thinks I am.

"What are you thinking?" she whispers.

"Depends. Do you want an honest answer, or what I *should* say?"

"I want both."

"We'll start with my original plan, then. I should tell you it's late and I'm tired. I should walk you out to your car so you can head home. I should say I'd be satisfied with gettin' together a few times a week. I should remind you we need to keep this casual because our time together has an expiration date."

"Suppose you *do* say all that." Her lip quivers. "If you were to lower your shield, who would I see?"

"A man who wants you to stay. One who wants to sleep with you wrapped in his arms so he can make love to you again in the mornin'."

"I want the second man."

"You don't know what you're doin' to me, Solana."

"What if . . ." She chews on her lip and stares up at the moon.

"What if, what?"

She meets my gaze. "What if we just let ourselves live? Indulge in each other and get what we need without the guilt or fear? Why can't we bask in the afterglow instead of looking for darkness?"

Because I'm afraid I'll fall for you.

"Because you'd be in my bed every fuckin' night, Solana."

"I'm not seeing a problem there."

"I don't want to make you feel used."

"You told me from the start, all you can give me is sex."

"But that doesn't mean it's the only thing I *want* to give you." I cup her face. "I don't want you feelin' like you're simply a body for me to fuck."

"So, basically, what you're saying is, you want to fuck me on a regular basis, while ensuring my sense of self-worth isn't tied to sex?"

"Right. Except, swap out regular basis for incessantly."

"Again, I'm not seeing a problem with *any* of this."

"Solana, you bring sunshine into my life." I point to the night sky. "And I'd give you the moon and stars if I could. All I can give you is sex, but you mean more than sex to me. Never doubt your worth—your shine—because it's fuckin' beautiful. I want you to keep that notion in the forefront of your mind."

She smiles and runs her fingers through my hair. "*While* you fuck me incessantly?"

I blink a few times, shocked that what I'm saying makes sense to her. "Yes."

"Then let's make it happen."

***

After a hot shower and a snack, Solana fell asleep in my bed with her perfect body pressed to mine. I dozed off after staring at the moon for a bit, but I'm wide awake now.

What started as a peaceful slumber is now anything but. Solana tosses and turns, flailing her legs and clutching the sheets. Her bare skin glistens with the sheen of sweat, and she's gasping for breath. She'd mentioned her nightmares, but it disturbs me to see one in progress.

My dad always told me never to wake someone having a nightmare, but my resolve not to intervene evaporates when her muffled moans become screams. I want to know what's tormenting her and why. More than that, I want to know what I can do to fix it.

"I can't get out. Mama, help me."

I grip her shoulders. "Solana, wake up." She thrashes in my hold, so I pull her closer. "Honey, you're all right. Wake up now."

Her eyes fly open and dart around the room. "I can't get my seatbelt off."

"Look at me. You're not in a car. You're safe in bed. I've got you."

The tension seeps out of her body when my voice registers. "Declan." The relief and desperation in her tone make my name sound like a prayer.

I smooth the hair back from her face. "I'm here. Everything's all right. Just breathe with me, honey."

She buries her face in my chest. Her tears come fast and heavy, the sobs wracking her petite frame. I hold her close and rub slow circles on her back in silence because I couldn't find words if I tried.

After a while, her tears slow, and her shoulders stop shaking.

She melts deeper into my embrace and sighs. "I'm sorry."

"For havin' a nightmare?" I cup her jaw and tilt her face to meet my gaze. "You've got nothin' to apologize for."

"But I woke you up."

"Forget about me. It's you who's sufferin'. Do you wanna talk about it?"

"It's always the same one," she whispers. "My father's already gone. The side of the van is crushed in, pinning me to the seat. My seatbelt is caught under a piece of metal, and I can't reach the buckle to free myself. I keep calling for my mom to help me, but she can't. She's fading, and I'm powerless to help her."

"*Christ.*"

"It feels so real. I *hear* the squealing tires and crunch of metal. The screams and sirens. I smell gasoline and smoke from the engine fire." She shudders and clutches at my back. "And I still can see—" She loses her words in a sob.

I tighten my embrace and run my fingers through her hair.

"Oh, God, there was so much fucking blood." Her whisper breaks my heart.

"I'm so sorry, honey. I wish I could do somethin' to ease your pain."

"You're already doing it. No one has ever held me after a nightmare."

"I'm glad I asked you to stay tonight. I hate the idea of you goin' through that alone."

"I'm used to it. But I hate how weak it makes me feel."

I stroke her cheek. "What do you mean?"

"It's bad enough to have scary dreams like a little kid, but then I need someone to coddle me?" She shakes her head. "It makes me sick how needy I've become. It's been fifteen years—I should have a handle on this by now. But I don't. Every day, it's some combination of a panic attack, a nightmare, or general anxiety about shit I can't control. I'm tired of feeling like a failure."

Rolling her onto her back, I brace my weight on my forearms and lean over so we're eye to eye. "Listen to me. We *all* need someone sometimes. We're not meant to take this journey alone. Turnin' to other people for comfort or support doesn't make you needy."

"I know," she mutters, chewing on her lip. "I just wish I was stronger."

"You *are* strong, Solana. It's not like you're cryin' over a broken fingernail—this is heavy shit you're dealin' with. Besides, there's no timeline for grief."

She sighs. "Maybe you're right."

"Think about it—no one can handle everything life throws at them with grace and dignity and strength. It's not possible to keep it together all the time. Sometimes, we drop the ball or stumble a bit before we catch ourselves. And other times, we fall and shatter into pieces. That doesn't mean you're weak or a failure, it means you're human."

"Yeah, but I do an awful lot of falling and shattering."

"Look at how many times you've gotten back up. Every time you fall, you gather your pieces and put yourself back together. Like a mosaic."

She looks up at the moon for a moment, deep in thought. "No. Mosaics make sense. I'm missing too many pieces for that. I'd say I'm more like a fucked-up jigsaw puzzle some old lady picked up at a yard sale."

I chuckle at the analogy. "Honey, we've all lost pieces of ourselves along the way."

"I've lost more than I can count."

"Not every missing piece is lost. Sometimes, life steals parts of us, like with your parents' deaths. You won't get those pieces back, so it doesn't make sense to pretend otherwise. But it's easy to forget about the pieces we leave behind on purpose."

"What do you mean?"

"The morsels we leave along the way. Think of them like breadcrumbs or seeds we scatter."

"Okay, Socrates." She giggles and kisses my cheek. "Are you always this philosophical?"

I laugh. "Wisdom comes with age, I guess."

"No, seriously. How come you're so smart about everything?'

"Trust me, there's a lot of shit I'm not smart about, and I've made plenty of mistakes. But I'd like to think I've learned from them. Anyway, to answer your question, this self-reflection stuff didn't start until after Liam was born. His birth—the whole idea of becoming a father—changed *everything* for me."

"What's it like to be someone's parent?" She peers up at me, her eyes shining in the moonlight. "How does it feel?"

"*Now* who's gettin' philosophical?"

She gives a wistful sigh. "I've always wondered about the nitty-gritty emotions behind parenthood."

I've never had a deep conversation about what it means to be a father—not even with Darcy. I've never talked with *anyone* as often, or as candidly, as I have with Solana. Something inside my chest tightens at the realization.

"Sorry for the midnight interview, but I never got the chance to ask my parents these types of questions."

"Don't apologize. I'm just tryin' to think of the best way to explain. I guess, to start, I'll say Liam is my greatest accomplishment. To tie it in with my Socrates speech, he is a piece of me—a seed—I've chosen to leave behind. In return, I'm gifted with the opportunity to watch him grow. I hope to guide him through life and teach him how to be a good man. Maybe one day, he'll remember something I've taught him, or some experience we shared, and he'll tell his kids about it. So, basically, my goal is to give him those morsels of nostalgia and wisdom to use how he sees fit."

"I totally get what you're saying with the breadcrumb analogy. It's kinda like Hansel and Gretel in the forest, except *you* are leaving the crumbs for Liam."

"Right. We never know when we'll leave behind a piece of ourselves that changes someone's life for the better." I kiss her forehead. "Like you did yesterday."

"Me?"

"Think about what happened with Liam. He'd had a shit day at school, then I hollered at him in the truck. Your kindness changed his mood and outlook. *You* made him feel excited about learnin' instead of discouraged. *You* reassured him about my love and pride. When you lifted Liam up, you gave him a piece of yourself. And when I saw him smile, that gift was passed along to me." She opens her mouth to speak, but I press a finger to her lips. "So, I don't wanna hear about you bein' a failure. With every fall, you've risen and stood taller, liftin' others up with you. Maybe you think your life is filled with chaos and fragments, but it's fuckin' beautiful too. Don't lose sight of that, Solana."

She pulls my lips down to hers in a kiss that touches my soul. Deep, full of passion and need, it speaks to parts of me that haven't listened in years. It's a kiss that might even have what it takes to fill up my hollow heart and make it beat again. Too bad I can't let that happen.

29

SOLANA

MOOD MUSIC: "SEX FOR BREAKFAST" BY CHRISTINA AGUILERA

The muted sunlight coming through a window illuminates Declan's bedroom in a soft golden glow. As I discovered at sunrise, the skylights are equipped with fancy automatic shades, programmed to close at a certain time.

Declan's on his side behind me, his arm draped over my hip, his breathing steady in sleep. Despite my nightmare and the actual number of hours we slept, my slumber was restorative. Something that hasn't happened in . . . well, fifteen years.

Our nakedness and tangled legs flood my mind with memories from last night. I couldn't imagine a better man to take my V-card. The experience was intense in every way. While my lady bits are a little tender, I want more. Burrowing closer to Declan, I release a blissful sigh.

He tightens his arm, pulling me flush to his body. There's no mistaking the prominent erection pressing into my lower back. Arousal pools at my core. I flex my hips, so my ass rubs against him in a slow tease. His breath catches, and he gets even harder.

I trace my fingertips down his arm. "Good morning."

"Mornin', Solana. You want somethin' from me?" The low rumble hardens my nipples.

"What if I do?"

He kisses the side of my neck. "Then, I'll give it to you." He reaches across me and snags a condom and the bottle of lube from his nightstand. I start to turn toward him, but he stops me. "Stay on your side like that. I wanna take you from behind."

The dominance in his tone ignites me. Not being able to see what he's doing heightens my other senses. I hear him tear the wrapper and roll on the condom. Then the cap and slick glide of lube as he coats us both. My heartbeat races when he settles behind me and coaxes my hips back. He lifts my upper leg and hooks it over his thigh, lines us up, and eases his cock inside me with measured strokes.

This angle feels much darker and more erotic than last night. Almost naughty or forbidden. *"Declan."*

"Baby, you feel so fuckin' good." He rains kisses on the back of my neck and my shoulders. "So perfect . . ." He slides a hand between my legs to tease my clit, and works his hips for several minutes in a slow, deep grind.

While it feels amazing, I crave the intimacy of eye contact. "I want to see your face," I say on a gasp.

Declan pulls out and rolls me onto my back. He presses my thighs open and settles between them. Bracing his weight on his forearms, he cradles my face in his hands and seals his lips over mine in a sensual kiss.

I tighten my legs around him and weave my fingers into his sleep-mussed hair. He strokes my cheeks with his thumbs while our lips and tongues dance. We both moan when he fills me again and starts to move.

Declan's weight on top of me, and looking up into his eyes while he thrusts, is exactly what I need. The sweet surrender intensifies when he interlaces our hands and presses mine into the bed at my shoulders. His pubic bone rubs my clit, and his powerful thigh muscles contract as his thrusts pick up speed.

"Oh, yes . . ." I grind against him, releasing a throaty moan as my orgasm draws nearer. "Don't stop . . ."

"Let me hear you." He follows up the low growl with a hard thrust, sending me over the edge.

My back arches off the bed. *"Declan."*

After a few more strokes, he rears up onto his knees like a stallion and lifts my ankles to his shoulders. He crosses his arms over my legs, holding them against his body. His gaze pinned to mine, Declan thrusts deeper. Harder. His control untethering as he draws closer to his own release.

The raw lust in his expression now is a thing of beauty. He's savagely sexy with his muscles and tattoos, and the feral grunts that leave his chest with each thrust. I love that *I'm* making him feel this good. Me. My body.

He moans and thrusts faster. Our gasps and the slap of our bodies joining is heady music to my ears. Suddenly Declan tenses and throws his head back, losing himself inside me on a groan. "Oh . . . *fuck* . . ."

My legs slide from his shoulders. He lowers himself to the bed and pulls me to his chest. He kisses me slowly and deeply, whispering my name over and over, and we come down from our high.

"Your O-face is sexy, Mr. O'Shaughnessy."

Declan laughs and kisses my neck. "You should see yours. I've got the sudden urge to swap out my skylights for mirrors."

"Funny, I thought *you* were the one who wanted to watch?" I flutter my lashes and give a playful shrug. "Guess that's not gonna happen."

Heat flares in his gaze. "Oh, it's happening. Preferably in the next twelve hours . . ."

"I can't do tonight."

He raises a brow. "And why's that?"

"Well, I work all day, and then I need to complete an assignment that's due by midnight. I need to keep my grades up or my old college won't let me back in." I chew on my lip. "I kinda forgot about the assignment when we talked about getting together. Can we reschedule for another day?"

"Of course." He brushes the hair back from my face. "School comes first."

"What are you doing on Saturday?"

"I've gotta help Ethan build a shed for his ma. Then, I've got my visit with Liam on Sunday. Ethan and I are takin' him to a hockey game at Moo U."

Damn.

"That sounds fun. Maybe you could come over on Sunday night? We can order takeout or something?"

He smiles. "Yeah, let's do that. I'm usually in a shit mood after I take him home, but that'll give me somethin' to look forward to."

Fifteen minutes later, I make my way into the kitchen while towel-drying my hair. "I'm going to head out to work now. Thanks for letting me stay over."

"My pleasure." Declan hands me a Dublin University travel mug and a brown paper bag. "Here's some coffee and an egg sandwich."

I blink. "You made me breakfast?"

He nods. "Most important meal of the day."

I'm not sure what's considered proper fuck-buddy etiquette, but I can guarantee it doesn't typically include sleepovers and breakfast. Or coffee in a mug from their alma mater.

I wrap my arms around him in a tight hug. "Thank you."

"You're welcome." He kisses my forehead. "Thanks for blowin' my mind last night and this mornin'."

"Likewise." I peer up at his face. "So, I know this is only about sex, but do you think it would be all right if I texted or called you sometime? You know . . . just because."

"Any time of the day or night." He pinches my ass. "Now, get goin' before you're late."

I pull his ear to my lips and lower my voice to a sultry whisper, "I look forward to blowing more than your mind on Sunday."

It occurs to me that I need to do some serious research in the blow job department, but *that's* what the internet's for.

30

SOLANA

MOOD MUSIC: "LONG DAY" BY MATCHBOX 20

Even though I'll always think of myself as a Colebury girl, the village of Hamilton is my official hometown. Situated about halfway between Montpelier and Colebury, Hamilton is basically a miniature—much less exciting—version of Colebury. We don't even have our own school district, so most kids are bussed elsewhere. Since my father taught at Colebury Elementary, I was lucky enough to ride with him for my first two years. After he died, I was subjected to the typical gum-in-your-hair school bus drama.

I cringe at the memory as I pull into Cody's driveway for our impromptu visit. With its sprawling front porch and old-fashioned white shutters, the yellow farmhouse I grew up in hasn't changed much in the five years since I've lived here. Not that I'm surprised. My brother is nothing if not stuck in his ways. The only difference is evidence of his new stepson: a large swing set in the yard, and a treehouse I would've killed for.

I park beside Cody's blue Ford pickup. Before I get out, I take a few deep breaths to steel myself for the encounter. I completely cut ties with him when I moved out. We only resumed speaking

161

last month, when I called to tell him I was moving back to Cole-bury for a bit.

After a quick pep talk reminding myself I'm a grown woman now, I climb from my car and head for the house.

The front door swings open when I reach the end of the path. Cody steps onto the porch with a broad smile, dressed in jeans and a black thermal.

"Sunny. It's been a while."

I trudge up the steps. "Hello, Cody."

At six-foot-one and built like a linebacker, women have always found him handsome. I never saw the appeal—he's my brother and a dickhead most of the time.

But now, the rare appearance of a smile, and the twinkle in his chocolate-brown eyes, makes him seem warm and approachable like our father. And with his dark hair closely cropped, and his skin bronzed from working outside, it *almost* looks like we shared the same mother too.

Cody lost his mom to cancer when he was eight. Our dad remarried a few years later after falling in love with my mother during a trip to Spain. Theirs was a whirlwind romance that soothed the ache of loss—for both Dad and Cody. Mom was the embodiment of maternal warmth and comfort. She loved Cody like he was her own, and he adored her. When I came along, we were the perfect family of four.

Then everything went to shit.

Cody holds out his arms. "Come here."

I stare at him for a moment. Cody *never* embraced me when I was little. Nor did he dry my tears or tuck me in at night. I got all my affection from my friends and their parents.

I raise a brow. "Huh?"

He laughs. "I can't hug my sister?"

"Of course you can hug me." I wrap my arms around him. "I'm just surprised, that's all."

"I've changed, Sunny."

"Me too."

He squeezes me tightly. "I'm glad you came."

"Thanks for the invite." I peer into the foyer. "Where's your lady love?"

He holds the door open. "Dee went to the grocery store to pick up school snacks."

"Snacks are good." I slip my shoes off and leave them on the mat by Cody's boots.

He points to the floor. "Be on the lookout for stray Legos. They hurt like a bitch to step on."

I want to make a snarky comment about how he never tolerated my Barbie stuff strewn through the house, but that would likely burst the bubble we're in. Instead, I say, "Everything looks so . . . homey."

He chuckles. "Yeah, well, I can't take credit for that. But thanks."

I follow him into the kitchen, which now boasts granite countertops and stainless-steel appliances instead of our old farmhouse wood and porcelain. The island remains, and the cabinets are still painted white, but everything else is sleek and modern.

"Wow. The kitchen's amazing."

"Thanks. We remodeled last spring." He points to the fridge. "Want something to drink? We have water, seltzer, and apple juice."

Cody also doesn't drink alcohol—one of the few things we have in common.

"I'd love a seltzer, please."

He opens the door. "Orange blossom or watermelon punch?"

"Since when do you drink flavored seltzer?"

He grins and opens a drawer. "Since someone else took over the grocery shopping. Do you still like to use a straw?"

"Yes, please." I tilt my head to the side. "I'm surprised you remember."

He cracks open a can, plops a straw inside, and hands it to me. "I'm thirty-seven. Not eighty-five. And just because you didn't think I was paying attention, doesn't mean I missed every detail."

He grimaces and touches my shoulder. "Just the ones that mattered to you, I guess."

"Cody, it's fine. Let's move forward."

He nods. "For what it's worth, I'm sorry I was such a shitty excuse for a dad. The accident wrecked me. After losing *two* moms, I checked out emotionally and bottled everything up. Not to mention, I had no fucking clue how to raise a seven-year-old girl. You deserved better than you got from me. I'm truly sorry, Sunny."

I stare up at his face. "Who are you, and what've you done with my brother?" The regret in his eyes makes mine burn. I blink rapidly and touch his arm. "Your apology means more than you realize. And I appreciate everything you did for me."

He nods. "How're classes?"

"Good. I did schoolwork all day yesterday and most of today, so I'm all caught up for the week."

"You staying in town for the whole year?"

"No, just the semester."

"You never explained why. I mean, you had a full scholarship . . ."

"The anxiety was so bad, I couldn't focus. I was afraid I'd wreck my GPA or flunk out, so I decided to step back for a semester and get out of the city to recharge. Hopefully, I'll get my shit together so I can go back in the spring."

"Makes sense. You should hang out and watch a movie with us after dinner. I'd say you've earned the break."

"Thanks, but I have plans tonight."

My innards flutter when said plans, and the stormy Irishman they involve, flit through my brain. I've been counting down the hours since I left Declan's house Friday morning.

"Okay, maybe next time." He motions for us to relocate to the living room. "How're your friends? I haven't seen either of them in years."

I settle on the couch and give him a quick update about River and Will. Cody asks questions and genuinely seems interested.

For the first time in our relationship, the conversation comes easily.

He eyes me. "You dating anyone?"

"Not really, no. It doesn't make sense to start something when I'm only going to be around until January, so I'm focusing on school."

"Good." He smirks and flexes his huge biceps. "Keep it that way." Outside, the rumble of an engine in the driveway draws his focus. He peers over my shoulder to the window behind me, and the man's face literally lights up with a smile. "L.J. is here."

"Jesus. I never expected to see you get so excited about a kid."

Cody stands and crosses the room to the foyer. "That's because you haven't met this one."

I stretch out on the couch. I don't know what this L.J. did to soften my ornery brother, but I love him for it.

Heavy footsteps sound on the porch, and Cody opens the door. "Uh, it's kinda late for a nap, man. How long has he been out?"

"He's been sleepin' for an hour. I tried to keep him awake, but he wasn't havin' it. Where's his ma?"

Oh.

My.

Fucking.

God.

DECLAN

MOOD MUSINGS: NEVER SAW THAT ONE COMING.

"Dee went to the store." Bridges juts his chin at Liam. "He enjoy the game?"

"Loved it. He and Henry were in their glory. I dunno if I've ever seen them so riled up. Don't be surprised if he's talkin' about hockey lessons when he wakes." I hand him Liam's backpack. "His inhaler's in the front pouch. Tell Darcy he needs it refilled."

"Did you have to give him a dose?"

"No, but the counter says he's only got six left."

"Did he have dinner?"

The aroma of lasagna wafts from the kitchen. It's one of my favorite dishes Darcy makes. My mouth waters at the memory. Her cooking is probably the only thing I miss about being married.

"No. We had a late lunch."

Bridges nods and steps aside so we can enter.

I shift Liam's sleeping body on my shoulder so his head doesn't hit the doorjamb. "Where do you want him?"

He points to the living room. "Stick him on the couch next to my sister."

"Didn't know you have a sister."

He rubs his jaw. "We just reconnected."

"Good for you." I carry Liam into the room, pausing near the couch. "Hello, I hope you don't mind compan—"

My gaze lands on a set of eyes the color of Irish whiskey. My knees buckle, making me nearly drop my sleeping child, but I regain control and roughly plop him onto the cushions. He stirs, then burrows into a little ball.

Solana stares up at me, wide-eyed and white as a ghost. She opens and closes her mouth, but no sound comes out.

Bridges appears at my side. "This is my little sister, Sunny."

"I got that." My scalp prickles, and my ears buzz as pieces of the story fit themselves together.

"Sunny, you'll meet the little guy when he wakes, but this is L.J.'s father, Declan." He opens an old chest and pulls out a blanket, draping it over Liam.

"Hello." Her voice is nothing but a strangled whisper.

I can't speak. I can't fucking breathe or think.

"Excuse me." Solana jumps to her feet, rushes down the hall, and shuts herself into the bathroom.

Bridges stares after her in confusion. "Sunny, what's wrong?"

No answer.

"Jesus Christ," he mutters, scrubbing a hand over his face. "I hoped she'd outgrown the drama queen phase." He meets my gaze. "Guess not."

I give a lazy shrug. "Women."

"Yep."

"Gotta go." I lean down to kiss Liam before turning back to Bridges. "Tell your sister it was nice meetin' her." I force an even tone when I feel like screaming.

"Will do," he mumbles. "Later."

I give him a wave and stalk to my truck when what I want to do is sprint. Hands shaking, I jump into the driver's seat and jam my key into the ignition. The engine starts. I ease my foot onto the gas pedal instead of stomping. The last thing I need is to peel out of here like I'm leaving the scene of a crime.

I glance in my rearview mirror. Solana's little yellow car is tucked on the opposite side of Bridges's truck. I was so focused on getting Liam home in time, I didn't notice it when we arrived.

I wait until I'm back on the main road before slamming my fist on the steering wheel. My battle-cry reverberates through the cab as questions circle my brain on an endless loop.

How did I not realize that Solana is Cody Bridges's little sister? Better yet, why did I have to be drawn to a woman so closely tied to my vindictive ex-wife? Solana told me her last name is Delgado. Why haven't Bridges or Darcy ever mentioned her? How did Solana not know our connection before? Then again, what if she *did* and chose to keep it from me? Judging by the sheer panic on her face, my gut tells me she figured it out when I did, which means we both missed the clues. I drive on autopilot, barely seeing what's ahead of me.

I need a drink.

I clench the steering wheel as the location of every bar and liquor store in the county drift through my mind.

How long have I been driving?

Blinking, I focus on the road to get my bearings. The Mountain Goat is closest to where I am now. A left-hand turn, not even a mile up ahead. I could stop for just a few minutes, maybe have a beer. No one there will try to stop me.

Four years! My inner fighter screams from the sidelines, begging me to drive past the bar.

I take a few deep breaths, but my mind goes back to Solana. If I want to keep my son, I have no choice but to cut ties with her. The Busy Bean Café is a thing of the past for me. In fact, I need to avoid that section of town—at least until January. A wave of pain slams me.

I need a drink.

While I can live without apple turnovers, I'm already grieving the loss of our conversations—those deep, meaningful interactions which touched places inside me I never knew existed. I'll never again kiss those soft lips or stare into her soulful eyes while we make love. The Mountain Goat is no more than a hundred yards ahead.

Just one sip of whiskey to calm me.

Kind, beautiful Solana. What a fucking hero I was to take her virginity. I flick on my turn signal.

I need a drink.

SOLANA

I'm standing in Cody's half bathroom, running cold water on my wrists—one of my go-to calming methods. Of course, the technique is only effective when there's a sink, so like someone with an overactive bladder who's always on the lookout for the closest toilet, I'm known for my dramatic exits. While they seek only bathrooms, my arsenal includes kitchens. Today's meltdown—courtesy of the Irish bomb that just dropped—required the privacy of a bathroom. Declan's been gone ten minutes, and I still haven't been able to regulate my breathing.

There's a tap on the bathroom door. "Sunny, what's going on?"

Cody's voice is soft. Concerned. This tentative behavior from him is new. When I was young, he'd pound on my door or just barge right in. Granted, it took five years with no contact, but I appreciate his developing respect for my boundaries.

Regardless, I need to get out of here before Liam wakes and lets it slip we've already met.

"I'm not feeling well."

"What's wrong?"

"I had a sandwich from the gas station, and I think something was wrong with the meat. The seltzer made my stomach bubbly. Now my lunch is gurgling. I feel like I'm gonna hurl."

"Can I get you something?"

If there's one thing my brother can't handle, it's barf. I make a few gagging noises and spit into the toilet. I hear Cody take a few steps back from the door. I fake a couple more dry heaves, then flush the toilet and wash my hands.

Opening the door, I clutch at my abdomen. "I think I need to take a raincheck for tonight. I'm so sorry."

"It's okay. I'm sorry the seltzer upset your stomach." He rakes a hand through his hair. "This sucks. I really wanted you to meet my family. Dee is going to be disappointed."

Dee.

Why does Cody have to call everyone by some choppy nick-name? When he told me his wife's name on the phone, I assumed it was short for Deanne or Darlene or Dierdre. Nope. Dee is for Darcy. Too bad I didn't fucking *ask.*

Of course, now that I think about it, Declan only mentioned Darcy by name once—usually it was *my ex* or *Liam's ma*—so I never would've made the connection.

And then, there's L.J. *Are you fucking kidding me?*

Liam James?

Liam John?

Liam Jacob?

Liam Jingle-heimer Schmidt?

My brain runs down the list of possible middle names like it's going to change the reality that he's Declan's son.

"Tell your wife I'm sorry." I make another gag and press my hand over my mouth.

Cody's eyes widen. His gaze darts to the newly carpeted floor. "Are you good to drive?"

"Yeah." I snatch my purse from the couch, rush to my car, and feign another dry heave outside the door for Cody's benefit. Then, I jump inside and leave, breathing a sigh of relief when I reach the main road.

I can't believe Declan's bitchy ex-wife is my sister-in-law. Or that *my* brother is Liam's stepdad. Sure, the nicknames muddled things a bit, but how did I miss the signs? Everything clicked the moment I heard Declan's voice in the foyer. I wanted to hide, but the panic paralyzed me. I'll never forget the look of betrayal on his face.

I need to explain. Make sure he understands I was just as blindsided as he was. Ask for his forgiveness for my brother's sins and beg him not to pull away from me. I turn onto the highway that leads across town to his cabin.

33

DECLAN

MOOD MUSINGS: BUT THEY ALL HAVE POWER OVER ME.

I storm into the Gin Mill like a pilot on a kamikaze mission. And who knows? Maybe that's what this is. Deep down, I don't want to crash and burn, which is why I came here instead of the Mountain Goat or a liquor store. A cry for help, as they call it.

Ethan's shift just started. He and Alec Rossi are behind the bar, engrossed in conversation. I march over and plop onto a stool.

Ethan blinks, his jaw dropping open. "Dec, what the hell're you doing here?"

"I need a drink."

"Well, I'm sure as fuck not serving you," he sputters, gripping the edge of the bar. "You gonna tell me what's up?"

Alec's gaze burns into the side of my head. "You all right, man?"

"No."

Ethan leans in. "Start talking."

"She's his sister." I rest my head on the edge of the bar and squeeze my eyes shut. "His fuckin' *sister*."

"Who?"

"Solana."

Ethan slaps the back of my head. "Fuck the riddles, bro. Who are you talking about?"

My patience wearing thin, I stare up at him in disbelief. "Which part of the disaster I've created are you not grasping?" I grit my teeth. "Solana. Is. His. Sister."

His eyes flash blue fire. "*Whose* fucking sister?"

I can't bring myself to say it aloud.

"If it's the Solana I know of, he means Cody Bridges," Alec says.

"Holy fuck." Ethan grabs my arm. "How'd you find *that* out?"

"She was sittin' on his couch when I dropped off Liam. Now, *please* give me somethin' to drink."

"You know I can't do that, Dec."

Alec pats my shoulder. "No one in my bar is gonna serve you alcohol, my friend. But if you want something NA, it's on the house. I know you like the oatmeal stout."

"That works. Thanks."

He pours one of the non-alcoholic beers he'd brewed with May's brother, then sets the glass in front of me. "What's going on between you and Sunny Bridges?"

"She told me her name was Solana Delgado."

Alec rubs his jaw. "Technically, it is. Rosita Delgado was her mother's name. Sunny's parents gave her a hyphenated last name when she was born. She must've dropped the Bridges part after her fallout with Cody."

"How do you know all this?" I ask, meeting his brown gaze.

"Small town, man. Besides, my family's known Sunny since she was born. Zara didn't mention anything to you?"

"Your sister hasn't been there the past couple times I've visited the Bean. Besides, it's not like I would've asked about her new employee like some creeper."

Alec chuckles. "Good point. That would've raised Z's hackles for sure." He lifts a brow. "So, are you and Sunny sleeping together?"

"It won't happen again. That's for damn sure," I mutter, scrubbing a hand over my face. "I'm not tryin' to lose my son."

He watches me chug the contents of my glass before speaking. "Does Cody know?"

"He's probably figured it out by now."

Ethan shakes his head. "I'm confused. How did *she* not know who you are to her?"

"She mentioned havin' a shitty relationship with her brother. And it's not like I drone on about Darcy. I guess the topic never came up."

"Did she say anything to you at his house?" Ethan asks.

"Nope. Just looked like she was gonna faint." I clench my jaw. "Or have another panic attack."

Alec is looking at his phone now, his brow deeply furrowed as he taps on his screen. Then he straightens and tucks it in his pocket. "No wonder you want a drink."

"Yeah." I rest my forehead on the edge of the bar and close my eyes.

Alec is wrong. I *always* want a drink. The only exception is during time spent with Liam or Solana. Now that seeing her has become an impossibility, the urge to drown my frustrations in a bottle of whiskey is all-consuming.

All around me, people are laughing and chatting in that jovial way people do at pubs. The music's playing an upbeat track, which almost makes me want to tap my foot. The place smells like beer and whiskey, cologne and perfume. *Like home.* A deep yearning bubbles in my veins.

Right now, I'm not an outsider in Vermont. I'm not some fuckup who can't get his shit together. I'm back home in Galway, on a barstool at Kings of Connacht, surrounded by people who like me. Laughing with my dad and his friends. Flirting for the sake of flirting. No frustrations. No responsibilities. Just me and my glass of Tullamore D.E.W.

My mouth waters for just a taste. One little sip. I can almost feel the warm burn sliding down my throat, heating my belly. I just want a taste—

An arm settles around my shoulders. "You look like you need a friend."

The feminine voice isn't one I expected, but it makes sense Alec would summon his girlfriend—their place is nearby. Not to mention, May Shipley knows all too well the struggle with alcoholism.

"Hello, May. What're you up to tonight?"

"I was doing some knitting, waiting for dinner to heat in the crockpot, but now I'm hanging out with you."

I meet her gaze, not at all surprised by the compassion reflected in her light brown eyes. "You don't have to do that. I'm all right."

She shakes her head, dark hair swinging with the movement. "You told me you haven't set foot in a bar in four years. You're not all right and we need to get you out of here. Let's take a walk."

I rise from the stool and glance at Alec. "Thank you."

He nods. "Got you covered, man."

May leans across the bar and kisses him. "See you in a bit. Love you."

"Love you too, baby doll." His eyes shine with affection, pride, and all those other feelings people get when they love someone. He gestures to May and me. "You two go talk. I've got a few things to finish up here, but I'll be home soon."

I give Ethan a wave and follow May, her long legs eating the distance across the bar. She's probably close to six feet—easily one of the tallest women I've ever met. Solana's petite frame drifts through my mind and my chest tightens. How the fuck am I supposed to stay away from her?

"Where're we goin'?"

"To our place. It's not far from here. Alec texted me at a good time—I was already on my way over to get him." She smiles. "I've got meatballs cooking for dinner."

"May, I appreciate you chattin' with me, but please don't let me interrupt your meal."

"You're eating too."

"Thanks, but you really don't have to feed me."

"I insist." Her gaze burns into me. "That's what friends do."

I don't have a rebuttal for that, so we walk the short distance to her place in relative silence.

She opens the front door and leads me inside. Delicious aromas waft from the kitchen, making my stomach growl. All I ate today was a soft pretzel at the hockey game, which tasted like cardboard compared with one of Roderick's pretzels.

May points to the couch. "Have a seat." She grabs us each a bottle of water and settles beside me. "I hear you're in a predicament."

A dark chuckle rumbles in my chest. "I wouldn't believe the level of irony if it wasn't happenin' to me."

"So, tell me about Sunny Bridges."

"I may have thought twice if that's how she introduced herself." I scrub a hand over my face. "Instead, she knocked me senseless the first time I looked at her."

"Then, go for it. Who cares what people think?"

"Somethin' tells me you don't have much experience with my ex."

"I've seen her in the courtroom a few times, and at legal events she's attended with her boss." She sips her water. "I know she's kinda bitchy, but your love life is out of her jurisdiction."

Sometimes, I forget May's an attorney. As such, she runs in some of the same circles as my paralegal ex-wife and her colleagues.

"In theory." I rub my temples. "But she's on a mission to keep Liam away from me, so she'll use any excuse to make that happen."

"Why?"

"Because I fucked up. Hence the divorce."

I squeeze my eyes shut and beat back the memories of that

night. How a single decision cost me my marriage, my son, and my job. How I've been a shell of myself ever since. But I don't feel like sharing those details with May. Then again, she's probably already heard all about it through the Darcy grapevine.

"Everyone fucks up," she murmurs.

"Yeah. But I didn't *just* fuck up. I fucked myself over in the process."

"How so?"

"Well, I was so desperate not to be written out of Liam's life, that I agreed to some things I shouldn't have. She's got me bent over a barrel, May."

"You mean with the terms of your divorce?"

While I'm pretty sure May doesn't practice divorce law, I'd imagine she's familiar with the basics, so it shouldn't hurt to get her take on things.

"Yeah. I've gotta remain sober and attend meetings, which I'd do anyway." I meet her curious gaze. "But *that* wasn't enough for Darcy. She's gotta have the upper hand with everything, so she used her legal connections to fuck me. Her lawyers added a clause stating *any* demonstration of poor judgment is grounds for the loss of my visitation rights. As it stands, I'm already limited to only twelve hours a week." I clench my jaw. "That kid is my everything. I can't risk losin' him."

"Who decides what counts as poor judgment?"

"The court."

"Okay, so it's not like Darcy can snap her fingers and make it happen. You'd have to make a serious misstep, like commit a crime."

"It says right in there that if I happen to get arrested for *any* reason—whether or not I'm at fault—I automatically lose visitation for thirty days, pending a court date."

She nudges me. "So, don't get arrested."

"Believe me, I'm *not* the kind of guy who looks for trouble." I sip my water. "But I'm tired of walkin' on eggshells."

"Listen, I know it feels like it, but she can't take away your son just because she disagrees with something. No judge will let that happen."

"Except, she knows *all* the judges," I mumble. "And I'm pretty sure me sleepin' with her husband's little sister counts as poor judgment."

"Who you sleep with is none of her business." May shakes her head. "Again, your love life should *only* be a factor in your visitation if you're involved with someone who's a danger to your son. I don't know Solana well—she's closer in age to my twin siblings —but I've never heard a bad thing about her. Besides, it's not like Cody would let Darcy label his sister as a predator."

"Nah, he'd just kill me for touchin' her in the first place."

"Look at me." I meet her gaze, and she gives me a sly smile. "Nobody has to know."

"But people *do* know."

"Outside of Alec and me, and I'm assuming Ethan, who else knows?"

"Her friends, River and Will."

"Do you think they'd want to hurt her?"

"No, definitely not."

"Then, my advice is to live your life. Keep things quiet and enjoy each other's company. Bottom line, you need to stop giving your ex-wife more power than she really has."

"Easier said than done. If Darcy wants to make my life hell, she will. That includes getting a court order."

She smirks. "Too bad you don't have someone in your corner with legal connections."

DECLAN

MOOD MUSINGS: I DON'T HAVE A CHOICE.

After a delicious meal with May and Alec, I turn onto the private road that leads to my cabin with a heavy sigh.

Stop giving your ex-wife more power than she really has.

May's words have circled my mind for most of the drive home. It's true—I *do* give Darcy a lot of power. The thing is, with all her connections and money, she *has* power. No one dares to cross the Jensen family. Her father owns the biggest logging operation in Vermont. She's a princess who gets what she wants when she wants it. Too bad I missed the fine print on her warning label.

May thinks I should take Darcy to court and demand equal custody of Liam. She listed off my four years of sobriety, property ownership, and successful business endeavors as evidence to support my case. Her reasoning seems logical, but what happens if I lose? Will the court revoke what I already have?

The sad truth is, no matter how much I want her, I need to stay the fuck away from Solana Delgado *aka* Sunny Bridges *aka* the definition of forbidden fruit. But that's going to be tough since the beautiful, sweet indulgence I desire is sitting on my porch with my dog across her lap.

35

SOLANA

Declan marches up the walkway to his porch, stopping at the bottom step to glare at Moira and me. He crosses his arms over his chest and glowers when Moira thumps her tail on the wooden floor instead of rising to greet him.

He and I stare at each other for a few moments before I break the silence, "You shouldn't leave your dog outside."

"Didn't plan on bein' gone that long." He points to my car. "How long have you been sittin' here?"

I peek at my phone. "Three and a half hours."

"Why'd you come?"

"Because I want to talk."

His scowl deepens. "Unless you're gonna tell me I imagined what I saw earlier, there's not much to discuss."

I stiffen my spine. "Maybe you don't have anything to say, but I've got plenty."

"You blindsided me, Solana."

"You make it sound like I knew our connection and kept it from you. I was just as surprised as you. Today was the first time I've seen Cody in five years. We only started talking again last month, and it's been superficial as fuck. He and I know nothing about each other. He told me his wife's name was *Dee*, and I only learned L.J.'s today."

Declan's face and ears turn bright red. "*Don't* call him that in front of me. His name is Liam Joseph O'Shaughnessy!" At his roar, Moira jumps to her feet and whines, pacing the porch between us. Declan narrows his eyes. "Your brother would love nothin' more than to make my son into L.J. Bridges, but I'll die before I let that fucker replace me." He climbs the bottom two steps and jerks his thumb toward the driveway. "Now that you're in the equation, it's only a matter of time before he shows up here with his rifle."

"He won't. I didn't let on that I knew you."

"You ran into the bathroom like a drama queen."

"Don't you *dare* call me a drama queen. That's straight out of Cody's arsenal, and I'll be damned if I let someone else insult me."

"Sorry, but you made it obvious by runnin' off like that."

"I told him I didn't feel well and was going to barf. I asked for a raincheck and left before Liam woke up. Cody's none the wiser."

"Maybe for now. But it's only a matter of time before you slip up." He knots both hands in his hair. "I can't believe you're his fuckin' sister."

"*Half*-sister. It's not like I had my choice of kin. Trust me, my blood is the only thing I share with Cody."

"It's one too many for me." Declan slowly shakes his head. "You need to leave. I can't do this. If Darcy ever got wind . . ." He squeezes his eyes shut. "I'm sorry, Solana, but I won't risk losin' my son. Not for you, not for anyone."

"So, that's it? You're just going to cut ties with me like nothing happened between us?"

"That's exactly what I'm gonna do." He climbs another step. "Because I don't have a choice."

"No one's holding a gun to your head."

"You can say that because you've got nothin' to lose." He runs both hands over his face. "I know I told you all I could give you was sex, but things have changed. I can't give you a damn thing. Please leave."

"Fine. I'll go." I slowly climb to my feet and blink back the tears threatening to spill over. "I'm sorry. I didn't mean to cause trouble in your life. The *last* thing I'd ever do is jeopardize your relationship with your son."

He clenches his jaw but doesn't speak.

"I appreciate our talks, and I enjoyed getting to know you. You're a decent man and an excellent father." I wipe an escaped tear. "Good luck with your tiny house resort, and thanks for uh . . . taking my virginity, I guess."

Pain flashes on his face, but he still doesn't respond.

I need to get out of here so I can cry in peace. I pat Moira's head and give Declan an awkward thumbs-up before stepping around him.

"Excuse me," I whisper, rushing down the stairs.

"Solana, I'm sorry." His voice is rough, but he stays rooted to the steps.

As I sprint past his truck to my car, I toss an envelope full of cash on the hood. It's the other two hundred and fifty dollars for my tires. One thing's for damn sure—I refuse to be a burden or owe anyone a fucking thing. Especially not a man who thinks my bloodline alone will ruin his life.

I jump into my car and crank the engine, peeling out of his driveway. I don't bother to look in my rearview mirror because what's behind me is in the past. All my life, I've done a shitty job of keeping my past from coloring my present and future. Fuck that. New plan: I'm going to focus on being present, so I can take charge of my future and push forward. That's right, Solana Delgado will not mourn another ghost—no matter how fucking perfect he is.

After a good cry on the phone with River and a pint of Ben & Jerry's Chunky Monkey, I wash up and put on my jammies. I slide between the crisp sheets and turn off my lamp. It's well after midnight by now, and I need to be at the Busy Bean by seven. Too bad I'm wide awake.

I stare at the ceiling and find myself wishing I had skylights. Maybe I'll see if River's mom minds me sticking some of those glow-in-the-dark stars up there. One of the few sweet things Cody did when I was little was put a galaxy of stars on my bedroom ceiling. I used to lie awake and make wishes on them. It was always for the same thing—a family. Now, my wishes have changed a bit, but the theme is still the same. I gaze at the smoke detector's blinking light and pretend it's one of my stars.

My phone chimes with a text. I snatch it and read the screen.

Declan: I'm sorry I hurt you.

A little freaked out he'd text me as I was thinking about him, I send him a thumbs-up emoji instead of any real reply.

Declan: Can we talk?

Solana: I thought you weren't interested in speaking to me unless I burned down my family tree?

Declan: Can you understand where I'm coming from?

Solana: Yup. Read you loud and clear. Especially the part where you cut ties and told me to leave.

Declan: I need to talk to you.

Solana:It's late. I've had a shitty day. We can chat some other time.

Declan: Fine. Please remember to lock your car doors.

I thought Cody talked in riddles, but he's got nothing on this guy.

Solana: That's a bit cryptic.

Declan: The money is under your passenger seat. Don't try to give it back to me again.

Wait, he's here? I sit up, clutching the phone.

Solana: Where are you?

Declan: Outside.

My heart picks up speed, which royally pisses me off. I shouldn't be sitting here all bated breath and fluttery, clinging to some fiber of hope like it's a lifeline. It's not fair he has this effect on me. But . . . it might be interesting to hear what he has to say.

Solana: Since you're already here, let's talk.

A minute later, I hear his footsteps coming up the deck stairs. I smooth my hair and try to make myself presentable, which is next to impossible when one wears a flannel Christmas nightgown in September. And I'm sure my red, puffy eyes will earn points for sexiness.

Declan knocks on my door.

"It's open," I call.

He turns the knob, cursing under his breath as the door swings inward. All six foot three of him appears in the doorway with a scowl on his face. "Why do you have an aversion to locks?"

I cross my arms over my chest. "Did you come here to lecture me about locks?"

"No, but the opportunity presented itself. *Again*."

"Are you going to stand in the doorway or come in?"

He steps inside, and his presence alone makes the room shrink. It does something to the ventilation, too, because somehow, my lungs can't pull in the oxygen I need. He's wearing jeans and a hunter green thermal shirt. His hair's a haphazard mess—no doubt from him knotting his fingers in it—and I hate that it makes him look so damn sexy. He has no right being gorgeous when I'm a train wreck.

I point to my bed. "Why don't you sit instead of looming over me all menacing-like?"

The corners of his lips twitch. "I'm not a menace."

"Tell that to my heart." *Fuck.* I shake my head. "Never mind. Just sit."

He settles on the foot of my bed then stares at me in silence, his gaze more turbulent than ever. Since he's the one who wanted to talk, I wait.

And wait some more.

"Are you going to speak?" I quip after the silence becomes unbearable.

"Sorry." He sighs and runs a hand through that silky, auburn hair I love to touch, then rubs his jaw. "Three hours, Solana." He shakes his head. "I lasted three fuckin' hours. What're you doin' to me? I can't stay the hell away from you." His tone is neutral, but it feels like an accusation, so I bristle.

"You make it sound like I'm some siren, luring you to destruction. For the record, no one told you to show up here, Declan. You wanted a clean break, and I gave it to you. I left your place when you asked and had no plans to reach out. I'm not a femme fatale—just a girl trying to live her life and be happy. Why do *you* have such an aversion to happiness?"

"I don't."

"Sorry, but I call bullshit." I meet his gaze. "I get that your son is top priority—as he should be—no one's debating that. But what bothers me is that you've closed yourself off to everything else.

Yes, you're Liam's father *and* a business owner who works incredibly hard toward his goals. But you won't allow yourself to have a life outside of those two compartments you've built. You forget you're also a *man*. Why is that?"

"I don't have a choice."

"There's always a choice." I wave a finger at him. "You're just too afraid to make one."

"You have no idea what I'm dealin' with."

"Then maybe you should tell me."

He glowers instead. The man does moody and sullen nearly as well as Cody.

I roll my eyes and flop onto my pillow. "Okay, since you're not in the mood to talk, you can sit there and watch me sleep."

"You're Cody's sister."

"I think we've established that."

"Yeah, but do you have any idea what that means?"

I sit bolt upright. "I grew up under his roof, so *believe* me, I'm well-aware of what it means to be his sister. Guess what? I'm a grown-ass woman. He hasn't run my life for five years."

"But you want him in your life."

I narrow my eyes at his accusation. "And what if I do? He's my only living family member. He invited me for dinner to meet his wife and stepson. For the first time *ever*, the man is trying to have a relationship with me. I have no clue where his efforts will lead. I learned a long time ago that it's best to have zero expectations with Cody, so I'm not idiot enough to expect some Hallmark Channel family dynamic." I shrug and study my fingernails. "I guess I'm tired of feeling like he's dead to me. Regardless of whether I've forgiven him, if he wants to extend an olive branch, I won't burn it."

"Why was he dead to you?"

"Because saving face with his buddies was more important than protecting me."

"What do you mean?"

"It doesn't matter." I tilt my head to the side. "Why do you care?"

"Because I wanna know everything about you." He runs a hand over his face. "I keep tellin' myself to keep my distance, but I can't. I'm drawn to you, Solana. I want you more than I want to breathe, and that scares me. If Darcy ever knew I was hookin' up with her sister-in-law, she'd lose her mind."

"I haven't even met the woman."

"I know her well enough for the both of us."

"So, what's the main issue here? You're afraid she'll find out and take Liam away?"

The pain on his face is a punch to my gut. "That's exactly what she'll do."

"I'm no lawyer, but I'm pretty sure she doesn't have the power to do that."

"Darcy's a paralegal. She knows every lawyer in the county. She has the power—and finances—to get what she wants. Trust me, she's done it before."

"I don't get it. Is there something in your divorce agreement that says you can't date?"

"No, but there's a clause in there which allows the court to revoke my visitation with Liam if I use poor judgment."

"What defines poor judgment?"

"No fuckin' clue. But I can guarantee sleepin' with her husband's little sister will make the list."

"So, basically, you think I'm a liability?"

He squeezes his eyes shut. "Yes."

His admission hurts more than I care to admit. All I've ever wanted was a family, a home, and the warm, fuzzy feelings that usually come with them. I want someone to lean on when shit gets hard. A hug now and then. I don't want to cause anyone's ruin—or be a source of resentment, guilt, or shame in their life. I've got enough of my own shame to deal with. While the idea of risking everything to be with someone is innately romantic, I hate that he thinks of *me* as a risk.

"Then you should probably stay away from me."

"That's the problem. I can't."

"I'll make it easier for you." I point to my door. "Get out."

His gaze snaps to mine. "You want me to leave?"

"If you feel like you need to, then yes." I rub my hands up and down my goose-bumped arms. "Look, I'm only in town for a few months, so I realize we could never have a conventional relationship. You set up those parameters from the get-go. I understand that it's even *more* true now that we know who we are to each other."

He nods slowly but doesn't move off my bed.

"You think you can't give me what I need. And maybe that's true. But what I *don't* need is any more guilt or shame. I'm not a homewrecker or some seductress who's hellbent on destroying your life."

"I never said you were."

"You implied it. See, here's the thing. I have no problem with being discreet. Outside of my two best friends, I don't broadcast details about my life. If being seen in public together is out of the question, I'm fine with that. But I won't tolerate the push and pull from you. Either you want me, or you don't. Choose one and stick with it because I can't handle being treated like a dirty secret. If the idea of being with me brings you shame, then stay the fuck away."

"Yes, I'm worried about losin' Liam, but *you* aren't a source of shame. Me pulling back has nothin' to do with you. I'm frustrated with the situation. Even if you were staying in Colebury, it's selfish for me to want you when I can't give you what you deserve. I can't be the man you need. You're young, beautiful, and kind. You've got a lot to offer and your whole life ahead of you. I hate the thought of you missin' out on stuff because of my baggage."

"I already told you I don't do picket fences. Let me worry about my needs."

"You keep sayin' that, Solana."

"Because I mean it. I've been taking care of myself for years."

His gaze darkens and sweeps over me. "So you've mentioned."

I flush and pull the blankets up to my chin. "Jesus Christ, Declan. I am not talking about my vibrator right now."

"Neither am I."

"Yeah, but you gave me *the look.*"

"The look?"

"Yeah, the one you get when you want to have sex with me."

"I *always* want that, Solana." He grips my shoulders. "But I happen to care about you too."

"Likewise." I chew on my lip. "So, what's your game plan?"

36

DECLAN

MOOD MUSINGS: PLANS CHANGE.

My game plan *was* to deposit the money and leave. Instead, I sat in Solana's unlocked car, staring at an old family photo I found in her center console.

She appeared to be around Liam's age, wearing a yellow polka-dot sundress, all pigtails and smiles. She stood in front of her father, a handsome, sandy-haired man who rested his hands on her shoulders and smiled down at her like she was the apple of his eye. Standing beside them was a stunning brunette in a red dress. Solana's ma had one arm wrapped around her husband's waist and the other around Cody, who towered over her. The palpable warmth and affection the family shared made my heart ache. Even Cody's smile was visible as he pressed a kiss to his ma's temple.

I sat there, breathing in Solana's scent while I studied the perfect family for a good fifteen minutes before I texted her.

"I see we're back to being silent and broody again?" Despite the teasing words, Solana's voice is soft, vulnerable.

"No. I'm just trying to make sense of it all."

"I stopped trying to make sense of my life years ago. Some things can't be explained."

"That's a good way of puttin' it." I reach for her hand and clasp her delicate fingers. "I don't want my family drama to bring any more darkness into your life, Solana. But more than that, I don't want to dim your light."

"You won't."

"You sound so sure of it."

Her small smile makes my chest tighten. "My mother always told me, 'Sometimes life gets dark, and even though we can't always see it, the sun still shines behind the clouds.' She taught me to watch for silver linings as proof, so that's what I do whenever the sky gets stormy. It makes me hopeful, you know?"

I lift her hand to my lips and press a kiss to each knuckle. "I'm not a man who turns my face upward, hoping to feel the sun's warmth, but I feel it when I'm around you."

She smirks. "So, I'm not just the flame to your moth, then?"

"Not entirely. Our circumstances are what could burn me—not you." I stroke her cheek. "You're the warmth and light."

"Then come hold me because *I* need a little warmth right now."

The vulnerability in her command has me kicking off my shoes and sliding beneath the covers with her. I pull her close, loving the way her body relaxes against me.

"You don't have to spend the night, but I want you to hold me and stay a while."

Hold me and stay. Those are both things I can give her.

37

DECLAN

Ethan leans against the workbench in our shop. I just finished telling him about everything that went down with Solana last night. He twists the cap off his water bottle and takes a swig, then eyes me warily. "Okay, so what happens when she falls for you?"

"She won't fall for me. She's leaving next semester, and I made it clear I can't give her anything conventional."

He punches my shoulder. "That's something *I'd* say to a woman."

"Well, it's true. We can't be seen in public at any place other than the Busy Bean, so we're limited to hangin' out at my place or hers."

He wags his brows. "So, essentially, what you're saying is, if I see a yellow Mustang in your driveway, I shouldn't barge into the cabin?"

"Unless you wanna watch me fuck her." The filthy bastard grins, so I shake my head. "Correction, you will *not* watch me fuck her."

"Damn." He laughs and humps the nearby table saw. "What's

the fun of having a tryst if you won't let me drop by to join the party?"

"You touch her, I'll kill you."

Ethan laughs harder. "Oh, Dec. I love you, man." He jabs his finger into my chest. "Look at you, getting all possessive and shit."

"I can't help it." *She's mine.*

"Looks like I've been asking the wrong questions." His face sobers, those cobalt eyes searing my skull. "What happens when you realize you're falling for her?"

I cross my arms and glare at him. "Who says I'm fallin' for anyone?"

He lifts a brow. "You can pretend with everyone else, but don't bullshit me. I know you, Dec. You keep insisting it's only physical, but this chick is doing something to you on a fundamental level." When I don't challenge him, he continues, "I just don't wanna see you get hurt when she leaves."

"I know." I sigh and rub a hand over my face. "I'm more worried about hurtin' her."

"That's because you're a good man." He shakes his head. "But until you grow the balls to take Darcy's ass to court, she'll always have a hold on them. Knowing Darcy, if she—or Bridges—finds out about your secret rendezvous, she won't hesitate to squeeze. Unless you make a change, you've got a lot more at stake than Solana."

"I know."

"You say you know, but you aren't doing anything about it."

"Darcy always wins. We've been over this, Eth."

"And I'm saying it again." He grips my shoulders. "Fight her. Take what you deserve."

"It's not that simple. I could lose everything."

"If you *truly* believed that you'd keep your distance from Solana."

I yank from his hold. "I can't stay the fuck away from her."

"You can't, or you *won't?*"

For all his teasing and joking, Ethan is the most intuitive fucker I know. It's infuriating, actually. My life would be much easier if he didn't call me out on my shit.

"Both."

His eyes widen at my admission. He stares at me for a moment, then sighs. Instead of a mocking retort, he steps closer and lowers his voice. "Then you need to let go of your fear."

"I'm not a coward."

"Then act that way. Stop being Darcy's puppet. Take back your fucking life and live it without fear."

I just finished washing some dishes when my phone rings in my back pocket. I grab it and glance at the screen, smiling when I see Dad's number. We usually talk once a week, but I try to text him more frequently than that. He's not overly tech-savvy, so we've yet to do the video chat thing, but I sent him an email with detailed instructions for downloading Skype. I may need to reach out to Siobhan for her assistance with that one. My cousin waits tables at Kings of Connacht on weekends. I can always count on her to check on Dad when I ask.

"Hello?" Galway is five hours ahead, so he's probably in the middle of the pub's dinner rush. "Don't you have Guinness to pour?"

He chuckles. "I've got people for that. Declan, my boy. How're you gettin' on?"

People tell me I have an Irish accent, but it's mellowed a lot since I moved to Vermont. My dad, on the other hand? Well, there's no mistaking he's an Irishman. Hearing his voice makes me miss home even more, which is why I can only handle weekly calls. Even now, that pang of sadness rises in my chest.

"Well enough. You? What's the craic?"

"I'm good. Puttin' together a package for Liam's birthday."

"Thanks, but it's not until next month. October thirtieth."

I can't blame him for mixing up the months because thanks to Darcy, the poor man has never gotten to meet his grandson. Another reason I need Skype figured out on his end: I'd love for him to see Liam's toothy smile and chubby cheeks. Every now and then, I see a bit of my father in Liam. They share the same fiery hair and infectious laugh. But while Liam has freckles, Dad is ruddy-complexioned and pale.

"I know. That's why I'm callin' for ideas ahead of time."

"Oh."

"Thought I forgot, did you?"

"No," I lie, smiling to myself at the indignance in his tone. He's always been a proud man. Clearly, that hasn't changed in the six years I've lived in the States.

"Don't give me that malarkey. You know I can smell a lie."

I chuckle. "Okay, Dad. You're right. I thought you'd mixed up the days. Sorry for doubtin' you."

"How's the wee boy doin'?"

"He's good. Having some trouble with his letters, but we're workin' on them."

"Got any gift ideas?"

"He's been collectin' rocks and treasures lately. I built him a treasure chest. Maybe grab him some pieces of Connemara marble."

The distinctive green stone comes from Western Ireland and is some of the world's rarest marble. It's frequently quarried and fashioned into jewelry. Liam will be happy to add it to his collection, especially since he loves all things green.

"I'll do that. Maybe I'll pop over to the Burren to get him some limestone too. Or make a trip to the Blarney Castle to see if I can find somethin' there. They have all those Blarney stone souvenirs, you know?"

"You don't need to make a special trip."

"He's my only grandchild. I'll make all the trips I want." He clears his throat. "You know, Declan, I've been doin' some thinkin'."

Here we go.

"And?"

"You need to put that ex-wife of yours in her place, so I get a chance to meet Liam before the Devil takes me."

"Tell Satan to go fuck himself. You've got a lotta years left in you. Besides, you're goin' to heaven."

"Doubtful." He snorts. "But anyhow, I'm serious. It's time to make some changes."

"Grand. Now I've got you *and* Ethan ridin' me about it."

I pace my kitchen, careful not to step on Moira's paws as she follows me around. She always does that. I swear, this dog has an emotion barometer because she just *knows* when I'm less than thrilled about something. And despite being the size of a small pony, she still manages to get underfoot.

"Well, it's true. Liam's been around half a decade, and the boy wouldn't know me from Adam. I'd like him to have a face to go with your stories. Maybe I'll have Siobhan take some pictures and send 'em to you."

"He knows what you look like, Dad. I show him pictures all the time."

"Yeah, well, I'm forgettin' what *you* look like, Declan."

"Then come see me," I challenge, knowing he'll never leave his precious bar in someone else's hands. Kings of Connacht has become a tourist attraction near Eyre Square. It's a leading stop on the Galway whiskey trail, and my dad takes serious pride in having that honor.

"Planes cross the ocean from both directions."

I clench the phone. The man wields guilt better than the nuns who taught me in primary school. I know I should make a trip back home, but I'm afraid it will only make me miss Ireland more, so I opt for my standard excuse, "I only get to see Liam twelve hours a week. I don't wanna miss any of them."

"Well, I hope I still have some hours left in *me* when you finally decide to deal with that Darcy situation." He sighs heavily.

"But knowin' you, you'll keep lettin' her run the show. Oh well. I guess you'll miss me when I die."

"I hate when you say that."

"And I hate to see you sellin' yourself short."

"I gotta go, Dad."

"I know a dismissal when I hear one. Fair enough. I love you, Declan. Never forget that."

"Love you too." I hang up and plop onto the couch. Moira rests her head on my knee, so I scratch her ears. "Everyone's tellin' me the same thing, girlie. They all want me to fight Darcy and win back Liam."

She whines and gives me her paw. I shake it and smile as she leans against my legs and stares up at my face. A wayward piece of fur blocks her doe-like eyes. I brush it back and kiss her snout. She rewards me with a nuzzle, then tilts her head to the side. Her scruffy eyebrows dance with a question I can almost hear.

"I know, I know. When am I gonna listen?"

38

SOLANA

Will and I are behind the Busy Bean's counter on Monday afternoon, dancing to Gloria Estefan's "Conga" like we have zero fucks to give.

Someone clears their throat.

I glance over my shoulder mid ass-shake, and freeze.

"Hello, Solana." Declan's amused expression makes me flush.

I spin to face him. "Hi. I was dancing."

"Yes. I got a good look at your moves. And please . . ." His heated gaze travels to my breasts and lingers, making my nipples tighten. "Don't let me stop you."

My insides quiver and clench. "Can I get you—" Will smacks my ass with a wooden spoon. "Ow." I swat his arm and cup my abused butt cheek. "You're a bastard, William."

Declan laughs.

Will grins at him. "Howdy, McFuck. How's it hanging?"

"Doin' just fine, Will. And yourself?"

"Living the dream." He points to the wall calendar. "It's Monday. Where's the little guy?"

Declan clenches his jaw. "Apparently, his class went on a field trip to the zoo today. They won't be back until later. His ma conveniently forgot to mention it to me until I arrived to pick him up."

"That's fucking inconsiderate," Will says.

I frown. "The zoo's like two hours away. I'm surprised they'd take all those little kids that far."

"They had chaperones in attendance." Declan gives me one of those dangerous smiles that isn't truly a smile. "Liam's stepfather went with him."

Fuck. I'm not sure what's an appropriate response to his revelation, but all I can muster is, "Oh."

"Yep."

"Okay, well, I'll let you two chat," Will says. The bastard is a pro at jumping ship when things get awkward. He quickly makes his way over to a customer who just walked in, leaving me alone to face a grumpy Declan.

"I'm sorry."

"You have nothin' to apologize for."

His words don't match his tone, making me feel guiltier than a fox caught in the chicken coop. Sure, *I* didn't withhold his son, but *my* brother took Liam on a field trip. Now Declan's missing out on precious time with his kid.

"I know, but I'm sorry you're upset."

"It's bad enough I miss out on a chance to see him," he mutters, rubbing at the back of his neck. "But what really burns me, is she found it necessary to wait until the eleventh hour to tell me. I fuckin' hate when she cancels like that. I've been lookin' forward to our visit all day. Feels like the rug's gettin' ripped out from under me."

He's venting. I don't want to trivialize any of what he's feeling, or make him clam up, so I simply nod and touch his arm.

He shakes his head. "I'm pissed I wasn't given the option to go to the zoo as a chaperone. I can guarantee the permission slip came home weeks ago. She purposely didn't tell me because she wanted *him* to take Liam." He meets my gaze. "I'm tired of missin' out on things in favor of Cody."

"I know."

"And what *really* grinds my gears is that I planned to take Liam to the zoo to celebrate his birthday. They have a Halloween festival where the kids get to wear their costumes when they visit the animals. I thought it would be something fun for us to do together, you know, since the wench excluded me from his fuckin' party."

I open my mouth to speak, quickly closing it when I realize he's not done.

"And another thing, why do I get stuck with Mondays, Wednesdays, and Sundays? Can't I have a Saturday now and then? Nothing fun is open on Sunday, so how am I supposed to make memories with my kid? How come they get to take him to all the fairs and festivals? Mini-golfin' and whatnot."

"Do you like golfing?" I ask, knowing how much my brother loves the sport.

He crosses his arms. "No. I hate golf."

"Well, maybe we can brainstorm some fun activities for you to do with Liam. You told me you like outdoorsy stuff, so why not take him fishing?"

"It's not fishin' season right now. But we went in the spring," he grumbles. His stomach growls, deepening the furrow in his brow.

"Can I get you something to eat?" I point to the kitchen. "Audrey made a maple bacon chive glaze for our scones."

"Sounds delicious, thank you."

"You thirsty?"

"I'll take some water, please."

Even when moody, he still remembers his pleases and thank yous—a civility Cody could never grasp.

"Coming right up," I sing-song, determined to dispel his clouds. I grab his scone and set the plate and water glass in front of him. "How's the tiny farmhouse?"

"Good." He chews for a moment. "Ethan's doin' the wiring this week."

"Wait, I thought you told me they used solar panels?"

He nods. "The houses will be solar-powered, but they still need to be wired. There has to be a way to get the electricity from the solar panels to the plugs. Also, since we want to operate year-round, we need the option of using grid electricity as backup."

"Makes sense. I imagine they don't have fireplaces?"

"Sadly, no." His posture relaxes a bit now that we're discussing his passion. "But some of them will have fire pits as part of the outdoor space."

"So, it's kinda like glamping?"

"I guess you could say that. But unlike an RV, we intend for these to stay where we put them. We'll offer up some of the houses as long-term lodging, so people can stay for weeks to months at a time. Others will be available for timeframes as short as one weekend."

"Playing Devil's advocate here, but what makes your tiny house resort more special than The Three Bears Motor Lodge Mrs. Beasley owns?"

He smiles. "I'm glad you asked. You see, those are a bunch of one-room cabins that haven't been renovated since the 1970s. There's nothing eco-friendly or efficient about any of them. They all look exactly the same. Yes, they have bathrooms, but our tiny houses will also have full kitchens. Albeit they're a bit compact, but guests will get a helluva lot more than a toaster oven. And we're situated right on the Winooski River, so it's a room with a view."

I flash him a wink. "Not to mention the eclectic design and superior craftsmanship."

Satisfaction diffuses his features. "Right."

"Do you do any of the electrical stuff?"

Shaking his head, he takes a long sip of water before answering. "No, I'd probably get us killed. Ethan has a degree in electrical engineering, so he takes care of it. My focus is on the architectural components and the actual construction." His lips twitch at the corners. "Because I like workin' with my hands."

Damn right, you do.

"Yeah, I've heard that about you."

"Oh? And what else have you heard?" Mischief glitters in his eyes.

Even though we're all alone at the end of the counter, I drop my voice to a whisper, "Tell me, what types of structures can you build with your tongue? Seems you enjoy working with that too."

He sucks in a sharp breath, his eyes darkening with lust. "Maybe I'll give you a demonstration tonight."

"I'd love that. My shift ends at six." I flutter my lashes. "Your place or mine?"

"Yours." A wicked smile curves his lips, and it sends a zing of electricity straight to my clit. "Because if I remember correctly, you owe *me* a demonstration."

My ears and face heat with his reminder. "Uh, about that . . ." Suddenly shy, I twirl a piece of hair and picture Bob, the little vibrator that could. I'd picked up the compact, hot pink pleasure wand at a sex shop in New York. "I kinda hoped you'd forgotten."

His attention sweeps lower, pausing at the juncture of my thighs. When his gaze flicks back to mine, it brings the heat of a blowtorch. "Not a chance, honey."

"What if the batteries are dead?"

He leans in close. "Then I'll stop at every fuckin' store in the county 'til we find some."

A few hours later, I'm all hot and bothered, seated on my bed while I await Declan's arrival. My insides flutter with a mixture of nerves and anticipation. I've been giving myself pep talk after pep talk, trying to convince my inner shy girl to go fuck herself. Literally.

I nearly jump out of my skin when Declan's knock sounds on my window. I peek through the blinds and point to the main door. "It's open."

He shakes his head and enters the inn. He's inside my room a moment later. He cocks a dark eyebrow. "What do you think I'm gonna say?"

"Before you start to lecture me, I'll have you know I *just* unlocked it when I got your text."

He chuckles. "Good. You're finally learnin'." He hands me a brown paper bag. "Brought you a present."

"What's this?" I open the bag, half expecting to find an assortment of batteries—or a backup vibrator. Instead, my hand closes around something hard and roundish, covered in tissue paper. I slowly withdraw the object, unwrapping an ornate wooden sun carving. The finish gleams in the light, and the edges are smooth to the touch. "Omigod. This is beautiful."

"You like it?"

"I love it." I throw my arms around his neck. "Thank you so much. Where did you find this? I'm always on the lookout for suns."

"I finished lacquering it today."

"Wait, *you* made this for me?" I whisper, staring up at his face.

"Yep. Sanded and stained it too." He smiles and touches my cheek. "I carved it on Saturday and planned to give it to you last night, but then things got crazy, and I forgot. You can use it as a paper weight, or if you want, I'll drill a hole so you can hang it."

"Actually, I'm going to sleep with it every night like a teddy bear."

He barks out a laugh. "Seriously?"

"Yes, seriously. No one has ever given me such a thoughtful gift." My eyes blur, so I blink rapidly and hug him again. "Thank you."

"My pleasure, Solana." His voice softens. "I'm happy you like it."

"I love it." I nuzzle into him. *And I could love you if you'd let me.*

The realization floors me. Tucked against his burly chest and wrapped in his warmth, we stand this way for a moment, just hugging. I breathe in his clean, masculine scent and listen to his steady heartbeat.

I lied when I told myself I wouldn't fall for him. Truth is, I'm already headed there. I need to pull back, but Declan's sweet gesture touches me deeper than he realizes. The only other person who ever gave me suns to collect was my mom.

"What's the occasion?" I ask.

"Just because." He brushes his lips over my ear. "But I won't deny havin' ulterior motives for givin' it to you tonight."

"You trying to butter me up for sex, Mr. *Oh* Shaughnessy?"

"Maybe."

I press a kiss to his throat. "Well, it worked."

Declan cups my face and devours my lips in a soul-melting kiss. Tongues twining, we sip from each other's mouths like we've spent years lost in the desert, parched and aching. His hands slide to the back of my head, tangling in my hair.

I love the way this man handles me with a fusion of tender and rough that makes my knees go weak. His dominance makes me want to grant his every desire and let him bend me to his will.

I slide my hands down his back to squeeze his perfect ass.

He groans against my lips. "Fuck, baby."

"I want you," I whisper, tugging at the hem of his shirt.

He lifts the blue Henley over his head and tosses it on my bed. Next comes his boots, jeans, and socks. He settles on my pillows, wearing nothing but a pair of grey boxer briefs, and crosses his arms behind his head.

"Well, don't you look mighty relaxed."

He grins. "Strip for me, honey."

Any awkwardness I felt earlier dissipates into thin air with his command. "In a second." I reach for my phone, which is paired with the Bluetooth speaker on my dresser. "I need some mood music."

"Mmm . . . can't wait. I loved the taste of your dancin' you gave me earlier."

"This is a different kind of dance." I bite my lip seductively. "I figure if I'm going to let you *watch*, why not start from the beginning?" I dim the lights and queue Bishop Bridges's "River" for the occasion. "Your job is to keep your eyes on me."

He licks his lips. "Won't be a problem. But I doubt I'll be able to keep my hands *off* you."

I give my sultriest smile. "Well, you'd better. Or else, you're gonna miss out on one helluva show." I move to stand at the foot of my bed. "You ready?"

"Fuck yes." Declan's raspy tone sets me free.

I start the song and stare into his eyes for a few beats before moving. Then, I lift the hem of my tank top inch by inch, exposing the skin of my belly in a slow tease. When I reach the bottom of my bra, I pause. "Want this off?"

"Yes."

I raise the shirt to my armpits, then whip it off and toss it onto my dresser.

Declan eyes the lacy, hot pink bra I've chosen. "So sexy."

"You'll notice a theme with my color choices."

"I love themes." He props my pillow behind him, angling his torso for a better view. The raw desire on his face damn near curls my toes. "But I *really* love to fuck you, so you'd better get movin' before I lose my patience."

I toy with my waistband. "Trust me, you don't wanna rush this." His gaze flares with lust when I slide the yoga pants over my hips and allow them to drop to the floor. I slowly turn in a circle, moving my hips in rhythm with the music.

"*Christ.*" His reverent groan is followed by a string of incoherent whispers when he sees my matching pink lace panties are, in fact, a thong.

Still dancing, I peer over my shoulder at him while I unhook my bra and let it slide from my body. My nipples harden in the cool air. My breasts feel full and swollen, aching for his calloused hands on them. I'm large-chested, but my boobs are no match for Declan's palms. No part of my body is immune to him. He's one hundred percent potent male, and I can't get enough of his touch. His kisses. His scandalous tongue. I want him to lick and suck my nipples so I can feel the scrape of his whiskers on my skin. But right now, I'm in the mood to tease him.

"Want me to turn around?"

"No, I want you to ride my dick," he growls.

I slowly turn to face him. "Getting ahead of yourself. If you want me to climb in the saddle, you'd better be patient." I feather my fingertips over my breasts and skate my hands lower. Then, I hook my thumbs in the lace panties and tug them off. I fling them at Declan and walk over to my dresser to retrieve my battery-operated boyfriend. "Your job is to keep your hands to yourself."

"No guarantees."

"I mean it. Touch me, and I'll stop."

He grunts.

"Because first . . . you're going to watch." I brandish my hot pink vibrator with a sultry flourish and crawl up the bed to Declan. I twist the bottom, and the toy hums to life.

His eyes widen with shock. "Holy fuck, Solana."

I turn the mode to a steady pulse of vibrations and settle beside him. "This *is* your fantasy, is it not?"

"Yeah, but I never imagined you'd actually do it for me."

"Maybe one day I'll tell you *my* darkest fantasies."

He grips my chin. "You'd damn well better."

"We'll see." With one hand, I trace my fingertips down his chest, relishing the feel of his hairs against my palm. He's hard and leaking for me, a small circle of moisture dampening the tented material of his boxers. "I like this," I murmur, tracing the happy trail that leads to his waistband. I slide my hand lower and grip his cotton-covered cock.

"Solana . . ." His breath leaves him in a hiss.

I release him and roll to my back. "Now, pay attention."

His jaw goes slack when I drag the toy across my nipples and gasp. I rub it in slow circles over my breasts before inching lower to skim the top of my lady bits. I find my clit and tease it with featherlight strokes. Little moans escape me while I focus on the sensitive nub.

I always start with my clit when I pleasure myself. It's like the appetizer before my main course.

"Tell me what you want to see," I say on a moan, arching my back up off the bed.

"Show me what drives you wild." His roughened voice makes me even hotter. "I wanna hear you scream."

I meet his gaze and hold it. Spreading my thighs farther apart, I glide the toy through my arousal until it nudges my entrance. I ease it inside, moaning as the delicious vibrations fill me. I thrust in and out, angling the tip to rub against my G-spot. My hips jerk upward to meet my strokes. "Ohhhhh . . ."

"Do it harder," Declan growls, pressing himself up onto his knees. The look on his face borders on savage as he kneels in front of me to get a better view. His chest heaves. "Fuck yourself for me."

This is, by far, the boldest experience of my life. Gone is the inexperienced young woman who first landed in bed with him. She's been replaced with a sexual prodigy, and I love this new version of myself. Then again, maybe she's who I've been all along, and I simply needed Declan to help me release her.

39

DECLAN

MOOD MUSINGS: IS DEATH BY DESIRE A THING?

Is it possible to simultaneously implode and explode? I need to know because it's about to happen. Right here, right now.

Watching Solana grind her hips while she pleasures herself with the little pink vibrator, blows my fantasy out of the water. My eyes travel her naked body, trying to memorize every inch. I want every second of this experience imprinted in my memory for the rest of eternity.

Her head's thrown back; hair spread across the pillow like a golden halo. Her eyes are closed, lashes fluttering on her cheeks. She's parted her rosebud lips in ecstasy as moans and whimpers spill from them. I wonder how amazing it would feel to have those lips wrapped around my cock. The graceful curve of her neck makes me want to suck on it, mark her so everyone knows she's *mine*. Because she is. Fuck expiration dates or anyone who says otherwise.

She arches her back, those glorious tits heaving with each gasping breath. She's spread her legs wide open for me. Her pussy glistens with the sweet honey I want to spend hours tasting. I lick my lips, aching to indulge in my favorite hedonistic treat.

"So close," she wails. Her thumb finds her clit and massages in circles. She picks up the pace of her thrusting, then suddenly stops. Her eyes fly open, seeking mine as she slowly withdraws her toy. She holds it out to me. "I want *you* to make me come."

I snatch the vibrator and toss it behind me. I dive-bomb her pussy, planting my face in the slick flesh. With my hands clenching her arse, I seal my mouth over her clit and hold her in place while I tongue her like a starved man at his last meal. All it takes is twenty seconds.

"*Declan.*" She spears her hands into my hair, pulling my head closer while she climaxes, bucking her hips against my face. "Yes!"

I ride out the wave of her release, then rear up. "Now you're gonna come on my cock."

At first, I wanted her to ride me. But now, I'm so far gone with lust, it feels like I'm going insane. I need to take control, show her just how badly I crave her. I tear open a condom wrapper and roll it onto my throbbing cock.

"How do you want me?" Her husky voice tightens my balls.

"Facedown." Flipping her over, I press her shoulders into the mattress and yank her hips up, so she's on her knees. "Bottom in the air just like this."

She peers back at me, those whiskey eyes stealing what's left of my sanity. "You gonna fuck me hard and dirty?"

I plunge into her wet heat instead of answering. Solana cries out and clutches the comforter. I grip her hips and start to move, her muffled moans spurring me on.

I'm a fucker for the view of my cock stretching and filling a woman. For some reason, the sex is a hundred times more intense with Solana. Probably because I've never wanted anyone the way I crave her. And no one's ever reached inside my soul like she has. Maybe I can't give her the moon and stars, but she can have every rock-hard inch of my dick.

"Oh . . . Declan," Solana wails into her pillow.

"Take it, baby."

I clamp my hands on her lush hips. God, I love her curves. Right now, fucking her the way I've always wanted to, I can't imagine ever being with someone else. Her body's so hot and wet. And the way she's squeezing my cock, bearing down on me like she's desperate to keep me inside, is going to make me lose my motherfucking mind.

I trace my fingertips over the colorful sun tattoo on her lower back, relishing her silken skin. I carved the wooden sculpture to match it. I almost wish I'd painted it with reds, oranges, and yellows instead. Because Solana is fire, warmth, and sunshine. She's everything bright and beautiful. And she's *mine*.

"You're fuckin' perfect, Solana." Her gasps and moans make me change pace to a slow grind. "Come for me, baby."

She arches her back, rocking into my thrusts. Her moans grow louder, her movements jerkier. "Oh, Declan . . ."

"Let me hear you."

A keening cry leaves her lips. She comes hard, her greedy pussy spasming around my cock. Her knees give out and she flops forward. I yank her hips back up and keep moving.

"Ungh. . ." I dig my fingers into her flesh as my release draws closer. "You feel so fuckin' good," I growl, punctuating each word with a thrust.

She looks back at me. "Gimme more."

Those two words break what's left of my control. I slam into her, delivering brutal, pounding thrusts. She screams into her pillow. Guttural groans rip from my chest as everything tightens. My body goes rigid.

"Solana, *fuck*." I explode on a feral snarl and pour my soul into her. I give a few more thrusts then collapse on top of her, both of us panting.

"You all right?" I gasp at her neck.

"Uh-huh."

My body is draped over her like a blanket. I interlace our

fingers, pressing her hands into the bed at her shoulders. I bury my nose in her hair and breathe her vanilla scent. Her head is turned to the side, so I press a kiss to her jaw. Her cheek. Her temple. Her earlobe. She giggles when I nuzzle her neck.

"Somethin' funny?"

"Your whiskers tickle." She releases a contented sigh. "But I like it."

I brush my lips over her ear. "I like *you*."

"I *more* than like you, Declan."

Her confession's barely audible, but my heart's playing a symphony. I swear, someone's plucking the strings of a harp while choirs of angels sing from the heavens.

I know it's dangerous to let myself feel what I'm feeling, but right now, I don't care. Darcy never liked me. We got together on a drunken night and wound up expecting a baby. Any affection she felt for me was tied to Liam. She didn't care about me as a man because she'd always been in love with someone else. I fucked up her plans. We married because it was best for our child—not us. Funny, I can see it so clearly now.

I never realized how refreshing it would feel to spend time with someone who enjoys my company. Someone who "more than likes" me. A woman who sees me for who I am—not the mistakes I've made.

I should be open and honest, but I hate the idea of losing Solana's respect. Or worse, having her turn her back on me like Darcy did.

But Solana is nothing like Darcy. She's warm and full of compassion. Whenever I'm around her, the whiskey's siren call fades to a whisper, and she's all I know.

After a few minutes, I pull out and remove the condom, tossing it in the trash can near her bed. I'm still hard, but she's clearly spent—facedown and spread out like a starfish. "You sure you're okay?"

"Mm-hmm." Her muffled reply is accompanied by a thumbs-up. "Please stay over."

"Honey, I can't. I need to let Moira out."

"Oh. Okay."

There's no mistaking the disappointment in her voice. Why the hell didn't I ask Ethan to check on my dog? The last thing I want to do is let Solana sleep alone tonight—especially not after the intensity of the sex we just had.

When we fucked, I was in primal claim-staking mode. Now, I've switched gears to quiet sentry. The desire to shelter, protect, and soothe her is all-consuming. I need to know she's safe and secure. And not just physically.

If I hadn't already felt the invisible bond tethering us, there'd be no denying it now. Solana calls out to something deep inside me, making me feel things I'd written off years ago. I've been hollow for so long, but this sweet girl—full of sunshine and honey —fills me. Mind, heart, and soul.

"What time is your shift tomorrow?"

"It's Tuesday, so I'm off. I'm always off on Tuesdays."

I perk up. "Come home with me. We can spend the day together."

She meets my gaze. "But you have work, and I need to study . . ."

"Bring your schoolwork. You can use my kitchen table while I work in the shop."

"You don't mind?"

"I don't mind at all. Come home with me, honey. I need you in my arms tonight." *And every night.*

SOLANA

MOOD MUSIC: "CHERISH THE DAY" BY SADE

I stretch like a cat and roll onto my side. Declan's not in bed. I can hear him downstairs talking to Moira. It's only five o'clock, but I feel like I got twelve hours of slumber. It's amazing what vigorous sex and a warm embrace can do.

I don't have words to adequately describe last night. Suffice it to say, it's a damn good thing I gave him a heads-up about being a virgin. My lady bits are more than a little tender this morning. Maybe it's weird, but I like that I can still feel him even hours after we've finished. It's almost like he gave me a sex souvenir. *Or would you call it a sex-venir?*

I snort at my own wittiness. Then my traitorous brain drifts to the time when I felt the aftereffects of someone *else's* touch. How, instead of remembered pleasure, it was pain. Betrayal. Shame. And that was only his fingers. How much more fucked up would I be if I hadn't gotten away? What if he'd ra—*Nope. Not going there. Deep breaths, Solana.*

I press my knees together and shudder, forcing my thoughts from the incident. Hopefully, that asshole doesn't get wind I've moved back to Colebury.

I nearly solved a differential equation in my head when I hear Declan's footsteps coming up the stairs. Then, a gallop of sorts.

"Incoming," he calls.

Moira bursts into the bedroom, all tail-wags and prancing. She comes to my side of the bed then politely sits on the floor, resting her muzzle on the mattress.

I scratch between her ears. "Good morning, Miss Moira."

Her tail thumps on the hardwood. She whines and licks my hand, then spins in a circle.

Declan appears in the doorway. "Sorry. The horse wanted to see you."

"No worries. She's super sweet." I lift my head. "And seriously well-behaved. I half-expected to be mauled when she came running in here."

"Moira knows better than to get in my bed. Right, girlie?"

Cue the tail thump. Declan approaches with the mugs of coffee he's carrying and hands one to me.

"Thanks." I take a slow sip. "Why don't you let her sleep with you?" I ask, indignant on Moira's behalf.

Declan chuckles. "I've spent a lotta lonely nights here, Solana. If I let Moira in my bed, I'd spend them spoonin' my overweight dog."

I stroke Moira's fur. "He called you overweight. You gonna stand for that?" She licks my hand again.

"Well, she *is* a bit hefty, don't you think?"

I glance at Declan. "Gee, I can't imagine *why* that is. I mean, croissants are totally a low-calorie food."

He grins. "You sound like my vet. Pen is always givin' me shit about what I feed Moira."

"Maybe you should listen to him." I poke his chest. "Also, don't knock spooning. I, for one, love spooning and snuggling. Cats, dogs, rabbits—I don't discriminate." I flash him a smile. "But in all seriousness, I'm more than a little happy you don't have tons of women in your bed."

He grips my chin. "Solana, you're the only woman who has

been in my home, period. Like I told you, there hasn't been anyone in my life since Darcy."

"But why? You're hella sexy."

He snorts and settles on the bed. "Thanks, but after a messy divorce, celibacy was more appealin'."

"Works for me. I wouldn't enjoy the thought of other women tainting you."

He laughs. "Oh, I'm tainted all right."

"I think you're wonderful."

His gaze softens. "Same." He sips his coffee, then smirks. "Tell me more about spoonin' rabbits."

I giggle. "I've never actually slept with a rabbit. Will had bunnies when we were kids. One of them, a flop-eared little guy named Edgar, was super-affectionate and loved to be petted. I totally snuggled up on him."

"Did you have pets growin' up?"

"We had a brown Dalmatian named Trixie. Cody gave her away when I was eight. I was heartbroken."

"He gave your dog away?"

I shrug. "Apparently, *I* was enough to handle."

He narrows his eyes into slits. "Your brother's a dick."

"I'm aware."

Declan rests a hand on my knee. "Listen, Solana, I want to apologize for bein' moody when I showed up at the café yesterday. I was pissed off at Darcy, but I took it out on you. I'm sorry."

"Don't apologize. I totally get where you're coming from. I knew it wasn't directed at me—you were venting. Just so you know, you can always vent to me. Even if it involves my idiot brother."

He squeezes my hand. "I appreciate that. I'm not someone who shares his feelings, but you're easy to talk to. That's part of why I'm so drawn to you."

"I love our talks."

"Same here." He touches my cheek. "Anyway, with that whole

thing yesterday, I guess I just hate feelin' like he's tryin' to steal my son away."

"For what it's worth, in the short time I was at the farmhouse, I noticed a change in my brother. He never liked kids. He barely tolerated me. But when he mentioned Liam, his face lit up. He genuinely cares for your son."

"Liam is easy to love," he retorts.

"Oh, absolutely. But what I'm saying is, as someone who has plenty of experience with Cody's cold side, I wish you could take comfort in the fact that he's so warm to Liam. It's not like he's over there being mean to him, you know?"

"Now you sound like Ethan."

"He's been around Cody?"

"Yeah. Eth's older sister is Darcy's best friend, so that lucky bastard gets to spend more time with Liam than I do. He's told me the same thing about your brother," he grumbles.

I touch his cheek, so he looks into my eyes. "I'm gonna tell you something. You probably won't like it, but you need to hear it."

"Sounds ominous."

"It's not. I just want to give you a different perspective."

"I'm listenin'."

"Okay, look at it this way. So, Liam is your heart and soul, right?"

"He's my everything."

"Right. So, naturally, that means you want him to always be safe, healthy, and happy. You want him to feel secure and well-loved. And you want him to *know* he has people in his corner."

"One hundred percent."

"So, what's the harm in having more people who love him?"

He stares at my face. "I guess there isn't any."

"I'm telling you there isn't. With love, it really *is* the more, the merrier. It's better that Liam has a hundred people who love him, than be stuck with one person who makes him question his worth. After my parents died, Cody was all I had. With me, he wasn't warm and loving. At best, he was dismissive. At his worst,

I lived with a dictator. Yes, he kept me healthy and safe to an extent. But I never felt secure or well-loved. I didn't have a rock to lean on or someone to turn to. Not a day went by that I didn't question *my* worth." I squeeze his hand. "I'm not telling you my sob story again because I want sympathy. I'm a grown-ass woman now. I don't need anyone's sympathy. I'm explaining this because I want you to understand what it could be like if Liam lived in a different environment. Like, say, if Cody hadn't changed over the years."

Declan nods slowly.

"My brother is not the man he used to be. He adores your son. I can't help but wonder how much easier and more enriched *my* childhood would've been if I had the support system Liam has."

"He's gonna take my place."

"I know you think that, but you're wrong. I've seen how Liam looks at you. You're his idol, Declan."

"I'm not fit to be anyone's idol."

"Well, Liam believes otherwise. You will always be his dad, and that child *adores* you. Instead of looking at the people who love him as threats, maybe think of them as enrichment opportunities."

"Enrichment?" he scoffs, still not completely sold.

"Yeah. You said you hate golf. Well, Cody loves it. Maybe that's a breadcrumb he shares with Liam."

His lips twitch at my use of his analogy, but he doesn't say anything.

"Meanwhile, you have your woodworking, architecture, and outdoorsy stuff. You and Liam made that birdhouse for Darcy together. You also have your jelly doughnuts, letter-learning, your Irish heritage. And many more things I don't even know about. Those are memories he has with you that he'll get to keep forever. Daddy breadcrumbs, right?"

He nods.

"So, what's wrong with Liam having a whole breadbasket? Maybe he's got some golf balls in there. Maybe he has fishing lures and sandpaper. Why not let him fill his basket with memories? We're not talking about bleached white bread—I'm referring to whole wheat. The organic kind with oats and shit."

Declan barks a laugh and pulls me into his arms. "When did you become my little philosopher?"

"When I started to pay attention." I peer up at him. "Instead of wasting your energy feeling jealous and insecure, why not channel those feelings into experiences? Don't view Cody as a threat. Think of him as motivation to make the time you spend with Liam even more memorable. Don't focus on what other people get to do with him. Focus on *your* impact on his life."

"You're wise beyond your years, Solana."

I snort. "That's debatable."

"No, really. I've never thought of it like that. I've always been jealous and resentful of your brother. Maybe I owe him some gratitude?"

"Hey, now." I hold up a hand and chuckle. "Let's not get too crazy."

"I'm serious. Thanks for openin' my eyes."

"Anytime." I point to the storybook spiral staircase on the other side of his room. "Now, talk to me about the stairway to heaven you've got going on over there."

He grins. "I'd rather show you."

In terms of rooftop refuges, Declan's secret oasis is epic. After climbing the gorgeous spiral steps he built, we went through a door and emerged on the back side of his cabin, where part of the roof is flat. The area is like a tiny courtyard of sorts. He's furnished the space with a wrought iron bistro table and chairs and a massive wooden chaise lounge. He's got a few terracotta planters filled with some type of vine, and a string of white lights hung around the door.

Declan opens the lid of a storage container and withdraws a

burgundy cushion for the chaise. "Welcome to my favorite place this side of the Atlantic."

"This is amazing. Do you frequently hang out up here?"

He points to the chaise. "Yep. Do a lotta thinkin' on that chair."

"I'm intrigued by what prompted this hideaway."

He sets his coffee on the little side table next to the chaise and settles, motioning for me to join him. "Sit with me, and I'll tell you all about it."

I place my mug beside his and ease into the place he's made for me between his bent legs. I lean back against his chest.

He gestures to the east where a palette of pastel pinks and oranges illuminate the sky. "Perfect timin'. The sun's about to rise."

"Now, *this* is a room with a view."

"When I built the cabin, I purposely designed this rooftop area so it faced east."

"To watch sunrises?"

"That's part of it, but more importantly, Ireland is east of Vermont."

"You really miss home, don't you?"

"More than I can put into words. I told you my father owns a pub in Galway, right?"

"Yes. King something."

"Kings of Connacht. Anyway, Dad owns the whole building. The pub takes up the entire bottom floor, and we lived on the upper two. Dad still lives there, actually."

"What's his name?"

"Eamon Padraic O'Shaughnessy."

"That's a cool-ass name."

He chuckles. "It is. He used to run around sayin', 'Why's everyone blamin' Eamon?' He's got a thing for rhymes. Anyhow, our building has a rooftop area much like this. I used to hang out up there when I was young. Felt like king of the world back then."

The warmth and affection in his tone when talking about his father moves me.

"What would you do up there?"

"I'd stare at the moon and stars for hours. I've always had a fascination with the night sky. Dad used to tell me, 'No matter where you are on this Earth, we all share the same moon.' I know it sounds silly, but it comforts me to look up there and know he's seein' it too. Makes me miss him a little less."

"I don't think it's silly at all. That explains why you have skylights over your bed."

"Yep. I have a hard time fallin' asleep sometimes. When I look at the constellations, it gives me something to think about."

"Why don't you go to Ireland for a visit?"

"Because I know once I step off the plane in Dublin, I'll never want to leave. And since I've got Liam, Vermont's my home now. Here's where I belong—whether or not it feels like it."

I wriggle so I'm straddling his lap. This way I can see his eyes. "That makes me sad."

"Me too, honey. That's what makes dealin' with Darcy so frustrating. She's got her whole family here, her career, and plenty of friends. She's got a husband *and* the joy of spendin' more than ninety percent of each week with Liam." He squeezes his eyes shut. "Liam's the only thing keepin' me here, and all I get is ten percent."

"That's not fair. It should be fifty-fifty."

A dark laugh rumbles in his chest. "Maybe in a dream world."

"Why don't you take her to court? See if you can't get it changed?"

He tenses. "It's complicated."

Since he doesn't elaborate and the hard set of his jaw tells me it's a sore subject, I change topics. "You should ask your dad to visit."

He shakes his head. "He's got a business to run."

"Yeah, but I'd think his son and grandson are worth making the trip for."

Declan's pain-filled gaze squeezes my chest. "Again, maybe in a dream world."

DECLAN

MOOD MUSINGS: THERE IS NO HIDING WITH HER.

Feels like heaven to sit here with Solana in my arms and the sun's rays warming our faces. I still can't get over how easily she gets me to open up. Sure, I talk to Ethan all the time, and I've recently opened up to Penley, but those are typically man-to-man conversations where we barely scratch the surface with things like feelings. Yet Solana's got me baring my soul.

"I remember you saying you've never met your mom. Does that make you sad?" she asks softly.

"It did for a long time, but now I'm at peace with it."

"Did you ever try to find her?"

"She wasn't lost, love."

"I'm confused. Did your parents have a bad relationship or something?"

I take a deep breath. "They didn't have a relationship at all. I guess you could say I was the product of a scandal."

"What do you mean?" When I hesitate to respond, she touches my arm. "I'm sorry for being nosy. I just want to know you."

"I don't think you're nosy. I'm a little surprised—no one's ever wanted to know my story from cover-to-cover."

She smiles. "Remember what I said when we met? I'm not like everyone else."

"No, Solana, you're not." I stroke her cheek and press a kiss to her lips. "You're a treasure."

"Then let me in. Give me your bonus chapters and deleted scenes."

My chest tightens, and I force a swallow. I wish I could tell her everything, but that's a slippery slope. I'm not ready for her to know my whole truth. I don't want to lose this closeness we share.

"Well, my ma was married to a prominent politician in Ireland. A wealthy, powerful man who no one dared to cross. She made a huge mistake when she had a one-night stand with my dad because she became pregnant despite using protection. Apparently, she tried to play it off as her husband's baby, but unbeknownst to her, he'd had a vasectomy after their three children were born."

"Holy shit."

"Yep. So, the husband gave her an ultimatum and threatened divorce. Either she terminated the pregnancy right then and there or kept it a secret and surrendered the baby to an orphanage at birth. Lucky for me, she decided to go with the second option. Although, how they would've managed termination back then is beyond me. It only recently became legal in Ireland." I meet her widened gaze. "Anyhow, instead of an orphanage, she showed up on my dad's doorstep with a newborn."

"Oh my God. Did he know she was pregnant beforehand?"

"Nope. She told him her predicament and explained that she went into hiding for the duration of the pregnancy. The public never caught a glimpse of her growing belly. Not sure how she managed it, but whatever."

"Did your father ever question his paternity?"

"No. The math made sense, and I had his eyes. *I'm* the one who needed confirmation, so at thirteen, we did a cheek swab test, which came back positive."

"But what about her other kids? Wouldn't they have noticed their mom was knocked up?"

"My half-siblings are triplets, and from what I understand, we're all close in age, so they were toddlers back then."

"You've never met them?"

"Nope. I doubt they know I exist." I stare at the horizon for a few beats. "I didn't know my ma's identity until after her death."

Solana wraps her arms around me in a tight squeeze. "I'm so sorry. When did she pass away?"

"She died of breast cancer four years ago."

"Are you angry with her?" she asks, after a few minutes of silence.

God, this woman is ripping my heart open.

While Ethan knows the story of my secret birth, I've never confessed to its emotional impact. Mainly because I don't want to dissolve into tears in front of him. Yes, he's seen me cry, but it usually has something to do with Liam. For some reason, I become a blubbering idiot whenever my kid is involved, so he's learned to expect it.

"Yes and no."

She touches my shoulder. "It's okay. You don't have to tell me."

Except, I want to tell her. Deep down, I need to confide in Solana about how the situation with my ma irrevocably fucked up my head.

"I've tried to pretend I'm indifferent, but I'm really not. I've never shared this with anyone, not even Darcy, so bear with me if I don't make sense."

Her eyes widen. "You never talked to your wife about this?"

"Darcy didn't like me much."

"Why?"

"Long story. Maybe I'll tell you some other time."

She nods. "Back to your mom. You said, 'yes and no,' but I can see the anger in your eyes. Talk to me."

"It's a shitty feeling to grow up thinkin' your ma didn't want you."

"Is that what your dad told you?"

"No. Dad said a fairy dropped me on his doorstep wrapped in a shamrock."

She giggles, and the sound warms my heart. "My parents found me under rocks in a cabbage patch if that makes you feel any better."

I chuckle. "Liam thinks the stork brought him. Anyway, when I was around five, my uncle told me the truth. He'd had a fight with my father over somethin' stupid and felt the need to hurt him."

"He hurt you, instead."

"Right. After that happened, I started askin' questions about my ma. Dad was extremely vague, but he had good reason to be. I later found out she'd given him a lump sum of money—with an attached confidentiality clause—to help cover the cost of raisin' me."

"Hush money?"

"Pretty much. But I don't blame Dad for acceptin' it. I mean, he didn't know he was gonna be a father until she left me with him at three days old, so it's not like he could've prepared financially or mentally. He'd just started a business, so a screamin' baby wasn't part of his plan. I'm just happy he kept me."

"You speak very fondly of him, so my guess is he did more than *just* keep you."

"And you'd be right." I clench my jaw and blink a few times. "He raised me with nothin' but love and selflessness. He didn't expect me, but he *wanted* me." I finish what's left of my coffee before continuing, "When I think about my ma, I'm a mixture of angry and grateful. I'm angry she two-timed her husband but grateful she didn't abort me. It hurts that I was treated like a dirty secret, but at the same time, I'm fortunate she approached my father instead of an orphanage." I'm trying to keep it together, but my vision's starting to blur, and my nostrils flare with each breath.

Solana squeezes my hand, stroking her thumb over my knuckles. It's something I've done when comforting her, but I didn't understand its impact until now. I never imagined I'd be a man who loves to hold a woman's hand. God help me, I never want to let go of this one.

I force a swallow and continue, "I'm furious I missed out on having a mother and siblings. I spent so many years feelin' lonely when all along, I had a sister and two brothers livin' in the same city as me. While I hate that I never had the chance to meet my ma," my voice breaks, and a lone tear escapes, but I quickly brush it away, "what kills me most is that I didn't know she loved me until it was too late."

"Declan, everything you're expressing makes sense."

I didn't know I needed the validation until she said those words. My posture relaxes a bit, and I pull her closer. The more we talk, the easier it becomes to open up. I've been stewing over this for decades, so it's a relief to finally get it off my chest.

"That means a lot, Solana."

"Well, it's true. You have every right to feel abandoned. You've earned every shade of hurt and angry. Yet you're smart enough to recognize the hidden blessings. Silver linings, right?"

I bop her on the nose. "Wise beyond your years, love."

She kisses my cheek. "Tell me more."

Hearing the telltale sound of wheels crunching on gravel, I straighten. "Hold that thought. We've got company."

"Who's here so early in the morning?"

"Ethan."

"I'm sorry, I didn't realize you'd have visitors today."

I snort. "Eth's not a guest. He's my business partner, remember? His arrival is a daily occurrence."

"Right. I guess I didn't realize he built stuff in your workshop."

"While it's on my property, we consider it *our* shop. It doesn't make sense for us to have two, so we do all our work here. We borrow his cousin's flatbed when we need to transport the stuff our vehicles can't handle."

"That makes sense. What about the rest of the business? How do you divvy it up? Sorry, I'm being nosy again, but I'm a numbers girl, and this fascinates me."

"Eth owns the riverfront land in Kingsbury where our resort will be. I own the workshop and recently invested in an equitable share of the resort property. We split the cost of everything else, like tools and materials, fifty-fifty."

Moira barks, and Ethan's voice rings out from someplace inside the cabin. "Dec, where the hell are you?"

"On the roof," I yell.

A few moments later, he appears in the doorway. "Why are you hanging out up here when—" His eyes widen when he spots Solana. "Good morning. I didn't see a yellow Mustang in the driveway." His gaze briefly darts to me, then refocuses on her.

"Hi, Ethan. My car's at Maple Haven. I rode with Declan last night."

The bastard's lips twitch, but shockingly, he suppresses the urge to make a dirty joke about riding. "Nice. I wish I'd known you were here. I would've brought you a bagel too."

"She can have mine," I say.

Solana waves me off. "Don't be ridiculous. You need to have breakfast if you're gonna be hefting all that big wood."

Ethan snorts. "That's what she said."

She realizes her mistake and flushes bright pink, then bursts into laughter. "Jesus, you're as dirty-minded as Will."

"Oh, I can guarantee you, Eth's much worse."

"Who, me?" He flashes her a wink and points to me. "Someone's gotta lighten this moody fucker up, am I right?"

I give him the finger. "Bite me."

He chomps his teeth in challenge. "Think I won't?"

Solana giggles her little tinkling fairy laugh, and it makes me warm inside. "Wait, would you actually bite him?"

"I've done it before." He plops onto the foot of the chaise. "Remember that, Dec?"

"How could I forget? You left a mark, dickhead."

She looks between us. "Um, I need to hear this story."

"Let's put it this way, I have three sisters, so Dec's the big brother I always wanted. Naturally, that means I seize every opportunity to act the part of the annoying little brother."

"Older brothers are just as annoying," Solana mutters.

Last night on the phone, she told Cody she met Liam and me at the Busy Bean and recognized us from his living room. Said we chatted a bit, and she fell in love with Liam. This way, it'll seem more natural when she walks into his house and Liam already knows her—or if her name happens to come up in conversation.

That factor has been on my mind, so I'm relieved to have a story in place. While I'm not thrilled about Cody being in her life, I won't be the dick who discourages a girl from having a relationship with her only sibling. Especially since I'll never meet mine.

Ethan nudges her. "Knowing your brother, I can only imagine."

She gives a dramatic eye roll. "Trust me, you don't know the half of it. Anyway, you still haven't told me why you bit Declan."

"We were in college. I was trying to get into a fight with some asshole who banged my girlfriend, but Dec wouldn't let me."

"I restrained you for your own good," I say. "Nothing positive could've come from hittin' that guy."

She raises a brow. "Did you two get into a lot of brawls in Dublin?"

"Nah, no brawls. I got into one scuffle at a pub, but otherwise, we behaved." Ethan points to me. "Declan's never been in a fight."

"Really?"

I nod. "I'm a yeller, but I've never hit anyone."

"Have you ever wanted to?" she asks.

"Countless times, honey."

"Wow, that's admirable you're able to keep your cool. You must have really good self-control."

No, I used alcohol to numb the urges.

She chews her lip. "I kicked my brother in the balls once."

Ethan and I reflexively wince. There's nothing like the mention of a junk shot to make a man panic and curl into a ball.

"How'd that work out for you?" I ask.

"Not well. He slapped me, and I had to miss school for two days so no one would see the handprint on my face."

My blood boils at the thought of anyone raising a hand to her. I clench my jaw to hold back a snarl.

Ethan's gaze flicks to mine and lingers for a beat before finding Solana's again. His jaw tightens. "Dare I ask *why* you kicked Bridges in the nuts?"

He knows all too well what it's like to be hit. His father knocked him around for years. The bastard beat Ethan's ma and oldest sister too. He never struck the younger two girls, but that was only because Ethan protected them. One night, his father went too far and broke Ethan's arm. Only then did his ma finally gain the courage to leave with the kids.

Solana looks away. "It's a long story, but I went to him about a situation I needed his help with. Instead of coming to my defense and protecting me, he blew me off and called me a lying drama queen." She shrugs and picks at her nails. "I sorta lost my shit. Granted, I shouldn't have kicked him, but I was livid. After he hit me, I packed a bag and stayed with River until high school ended. Then, I went away to New York for school. Thanks to the incident, my brother and I didn't speak for five years."

"Hopefully, you two have worked everything out by now," Ethan says.

"We've never really addressed it, but he seems to be a different person." She sighs. "Time will tell, I guess."

"He hit you often?" I growl, finally able to speak through my fury.

"No, just the one time," she replies quickly.

I grip her elbow. "What did you need protection from?"

"I don't wanna talk about it." She's made multiple mentions of her and Cody's fallout but offers zero elaboration on the catalyst. And every time I ask, she shuts me down and changes the subject. Maybe she's not interested in discussing the issue, but I am.

"Did someone hurt you?" I tighten my grip. "Tell me."

She pulls her arm from my grasp. "Don't worry about it."

I use those exact words when someone calls me out. There's no question in my mind now. Someone definitely hurt her. I stare her down, hoping to get some answers, but she avoids eye contact.

The morning flew by. Ethan and I have been in the workshop, focusing on jobs not related to our resort. Sometimes, I wish we could ignore all the cabinetry and custom build orders, but we need a steady cash flow if we're ever going to make our dream happen without tapping into our reserves.

Solana is hard at work, studying. I set her up in the dining room with water, coffee, and snacks. She looked so cute sitting there with her books spread across the table.

Ethan lifts his safety goggles onto his forehead. His blue gaze burns into me. "We've been working for almost four hours. I figured you would've broached the topic by now."

"What topic?" I grunt.

"Oh, I dunno, maybe how you looked like you wanted to rip someone's throat out." He leans against the workbench and waits. When I don't say anything, he adds, "Any idea what happened to her?"

"Dunno." I set aside the sander I've been using. "She shuts me down when I ask for details."

"Maybe because I was sitting there?"

"Happens every time, so I don't get why she bothers bringin' it up in the first place."

He sighs. "I used to do that."

"Do what?"

"Drop subtle hints about the shit that went down behind closed doors, then clam up when asked about it."

"Why?"

"I hoped that someday, somebody would care enough to dig deeper. Hint, hint, no one ever did. It took a compound fracture to get people's attention."

"Bridges called her a drama queen when she went to hide in the bathroom."

"Yeah, and Solana coming face-to-face with you in her brother's living room gave her a damn good reason to panic, right?"

"I guess. But I'm not sure what you're gettin' at."

"Look, you saw firsthand how he dealt with her distress, and this is *after* he supposedly became a different man, or whatever. Think about it, Dec. If she grew up being blown off all the time—or accused of drama queen behavior—why would she expect anyone to listen? Trust me. It's bad enough to go through the shit, but when someone tries to trivialize it or tell you it didn't happen, it's easy to make yourself believe you deserve the abuse." Pain flashes across his face, but he quickly recovers. "She's feeling you out, bro."

"You think she wants to tell me?"

"Yeah, I do. But she's scared, so don't expect her to open up easily. Whatever happened was enough to make her move out and cut ties for half a decade. If she's dropping hints, she wants you to know."

"What should I do?"

"Never stop asking questions." He jabs his finger in the middle of my chest. "And when she talks, you'd better listen."

"I will."

His gaze darts over my shoulder. "Incoming."

I spin around. Solana's crossing the driveway carrying a tray of food. Moira follows close behind, tail wagging, doing her typical trot that borders on a gallop. My enormous dog dwarfs

Solana's petite frame, making me chuckle. "Looks like I'd better get a saddle so you can ride her next time."

Solana laughs and tips her imaginary cowboy hat. "Howdy, boys." She enters the shop. "Declan, I hope you don't mind me raiding your fridge. I figured you two might be hungry, so I made lunch."

Sure enough, she's got a pair of sandwiches, some chips, pickles, and two glasses of lemonade.

"You didn't have to do that, but thank you, love."

"Thanks, Solana." Ethan tears into his sandwich, then crunches on his pickle. "I'm starving."

"You're welcome. I needed a break from school stuff." She looks around the workshop, taking in the tools and partially finished projects with an appreciative nod. "So, this is where the magic happens, huh?"

Ethan snorts. "Maybe for Dec, but *my* magic happens in the bedroom."

I roll my eyes at the cocky bastard.

Solana giggles and hands me a sheet of paper. "So, I did some research during one of my snack breaks."

"What's this?"

"I've compiled a list of every fun, kid-friendly activity in the Colebury area and surrounding counties. Up to and including Burlington."

"Uh, you were supposed to be studyin'."

She waves me off. "On here, you'll find everything from pick-your-own pumpkins to parades and festivals. I found aquariums, museums, zoos, and nature preserves. There're tons of playgrounds and this cool place with mini-golf and bumper cars. I even listed a few music classes and sports teams. I sorted them into columns based on the day of the week. The highlighted activities coincide with your Liam visits."

My chest tightens. I open and close my mouth a few times but can't find words.

She touches my arm. "Hopefully, this will help with the

enrichment thing we discussed. Don't forget he'd be just as happy traipsing through your property in search of animal footprints or salamanders."

"Thank you," I finally whisper.

"You're welcome. Well, I'd better get back to studying. Enjoy your lunch, gentlemen." With that, she kisses my cheek and heads inside.

I stare after her in disbelief. She's full of malarkey—a list this detailed had to eat up her study time this morning.

"Lemme see," Ethan murmurs, coming up beside me. I hand him the list, watching his smile grow as he reads. He lifts his gaze to mine. "Wow."

"Wow," I repeat, nodding my agreement. "I'm just . . . wow." Because that's exactly what I am—completely in awe of Solana. Her sweetness. Her spirit. Her pure heart and beautiful soul.

I'm falling. Hard. I need to pull back before we both get hurt.

42

SOLANA

It was midafternoon by the time Declan and Ethan finished up in the shop. Declan just showered, so now he's chatting on the phone with Liam while Ethan showers. Then, we're taking a ride over to the resort property so they can show me the tiny houses they've built.

While I only got through a fraction of what I hoped to accomplish today with my schoolwork, the time spent making the activity list for Declan was well worth it. I knew he'd appreciate the gesture, but I never expected to render him speechless. He followed me inside a few minutes after I left the workshop for a scorching hot kiss. My insides quiver at the memory.

I glance over to where he's seated at the kitchen island. His back is to me, but I can hear his smile.

"Yeah, buddy. As long as the weather's good, we can pick as many apples as you want." He chuckles. "I'm sure I could figure out a pie. We can look for a recipe and bake one afterward. Sound good?"

I'm swooning hard at the image of them baking together. Especially since I'm so useless with ovens.

234

"Oh, did she, now?" He pivots on his stool to face me and grins. "Mrs. Parker says you wrote your last name perfectly, huh? Buddy, that's fantastic. I'm super proud of you. Maybe we'll pick up some treats at the Busy Bean tomorrow to celebrate."

Yay, Liam. I smile and give Declan two thumbs-up.

"Oh, I dunno. I *think* she works Wednesdays." He flashes me a wink. "But I guess we'll have to wait and see. Yes, I'm sure she'll save you a jam doughnut if she's there." Declan's gaze burns into me. "Yes, bud. Solana will be *very* proud to hear you're making progress."

My God, this child. It's no wonder Cody's a changed man. I can't imagine how amazing it must be to live with the world's cutest little boy. Or how much it hurts Declan to miss out on time with his son.

"Keep up the good work, Liam. I love you to the moon and stars." He closes his eyes. "And beyond. See you tomorrow. Okay, bye." He hangs up and sets his phone on the counter. "Come here."

I make my way over to him. "You must be on cloud nine."

He wraps me in a hug. "You should've heard his excitement. The teacher gave him two gold stars for spellin' his name aloud and writing it perfectly. You would've thought he won a Ferrari."

"That's awesome."

He rubs his hands up and down my back. "Thanks for your part in that." He releases me enough to capture my face between his palms. "And for makin' me that list. I can't tell you how much I appreciate it."

"I know you do. I'm glad I could help."

He takes my lips in a bone-melting kiss that's as relaxed as it is hungry. His tongue rubs against mine in a languid tease, setting my insides on fire.

From the doorway, Ethan clears his throat. "I'm guessing you two want to skip the field trip?"

Declan breaks our kiss with a chuckle. "That's up to Solana."

"I really want to see the tiny houses. I'm hella intrigued by the whole concept and can't wait to hear all about your business plan."

Ethan snorts. "Yeah, okay."

"No, seriously. I love talking numbers."

Declan stands. "Lemme take Moira out for a piss, and then we'll get goin'."

Ethan watches him leave, then turns to me. "In case he doesn't mention it, Dec was really moved by what you did for him and Liam." He gives me a warm smile. "Sometimes he has trouble expressing his feelings and shit, so I wanted to make sure you knew." He looks over his shoulder to make sure we're still alone. "Listen, Dec's not much of a talker, and he gets moody sometimes, but he's a damn good guy. He's been through a lot of shit. Just bear with him, okay?"

The three of us chatted throughout the ride to the resort site, Ethan's words echoing in my mind. I get the feeling there's more to Declan's story than he's told me. I really wish he'd let down his guard. Of course, that's pretty hypocritical of me, no?

They filled me in on what it was like to go to school in Dublin. Ireland has always been on my travel bucket-list, but after hearing them describe the countryside, food, music, and people, I've moved it to the top.

Ethan raved about Declan's father, echoing the sentiments he's shared with me about Mr. O'Shaughnessy's warmth and jovial nature. Declan got a wistful look on his face again, so I squeezed his hand. He'd taken hold of mine the moment I fastened my seatbelt, and he's still holding it twenty minutes later.

I'll gleefully hold the man's hand all day, but there's a little voice inside my head that keeps reminding me we're only temporary fuck buddies. This begs the questions: Are fuck buddies supposed to hold hands in the car? Or have meaningful conversations about the other person's hopes and dreams?

Declan glances at me before turning down a winding, gravel driveway. "Almost there."

"So . . . is River single?" Ethan asks from the backseat.

I spin to face him. "That was random. Why do you ask?"

Mischief flashes in his royal blue gaze. "Just curious."

"Stop tryin' to hook up with her friend," Declan warns.

Ethan flicks his earlobe. "I'm asking a simple question, Dec. Mind ya business." He meets my gaze once more. "So, *is* she?"

I debate the best way to answer. Yes, she's single, but she's not available. River is a complicated woman. She knows what she wants in life and how to get it. Unlike me, once she commits to something, she sees it through. She's ambition personified with an even bigger fear of failure, so she's guarded as fuck. While she enjoys a romp now and then, she's wary of playboys. Especially ones as sexy as Ethan.

I decide on a diplomatic answer. "She doesn't have time for guys. Med school keeps her occupied." She certainly won't mind hearing that Ethan asked about her, though.

He nods. "I bet. What kind of doctor is she planning to be?"

"A psychiatrist like her dad. He's my doctor, actually."

Both men are silent for a few beats as if waiting for me to continue, but that was all I planned to say.

Declan speaks first. "Do you see him regularly?"

"No, but I should." I stare out the window for a moment, calculating the time since my last appointment. Six months—far too long for a woman with crippling panic attacks.

He pulls the truck to a stop beside a large weeping willow and turns off the engine. "Then why don't you?" I shrug instead of answering, so he changes topics with a grunt. "We're here. Welcome to the future home of . . . whatever we decide to call the place."

"Seriously? You haven't chosen a name?"

"Nope. We can't find anything that suits it," Ethan explains.

"Maybe I can help. I love naming things." I purposely leave

out the story about my baby name lists because it tends to freak dudes out.

We climb from the truck, and I take in the view of the Winooski River. This section is rockier than the spot near the Busy Bean. The current seems stronger—that place between babbling brook and whitewater rapids—one might even call it wilder. Pristine forest greets us on the opposite bank, thicker than the wooded area by the old mill. The trees are mainly evergreens interspersed with oaks and maples cloaked in burnished reds, golds, and oranges.

I've always loved the New England fall foliage. When I lived in New York, my roommate and I took a trip upstate to explore the Hudson River Valley and Catskills. The region reminded me so much of Vermont.

Right now, standing on a bed of fallen pine needles, at the future home of Declan's dream, I realize the Green Mountain State is where I belong. Too bad my ideal school is in the Empire State. The more time I spend with Declan, the less I like the idea of returning to New York.

Feeling preemptively homesick, I scan the property in silence. On this side of the river, there are fewer trees. As we walk toward the cluster of buildings in the distance, Ethan explains how he inherited the piece of land from his grandfather, who, in a deathbed legacy speech, made him promise never to sell. Ethan lives in a cabin not too far from Declan's and spent years trying to figure out what to do with this glorious slice of riverfront property.

The idea to tap into the region's tourism market was originally Ethan's, but Declan came up with the eco-friendly tiny house concept. It warms me to hear them discuss the joint business venture as if it's their baby, and I love seeing the fire in Declan's eyes when he talks architecture.

Finally, we reach the group of eight buildings. There are four that resemble tiny log cabins, two modern ones, a French cottage one, and the tiny farmhouse they recently finished.

"These are incredible."

Declan beams. "Which one's your favorite?"

"Hmm . . . that's tricky. I grew up in a farmhouse, so I've always loved that vibe, but having spent time at your cabin, the rustic design is also appealing. But if I had to choose . . ." I make my way over to the tiny French cottage. "I'd pick this one. It reminds me of my old dollhouse."

Ethan laughs. "That's my little sister's favorite too. Dalia calls it the 'chic shack.' "

I turn to Declan. "Does Liam have a favorite?"

He points to one of the modern structures. "He likes that one. Said it looks like a spaceship."

The guys give me a tour of each building. What strikes me most is how huge they seem from the inside. Not only are the houses fully equipped with all the amenities one might need, but every inch of space is utilized to its full potential.

"So, let's figure out a cool name, shall we?" I suggest.

Ethan nods. "We'll take all the help we can get."

"What've you come up with so far?"

Declan rubs his jaw. "We've tossed around a few ideas, like Tiny Town and Tiny Village, but they make it feel like a kids' park or somethin'."

"We liked River Haven, but it sounds too much like the Maple Haven Inn." Ethan quirks his eyebrow at me. "And now that I know your friend's family owns it, that name's outta the question. We don't wanna start shit with our competitors."

I chuckle. "Good call."

Declan surveys the area. "We want a name that'll convey both the beauty of the property and the homes' eclectic designs. But I think Eth should have the final decision since it was his idea."

"We're a team, bro."

I point to the river. "I think much of the property's appeal comes from your view of the Winooski. If you close your eyes and listen, all you can hear is the rush of water and birds chirping. It feels so wild and free here, so it would be awesome if you could capture that vibe."

Declan straightens. "What about Wild River somethin'?"

"Wild River Resort?" Ethan smiles and turns to me. "Thoughts?"

"Well, I *love* the Wild River part, and it's extra cool since your last name is Wilde."

"Holy shit, I didn't even think of that."

Declan grins. "I love it. It's a perfect way to pay tribute to you *and* your grandfather." He glances at me. "Eth's namesake was Ethan Wilde the first."

"*Damn.* That's a sexy name for a grandpa," I blurt. The guys laugh heartily as heat creeps across my cheeks. "Sorry, Ethan."

He squeezes my shoulder. "No worries. I'll take all the compliments I can get."

I clear my throat. "Back to the name. When I hear 'resort,' it makes me think of those big, commercial places." I motion to the property. "This place feels like an escape from all that. And you guys want to capitalize on simplicity with your tiny houses, so I don't think resort works."

"Refuge?" Declan offers.

Ethan shakes his head. "Nah, dude. Makes me think of safaris. Lions and shit."

I perk up. "What about Wild River Retreat?"

"Wild River Retreat," Declan repeats. "I really like it. What do you think, Eth?"

"I love it." Ethan embraces Declan in a back-slap man hug. "We've got a name, brotha."

43

SOLANA

MOOD MUSIC: "AWAKE" BY JOSH GROBAN

It's Thursday afternoon. I took the day off to study for a statistics exam, but I texted Declan when I started to get bored and antsy. His solution was an impromptu date, so now I'm heading to his cabin. He won't tell me where we're going or what we're doing, so my stomach is extra fluttery when I pull into his driveway.

Declan greets me on the front porch with a smile. "Hello, beautiful."

I kiss him. "Hey. Did you finish that table for your customer?"

"Yep. I got it done ahead of time, so that frees me up for our pizza-making plans on Saturday night." He takes my hand. "You ready?"

It's then I notice he's holding a basket. "We're having a picnic?"

Declan grins. "Somethin' like that." He leads me toward the pristine lake on his property and points to a rowboat secured to a wooden dock. "How about a boat ride?"

I raise a brow as we approach. "Promise not to throw me in?"

He laughs. "Maybe in the summer, but the water's too cold now." He hands me a life vest. "Put this on."

"What about you?" I ask, buckling the vest. "Don't you have one?"

"You're wearin' it, love." He tightens my straps. "I don't plan on us capsizing, and I'm a strong swimmer."

The man has been looking out for me ever since that day outside the grocery store. His concern makes my heart swell.

"In that case, take me away, Captain."

He helps me inside and settles on the middle bench, grabbing the oars. "Where to, milady?"

"The canals of Venice."

"I dunno much about Italy, so how about a float down River Corrib?"

"Is that in Ireland?" I ask, eager to hear more about his home country.

"Yes. It flows from Lough Corrib, which is how we say lake, through Galway, out into the Atlantic in Galway Bay. Believe it or not, it's the fastest flowing city river in Europe."

"Did you spend time on it when you were young?"

Declan rows us along the edge of the lake, beneath trees cloaked in burnished reds and oranges. "Yeah, I did some kayaking with my dad."

"If you could go anywhere in the world, where would you go?"

He smiles. "Ireland."

I giggle. "I had a feeling you'd say that. Even though it rains so much there?"

"I love the rain." He sets the oars inside the boat and hands me a bottle of water. He cracks open his own and takes a swig. "I love listenin' to it on my roof and goin' for walks in it. It's hard to explain, but it soothes me."

"Have you ever danced in the rain?" I ask, watching the wind whip through his auburn hair.

He pulls out a block of cheese and slices off a few chunks. I recognize the Garden Goat Farms label, and my mouth waters. I never met a cheese I didn't like, and their goat cheese is to die for.

"I'm not much of a dancer."

"I love dancing. River and I used to dance in the rain every summer. You should try it sometime."

He leans forward and touches my knee. "If given the opportunity, I'll dance anywhere with you."

"I'm gonna hold you to that, Declan." Although, if everything goes as planned, I'll be in New York next summer. A pang of wistfulness squeezes my chest at the thought of leaving Colebury.

What if I don't have to? Maybe I could stay in Vermont for a year instead of just a semester? As it stands, I'm acing my online courses. As long as I get my degree, does it really matter if it isn't from my dream school?

"What about you? Where would you go if you could travel the world?"

"I'd love to visit Barcelona to see where my mom grew up." I tuck a wisp of hair behind my ear. "Although lately, Ireland tops my list."

"Oh?" He hands me a sandwich and a napkin with chunks of goat cheese on it. "And why might that be?"

"Maybe I'm captivated by a certain broody Irishman."

A comfortable silence stretches between us as nature's tranquility provides the soundtrack for our meal—leaves rustling, birds chirping, and the creak of the old wooden boat.

"How do you imagine your future?" Declan asks after a while.

With you. "Like, my *ideal* future?"

"Yeah. If someone gave you a clean slate, where would you see yourself?" He rubs his jaw. "Forget about jobs and money, your anxiety, or anything like that. Paint me a picture of your dream life. What would you want?"

"All I want is a family and a safe place to live. Food on the table. Everyone happy and healthy. Warmth and togetherness."

"You want kids?"

Desperately. "I think so. I mean, I'm young, so I have plenty of time to worry about it, but I'd love to be someone's mom. Someone's wife."

Pain flashes across his face as he stares out at the lake. "And what if you couldn't have that?"

That's his way of reminding me he can't give me those things. While we have incredible conversations and mind-blowing sex, that's where it stops. *We're just fuck buddies.* For some reason, that fact hurts a little more right now.

"I'll embrace whatever warmth I'm given," I whisper. "I'll enjoy my chosen family and be grateful for the relationships I have for as long as I have them." I chew my lip. "Which is what I've been doing all along."

His eyes find mine. He doesn't speak, but the sadness in his gaze is enough to drown in.

44

DECLAN

MOOD MUSINGS: SAY WHAT YOU MEAN AND MEAN WHAT YOU SAY.

It's Saturday night. Solana and I finally finished cleaning up after making homemade pizzas. Watching her move around my kitchen like she belongs here makes me ache to share every meal with her. I keep thinking about our boat ride the other day. The wistful look on her face when she spoke about having a family. How it made me wish I could give her everything she wants. All I can give her is my time, but I'll make damn sure to fill every moment we share with warmth.

Right now, we're headed to the roof to watch the sunset. It's getting chillier in the evenings, so I gave her one of my college sweatshirts to wear. I love seeing her in my clothes. Her ponytail is a river of honey against the dark green material, and I'm enjoying the view of her lush backside as she climbs the steps in front of me. I pinch a cheek because I can't help myself.

She laughs. "Consider yourself warned; I pinch back."

"Please do."

I usher her outside. After grabbing the cushion from the storage bin, we settle on my chaise, and I recline us into a lounging position.

The sunset doesn't disappoint. Reds and purples paint the sky as a blood orange sun dips below the horizon. We sit in comfortable silence, basking in the afterglow. Not only do we have the deepest conversations of my lifetime, but these moments of simply *being* together feel just as nurturing. Time spent with Solana is equal parts effortless and engaging. Calm and wild. A symphony of peace and chaos. And, God help me, I can't get enough of her.

She sighs. "I wish I was a painter because that was stunning."

I run my fingers through her hair and kiss the side of her neck. "Not as much as you."

She traces the lines on the palm of my other hand. She's been holding it since we sat down. "I should probably head home."

I tense. "Why?" When she doesn't answer, I nudge her to shift position and face me. "I thought you were spendin' the night?"

Please don't leave.

"I want to, but I can't." Her cheeks turn pink. "I mean, we can't . . ."

I tilt her chin up. "We can't what?"

"We can't have sex, so I figured I shouldn't stay."

It takes a moment for me to understand what she's getting at. Clearly, she forgets I've lived with women before. "Solana, I don't care that you have your period."

Her eyes widen. "You're not going anywhere near my lady bits tonight." Then she turns an even brighter shade of pink and looks away.

"That's not what I'm sayin'. Look at me." I wait until I have her attention before speaking. "You think I want you to leave?"

She gestures between us. "You told me this is only about sex. Since that can't happen for a few days, I don't want to waste your time."

"Are you serious?" I stare her down for a few beats, both shocked and pissed she'd think that. And disgusted with myself for my part in making her feel that way. When she squeezes her eyes shut, I cup her face in my hands. "You obviously misinterpreted what I meant when I said sex was all I could give, so let me make myself *crystal* clear." I clench my jaw. "I want *everything* with you."

Her lower lip quivers. "I thought we were only fuck buddies?"

"I wouldn't be risking my visitation rights for a simple fuck." I rest my forehead against hers. "Solana, you're wrong if you think you don't mean somethin' to me."

SOLANA

MOOD MUSIC: "I MISS YOU" BY ADELE

All day, I worried about telling Declan I have my period. While I wanted to spend time together, I hated the thought of disappointing him with the news. I never expected his reaction to be so . . . vehemently . . . the opposite.

His stormy gaze scorches me with its intensity. "You understand what I'm tryin' to tell you?"

"You like me?" I whisper.

Declan kisses me instead of answering, and there's nothing slow and tender about it. He palms the back of my head and pulls me closer. I moan into our kiss and give it back just as hard, surrendering to the clawing need that grips me whenever we're together.

I shift to straddle him, feeling his hard cock press between my legs. He groans when I roll my hips and grind in his lap. I tangle my fingers in his hair and kiss him harder. Deeper. But it's not enough.

Tearing my lips from his, I flash a devilish smile before kissing my way down his neck. Declan's pulse throbs against my tongue, so I suck on his throat.

"God, Solana . . ." He groans. "You're killin' me, honey."

"That was a preview. I'm just getting started." I reach for the button on his jeans.

"Hey," he snatches my hand, "I don't want you feelin' obligated to do anything for me. Especially given what we just talked about."

"I know." I tug from his grasp and scooch so I'm nestled between his thighs. "But I want to make you feel good." Chest heaving, he watches me unzip his pants and pull out his cock. I stroke it up and down, relishing the satin-covered length of steel. "I like giving you pleasure," I whisper, adding a second hand to the mix.

"You're doin' great." His voice is ragged, just like his breaths.

A bead of moisture eases from the head. I hold his gaze and lower my lips to him.

DECLAN

MOOD MUSINGS: TODAY IS MY DAY.

I've fantasized about this since the moment I laid eyes on Solana's rosebud lips, never dreaming I'd be lucky enough for it to happen.

I blink to make sure I'm not imagining it. "You don't have to—"

"I *want* to. But be forewarned, I might suck," she flushes a pretty pink, "even though that's the point, I guess."

My reply comes out as a strangled moan when she puts her mouth on me. At first, she tentatively licks the head of my cock like an ice cream cone. Then, she takes me deeper, her perfect tongue rubbing the underside.

"Oh, fuck."

She stops. "Is it bad?"

"No, baby, you're perfect. Please don't stop."

"You're really big. I can't take you in that far. Can I use my hand too?"

I give a jerky nod. "Move it in rhythm with your mouth."

"Okay." She grips my shaft and starts to suck me again.

"So good."

Emboldened by my praise, she tightens her grip and moves a little faster. I keep my clenched fists at my sides, fighting off the urge to knot my fingers in her hair. I want to pull her closer, but I'm afraid that'll overwhelm her. I grit my teeth and squeeze my eyes shut, trying so hard to keep my hips still. I tighten my thighs and arse cheeks too. Anything to keep from thrusting into the wet heat of her mouth.

Solana stops suddenly. "Declan."

My eyes fly open. "Yeah?"

The heat in her gaze turns her eye color molten amber, and she's flushing like a wild Irish rose. She flashes a smile that could turn the Pope to sin. "Watch me."

My breath leaves me in a rush. She waits until my gaze is pinned to hers before continuing. Her eyes flutter closed when she takes me into her mouth and starts bobbing her head.

"Oh, *fuck* . . ."

The pleasure is incandescent. I lose the battle against my hands and knot one of them in her hair. Her moan reverberates up my shaft, tightening my balls. She doubles down on her efforts. The friction and gentle suction make my legs shake. Then she swirls her tongue.

"Solana . . ." I pant, rubbing my hands up and down her back. "Feels so good." I grip her ponytail and wind the hair around my wrist. "Keep doin' that, baby." She picks up her pace and my thigh muscles tighten along with my hold on her hair. My hips jerk upward. "*Fuck.*"

She moans around my cock and moves faster, taking me even deeper. Every nerve ending zings like a livewire. She's got me coiling tighter and tighter.

So close.

"Gonna come," I growl, pushing at her shoulders. Instead of stopping, she sucks me harder. My entire body pulses with my release. "*Solana* . . ."

Solana peers up at my face as I orgasm, no doubt proud of herself for getting me there. And she should be. Maybe it's because no one has sucked me in years, but that takes the record for fastest blow job in history. Part of me feels embarrassed for finishing so quickly, but it's a testament to her skill. Given that it was only her first time, I can't fathom the experience once she's had some practice.

"Did I do okay?"

"God, yes." I pull her up my body so she's lying on top of me. I kiss her cheeks. Her forehead. Her temples and the tip of her nose before I brush my lips over hers. "Best of my life."

Her eyes widen. "Really?"

"Yes, really. Had somethin' to do with your enthusiasm. Consider yourself a fuckin' expert."

Her eyes darken with satisfaction. "I hope you think about me when we're not together."

"I never stop thinkin' about you." I kiss her neck and gently suck the sensitive spot beneath her ear. "Trust me, love, I won't be able to get that vision out of my head."

She tilts her head, giving me more access to her neck. "Good. I want you just as crazy for me as I am about you."

"Wish granted." I tip her chin up so I can look into her eyes. "I didn't mean to pull your hair. I tried to pull out before I came. I'm sorry I got carried away."

She flushes and chews her lower lip. "Can I tell you a secret?"

"Tell me *all* of them."

"I love when you get carried away. It's hot as fuck. Your take-chargey-ness is hella sexy during ordinary circumstances." She brings her lips to my ear and whispers, "In the bedroom, it drives me wild."

"You drive me wild too." I hug her tighter and kiss the top of her head. "And to answer your question, yes, I like you."

She nuzzles her face into my chest. "I more than like you, Declan."

47

SOLANA

MOOD MUSIC: "REMEMBER WHEN IT RAINED" BY JOSH GROBAN

I lurch upward in bed, clutching my chest, sweat-covered and gasping.

Declan is awake beside me, his concerned gaze focused on my face. "You all right?"

Tendrils of the dream retreat to the darkened corners of my mind where they belong. "I had a nightmare."

"I know." He rests his hand on my shoulder. "You've been thrashin' around for a while, but I wasn't gonna wake you unless you screamed."

"If it happens again, please wake me right away."

"Will do." He reaches for the glass of water on his nightstand and hands it to me.

I swallow a few gulps and force my breathing back to normal. "Thanks."

He brushes the hair off my forehead. "Was it about your parents again?"

"No," I whisper. "Something different."

"Wanna talk about it?"

"Not really."

"Can I do anything for you?"

"Hold me."

Wordlessly, he pulls me close. Facing him, my cheek rests on his bicep, his chin on top of my head. He rubs slow circles on my back.

"Someone hurt me a long time ago," I say after a few minutes. "The dream felt like a flashback."

Declan stills. His muscles tense, but he doesn't say anything. Then his hands start moving again as if in a silent plea to keep me talking.

"He was someone I trusted."

"Who?"

"A friend of my brother's." I take a deep breath. "He tried to take something I wasn't willing to give."

He hugs me tighter and waits. While I don't want to relive the incident, I've talked about everything else with him, so I need to get it off my chest.

"His friend was staying with us temporarily. Cody was at work, so we were alone when I got home from school that day."

"How old were you?" His voice is low and even, but I can tell his jaw is tight.

"Sixteen. He was thirty-two." Another slow, deep breath. "I went downstairs to do a load of laundry. He followed. When I left the laundry room, he was standing in the hallway. At first, I didn't think anything of it, but he had a strange look in his eyes. He grabbed me when I went to pass him. Then I smelled the alcohol on his breath."

Declan's body goes rigid again. This time, his hands stop moving.

"I asked him to let me go, but he kissed me instead." I force a swallow. "He groped my breasts, then took it further. A lot further." My eyes well with tears, but I blink them away. "I was wearing a skirt, and he shoved it up around my hips and ripped my panties." A tear escapes. Then another. "He . . ." *Breathe, Solana.* "He was really rough with me."

"Did he rape you?"

"Not with his penis," I whisper, clinging to Declan's shoulders. "But his fingers made me bleed."

He sucks a sharp breath. "I'll kill him."

"That's what I thought Cody would say when I told him what happened."

"What *did* he say?"

"He called me a drama queen and told me to stop making up stories. But I wasn't the one who lied."

"What do you mean?"

"The bastard who hurt me knew I had a crush on him for years. My brother had an inkling too. The conniving fuck told Cody I offered to suck his dick in the basement. Said he turned me down and I didn't take it well."

"Motherfucker."

"Yeah, so instead of kicking the guy out, Cody made me feel like a slut. He allowed a sexual predator to stay in our home when he should've protected me. Or at the very least, believed *me* over his friend. That's when I kicked him in the nuts. After he slapped me, I was done. The day you saw me in the living room was my first time inside that house since I packed my shit and left."

"Tell me his name."

"No."

"Why not?

"Because it doesn't matter anymore."

"You're havin' nightmares. Don't tell me it's not affectin' you."

"I never said it's not affecting me. I said it doesn't matter."

He grips my chin. "Solana, no matter what happens between us, I'll never let anyone hurt you. If you need someone to protect you or stand up for you, I'll be there." Fire flashes in his gaze. "But don't fool yourself into thinkin' I won't hunt that fucker down if given the chance."

"Which is *exactly* why I'm not giving you his name. While I appreciate your concern, I didn't tell you the story so you could run out and avenge me."

He stares at my face for a moment. "I'm gonna have a hard time lookin' Cody in the eye after hearin' that story."

"Great. The *last* thing I wanted was to create more tension between you." I release a heavy sigh. "Listen, I told you what happened because keeping it from you felt dishonest. You deserve better from me." I cup his face in my hands like he does to me when he wants my full attention. "Declan, I'm falling for you." He opens his mouth to speak, but I hold a finger to his lips. "Maybe I'm being reckless, but you make me want to let go of my fear and bare my soul." I trace his chiseled jawline, indulging in the feel of his bristly hairs against my fingertips. "So, I hope you can understand why I don't want there to be any secrets between us."

"Solana, I . . ." Some unnamed emotion flares in his eyes before he quickly squeezes them shut. "I need to—"

Moira's vicious bark reverberates through the cabin. Followed by a series of snarls and more barking.

Declan sits up. "What the hell's she carryin' on about?" A loud thud from outside makes him jump out of bed. He rushes to the window and lifts the shade. "Fuck. I forgot to bungee the trash can lid and the bear got it again."

He lowers the shade and nods to the bed. "Let's get some sleep. I'll deal with the mess in the mornin'."

I've always loved chilly fall mornings. Turns out, I like them even more waking up at Declan's cabin. He's not in bed, but the aroma of coffee wafts from downstairs.

"Good morning," I call.

No answer. Panic flares for a moment. Then, I hear his muffled voice coming from outside. *Oh, right. The trash can.*

Curious who he's talking to, I peek out the window. Moira stands guard while a gloved Declan gathers the garbage strewn across the driveway. I pull on one of his sweatshirts and head downstairs to help.

As his fuck-withholding fuck buddy, it's the least I can do. I know Declan's words and kisses last night should've reassured me, but my insecurities have reared their stupid heads as usual. He told me from the start that all he can give me is sex, so I probably shouldn't have mentioned the part about falling for him. The voices in my mind were quick to point out he didn't say it back.

I certainly didn't plan to fall for him. It just kinda happened.

He looks up when I step onto the porch. "Mornin'. What're you doin' up so early?"

"I came to help you clean up."

He shakes his head. "Thanks, but I've got it. You're not wearing gloves, and I don't want you touchin' this shit."

Determined to serve a purpose, I descend the steps and make my way over to him. "That's what soap's for." I reach for an empty egg carton.

"Wait," he grumbles, pulling off his gloves and handing them to me. "If you're gonna be stubborn, be safe about it."

I slide my hands into the warm gloves and smile. "They're yellow."

"Most rubbers are."

Rubbers. I can't help but laugh at his word choice. "Are those the right equipment for this job?"

"It's not the kind of rubber I wanna be wearin', that's for damn sure."

"Glad to know we're on the same wavelength," I mutter, feeling my face heat. I point to his hands. "Don't you have woodworking gloves you can wear?"

He jerks his head toward his shop. "I was too lazy to walk that far." The corners of his eyes crinkle with his smile. "Haven't had my coffee yet."

"Well, let's get this over with, shall we?"

I help him gather the rest of the garbage while supervisor Moira prances around, hitting our bent heads with her wagging tail. Together, we make short work of the task.

Finally, we head inside and scrub our hands. I could get used to doing chores with Declan. There's something so beautiful and domestic about completing household work together. I can't help but fantasize about being part of his daily life. Sharing a home. Being normal.

Instead of the usual chorus of insecurities and failures that fill my mind, I get a taste of peace. Declan's presence quiets the voices. Takes the edge off my fears and worries. This must be what tranquility feels like.

He pours coffee for us and hands me my mug. "What're you thinkin' about?"

"You." I sip the life-giving nectar and release a happy sigh. "Thanks for the coffee."

"Thanks for helpin' me outside."

"You're welcome." I touch his cheek. "I like being here with you."

He sets his mug on the counter and pulls me into his arms. "I like havin' you here."

Declan's kiss is slow and deep. As hungry as it is tender. Bottomless. Exactly the solace I need.

Wrapped in the shelter of his warm, strong embrace, I moan into his mouth and pull him closer. He lifts me onto the counter without breaking the kiss and stands between my parted legs. I hook my ankles behind him, hugging his hips with my thighs. His erection presses against my core, and I silently curse my menstrual cycle.

He weaves his hands into my hair and cups the back of my head while we make out in his kitchen like a pair of horny teenagers.

God, I can't get enough of this man's kisses. Or his hugs and encouragement. Being in his home. His bed. His life. More than that, I love just *being* with him in whatever capacity he allows—even if I'll always want more.

Because finding my calm in Declan's storm feels a lot like love.

48

DECLAN

MOOD MUSINGS: IT ISN'T ABOUT ME.

I used to spend my days counting down the time until my next Liam visit. I still look forward to Mondays, Wednesdays, and Sundays for that very reason. Thanks to Solana, I've added Tuesdays and Saturdays to my list of good days—and my frequent pop-ins at the Busy Bean, of course.

I wish I could see her every day, but I can't. She needs to devote time to studying, and the last thing I want to do is distract her from her schoolwork. Besides, evenings are a bit tricky with my visitation hours and AA meetings.

Today is Friday, so I have a meeting tonight. As a rule, the Friday ones aren't an issue. Monday is another story. Now that school is in session, it has become challenging to take Liam home and make it to the church on time. I usually arrive ten minutes after they've started, which means I walk in when someone's speaking. Since I'd rather skip it entirely than be a rude interruption, I've missed two Monday meetings this month. Not a smart move for a recovering alcoholic with mandatory AA meetings.

Currently, it's midafternoon. I was up late working on a project for Solana's birthday, so I'm starting to fade. Lucky for me, my caffeine break comes with a shot of gorgeous blonde. I lock up my truck and head into the café, smiling when I see the new addition to the chalk beams. *Practice makes progress.*

Zara is behind the counter, rewriting one of the little boards that lists the drink specials. Her dark gaze lifts to mine. "Hey, you."

"Hello, Zara. How're you gettin' on?"

"Doing great. How about you?" Her nose ring flashes in the light when she smiles.

"Hangin' in there like always. How's the family?"

She tosses her long, black hair over a shoulder. "You just missed them. They stopped by for a quick visit on the way to the park."

I glance around the café. A few customers are milling about, but there are no employees to be seen. I know Solana is here because I parked beside her Mustang, but it's not like I can come right out and ask for her. Then again, it's possible Alec gave Zara a heads-up. I'm not sure about the typical brother-sister information exchange because I've never met any of mine.

"You workin' by yourself today?" I figure the question seems innocent enough.

"For now, yes. My baristas went for a walk." She points behind her. "Do you want coffee or hot cider today?"

"Coffee please. I need the caffeine break."

She chuckles. "Don't we all?"

"Damn right." I jut my chin toward her. "You let your employees take breaks at the same time?"

"Not usually, no." She sighs and shakes her head. "This wasn't really a break. It was more of a crisis thing."

My scalp prickles. "Everything okay?"

Zara stares up at my face with the same assessing look Alec gets when he's trying to decide how much to reveal. The bell on the door jingles as another customer walks in.

"Hold that thought." She points to my usual spot at the end of the counter.

I plop onto a stool and retrieve my phone to see if Solana contacted me. She didn't, which bothers me more than a little. I want to be the one she reaches for when she stumbles.

Zara finishes up with the woman at the counter and pours me a coffee with the perfect amount of milk, cream, and sugar. I come here often enough that she knows my order by heart.

She sets the mug in front of me. "I'm alone because Sunny, my new girl, needed some air, so Will went with her."

The pulsing in my head tells me my blood pressure's increasing. "Was someone givin' her a hard time?"

She purses her lips. "I really don't know why she was upset."

"Did she have another panic attack?"

Surprise flashes across her face. Either she's being coy, or Alec is a better secret-keeper than I expected. Her neutral expression returns. "How do you know about those?"

I shrug. "Small town."

She arches a brow. "Don't bullshit me, O'Shaughnessy."

"We . . . uh . . . spend time together."

"Wait a minute." Eyes widening, she snatches my wrist. "Do you have any idea who her brother is?"

"Funny you should ask—I recently discovered that little tidbit."

She slowly shakes her head. "You really know how to complicate your life, my friend."

"Understatement of the year right there, Zara."

"So, tell me," she begins, her lips curving into a scandalous smile, "does the super bitch know her sister-in-law is your fuck buddy?"

Zara is the queen of no-nonsense bluntness, and I love her for it. Some people find it off-putting, but I think it's refreshing.

"Well?" she probes, propping her hands on her hips.

"No, Darcy doesn't know." I give her a hard stare. "And I'd like to keep it that way."

"She sure as hell won't hear it from me. But wait . . . I thought you'd sworn off all women?"

"Yeah, well, so did I. Now, please tell me what's goin' on with Solana."

"She had a panic attack." She points out the window. "I told her to take a walk by the river to clear her head. Some creep had been hanging around the lot earlier, so I sent Will with her." She studies my face for a moment. "Are you aware of how her parents died?"

"Yeah." I sip my coffee. "And I know it's coming up on fifteen years."

"Is that causing tension between you? I mean, with your meetings and all?"

"She doesn't know."

Her mouth drops open. "How's that possible?"

"Hasn't come up in conversation, and I'm not in a rush to tell her." I pick at the callus on my palm to avoid looking at Zara's face, but it doesn't matter. The weight of the Rossi glare presses on my shoulders.

"Weaving a web for yourself, Declan."

"No kiddin'," I mutter, finally risking a glance. To my surprise, there's no judgment in her gaze—just genuine concern.

She releases a heavy sigh. "Look, I've known Sunny since she was born. I just don't want to see her get hurt." While her tone is even, the warning in it is crystal clear.

"I don't wanna hurt her, Zara."

"Then, be honest."

The door's bell jingles, and Will and Solana enter the café. He's got a protective arm wrapped around her shoulder. I know he's just a friend—and he's gay, so he isn't a threat—but still, a trace of jealousy bubbles in my veins. *I* want to be the rock she leans on when the rest of her world crumbles.

"You okay, Sunny?" Zara calls, as Will waves and disappears into the back.

Solana nods, joining her behind the counter. "Yeah. Sorry about that."

Zara squeezes her shoulders. "Don't apologize. Shit happens."

She jerks her thumb in my direction. "This customer was asking about you."

"How are you today, Mr. O'Shaughnessy?"

"Oh, puh-lease." Zara elbows her. "Skip the formalities, Juliet. I'm on to your little tryst with Romeo." Then she winks and heads to the kitchen.

Solana peers up at me with widened eyes. "Uh . . ."

"I told her."

"I thought we were supposed to be a secret?"

"We are." I squeeze her hand. "But I trust Zara. Now, tell me what's upsettin' you today."

"Just one of those days, I guess."

"Talk to me, honey," I coax, leaning in to listen.

She hesitates for a moment, then sighs heavily. "I tossed and turned last night, worrying about school."

"How come?"

"I'm not sure if going back to New York in January is the right decision."

Hope flickers to life in my chest, but I quickly squash it. I won't allow Solana to jeopardize her future over my selfish desire to keep her. I force a neutral expression. "Why wouldn't it be?"

"Because every time I think about moving away from you, it makes it hard to breathe."

"Solana," I whisper. "Don't factor me into decisions regardin' your future. You'd be a fool to stay in Colebury."

"Well, okay then." Tears well in her eyes, and her pain-filled expression is a knife to my chest. She looks away, her tone hollow when she finally speaks. "Maybe I've been reading this all wrong. We seem so good together."

"You're not reading anything wrong." I tip her chin up. "What I mean is, don't sell yourself short. I'm not worth it. I can't give you what you deser—"

"We'll have to agree to disagree." Blinking rapidly, she stiffens her spine. "So, anyway, I was comatose when I finally went under. Then, I woke up late. I skipped breakfast to make it here on time, but the morning crowd was busier than usual, so I didn't get a chance to eat. Then, someone broke a glass, which made me think of my parents' accident." She shudders and wraps her arms around herself in a hug. "I'm good now."

"Sleep at my place tonight."

"It's Friday." She eyes me cautiously. "I thought you had your Architect's Guild meeting?"

I hate lying to her about where I go on Monday and Friday nights, but that doesn't stop me right now. I ignore the prickly scalp that happens when I knowingly do something I shouldn't. "It got rescheduled."

She points to herself. "Are you sure you wanna spend your Friday night with this hot mess?"

I want to spend every night with you. "I wouldn't call you a mess, but you're right about bein' hot."

"Thanks," she mutters, flushing a pretty pink. She suddenly perks up. "I forgot to thank you for the surprise you left on my windshield."

"I'm not sure what you're talkin' about."

"Don't play games with me." She points to a long-stemmed red rose in a vase on the back counter. "It's beautiful, thank you."

A chill races down my spine. "That's not from me."

"For real?"

I shake my head slowly. "If I wanted to leave you a flower, I'd choose a yellow one—like a sunflower or daffodil."

She briskly rubs her hands over her biceps like she's suddenly cold. "Someone put the rose on my windshield after I got here. I found it when I took my actual break and figured you stopped by."

"I was in the shop until two. This is the first I've been here."

"Seriously?"

"Yes." Zara comes out from the back carrying a tray of scones, so I flag her over. "Zara, you mentioned somethin' about a creep in the lot earlier. Did you know him?"

She shakes her head. "I didn't see his face."

"Did he come into the café?"

"No. He strolled around the lot for a while, looking kinda shady." She cocks her head to the side. "Why? What's up?"

Solana points to the vase on the back counter. "Someone left a rose on my car."

"Lemme guess, it wasn't Romeo?"

"Nope." I scan the ceilings. "Do you have security cameras?"

Zara snorts. "Have you met my brothers and Griffin?"

"Good point."

"I'll have Benny stop by later to see if he can get a video still of the guy's face." She nudges Solana. "In the meantime, I'd feel more comfortable with you taking your breaks inside. I'll tell Will to walk you out when we close."

Solana gives a small nod.

Zara eyes her. "Any idea who could've left it for you?"

"No." She snatches the rose and drops it into a nearby trash can. "But if it's not from Declan, I don't want it."

Moira's excited barking signals Solana's arrival. I head for the front door and greet her with a smile. "Hello, love."

She wraps her arms around my waist. "Hi."

"How was the rest of your shift?"

"Uneventful, thank God." She rests her cheek on my chest and sighs. "I hate that Zara had to see me like that. Not to mention my complete and utter lack of productivity. One of these days, she and Audrey will get tired of wasting payroll on me."

"Zara flat-out told me she cares about you, and I'm sure Audrey feels the same. Stop worryin' about their business choices and turn your focus to making yourself feel better." I stroke my fingers through her hair. "You've mentioned River's father is your psychiatrist. What're his thoughts on how deeply the fifteen-year mark is affecting you?"

She shrugs. "Dunno. Haven't been to an appointment since I moved home."

I tilt her chin up. "And why not?"

Her body deflates on another sigh. "Because I didn't want to admit to myself—or anyone else—how bad it's gotten since March."

"Remind me what happened in March. That's when you caught your boyfriend steppin' out on you?"

"No, that happened in May. On March fifteenth, the drunken piece of shit who killed my parents got paroled." The words drip from her tongue like acid.

My stomach clenches. Darcy called me that on more than one occasion. And it was true. While I didn't kill anyone, I fucked up plenty of lives.

"Beware the Ides of March, right?" Her voice slices through my thoughts. "I never expected Shakespeare to be so relevant to my life. Anyway, the bastard went on to get another DWI in May. That's when shit really hit the fan for me, anxiety-wise."

"I'm sorry."

She touches my arm. "What are you sorry for? You didn't do anything."

I'm sorry for my likeness to the man who robbed her happiness. And the smoke and mirrors I've used to hide my alcoholism. My lies of omission are eating away at me. I force a swallow. "I assume he's behind bars again?"

"Dunno. I stopped following the news stories because they made me sick. The reporters kept mentioning his previous offenses, and I couldn't handle it. A few weeks later, I caught Chris fucking Jessica after my Calculus final. So, yeah, I kinda shut down."

"Is it any easier bein' back home?"

"Yes and no. On one hand, the familiarity and slower pace of Colebury is a comfort. I mean, I love my job at the Bean. Not only do I get to see Will more often, but I truly enjoy working for Zara and Audrey. School is going great, so that's not an issue. And I love spending time with you on my days off." She looks away. "But being home dredges up memories of the accident and some other shit I don't want to think about."

"Which is exactly why you should be meetin' with your doctor."

"I don't have time for therapy."

Realizing I'm not getting anywhere with the conversation, I change topics. "Was Benito able to get a picture of the guy who left the rose?"

"No. Nothing useful, at least. He was at the very edge of the frame, and Benny couldn't see his vehicle."

The thought of someone making an unwelcome advance stirs my protective instincts. "Do *you* have any idea who it could be?"

I know Zara already asked her, but my gut is telling me to revisit the question.

She shakes her head, but her eyes—and the tense set of her shoulders—tell a different story. The hairs on the back of my neck stand on end as the pieces fall into place. Solana does have a theory about the man's identity, but she doesn't want to reveal it.

Mulling the thought over, I watch her for a few beats before speaking, "Has he contacted you since the incident?" Her face goes ashen, confirming my suspicions. She tries to turn her head, but I capture her chin once more. "Answer me."

"No."

"Is your brother still in contact with him?"

"No clue."

"Tell me his name."

"No." She pulls from my grasp. "We've been over this. I'm not going to tell you."

I clench my jaw. "Why?"

She crosses her arms over her chest. "Because I'm just not."

"That's not an acceptable answer."

"Well, it's the only one you're gonna get," she snaps, turning away from me. "You know what? I think maybe it's better if I head home tonight. I've had a shitty day, so I'm really not in the mood to hang out," she mutters, making a beeline for the door. "Goodnight, Declan."

It takes a full ten seconds for my brain to start working again after she disappears onto the porch. And another ten for my legs to move.

"Solana, wait." I gallop down the porch steps and catch up to her in a few long strides. "Don't leave. I'll stop interrogatin' you."

"I should really go. I'm a bit of a wreck." She stares up at my face with wet eyes. "It won't be fun to have me around tonight."

"I'm not lookin' for fun."

"What are you looking for?" she whispers, her lower lip quivering.

"I just wanna hold you."

49

SOLANA

I'm rinsing the suds from the decadent bubble bath Declan drew for me when he reappears with a pair of fluffy white towels.

His gaze darkens, admiring my nakedness, but then he quickly wraps me in warm terry.

"This feels toasty." I lean against him as he towels my hair.

He touches my cheek. "I warmed them in the dryer for you."

"No one has ever done that."

"Warmed your towels?"

"Any of it. Not only did you feed me dinner, but you let me take a long bath, warmed my towels, *and* made me tea. I feel like a queen."

His eyes soften. "That was my plan."

While it's clear he's being tender, that same tenderness is tearing my heart in two. *Don't factor me into decisions regarding your future.* How can he push me away one minute, then sweep me off my feet, the next? Since it's clear he doesn't see a future for us, I need his current plan to involve hard thrusts.

I allow the towel covering me to fall to the floor between us. His breath catches, but he doesn't move.

"I want you to fuck me."

His eyes widen. "I didn't want tonight to be about sex."

I stand on my tiptoes and brush my lips over his neck. I drink in his clean scent and press wet, open-mouthed kisses to his throat. Flattening my hands on his chest, I suck on his earlobe, then pull back to make eye contact. "I *need* you to fuck me."

"Solana, you're killin' me," he rasps.

My nipples harden with the rumble of his voice. His hot gaze lingers on the swells of my breasts, before drifting lower. Heat pools between my thighs when he licks his lips. The desire written on his features is enough to burn me to ash. I know just how amazing it feels when he licks me like he can't get enough of my taste. But right now, I need more than his wicked tongue.

"Declan, please . . ." He's got me so desperate and achy for him, I'm willing to beg for it.

He slides his hands to my lower back, his fingers brushing the curve of my butt. "Tell me what you need."

I roll my hips. "You."

He cups my ass cheeks and tugs me closer. His erection presses into my belly, making my inner muscles clench in welcome. I *ache* for him. His touch. His ragged breaths. His heavy weight on top of me. I need his thick cock to stretch and fill me, chase my worries away as his thrusts pin me to the bed. Most of all, I need him to anchor me in this moment so I can shake off my demons and the pain of his earlier rejection.

"Please . . ." I stroke him through his jeans. "Make me forget about today."

He groans deep in his chest, then scoops me into his arms. We make it to his room in no time. My back collides with his plush, down comforter. Resting my head against his pillows, I watch him shed his clothes with a primal efficiency that tells me he wants this just as badly.

He snatches a condom from the nightstand drawer and tears open the wrapper. I'll never get tired of watching him roll one onto his beautiful cock. Or the heat that flares in his eyes the moment he's ready to go.

He looks me over and settles on top. "You're so fuckin' sexy."

I make room for him in the cradle of my thighs and hook my ankles behind him. His first thrust makes me cry out and clutch his shoulders.

He pulls back, then sheathes himself inside me once more. "Fuck."

"Harder." I moan, thrusting my hips to meet him. "Fuck me. And don't go slow."

He lifts my hands over my head, guiding them to the bedrails. "Hold on." He tongues the side of my neck and kisses his way to my ear. "Don't let go, or I'll stop." His slow hip-roll is a delicious tease, but I need more.

After the day's vulnerability, I need his direction. His dominance. My veins pulse with the desire to surrender to him and everything he has to offer. As much as he brings out my boldness, he stirs the side of me that wants to be claimed. I need to belong somewhere. Belong *to* someone. *To him.* Even if it's only for a little while.

"Declan?"

He lifts his head, and his molten gray gaze finds mine. "Yeah?"

"Tie me up."

Blinking, he stares at my face like he's not sure he heard me correctly. "What?"

"I gave you your fantasy. Now, give me mine."

DECLAN

MOOD MUSINGS: WE'RE ON DIFFERENT PAGES.

I've never tied someone up. Never really had the urge. But now, with Solana on her back beneath me, begging me to fulfill her fantasy, it becomes my life's sole mission.

I scan the room. "With what?"

"A belt? A tie? I don't care. Just do it."

My dick throbs at the desperation in her voice. I rush across the room, flinging my closet door open.

My gaze settles on a dry-cleaning bag in the far corner that has been hanging there since a friend's wedding two years ago. I own one suit and one tie. And I hope to God they're together. I shred the bag open.

"Thank fuck." I snatch the burgundy silk tie draped over the hanger.

"Did you find something?"

Wordlessly, I hold up the tie and prowl across the room to her. The devious smile on her face makes my cock jerk.

She offers her wrists. "I'm yours for the taking."

"Goddamn," I groan, lifting her arms over her head once more. "You don't know what you're doin' to me."

Using care to ensure my knot isn't too tight, I quickly secure her to the bedrail. Then, because she's powerless to stop me, I lower my mouth to her honeyed pussy and lazily drag my tongue through her arousal. I moan at the addictive, musky sweet taste of her.

I've never minded giving oral sex to a woman, but with Solana, it's different. I *crave* her. Harder and deeper than any whiskey that ever crossed my lips.

"I could savor you all night."

"Declan," she gasps my name, hips writhing. "Please fuck me."

I give one more slow, deliberate lick before moving into position, resting on my forearms. My cock nudges her entrance, but I don't push inside just yet. Instead, I slant my mouth over hers.

Solana's lips open for me immediately. Groaning, I hungrily sip from her mouth. Lips and tongues twining, we kiss without coming up for air.

I slam my hips forward. She screams against my mouth and clamps her legs around me. Without breaking the kiss, I fuck her hard and deep. My body moves like pistons in a well-oiled machine. Solana arches and writhes beneath me, absorbing each thrust like she was made for my cock.

"Declan," she wails, throwing her head back. Her lush breasts on full display, she struggles against the tie. "Give it to me."

I suck one of her nipples into my mouth and deliver a brutal thrust. "Like this?"

"Yes. Oh, God, please don't stop." The plea leaves her lips on a whimper, breaking the last filament of my control.

I clutch her hips and drive into her. Again and again. And again. She clenches and shudders, then climaxes with a wail. Her pussy squeezes my shaft, milking my sanity with each spasm, until I finally explode.

"Solana!" I bellow her name and give one last thrust before I collapse in a heap on top of her. Gasping, I bury my face in her neck.

"Untie me."

I lunge for the knot and release her wrists. "You okay?"

She nods, peering up at me with wide eyes. Her kiss-swollen lips are slightly parted, quivering with each panting breath. She's flushed from the sex and scrape of my whiskers on her cheeks. And she's never looked more beautiful to me.

I kiss her temples, then rest my head on her chest. She weaves her hands into my hair, tenderly stroking the strands. Her heartbeat races beneath my ear.

"I love you, Declan." Her whispered proclamation leaves her lips on an exhale. It's so faint, I wouldn't have heard it if my ear weren't pressed to her chest.

I close my eyes and tighten my arms around her instead of a verbal response. I know I should say something, but I'm too raw from hearing the words.

Darcy never loved me. I wasn't in love with her either. We married because I got her pregnant. It was a stupid, irrational move, but I thought I was doing the right thing. Sometimes, I think everyone would've been better off if I'd just gone back to Ireland when she called to tell me her period was late. I could've sent her money every month and otherwise washed my hands of the situation. We could've been free to live our lives separately.

But that's not what happened.

When I found out I was going to be a father, I felt a surge of affection for Darcy. I vowed to support her during the pregnancy —and after—because she was giving me the most precious gift I'd ever been given. I'd mistaken my gratitude for love, but by the time I figured that out, it was too late. We went through the motions for the sake of Liam, so I couldn't even blame her when she strayed. Too bad it didn't hurt any less.

After my wife's affair, I promised myself I'd never again tell someone I loved them unless we were both on the same page.

Do I love Solana? Yes. But the problem is, I can't give her the life she deserves. I won't lead her on with a false sense of normalcy when I can't deliver. She should be with a man who will make her his everything. Someone who will treat her like the treasure she is. As long as Darcy has me under her thumb, I can't be him. More than that, I refuse to jeopardize her schooling. Her future.

I'll fuck her until we don't know our names, but as much as I want to, I can't tell Solana I love her. Bottom line, we're not on the same page because I'm living a lie.

SOLANA

MOOD MUSIC: "LOST" BY DERMOT KENNEDY

Across the table, River drums her fingernails on the formica and stares at me with an expectant look on her face. "Well?"

"Well, what?"

Her surprise visit comes on the heels of my disastrous Friday at work, about which bigmouth Will found it necessary to inform her.

So, here we are, seated in a booth at the Colebury Diner, waiting for Will to arrive for our impromptu Saturday brunch. He's running a few minutes late because one of his sisters hogged the shower as usual.

"I asked you what's wrong." Her dark eyes search mine. "Talk to me, Sunny."

"I'm waiting for Will to get here so I don't have to say it twice."

"Fair enough." She points to the window. "He just pulled in."

A few moments later, our third Musketeer approaches the table with a grimace. "Sorry. Julia took for-fucking-ever to shave her stupid legs."

River waves him off. "No worries. We waited to order."

He plops onto the bench beside me and kisses my cheek. A droplet of water from his damp hair lands on my shoulder. "Howdy, Sunny-D. Didja get any D last night?"

My ears and face heat, making River snort. "Looks like she did." She reaches across the table and tugs a strand of his hair. "How about *you*, Big Willy Barnes?"

Will grins. "No comment. Besides, I asked first." He nudges me. "So?"

I stare at my menu, feeling the weight of both their gazes. Finally, I let out a heavy sigh. "Pick your food. Then, you can interrogate me."

We peruse our menus, placing our orders when the waitress drops off a carafe of coffee. I pour myself a huge mug. Lord knows I need it. Despite being in Declan's bed, I slept like shit. My brain refused to shut off, tormenting me into the wee hours with a multitude of real and imagined problems.

"I don't hear you talking, Sunny," River murmurs, taking a swig of her coffee.

"It's everything." I yank the foil top off one of those wasteful individual creamers and dump it in my cup.

"Give us the top three on your list," Will suggests.

"Here's a big one." I gesture to River. "Are you aware your parents are considering putting Maple Haven on the market?"

I learned that juicy morsel this morning after I got home from Declan's. Shortly after my shower, River's mother came to my room to talk. Evidently, she received some complaints from other guests about loud sex. So, yeah, *that* was awkward. Then she mentioned the part about selling, and I've been sick to my stomach ever since. Even if Declan had been receptive to the idea of me staying in Vermont, exploring a future together, that concept has gone down the tubes. Without a place to live, I have no choice but to move back to New York in January.

River curls her lip. "Not if I have anything to do with it. They can't sell. That place is way too important to me. I mean, it's like my childhood memory headquarters. I'd be heartbroken. Besides,

I doubt my parents are serious. They're just tired and over-whelmed."

"Your mom sounded pretty serious when she told me."

"Because the woman hasn't had a vacation in years. Maple Haven is everything to them, and it's taking its toll. As a compromise, I convinced them to close down for a bit to do some traveling. They're spending a week in Nashville."

"When's that?" I ask.

"Last week of October. They come back November third." She squeezes my hand. "Don't worry. You can stay at the inn while it's closed. You'll just have to fend for yourself for food."

Nodding, I arrange the little packets of jelly in the metal display. "I guess I'm kinda freaked about leaving Vermont next semester."

"Why?" Will asks.

"I'm having panic attacks just *envisioning* all the panic attacks I'll have when I go back to Manhattan."

"You need to stop doing that," River chides.

"Doing what?"

"Jumping to the worst-case scenario. You create unnecessary drama for yourself. Stop making every roadblock into a catastrophe and creating problems before they exist. There's always a solution if you're willing to look for it."

"Jesus. You sound like your dad."

"Speaking of my father, I hear you've yet to make an appointment."

Here we go. "I don't have health insurance right now."

River points a manicured purple fingernail at me. "That's a cop-out. You know damn well he'll see you at no charge."

"Don't you get it, Riv? I'm tired of being everyone's burden. Your parents are already helping me out with housing. I refuse to take advantage of your dad's kindness."

"You're family, Sunny. It's not taking advantage—family helps family. We love you and we're all worried about you."

"Wait, did you tell her about the flower?" Will asks me.

"Not yet." I raise a brow at him. "You mean *you* didn't open your mouth about it when you summoned her?"

He sticks out his tongue.

"He didn't summon me."

"Yeah, okay." I meet River's gaze. "Someone left a red rose on my windshield outside the Busy Bean."

She leans in. "Dublin's finest?"

"He's from Galway. And no, it wasn't from him."

"Then, who?"

"I don't know."

She stiffens and glances at Will before staring me down once more. "Do you think it could be from *him*?"

After the incident, we made a pact to never speak the bastard's name. It aligned nicely with my "sweep everything under the rug" default mode. Even now, I can't say it.

"No clue. Besides, why would he give me a flower?"

"Because he tried to take yours?" Will offers. "I mean, that's a damn good reason to apologize to someone."

I huff out a breath. "He's not the type of man who'd apologize."

He narrows his eyes. "Does McFuck know about that situation?"

"Yeah. I told him what happened, but I didn't mention the asshole's name."

"That's probably wise. He seems like the kind of dude who'd hunt him down."

The waitress arrives with our food, and we dig in. Silence settles over the table as we devour our pancakes. Funny, my appetite seems to have suddenly gone AWOL.

River plunks her fork on the table. "What *else* is bothering you?"

"What makes you think there's something else?"

She rolls her eyes. "Oh, I dunno. Maybe the way you've been swirling the same bite of pancake in syrup for five minutes?"

I quickly stuff said bite into my mouth and watch her irritation grow.

"I hate when you shut us out."

Will wraps his arm over my shoulder. "We only interrogate you because we love you."

Too bad someone else doesn't. "I know. I'm an idiot."

"Why?" Will asks.

"Because I told him I love him," I mutter, hiding my face in my hands.

He peels my hands away, his warm chocolatey gaze meeting mine. "McFuck?"

"Who else would I be talking about?"

"When was this?" River asks.

"Last night, after we had sex."

Will squeezes my hand. "I'm assuming he didn't say it back?"

"Nope. He got really quiet for the rest of the night, and this morning. I feel like a tool. He told me our arrangement was no-strings sex from the start, you know? But I had to go and ruin it."

River touches my arm. "What makes you think you ruined anything?"

I meet her gaze. "Don't you ever get a gut feeling?"

DECLAN

MOOD MUSINGS: CALL IT ENRICHMENT.

Darcy pulls in beside me at the Busy Bean and gives me a nod as she turns off her car. We step out of our vehicles at the same time.

She walks around to where I'm standing. "What do you have planned for today?"

"Dunno yet. Why?"

"Cody's sister is coming over for dinner, so you need to bring Liam home on time."

I always do. "You're eatin' dinner right at two?" Since Solana told me her plans yesterday morning, I already know the answer, but I figure I should probably play the idiot.

"Well, no. Dinner isn't until six, but I'm sure she'll visit for a while beforehand." She tucks a strand of red hair behind her ear and chews her lip. "You know what? On second thought, I should probably give the house a quick cleaning before she comes. Why don't you keep him until five?"

"Why're you so nervous to meet his sister, Darce?"

Her green eyes flare at my observation, but she quickly recovers and arches an indignant brow. "Who said I'm nervous?"

I shrug. "You're lettin' me have three extra hours so you can clean."

"Don't get used to it," she snaps, yanking Liam's door open.

"Hi, Daddy."

"Hey, bud." I point to the rock he's holding. "What's that you've got there?"

He unbuckles his seatbelt and holds it out to me. "Me and Cody found a fossil."

"Oh, yeah?" I accept the rock and turn it over in my palm. "Where'd you find it?"

Darcy hands me a bottle. "Here's his water."

"We were digging a hole, and Cody's shovel hit it, so he let me keep it for my treasure chest. But I wanted you to see it first."

"That's very cool, bud. Maybe we'll look for some more." I toss Liam's water into my truck and turn to Darcy. "Did your other half tell you Liam needs his albuterol refilled?"

"We took care of that last week, Declan."

My lips twitch. "No need to get yourself in a snit. I'm just checkin'."

"I don't need any reminders from you." She curls her lip. "And I'm not in a snit."

You sure about that, Bitcherella? Although, Darcy's more like the evil stepmother than Cinderella. Plus, she hates birds, so she'd never survive with Cinderella's little animal friends. I smirk at the visual.

"What's so funny?" she snaps.

"Mommy, why are you being mean to Daddy?" Liam says.

I raise a brow—mimicking her signature move—and Darcy squeezes her eyes shut.

"Sweetie, I'm not being mean to your father," she clenches her jaw, "he's aggravating me."

He frowns up at her. "He's just asking about my medicine, Mommy."

Yeah, Mommy. Stick that in your pipe and smoke it.

Darcy kisses the top of his head. "I'll see you later. We have our dinner tonight, so don't get filthy."

"Yay. I'm so excited!" He jumps up and down. "Wait until you meet Solana. She's super nice. Right, Daddy?"

Fuck.

"She seems like a very nice person, yes."

Darcy eyes me. "How would *you* know?"

The hint of jealousy in her tone is rather amusing. Is it possible Cody never mentioned Solana had already met Liam and me? Or maybe Princess Darcy isn't too keen on the idea of her man having another woman in his life. Either way, it gives me joy to see her so uneasy. Maybe that makes me a dick. Whatever. It's not like I haven't been called worse.

I point to the café. "She works here, remember? Always gives Liam the best jam doughnuts."

She glares at me. "We really need to discuss the way you feed him. Unless, of course, you *want* our son to be a diabetic?"

"Nope. Can't say that's on my list of goals for him."

"You're unbelievable."

I smile and take Liam's hand in mine. "Have a wonderful day, Darcy."

She marches around the car, muttering to herself the whole way. She hops inside, slams the door, and takes off.

"Why's she mad?" Liam asks, staring after the retreating Mercedes in confusion.

"Your guess is as good as mine, bud."

After swinging by the Colebury Diner for scrambled eggs because I *don't* want to make my son diabetic, Liam and I are cruising along the highway with the windows down. I left Moira home so I could run a few quick errands before Darcy dropped him off, which worked out nicely given the extra time we have today.

I've memorized the Sunday activities on the list Solana made me, and we've been debating our options.

"Today, you get to choose where we go. I want to do somethin' special."

He perks up. "Oh. I know what we can do." Then, his face falls just as quickly. "Never mind. You won't like this idea."

"Why don't you let me know what it is, and we'll go from there?"

"Well . . ." He chews his lip. "Cody took me to this super fun golf place."

It had to be golf? I cringe inwardly but force what I think is a neutral expression. "Oh, yeah?"

"It's not the boring, old people kind, Daddy. This place is the awesomest."

I chuckle. "Mind telling me what 'boring old people golf' is?"

"The kind Cody plays where he walks a hundred miles. The only fun part about that is the golf cart, but he never lets me drive," he says wistfully.

"Tell me about the fun kind of golf."

"The balls are colorful, and each hole has something cool like a pirate ship or skeleton."

"You mean mini-golf?"

"Yes." He touches my arm. "Daddy, you don't realize this, but I'm great at golf. Cody taught me everything, but guess what?" He lowers his voice like what he's telling me is scandalous. "I'm a better golfer than him now. He's not very good at putting."

"Is that so?"

He nods excitedly. "I always get a better score. Cody tells me I'm the next Tiger Woods."

I can't help but smile. Kudos to the guy for letting Liam win and boosting his ego a bit. As much as I hate to admit it, he's scored a few points with me. I think I'm starting to understand what Solana meant by filling Liam's basket.

"Do you think you could teach me?" I ask, meeting his big,

gray eyes. "I'm probably a lot worse than Cody, but maybe you can show me how to play?"

Liam's smile is one for the record books. "We can play golf?" he squeals. "You and me?"

"Sure, bud. If that's what you'd like to do, I'm happy to learn."

"This is the best day ever."

Liam peeks out from behind a red and white windmill. "Your stance is all wrong, Daddy."

I chuckle and point to my putter and the yellow ball I selected. "Come help me out, then."

He appears at my side. "Put your feet as wide as your hips. Try not to lean forward too much. Line up your putter with the ball and use your imagination to draw a line to the hole."

I follow his instructions and adjust my stance. "Okay, now what?"

He points to the wooden sign on our left. "This hole is a par four. That means you only have four tries to get your ball in."

"Wait, you can read the sign?" I ask in amazement.

"A little. Cody told me to use the letter sounds to make a word, so I know p-a-r is par." He grins. "And we played here before, so I remember it from then."

"Does he usually teach you things? You know, like reading?"

Liam nods. "All the time. Guess what I learned last night."

"What's that, bud?"

"I was helping Cody roll up his coins, and he showed me the man on the penny. His name was Abe Lincoln, and he was a president a long time ago. Did you know that a hundred pennies is a dollar?"

I smile. "Yes, but I'm really proud of you for learning it."

He hugs me. "Thanks, Daddy. I'm super rich now." At my raised brow, he adds, "Cody let me keep all the money we rolled up. I put it in my treasure chest."

"That was nice of him."

"He does a lot of nice things for me. One time I asked why, and Cody said he made some mistakes a long time ago and wasn't nice to someone he loves, so he's trying to do better."

I wondered if Solana ever came up in conversation. "I'm glad he's kind to you."

"He said he loves me." He peers up at me. "Does that make you mad?"

"Not at all."

"Sometimes I worry about loving him back because I'm afraid it will hurt your feelings."

My breath leaves me in a rush. For a child who isn't even five, his intuition surpasses that of most adults. Liam carries the weight of the world on his shoulders with his desire to protect everyone's feelings. It's high time I do my part to take back some of the burden.

I squat and pull him into my arms. "You are the kindest little boy in the world. Everyone who meets you, loves you. I would never be mad at you for lovin' Cody—or anyone else—who treats you with kindness and respect."

"Really?" His voice, and his big, gray eyes are full of hope.

"Yes, really. Now, let's play some golf."

53

SOLANA

From my place on their cushy couch, I smirk at Cody when Darcy leaves to check on the lasagna. Looks like that's her go-to *meet-the-sister* meal.

"Why're you making a face?" he asks.

"It's funny to see you so whipped."

He raises a dark brow. "What makes you think I'm whipped?"

"You look at her like the sun shines out of her ass or something."

"She's my wife, Sunny." He chuckles and rubs his jaw. "I'm *supposed* to look at her that way."

Not that I can blame him. With thick, red hair cascading to the middle of her back, and piercing emerald eyes, Darcy is painfully gorgeous. She's a good six inches taller than me with a gymnast's figure. Her high cheekbones and porcelain skin give her a doll-like beauty I'd kill for.

She seems to adore Cody, so at least his googly-eyed stupor is reciprocated. I'd hate for him to be married to someone dismissive or cold.

It's weird to sit on the couch and observe her as not just my sister-in-law, but also my fuck buddy's ex-wife. Despite what I've heard from Declan, she seems relatively sweet. Of course, that could just be an act for her first time meeting me. Time will tell, no?

She reenters the room with a smile. "I hope you brought your appetite."

I pat my stomach. "Oh, absolutely. It smells divine."

"Thank you. Cody loves my lasagna." She settles on the couch beside me. "So, I hear you're good with numbers?"

"Yes. Math has always been one of my strengths. My major is in accounting, but I'd love to be a math teacher."

"What's holding you back?"

Anxiety. "Time and money, I suppose."

Darcy touches my arm. "You're so young. Don't stress about that stuff yet. Try to enjoy the fun parts of college."

"And they are?"

"Parties and boys, of course." She winks at Cody. "Sorry, babe."

He grimaces. "Boys bring nothing but trouble."

Darcy rolls her eyes. "So, what do you do for fun?" Her vivid green gaze makes me feel suddenly naked.

Funny you should ask. I thoroughly enjoy fucking your ex-husband. "I don't have a ton of free time, but I like making jewelry and reading romance novels and thrillers."

"Nice. Are you seeing anyone?"

"Nope. Don't have time for that, either."

"Keep it that way," Cody says with a grunt.

Darcy waves him off. "Quiet, you. Leave her alone."

My stomach flip-flops at the sound of a vehicle pulling into the driveway. I force myself to breathe and maintain a relaxed exterior.

She peeks out the window. "L.J. is home."

"He's a sweetie. Can't wait to see him again."

"That's right. I keep forgetting you've already met." She

stands and looks at the clock, then addresses my brother, "I wonder what they did for an extra three hours."

"I'm sure Liam will tell us all about it," Cody says with a warm smile.

Clomping footsteps on the front porch make my heart race. At least this time, I *know* it's Declan, but it still feels a bit déjà vu-ish. Today's difference? I'm determined to keep my cool and act normal.

He knocks.

"It's open," Cody calls.

Liam dashes inside with Declan on his tail. He's as sexy as ever, wearing jeans and a navy thermal. His sleeves are pushed to his elbows, so his tattoos and muscles are in full force. "Hello, everyone."

"Hi." I give him a cheerful wave when I really want to run into his arms. I haven't seen him since the weirdness of my declaration of love, and I miss the hell out of his hugs.

"Solana!" Liam's smile could light up the darkest room as he rushes over and wraps me in a tight squeeze.

"Hey there, Mister Liam." I ruffle his hair.

Cody chuckles and turns to Darcy. "Looks like we've been replaced."

Liam runs over and hugs his mom, then makes a beeline for Cody. "Guess what me and Daddy did!" He does a happy dance and jumps up and down a few times.

"Did you build something cool?"

"Keep guessing." He rubs his hands together with glee.

Darcy turns to Declan. "When did he eat last?" Any trace of warmth in her voice is gone now.

"A little snack about an hour ago. Why?"

"He's all wound up. How much sugar did he have?"

The subtle accusation makes me shift uncomfortably. I glance at Cody to watch his reaction, but he's too focused on Liam to notice.

Declan stares at her for a moment before speaking. "Just some apple slices after lunch. Now, if you're ready to listen, he'd like to tell you about somethin'."

She presses her lips in a thin line and turns away from him.

Cody steeples his fingers in front of his face and pretends to be deep in thought. It warms my heart to watch him with Liam. He never entertained any of my guessing games when I was little.

"Hmm . . . let's see. Did you guys go hiking?"

"Nope. We went *golfing.*"

"Really?" He looks at Declan. "Thought you hated golf?"

"So did I, but it was fun to try somethin' new together." His gaze flicks to mine for all of a millisecond, but my heart swells at the gratitude in his expression.

"Don't worry, Cody. I beat Daddy too."

Cody gestures to Declan. "I guess you'd better build some shelves for his golf trophies."

Declan's smile is genuine. "I'll see what I can do." He squats and motions to Liam. "All right, come give me a hug." Liam plows into him. "Oomph."

"Sorry, Daddy."

"Got my spleen this time, bud." He hugs Liam and presses a kiss to his cheek. "Love you to the moon and stars."

"Love you too, Daddy."

Declan gives everyone a wave and leaves.

Darcy huffs out a breath and stalks to the kitchen. I watch Cody's face as he stares after her. An unmistakable hint of sadness passes over his features. Then, he shakes his head and regains his neutral expression. "Did you go to the same golf place we go to?"

"Yeah. I didn't think Daddy would want to, but he surprised me." He looks up at him. "Are you mad?"

"Why would I be mad?"

"Golf is our thing," he whispers. "I just wanted to show Daddy how fun it is."

Cody pulls him into a hug. "I'd never be upset with you for having fun with your dad."

"But Mommy is always mad at Daddy, so I thought you hated him."

My brother tips Liam's chin up to make him look into his eyes. "Listen to me. I don't hate your dad. I'm happy you had fun with him, and I never want you feeling bad about that. Mommy's issues with him are between them, so I don't want you worrying about it, okay?"

"Okay."

"Now, go wash up for dinner."

Liam nods and heads for the bathroom I hid out in the last time I was here.

Cody glances at me, and for the first time in my life, I see our father's heart in him. I see a man who's trying to do right by the child he loves. He moves to follow Darcy into the kitchen.

"Cody."

He turns to face me. "Yeah?"

"That's how Dad would've handled it."

His faint smile is at odds with the pain in his eyes. "Sorry I didn't channel him when you were little."

The lasagna was to die for, and Darcy is back to her cheerful self. We're chatting in the kitchen while she loads the dishwasher. Liam and Cody are watching a movie in the den.

"Can I give you a hand with anything?" I ask.

She smiles. "You relax. I've got it." She points to the Keurig on the counter. "Would you like some coffee or tea?"

"No, thank you. I'm a shitty sleeper, so I try to avoid caffeine in the evenings."

"Your brother has insomnia too."

"Really?"

She nods. "He sleepwalks sometimes. It usually happens when he's stressed at work."

"Wow. I lived with him until I was sixteen, and I never knew he sleepwalked. But now that I think about it, he *did* roam the house at night." I meet her gaze. "His eyes were open, so I assumed he was awake. He always ignored me, so I thought he was angry because my screams woke him."

"No, he was probably asleep."

Maybe *that's* why he never comforted me.

"Do you still have nightmares?" Darcy asks.

"All the time."

She touches my arm. "I'm so sorry you went through that. Cody's having a hard time with the upcoming anniversary."

"Wait. My brother talks about his feelings?" I raise a brow. "Are you sure this is the same Cody?"

She gives me a thoughtful look. "He's matured since you last dealt with him. And by the way, he's really happy to have you back in his life."

"I'm happy to reconnect now that we're both in better places." I nudge her. "I get the feeling you have something to do with the new and improved version of him."

She laughs. "I'd like to think so. But let's be real—Liam is the main catalyst for his transformation. Cody *adores* him."

"I can tell. People-watching happens to be my forte." And then, because I'm sleuthy as fuck, I say, "Liam seems to have that effect on the men in his life. I've seen him at the café with his father a number of times, and *he's* just as smitten."

She stiffens. "He should be. Liam's a great little boy."

Her sudden change in demeanor intrigues me. "The dad seems pretty nice. We've chatted a bit."

Her lip curls in disgust. "He's not high on my list."

"Professional people-watcher over here, remember?"

"Don't let Declan's *Father-of-the-Year* act fool you. He's a piece of shit."

Whoa.

I must be making a face because she sighs heavily. "I'm sorry. That came out really bitchy. Just know I have my reasons."

What could Declan have possibly done to her?

"I know this is none of my business, but the way you've described him seems at odds with the guy I've met."

"Like I said, don't let him fool you." The venom in her tone gives me goosebumps. She looks over her shoulder to make sure we're still alone. "Declan has always been—and will always be—a worthless *drunk*."

I blink a few times, and my jaw drops open. "Huh?"

Darcy's eyes flash fire. "Supposedly he's sober now, but I doubt it. Next time you chat, ask him how his Monday and Friday AA meetings are going, would you?"

My heart plummets to my feet. "AA meetings?"

"Yeah. They're court-mandated, but I hear he's been skipping quite a few of them." She looks over her shoulder again. "Declan's been an alcoholic since he was fourteen. It's not entirely his fault. He grew up in an apartment over a bar in Ireland somewhere. His mom wasn't in the picture, and his father's an enabler. He was doomed from the start. Unfortunately, I can't keep him out of Liam's life, but I can at least keep toxic grandpa away. I've never allowed Liam to meet him." She twists the dishtowel in her hands. "Everyone thinks I'm a bitch, but I'm just trying to protect my child."

"From what?" I croak.

"Declan's love affair with Irish whiskey nearly killed our son."

Ice fills my chest. "I'm sorry, *what*?"

Her hands shake as she rehangs the dishtowel. "That bastard drove drunk with my baby in the car."

DECLAN

MOOD MUSINGS: THE CAT'S OUT OF THE BAG.

Today is Wednesday. I haven't heard from Solana since we texted on Saturday night. Other than when I dropped Liam off on Sunday, I haven't seen her either. I stopped by the Busy Bean on Monday. Audrey told me she'd called out sick with a migraine. I didn't reach out that night because I figured a chiming phone was the last thing she needed with a headache.

Yesterday was Tuesday—her day off. Ethan and I had tons to accomplish, but I kept my phone close by in case she called.

She didn't.

So, here I am, parked beside her Mustang in the Busy Bean's car park, trying to get the balls to go inside. I know my failure to return her declaration of love hurt her. She was so quiet afterward. I'd like to think that's the only reason for her distance, but my gut tells me I'm wrong.

I take a deep breath, climb from my truck, and head into the café. Solana is behind the counter with Will. They look up when I enter. She immediately turns away and starts stacking mugs.

What the fuck?

"Hello," I say.

Will nods. "Howdy. Coffee and a turnover?"

"Please."

"Coming right up." He plates my pastry and pours some coffee. "You want milk or cream?"

"Half and half, please." I turn my focus to Solana, who still has her back to me. She's organizing the tins of herbal tea now. "Good mornin', Solana."

"Hey," she says, without turning.

"Are you all right?"

She rearranges the tins she'd just lined up, then puts them back how she had them before. "I'm fine."

I raise a questioning brow at Will as he hands over my coffee.

"No clue," he mouths with a shrug.

I pay for my purchases and head for my usual stool. Instead of approaching me, Solana disappears into the back.

For a fucking half hour.

I wave her over when she returns. "Do you have a minute?"

"Not really, no." She points to the counter. "I'm working." In what I assume is an attempt to place some distance between us, she crosses the café to the display of artisanal honey and starts organizing them too.

She definitely knows. My scalp prickles in awareness, and the hairs on the back of my neck stand on end. As much as I prayed Darcy wouldn't run her mouth, it's crystal clear she did. That is the only logical explanation for Solana's iciness.

I launch myself off the stool and cross the café, stopping behind her. "What's wrong?"

Solana yelps, and a bottle of honey slips from her grasp. Stooping to retrieve it, she places it on the shelf with shaking hands and turns to face me. She crosses her arms over her chest. "I already told you. I'm fine."

"Don't lie to me, Solana. Did I do somethin' to upset you?" I already know the answer, but I need to hear it from her. Just like she needs to hear my truth—the whole truth—from me. *Not* the vindictive woman I divorced.

She narrows her eyes and her perfect nostrils flare. Her searing gaze is telling a million stories. None of them look good for me. "Actually, it's more what you *didn't* do. Now, if you'll excuse me, I'm on the clock," she snaps, stepping around me.

I block her path. She collides with my chest, and the mere second of contact sets my body on fire. "When you're ready to listen to my side of the story, you know where to find me."

She gives me a thumbs-up and stomps away.

This time I let her.

55

SOLANA

MOOD MUSIC: "SURROUNDED" BY CHANTAL KREVIAZUK

The church parking lot is full for a Friday night. I guess there are more closet alcoholics in Colebury than I thought. Declan's silver truck is parked in the same place it was for my tearful drive-by on Monday.

Darcy's revelation gutted me. At first, the shock and disappointment outweighed my anger. Tonight, the tables have turned. Now that I have two reconnaissance missions as confirmation, I'm fucking fuming.

I ignored Declan all week, hoping to get a handle on my emotions, but it's no use. Sometimes a girl needs a good explosion before she can let things go. Beyond that, I need to hear it from him. *He* needs to tell me about his alcoholism—and what happened with Liam—because the man I know wouldn't drive drunk.

If I'm being honest, it's not the anger that's tearing me up inside. It's the pain of betrayal. The man who I bared my body, heart, and soul to, *lied* to me.

I step on the accelerator and speed past the church. That's okay. I'll get my answers tonight.

DECLAN

MOOD MUSINGS: THE TRUTH WILL SET ME FREE. MAYBE.

It's pouring rain. I just got home from my meeting. Solana's car is in my driveway, but she's not in it. I try the handles out of habit, and for once, she locked the bloody thing.

"Solana?" I shout.

"In here." Her voice comes from inside my workshop.

Ethan must've left the door unlocked. It infuriates me to think someone could've stolen the tools we bust our arses to pay for.

I enter the shop to find Solana seated on my workbench, swinging her dangling legs like a kid on a too-tall stool. She's plugged in one of my spotlights and has an open book in her lap.

"Howdy," she says, in a tone that's far too cheerful for the conversation we're about to have. "How was your AA meeting? I didn't realize that's what the Architect Guild was calling themselves these days."

I walk over, stopping a few inches in front of her knees. "Solana, honey, I'm so fuckin' sorry."

"*Why* are you sorry, Declan?"

"Because I fucked up."

"*How* did you fuck up?" She cocks her head to the side. "Please be specific."

"Because I'm an alcoholic." The shameful words burn my throat.

"Wrong answer." She crosses her arms. "While I admit that if I'd known about your alcoholism from the get-go, I *might* have run the other direction, your addiction is not why I'm upset."

I blink. "It's not?"

"No. I'm angry you kept it from me. I bared my soul to you, but you kept something so incredibly vital to who you are, a secret. And you fucking *lied* to me in the process. That hurts, Declan." She thumps her chest. "It fucking hurts a lot."

"What was I supposed to say?"

"*Anything* would've been better than hearing about it from Darcy."

I run both hands over my face. "I can't imagine how she spun the tale."

"I'm more interested in your side of it." She grabs my wrist. "Because the man *I* know wouldn't do what she said you did."

"What did . . ." I force a swallow. "What did Darcy tell you?"

She tightens her grip. "Did you drive drunk with Liam in the car?"

I squeeze my eyes shut. "Yes and no."

"I need more than that, Declan."

I point to the house. "It's a long story. My couch would be a lot more comfortable than a sawdust-covered workbench. Let's go inside."

"Nope. Here's fine."

I hoped she'd agree to a change of scenery. I could've made her some chamomile tea. I would've built a fire to relax us and rid the damp chill clinging to my skin. Moira would've rested her head on Solana's knee while we talked, her ever-present tail thump providing the moral support I so desperately need. But no, I've got to stand in front of her while she plays the judge, jury, and executioner. Confess to my sins with a spotlight on my face. For her forgiveness, I'd do it beneath stadium lights, but that doesn't mean I'm not scared out of my mind.

I take a deep breath. "I already told you about how I grew up over a bar, but I left out the part where I started drinkin' at fourteen."

"Why would you start at such a young age?"

"I was young, stupid, and lonely. My dad worked all the time, so I had no one to turn to. Fast-forward to college. I met Ethan, and we became close. He was, and still is, the brother I've always wanted. Eth's three years younger than me, so he was still in school after I graduated, which meant I got to keep him around a little longer. Anyway, when he moved back to the States after his graduation, I missed him terribly. I felt so alone, you know?"

"I felt that way when River moved to Boston."

"Yeah, I bet. So, Ethan invited me to visit him in Colebury for a few months. Since my job situation back home wasn't ironed out yet, I figured it was my only chance to take a decent chunk of time off. A week after I arrived, I received a call from a company in Dublin, offering me an architect position with a start date three months out. I was ecstatic. Everything was coming together."

"I'm assuming this is when you met Darcy?"

"Yeah. I'd just turned twenty-eight. Ethan's older sister had a huge party, and since Kelly is Darcy's best friend, she was there. We were both drinkin' when we hooked up. After that, I didn't see her for about a month. Then she called to tell me her period was late."

"And you automatically believed you were the father?"

I rub the back of my neck. "The timeline made sense. Like I said, we were drunk when we got together, so we weren't safe about it."

"Did you ever have a paternity test?"

"Yes. After the divorce."

"And?"

"Liam is mine." I release a heavy sigh. "Getting pregnant

wasn't part of Darcy's plan. She wanted to go to law school in Boston."

"Let me guess, she resented you for tying her down?"

"Yeah. Funny, she seemed to forget how I gave up my dream job too." I shake my head at the memory of the phone call with my prospective boss. He told me I was making a terrible mistake. He was right.

"Did you resent her?"

"We resented each other. I wanted to do the right thing, so I asked her to marry me when she was about four months along in her pregnancy. I promised to take care of her and Liam. What I didn't realize is her resentment ran much deeper than she let on."

Solana cocks her head to the side. "How so?"

"Unbeknownst to me, she was in love with someone else at the time. Essentially, I fucked up *all* her plans."

"Yeah, but it takes two to tango."

"It does." A hollow laugh leaves my chest. "But Princess Darcy didn't see it that way."

"Then why'd she marry you?"

"Her family pushed her into it. Much like my ma's family, Darcy comes from tremendous wealth. Her dad was only concerned about appearances. Last thing he wanted was some punk from Ireland walkin' out on his daughter after knocking her up. Darcy agreed to marry me, but only if I stopped drinkin'."

Solana eyes me. "Did you?"

"Yeah. I was sober until Liam was six months old. Then every-thing went to hell."

"How?"

"She started workin' late several nights a week."

"Okay?" She raises a brow. "Did you hate watching your own kid or something?"

"No, I loved spendin' time with Liam."

"Then what was your issue?"

"Darcy's a paralegal in a small town. She wasn't workin' late, Solana. She was steppin' out on me."

"Holy shit. Is that confirmed?" Her eyes are wide and full of empathy.

"Liam and I took a ride one night when she was supposedly workin'. I saw Darcy's car parked at The Three Bears Motor Lodge. That was all the confirmation I needed."

I'll never forget how that felt. Deep down, I'd known she'd been lying to me for weeks, but to actually see it was a punch to the gut. What killed me most was when I saw whose vehicle was parked beside her Mercedes.

Solana touches my cheek. "What happened next?"

"We went back home. I put Liam to bed and drowned my sorrows in a bottle of whiskey. The next night, I did the same thing. And just like that, I fell back into the habit."

"Did you confront her?"

"Nope. What was the point? I was head over heels for Liam, and I took my vows seriously."

"So, I'm assuming Darcy found out you were drinking even though you'd promised not to."

"Yep. But not the way you think. One night, a few weeks after I found out about the affair, she was *workin' late* again." I rub my temples and take a few breaths. "I put Liam to bed and cracked open a bottle. A little while later, my father called with news of my ma's passing. He said she left me a ton of money and an apology letter for kickin' me out of her life." My eyes start to burn, and my throat goes dry. "It gutted me, you know? Findin' out she loved me after she died."

Solana squeezes my shoulder.

"Anyway, Darcy's affair was still goin' strong. I really needed her that night, but she wasn't there. I cried harder than I'd cried in years, but my *wife* wasn't answering her phone."

"So, you turned to alcohol again?"

"Yep. Drank a bottle and a half of whiskey."

"Is that the night you got behind the wheel?"

I nod and swipe at an escaped tear. "Liam woke up coughin' a couple hours later. I don't know how much experience you have with kids, but if you've ever heard an asthmatic baby with croup, you'll understand what I'm talkin' about."

"That cough is scary."

"For a new dad, it's fuckin' terrifying. His lips were turnin' blue, and his little heart was racing, so I panicked. And Darcy *still* wasn't answerin' her phone." I try to hold back my tears, but it's a lost cause.

"Did you call an ambulance?"

"No. Maybe I would've thought to call one if I wasn't *drunk*. Instead, I buckled Liam into his car seat, ready to drive him to the hospital myself." I don't bother to brush my tears away. "When I got to the end of the driveway, after nearly hittin' a tree, it occurred to me that I had no business drivin'. *That's* when I finally called for help." I look into her eyes. They're wet now too.

"Oh my God," she whispers.

"So, to answer your question, yes, I drove drunk with my baby in the car. Doesn't matter to Darcy—or the law—that I never left the driveway. The real problem is that my child was in danger, and I was incapacitated by choice."

"You were upset about your mother's death. Your wife should've been there to comfort you." She touches my cheek. "When did you finally get ahold of her?"

"She rolled up after the police and ambulance had already arrived, took one look at me and told the cops I was drunk. She had me arrested."

"Are you serious?"

"Dead serious. That night, I lost my marriage, my son, and my job."

"Your job?"

"At the time, I worked for Darcy's father. He was quick to toss me out. I'm sure you've heard of Jensen Lumber? Well, I was Dean Jensen's foreman for a bit."

"Holy shit. *That's* her family? Cody works for them."

"Yep. He's the foreman now. Anyway, I lost all rights to Liam for six months."

"Because you were drunk?"

I nod slowly. "They called it 'endangering the welfare of a child.' Darcy's lawyers stuck it to me any way they could. Like I told you before, I agreed to some things I shouldn't have. Case in point: it's been four years and I still only get to see Liam twelve hours a week."

"Where *was* Darcy that night?"

I really hoped she wouldn't ask this question. I sigh heavily and rub my temples. "You don't wanna know."

"Tell me."

I meet her gaze. "Sleepin' with your brother."

57

SOLANA

My lungs constrict as I try to process Declan's words. "Darcy cheated on you with *Cody?*"

He nods. "He's the guy she was in love with when we first met. He'd just broken things off with someone else at the time, so he wasn't in the mindset for a relationship then."

"How do you know all this?"

"We worked together, and Cody was a good friend of mine. He spent a lot of time at our place. Things weren't great with Darcy and me. She had terrible postpartum depression, which made it hard for her to bond with Liam. But instead of lettin' me be there for her, she turned to him. *That's* why I went crazy when I saw you in his house."

"Why didn't you tell me sooner?"

"It wasn't my place to color your opinion of your brother. Especially when he's your only living family member, and you're tryin' to fix your relationship." He cups my face. "I feel terrible about tellin' you, but I don't wanna lie anymore."

"My brother caused you a lot of pain." The words are as heavy as the lead in my chest.

"No. I caused my own troubles, Solana. When the Devil hit his second stride, I turned to alcohol." He squeezes his eyes shut. "But that's why it's so hard for me to see Cody with Liam. Darcy replaced me as her husband, and she'd replace me as his dad in a fuckin' millisecond if she could."

I wrap my arms around his neck and rest my head on his shoulder. "I'm so sorry."

"Honey, you have nothin' to apologize for."

"Yeah, I do." I meet his gaze. "I was so fucking angry with you, Declan. When she told me—"

"You should've heard it from me." He brushes his thumb over my lip. "I never meant to hurt you, but I couldn't bring myself to tell you I was guilty of doin' the same thing as the fucker who killed your parents."

"You're *nothing* like him."

"We have more in common than you think." He shakes his head. "I'm an alcoholic, Solana. Just like him."

"Yeah, but when was the last time you drank?"

"I haven't had a drop in four years. Not since that night."

"When was the last time you *wanted* to?" I ask, almost afraid to hear his answer.

"An hour ago." His eyes well with tears again. "I think about it every fuckin' day. Sometimes it's a roar. Other times, a whisper. But the cravings are always there. Alcoholism is a part of me I can't escape. I fight and fight and fight, but sometimes I get tired of fightin'. Sometimes, I'd kill for a taste of whiskey. Just one sip." He wipes his cheeks. "Then I think about everything I stand to lose."

"And you keep fighting," I whisper.

"And I keep fightin'," he repeats, cupping my face. "So, imagine how it feels to meet someone who sees me for who I am—not the mistakes I've made. A beautiful woman, with honey-blonde hair and eyes the color of whiskey, who makes me forget about the cravings whenever I'm around her." He brushes his thumb over my lips and continues in a ragged voice, "This girl lights up my life with her warm smile. Her lips remind me of a wild Irish rose and her kisses send the pain away." He stares deep into my eyes and whispers, "And then, try to imagine how it feels to tell her I'm not the man she thinks I am."

"You're better than the man I thought you were. I meant what I said to you last week. And I mean it right now. I love you, Declan." His eyes are so full of longing, it breaks my heart. "You don't need to reciprocate, but I need you to know how I feel."

Declan threads his fingers into my hair and kisses me soft and slow, then pulls back to rest his forehead against mine. "Solana, I've loved you since the night I drove you home from the Gin Mill."

"You mean when I kissed you?"

"No, before that. I'm talkin' about when you held my hand in the truck like I was your hero. You made me feel like I was worth somethin'." He swallows tightly. "And I've never had that before."

"You *are* worth something, Declan."

This time, I initiate the kiss. And there's nothing slow or tender about it. His lips part for me, and I sweep my tongue into his mouth to tangle with his. I wrap my legs around him and scoot my butt to the edge of the workbench, bringing our torsos flush. His hardening cock presses between my legs, so I roll my hips in welcome.

He groans and pulls me closer, deepening the kiss. Fire meets fire as our hurt and anger dissolve into white-hot need.

I grip the hem of his shirt and lift it. He breaks the kiss long enough to tug it off. Next, comes my sweater.

Declan unhooks my bra and tosses it onto his nearby table saw. Roughened palms cover the swells of my breasts. He kisses his way down my neck to the valley between them and then sucks on my nipples. His tongue rasps the delicate peaks before he seizes my mouth again.

My hands roam his warm skin, exploring his chest and shoulders while we kiss. But I need more. I lower myself onto my back, tugging him along.

Declan climbs up onto his workbench with a low growl and settles on top of me, knocking a hammer and container of nails to the floor. We're so lost in each other the crash doesn't even faze us.

I tug his belt free and unbutton his pants. He does the same to mine, then yanks them down over my hips. I kick them off. My lace panties follow. I shove at his jeans and boxers, springing his heavy cock.

He moans into my mouth when I stroke him. Our kisses become desperate. Tongues sliding, teeth clicking. Bodies rubbing against each other. I roll my hips, rubbing my drenched pussy on his shaft. Before I know it, he's fully seated inside me.

"Oh . . . fuck," he groans, burying his face in my neck. "Tell me to stop."

"I need you," I whisper, clinging to him.

"Need you more, honey." His ragged voice reverberates in the silent shop.

His cock hits home. Again, and again. I tighten my legs around him and dig my nails into his back as he fucks me hard and fast. I meet each driving thrust like I'll die if we stop.

"Feels so fuckin' good." His moans are a thing of beauty.

"Give me everything."

His response is incomprehensible. He knots one hand in my hair and clamps the other behind one of my legs, allowing him even deeper. "Oh, God, Solana," he rasps, clinging to me for dear life. His entire body trembles as he takes me higher and higher.

Nothing compares to this. I love this man and everything about him. His strengths, flaws, successes, and failures. Every jagged edge makes him more beautiful to me. I love him for who he is, and for everything he's not.

"So close," I wail, arching into him. My body tenses and shudders and I lose myself moaning his name. My pussy spasms around him, and he follows me into oblivion after a few more thrusts.

We're both gasping and shaking. His cock is still pulsing inside me. I keep expecting him to pull out, but he doesn't.

I run my fingers through his hair and stroke his back. His sides and butt. Everywhere my hands can reach.

He lifts his head and stares into my eyes. "I keep wantin' to give you the moon and stars, but I had it all wrong."

"What do you mean?"

"You bring them to me." He kisses my forehead. My cheeks and nose. Both temples. "I love you, honey."

DECLAN

Two Weeks Later

MOOD MUSINGS: STRENGTH IS SUBJECTIVE.

Maybe I've always been a closet voyeur, but Solana brings out my inner watchman. Why is everything she does so goddamn sexy? Right now, I'm perched on my usual stool at the Busy Bean, watching her grind some coffee beans the guy from Dark Horse delivered. I can't stop staring at her arse. She knows it too. Her little hip shimmies are totally for my benefit.

"Oh, I meant to tell you . . ." She glances over her shoulder. "Remember when you were trying to come up with gift ideas for Liam's birthday?"

"Yeah."

"I thought of the perfect thing. You said he loves collecting rocks and stuff for his treasure chest. Well, when I went over there the other day, he was outside with a magnifying glass *looking for treasure*. It was hella cute. Anyway, I think you should get him a metal detector. They make kid ones."

I perk up and pull out my phone. "That's a great idea. Where do you think I'd find that?"

"You're probably gonna have to order it online. They also make these mock archaeological dig things where the kid chisels some clay to find a bunch of polished rocks inside. Oh! And you could get him a rock tumbler. Those take a while, but it would be cool for him to see the transformation from rough to smooth."

"You mean like you've done to me?"

She flushes. "You're still the perfect amount of rough for my taste."

Images of last night surface, and just like that, I've got a hard-on in a coffee shop. Sex with Solana is the kind of toe-curling ecstasy people write novels about. She gives it back as good as she takes it, always eager to please me. I'm not used to a woman touching my body with reverence. Someone whose desperate kisses ignite and soothe. It's like she wants to be just as deep inside my body. She loves when I run the show, and while I've never considered myself an alpha male, she brings it out in me.

Last night, I had her on her hands and knees in my bed. I clutched her hips and drove my cock inside her like my life depended on it. On a whim, I swatted her arse. Her moan nearly made me come. So, I did it again. Turns out, Solana has a wild side. My hand twitches at the memory.

"What are you thinking about?" she purrs, fluttering her lashes.

I lean in close. "Makin' that pretty little arse pink."

She bites her lip. "Good. I've been thinking of ways to misbehave . . ."

"Why're you so fuckin' sexy?"

Her slow smile goes straight to my lap. "I've got a *big* incentive."

The woman loves my body—a welcome change after what I went through with the one I married.

I'll never forget the first time Darcy and I got together without alcohol involved. I went from thinking I was just a normal guy to feeling ashamed. God forbid someone come from a country where more than ninety percent of men are uncut. When Liam was born, Darcy insisted on having it done. I agreed because I didn't want someone to ever ridicule him like she did me, but sometimes I wonder about the decision. Especially now that I'm seeing someone who thinks my body is perfect. And when I told Solana about what happened, her indignance on my behalf made me love her even more.

"There's something I need to ask you," Solana says, jolting me back to the present.

"What's up?"

"Well, Darcy invited me to Liam's birthday party, but I said I had to get back to her." She nervously toys with a strand of her hair. "I wanted to check with you first. I won't go if it hurts you."

"No, it's okay." I sigh. "Liam would love havin' you there. I'm just upset I can't be part of it."

"The whole thing is so fucked up." She squeezes my hand. "I mean it, Declan. I don't want to cause you any pain."

"I know, love. Just do me a favor, would you?" My chest tightens. "Please take lots of pictures. I never get to see him blowin' out his candles."

"Don't worry, I'll take tons." She cocks her head to the side. "You should stick a candle in a cupcake or something."

"I always get him a little cake and sing to him during whatever visit is closest to his birthday. But it's not the same, you know?"

She gives a sad smile. "I'm sorry."

I hate that my family drama made the mood somber, so I attempt to change the subject. "Speakin' of birthdays . . ." Liam's party is the day after his and Solana's shared birthday.

"I don't celebrate mine, Declan."

The pain in her voice burns me. I've been trying to figure out how to acknowledge the day without reminding her of her parents' deaths.

"What do you usually do on that day?"

"I get up, choke down breakfast, and head to the cemetery. I usually sit there for a few hours and cry. Then, I head home and cry some more. There's typically a pint of ice cream involved, though."

I scrub a hand over my face. "I'm so sorry, honey."

"Please don't say that. I can't tell you how many times I've heard it in the last fifteen years."

I squeeze her hand. "This year, you're spendin' the day with me."

"I'll be miserable company," she warns.

"I'll stock up on tissues and ice cream. You can cry on my shoulder as much as you need."

"Thanks. It'll be nice to have someone hug me for a change."

"Honey, I'll hug you until my arms fall off."

I don't usually stay at the café this long, but I had some bookkeeping shite to take care of. And let's be honest—I'd rather do my paperwork here, sipping coffee with a view of Solana, than alone in my cabin.

Currently, she's in the back, helping Audrey with something. Will is behind the counter, waiting on customers with his usual friendly smile. The door jingles, and in walks some idiot I used to work with at Jensen Lumber.

Will's face turns to stone, and his relaxed posture goes rigid. "What can I get you?"

"I'd like to speak to Sunny."

The hairs on the back of my neck prickle. I sip my coffee and morph into the quiet sentry, on full alert now.

Will crosses his arms over his chest. Tall and well-built, he's now a formidable wall of muscle. "She's not here."

The other guy smirks. "You sure about that?"

"What do you want, Markle?" Will's low growl sends a chill down my spine.

"I already answered that question." The guy leans a hip against the counter. "I want to talk to Sunny."

"About what?"

"I don't think that's any of your business."

Will grips the edge of the counter and leans in. "See, there's where you're wrong. She always has been, and always will be, my business. So, I think it's best if you head on out of here and get yourself a gas station coffee."

At that moment, Solana comes out from the back, carrying a tray of scones. "Beep, beep. Coming through."

"Long time no see, Sunny Bridges."

Solana's face turns ashen, and she drops the tray onto the floor, scones flying everywhere.

59

SOLANA

I can't move or think. Air refuses to fill my lungs, and my knees buckle.

"Get the fuck out, Markle." Will positions himself between me and one of the men I hate most in this world.

"Not until Sunny and I have a little chat."

"I have nothing to say to you," I croak, hating how strangled I sound.

I always envisioned this moment happening differently. I thought the years of anger I've harbored would give me a spine of steel and enough venom to kill an army. But nope. My heart's racing, and the buzzing in my ears grows louder. Sweat coats my shaking hands, and my stomach twists into knots.

"Not even a thank you?" Phil looks me up and down, making my skin crawl. "Surely, you liked the flowers I've been leaving for you?"

Movement at the end of the counter draws my attention. Declan sips from his mug, watching the scene unfold like a lion waiting in the shadows. Despite the turbulent expression on his face, his presence calms me. Because I know he'll pounce if I need him to.

I force an even tone. "I hate roses."

"Maybe you'd enjoy a nice dinner?"

"I'm not going anywhere with you."

He narrows his eyes. "I just wanna talk."

"I already told you I have nothing to say to you."

"Look, I came here to apologize. Why're you making this so difficult?"

"I'm not interested in your apology. Or your flowers and dinners. Leave me the fuck alone." I bolt past Will and retreat into the kitchen. Clutching my chest, I lean against a wall and try to breathe.

Audrey looks up from where she's flipping bacon. "What the hell? Are you okay?"

"No."

She turns off the burner and rushes over to me. "What's wrong?"

"The rose offender strikes again."

I haven't told Declan this, but since the first flower showed up on my windshield, I've received three more. Not once have the cameras outside the café captured a clear image, but it doesn't matter—Phil's appearance confirms my suspicions. I don't know who told him I moved back to town, or why he has the sudden urge to apologize, but seeing him again brings me right back to that darkened hallway from five years ago.

Audrey's eyes widen. "Wait, another?"

I shake my head. "Not a rose. This time, he graced me with his presence."

"Do you know him?"

"Far better than I'd like to."

Nothing fucks up your day quite like coming face-to-face with your abuser. After Audrey went out front and told Phil to leave, I headed for the riverbank to clear my head. I've always found the Winooski soothing. Seated on a bench, watching the flowing water, I replay the scene and stew over everything I wish I said.

I feel Declan's approach before I see or hear him. It's always like that—a soul-deep awareness.

He settles beside me and takes my hand, interlacing our fingers. He doesn't speak for a few moments, so I savor the connection we share. The warmth of his palm, his strong grip, the way his touch anchors me.

"Was he the one?" His voice is calmer than I expected.

It doesn't make sense to lie to him when he watched the whole thing play out, so I nod.

"I used to work with the fucker."

I look up at him. "At Jensen Lumber?"

"Yep. That's the only reason I didn't intervene. He knows who I am, and it would've gotten back to Cody." His gaze burns into me. "How come you didn't tell me you've gotten more than one rose?"

"I didn't want you to worry or feel like it's your problem to solve." I stare at my hands. "You have enough on your plate dealing with Darcy."

"If you haven't noticed, I worry whether or not you want me to."

"Yeah, but I'm supposed to be the person who eases your stress."

"Solana, my feelings for you aren't some hardship, okay?"

"Okay," I whisper.

Ever since Declan confessed to his alcoholism, things between us seem to be getting more serious. The man has told me he loves me on more than one occasion, so I'm trying my hardest to trust his words. I haven't brought up New York since the day I received the first rose at the Busy Bean. I secretly hope Declan will ask me to stay in Vermont, but even if he doesn't, I don't want to ruin this closeness we share. I promised myself I'd enjoy our time together, even if it ends before I'm ready.

He lifts my hand to his lips and presses a kiss to each knuckle. "Do you want to talk about that encounter, or should I leave it alone?"

"I'm angry with myself."

"Why?"

"Because I've imagined coming face-to-face with him for years. I rehearsed a scathing speech and everything. Instead, I clammed up and panicked. He wins again."

"He didn't win, love. You stood your ground and told him to fuck off."

"But I hate that he saw my fear."

He squeezes my hand. "Honey, we can't control how other people view us. People see what they wanna see, and there's nothin' you can do to change that. Lemme tell you what *I* saw in there." He strokes my cheek. "I saw a woman with steel in her spine. One who looked her abuser in the eye and told him he lost his power. Don't discredit your strength."

It's Tuesday morning. After a hot shower, I slip into clean pajamas and settle on my bed to study. I have two tests this week. I've been neglecting my schoolwork to spend time with Declan, but today I really need to focus.

My phone chimes.

Declan: I have something for you.

Solana: Pretty sure you gave it to me last night. ;)

Declan: Haha. No, I mean an actual gift.

Solana: My birthday isn't until Saturday.

Declan: Yes, but I'm too excited to wait that long. Can I come up?

Solana: Of course!

I debate changing into more presentable clothes, but I can already hear him clomping up the steps. I smooth my hair and wait.

Declan enters my room with a wooden object tucked under his arm. "Hello, love." He closes the door behind him and settles on my bed, handing over the most exquisite jewelry box I've ever laid eyes on.

"Oh my God. Did you make this?"

"I did."

"Declan, this is beautiful," I whisper, peering at the lid. My breath catches. On the top, he's carved a large, ornate sun, which is protected by a clear layer, making the surface completely smooth. "How did you do this?"

"Tricks of the trade, honey." He touches the top. "This part is scratch resistant and easily cleaned, so you don't have to worry about anything happening to your sun. I made it from oak because I've always loved the grain."

"The color is beautiful," I say.

"The stain is called honeyed. It reminds me of you. I figure you can keep your treasures in here. Or your vibrator."

I burst into laughter. "Math makes me really horny, so you never know."

Declan grins. "I dunno much about X and Y equations, but I'll gladly give you the D."

"Oh my God, I love you." Cackling, I throw my arms around his neck. "Thank you so much. It's gorgeous."

"You're welcome." He rubs my back. "Look inside."

I lift the lid. The box contains a blueprint for a structure. "I'm confused."

"Can't have my woman gettin' distracted. You told me yourself it's too loud here sometimes. Thought you'd like your very own she-shed for studyin' purposes. We can put it on my property."

"Wait, you're building me a tiny house?" I breathe.

He nods. "That's the preliminary design. We can change whatever you like. I want you to make it yours."

My eyes fill with tears as I hug him tightly. "Thank you so much, Declan. I love you."

"Love you too, honey." He kisses my forehead. "It'll take some time to build, but Ethan and I plan to start workin' on it next week."

After staying with River's family, then in college dorms, I've wanted my own space for years. Declan has no idea how much his gift means to me, but I'm going to thank him every way I know how. I stroke him through his jeans, making him hard in an instant.

He groans. "Fuck, Solana."

"Get on the bed," I command in my sultriest voice.

He shakes his head. "You need to study."

"There's always time for a quickie." I unfasten his belt and pop the button on his jeans.

"You have a point." He kicks off his shoes and steps out of his pants. "I want this off," he growls, tugging my nightgown over my head.

His breath catches at the sight of my bare breasts. He always looks at my body with pure reverence. Almost like it's his first time seeing a naked woman. I snatch a condom from my dresser drawer and hand it to him before shoving at his boxers. He drags my panties down over my hips. Soon, we're both completely naked.

He cups my breasts, rubbing his thumbs over my nipples. "How do you want me?"

I point. "Lie on your back. I wanna ride you."

His breath rushes out of him as he rolls on the condom and

settles like I asked. Straddling his hips, I grip his cock and ease down onto him.

We both groan, and Declan clutches my waist. I love this part of sex. The glorious shift from empty and aching to being completely filled. I steady myself by gripping his shoulders. Then I start to move. Rolling and grinding my hips while I stare into his gorgeous eyes.

He skims his hands up my sides to stroke my breasts, cupping them and rolling my nipples. I love feeling the scrape of his work-roughened hands. I arch my back, pressing my breasts deeper into his palms.

"You're so fuckin' beautiful."

"And you're hella sexy."

He chuckles. "Come here. I want your mouth."

I lean forward, so our chests are touching, and take his lips in a slow, deep kiss. He tangles his fingers in my hair, kissing me with growing desperation. I match his rhythm with my hips.

"That's it, honey," he rasps. "Take what you need."

I close my eyes and let my body take over, my movements wild and frenzied. It doesn't take long before I shatter around him. *"Declan . . ."*

He rolls me onto my back and takes over, fucking me hard and fast. The headboard slams the wall with each thrust until he loses himself inside me on a guttural groan of my name.

Gasping, he buries his face at my neck. "Thanks for lettin' me give you the wood."

"Well played, O'Shaughnessy."

DECLAN

MOOD MUSINGS: WHY NOT HIT ME WHERE IT COUNTS?

Halloween is this upcoming Sunday—the day Darcy scheduled Liam's fifth birthday party. Since I'm banned from those festivities, I'll also miss out on my regular visit with him. When I asked if I could make up the hours another day, she blew me off.

Today is Wednesday. I didn't waste my breath—or time—bickering with Darcy when she dropped Liam off at the Busy Bean.

Zara is here today. Liam is telling her all about his costume party and how Solana's going to be there. Ethan is going too. Even Pen and Henry were invited. But here I am, the odd man out like always. Jealousy sears me, burning a path from my heart to the lead pit in my stomach. I know I'm not great company right now because I'm stuck in my head, busy cataloging everything so I can stew over it some more in private.

Why can't I attend? It's not like I'd be a nuisance. I'd gladly clear tables or do any job I'm given. It's not like I'd try to be chummy with anyone. I'd keep to myself and stay the fuck away from Darcy's entourage. But nope. I'm just the boy's father; I don't matter.

After the party, Darcy and Cody will take Liam trick-or-treat-ing. Another thing I miss out on. When I was young, my father used to say, "Declan, me boy, don't be that feckin' eejit who thinks life's supposed to be fair. It isn't, and the sooner you accept it, the better off you'll be."

Truer words have never been spoken.

Solana touches my hand. "Would you like more coffee?"

"No, thanks."

"You're really quiet today. Are you okay?"

"I'm grand."

"Daddy's upset he can't come to my birthday party," Liam explains.

My head jerks in his direction. I haven't said a word about the party in weeks. Clearly, I underestimate the child's intuition. So much for keeping my feelings under wraps. I'm so stunned, I don't even have a response.

Zara squeezes Liam's shoulder. "Well, your daddy loves you an awful lot, so that makes sense, right?"

He nods. "Mommy finally told me why, though."

"What do you mean?" Solana asks.

Liam takes a sip of chocolate milk and looks up at me. "Mommy said you can't come cause you're a akohaulick."

Solana and Zara gasp. The apple turnover I was holding hits my plate with a thud. My ears buzz like I'm trapped in a nest with a thousand hornets. Face heating, throat closing, I stare back at my son. There's no *way* he just said what I think he said.

"She called me a *what*?" My mouth goes dry, and the voice that leaves my lips isn't mine.

"Akohaulick." Liam's eyes widen. "Why do you look mad? What does that mean, Daddy?"

All I can do is stare. I try not to blink. The tears well in my eyes, burning like acid.

Zara grips Liam's hands, her dark gaze flashing fire. "It's not a nice thing to call someone."

Solana's still speechless, opening and closing her mouth as she stares at my face with a mixture of shock and pain.

"Then, why'd Mommy say it?" he whispers, his lip quivering.

Zara's nostrils flare. "That's a question for Mommy." She straightens and points to the back. "Do you want to see how pretzels are made? Roddy is about to start a batch."

Liam perks up. "Yes, please. Daddy, can I go with Zara?"

I nod.

Zara points to Solana and me. "Why don't you two go for a walk? I'll take over behind the counter, and Liam can hang with Roddy for a bit."

Solana removes her apron and walks around the counter. She gives my hand a gentle tug. "Let's go."

61

SOLANA

My heart breaks for Declan. We're seated on the same riverfront bench as the other day, but this time, I'm comforting him. And trying to suppress my anger on his behalf. I'd like to choke Darcy.

A tear rolls down his cheek. "I've *never* badmouthed that woman to our son."

And he wouldn't. He built the bitch a birdhouse for her birthday and makes sure Liam always has something to give her for holidays.

"I know, babe," I whisper, wiping at his cheeks. "She's an asshole."

"She fuckin' hates me *so much*, she wants to tarnish Liam's perception of me too. Turn him against me like everyone else. I'm not denyin' I fucked up when he was a baby, but I wasn't the only person in the wrong that night. Why are *my* sins the only ones that count? Why does she hate me so much, Solana?"

"I wish I had an answer for you."

"I could've told Liam his ma's an adulterer, or how vindictive she is, but I'd never do that."

"I know you wouldn't. You're a better person. Honestly,

325

Declan, I'm furious right now. I can't believe she'd say something like that to a little boy."

He looks over at me. "The sad part is, it's the truth." His hollow tone squeezes my chest. "I *am* an alcoholic. That's never gonna change."

"You're a *recovered* alcoholic."

"Recover*ing*," he corrects me. "That side of me isn't gone, Solana. It'll never go away." He points to the Gin Mill. "You don't know how badly I wanna march in there right now." He flattens his palm over his heart. "A fifth of whiskey would make the pain go away. Make me forget my ex-wife is tryin' to take my son from me."

"Alec would never serve you."

"Thank fuck for that. But if it were any other bar . . ." Fresh tears roll down his cheeks. "If it were any other bar, I can't guarantee I'd be able to stop myself."

"Yes, you would." I cup his face. "You're stronger than the alcohol, Declan. You have a lot to fight for."

"All my battles are rigged," he whispers. "I'm gettin' tired of fightin'."

"I love you and I'm here for you." I press a tender kiss to his lips. "I'm not like Darcy. I won't turn my back on you, Declan. I'll fight with you."

He clutches my shoulders, wordlessly pulling me into a hug.

I stroke his back. "I understand what it's like to deal with something you can't control, and I know how frustrating it is to feel alone. I want you to remember you're never truly alone. You'll always have Ethan, your dad, and me on your side."

"Thank you." He strokes my cheek. "What do I say to Liam?"

"I think you should cut Darcy off at the pass."

"What do you mean?"

"Make sure he hears it from you, first. Sit him down and have a serious conversation about alcohol."

He raises his brows. "Isn't he a little young for that?"

"Maybe, but Darcy started it. Besides, the schools start talking to kids about drugs at an early age. Why not have Liam's information about alcoholism come from the source. That way, when Darcy runs her mouth, he'll remember what you said. He's a smart boy, and he adores you. He'll respect you for being honest." I run my fingers through his hair. "If he has questions when he's older—or God forbid, gets himself into a situation—he'll know he can come to you."

"How'd you get to be so good at bein' a parent?" he asks.

"I had to parent myself, remember?" I straighten and meet his gaze full-on. "Listen, I know you don't wanna hear this right now, but I think you need to push back a little. Don't let Darcy bulldoze you. She has no right to badmouth you or deny you your visits. Take her ass to court and win back some of your power. Fight her, Declan."

"Honey, I wish I could."

"But you *can*." I grip his chin. "You're just afraid to."

After Declan and Liam left the Bean, the rest of my afternoon flew past. I'm headed home now. While I'm drained from the day, I need to do some studying before I go to sleep. That is, *if* I can concentrate. I seriously can't wait to study in my she-shed instead of hunched over on my bed. I still can't get over Declan's heartfelt gesture. God, I love that man.

Suppressing a yawn, I pull from the lot onto the main road. It's drizzling, so I crank my windshield wipers and turn on my high beams. I've never been a fan of the fall's shortening daylight hours because I hate driving after dark—especially in the rain. The glare from oncoming headlights fucks with my vision, and I usually see a shitload of deer on my way to the inn. Tonight's no exception.

As I drive through Colebury, I squint against the headlights coming from the car behind me. Like everything else on my crappy Mustang, my rearview mirror is busted, so I can't angle it properly. I hate tailgaters. I'm doing the speed limit, and it's not like I can go any faster in the rain. The idiot follows me along the winding roads, finally speeding past when I make the turn for Maple Haven.

I park outside the darkened bed and breakfast. River's parents are in Nashville, so thankfully, I've got the place to myself for the week. It's much easier to study without noisy guests around. Then again, I'm guilty of disturbing the peace with my carnal activities. I still can't believe I had to have that conversation with River's mother. Grimacing, I snatch my purse, lock up the Mustang, and head inside.

I pull out my phone to text Declan.

Solana: Just got home. Hope the rest of your visit went better.

His reply is immediate.

Declan: Glad you're safe. Liam and I had a long talk like you suggested. I explained alcoholism and told him I once made a stupid mistake his ma hasn't forgiven me for. I think he understands. I made sure he knows he can come to me about anything.

Solana: Excellent. I'm so proud of you!

Declan: You're one of the few. Thanks for having my back.

Solana: Always.

62

SOLANA

I didn't think it was possible for me to love Declan more until he showed up at the inn this morning with bagels, coffee, and a bouquet of sunflowers in honor of my birthday.

He drove me to the cemetery, our hands intertwined during the whole ride. We put flowers on my parents' graves, and he held me when I broke down in tears. For the first time since I lost them, I had someone to lean on. Someone who kissed my tears away and turned them into laughter.

We just arrived at his cabin for lunch. Ethan's Jeep is in the driveway.

I glance at Declan. "I thought Ethan had to help his sister with something today?"

He shrugs. "Maybe they finished early." He hops out of his truck and comes around to my side. I've learned to let him do the gentlemanly thing and help me out, even though I'm more than capable of exiting a vehicle. He opens my door and leans in, pressing a tender kiss to my lips. I moan and pull him closer, deepening the kiss because I simply can't help it.

He breaks the kiss. "Lunch first. Then we can get riled up."

"Or we can skip lunch?" I accept the hand he offers and hop out. "Maybe sample each other instead?"

Declan's low chuckle hardens my nipples. "Don't worry, honey, there will be plenty of that later."

We climb the steps to the front porch, and he ushers me inside. My jaw drops when I see Will, River, and Ethan seated at the kitchen island wearing birthday hats.

Ethan grins. "Welcome to the party, birthday girl."

"Surprise," River croons, crossing the room to me. She wraps me in a hug. "Happy birthday, Sunny. I love you so much, girl."

Will envelops us both and starts singing a boisterous rendition of "Happy Birthday."

"Who did this?" I ask, my eyes watering.

"McFuck planned the whole thing," Will announces. "He conspired with me on your day off from the Busy Bean because he wanted you to have your chosen family all in one place to celebrate your wonderfulness."

I release my friends and rush over to Declan, throwing my arms around his neck. "You don't know how much this means to me."

"You're welcome, Solana. Happy birthday, love."

I peer at the sunflower and Tigerlily floral arrangement on the island, the yellow and orange balloons scattered around the kitchen, and the assortment of my favorite foods on the table. I haven't had a birthday party since the day my parents died. Not only did Declan give me one, but the amount of detail he put into making it special for me, brings me to tears.

"I love you."

"Love you too, honey." He kisses my forehead. "Now, let's have some lunch."

I give Ethan a quick hug on my way over to the food. "Thanks for being part of this too. I'm happy to have you in my life."

"The feeling's mutual, kiddo. Happy birthday." Ethan points to a platter of deviled eggs. "Your buddy Brooke Lincoln hooked us up with food."

River rolls her eyes. "For the last time, it's *River Washington.*"

"Same difference," he says, blue eyes sparkling as he crunches on a carrot. "Body of water and a president."

She smirks. "Whatever you say, *Evan.* Pass me a napkin, would you?"

It's Halloween. I'm leaning against the counter in my brother's kitchen, peeling carrots and reminiscing about my birthday party. I still can't believe Declan went to such lengths for me. The party was wonderful. It felt so good to hang out with friends like a normal couple. There was laughter, singing, and we even had chocolate cake with a colorful fondant sun on top. Gigi from Oh, For Heaven's Cakes made it especially for me. Declan fed me bites of cake between kisses, and I sat on his lap while opening presents.

River gave me some hand-painted glass beads and a variety of jewelry-making stuff. Will had gotten ahold of my to-be-read list and ordered all the romance novels and thrillers I've been waiting to binge, including the new Elias Hawke novel everyone's talking about. I love that Will remembers the names of my favorite authors. Even Ethan had something for me—a funny T-shirt that reads, "Numbers girl." Declan's actual present is my forthcoming she-shed, but spending my day surrounded by people who love me, was the greatest gift I've ever been given.

After our friends left last night, he made me a romantic dinner of filet mignon and lobster tails, then we shared a pint of Karamel Sutra Core ice cream. Our evening culminated with slow, decadent lovemaking on his rooftop oasis. When we finished, sated and gasping, he gave me a little gift bag. Inside was a gorgeous pair of earrings—sterling silver suns with pieces of amber and tiny yellow sapphires. It was easily the best day of my life, and I have no doubt I'll be smiling for months to come.

I hum along to the Dermot Kennedy song playing in my head while thinking about my own sexy Irishman.

Cody comes up beside me with a basket of tortilla chips. "You're cheerful today."

"I'm at a birthday party. Why wouldn't I be?" I look up from the carrots and laugh. He's dressed up as Zorro—complete with an eye mask and cape. "Where's your sword?"

He grins. "The captain stole it."

Liam is wearing a Captain Hook costume, and he looks adorable with his eye patch and skull and crossbones garb. Darcy even painted a little mustache on him.

I tug on Cody's cape. "When's the last time you dressed up for Halloween?"

"Last year." He gestures to my jeans, work boots, and flannel shirt. "Where's your costume?"

"Uh, duh. This *is* my costume."

"Are you a lumberjack?"

I giggle. "I prefer lumber*jill*."

He wraps me in a hug. "Happy belated birthday. I wanted to call you yesterday, but I was in a dark place."

"I get it." *Sorta. Though it would've been nice to hear from you.*

"What did you end up doing?" His chocolate-brown eyes search my face. "I hope you weren't alone?"

"No, I spent the day with friends. It was lovely."

"Good." He lifts a hand to my earrings. "These are cool."

"Thanks." My ears and neck heat, but he doesn't seem to notice. "Once I'm done with the carrots, is there anything else you need me to help with?"

"No, we're good." He squeezes my shoulders. "I'm really glad you came. Please just have fun."

Liam gallops into the room. "Uncle Ethan is here! *And* our costumes match!" He disappears just as quickly, back outside with his friends.

Ethan and I had already discussed our plan to pretend we don't know each other, so I say, "Is Ethan Darcy's brother?"

Cody shakes his head. "No, he's the younger brother of Darcy's best friend. Ironically, he's also the best friend of Liam's dad."

"Huh. Small world," I say, as nonchalantly as I can manage. "Is Darcy an only child?" She seems like the type—one of those princesses who always gets her way.

"No, her younger brother passed away when she was thirteen."

"Oh my God. How sad."

Guilt squeezes my chest for mentally insulting her. In truth, Darcy has been nothing but sweet to me. I just can't get past how she treats Declan. As much as I want to hate her, it's hard when I see how much she loves Cody. I'm glad my brother found his person. Even if the stupid fuck stole her from another man.

It's weird. It's almost like Darcy *wants* Cody to have a relationship with me. Given what I know of her from Declan, I expected the opposite. Instead, when she overheard me mention to Cody that River's parents are considering selling Maple Haven, she said I was welcome to come live with them. After Cody left the room, Darcy confided that he always hoped I'd come back, so to this day, my old bedroom is exactly as it was. I might take a trip upstairs later to check it out.

Ethan enters the kitchen dressed like a pirate. "Ahoy, maties."

"What's up, Wilde?" Cody shakes his hand, then points to me. "Ethan, this is my little sister, Sunny." He clears his throat. "Actually, I think she prefers Solana now."

I shake Ethan's hand. "Nice to meet you, Ethan. Call me whatever you want."

"Well, shiver me timbers. She's *way* better looking than you, Bridges." His smile reaches his eyes as he presses a kiss to my hand. "Pleasure to make your acquaintance, milady." He grins at Cody. "Dude, where's your sword?"

"Liam took it." Cody jerks his thumb toward me. "My sister is off-limits."

Ethan's grin widens. "Wouldn't wanna end up in Davy Jones's Locker, now would I?"

I examine the contents of Cody's fridge and withdraw another seltzer. Orange blossom, this time. Liam skips into the room and tugs on my sleeve. "Solana, come see what Mommy and Cody got me."

I follow him outside to his cherry-red Power Wheels Jeep. "Oh, my goodness! This is so cool. I bet you can go really fast."

I desperately wanted a yellow convertible when I was younger, but Cody said it was too expensive. I'm happy to see Liam isn't being denied the cool toys.

"Uncle Ethan has a Jeep too." He hops inside and drives around me in circles.

I take a quick video to send to Declan, which I've been doing all day. I captured moments of Liam's laughter, and when he blew out his candles and opened presents. I took an action shot of him on the swings with Ethan and another little boy dressed as a pirate. I even managed to snag a cute selfie of Liam and me to add to his fridge collection.

I hope the pictures bring Declan joy and make him feel less excluded, but I know him better than that. They'll break his heart too. My guilt about being in attendance rises like a cresting wave.

The boy in the pirate costume gallops over to us. "Liam, can I ride too?"

"Sure! We can pretend it's our ship." Liam scoots aside so his friend can climb into the little Jeep with him. "Solana, this is Henry. He's my bestest friend in the whole wide world."

"Hi, Henry. Nice to meet you. Wanna know something cool?"

"Hi, Solana!" He bounces in his seat. "Yes, I love cool stuff."

"My best friend's name is William *Henry* Barnes."

Henry grins. "That *is* cool."

Liam nudges him. "Let's see if we can find more stuff for my treasure chest."

"Good idea." Hazel eyes flashing, Henry points to a handsome dark-haired man—also dressed as a pirate—conversing with Ethan nearby. "Then we can capture my dad and make him walk the plank!"

The boys release a collective "Argh!" as the motorized Jeep lurches toward the men. I hold up my phone, recording their adorableness with a wistful sigh.

"Sabotage!" Ethan yells, drawing his plastic sword and lunging into a defensive stance. The other man mimics his antics, waving a foam weapon, as the boys cackle with glee and circle them.

I tuck my phone in my pocket and make my way over. "Uh, did I miss the pirate memo, or what?"

Ethan laughs. "Nah, kiddo. It's a secret society. Those invites only go out when the fairies breach Neverland."

Henry's father snorts. "Dude, are you sure you're not seven?"

"Depends who you ask." Ethan gestures to me. "Pen, this is Solana Delgado. Solana, this is Dr. Penley Brooks, aka the dog whisperer, aka one half of Colebury's chillest bromance, aka co-founder of the single dads club."

Penley laughs. "How's *that* for an introduction?" He clasps my hand. "Nice to meet you, Solana. I'm a friend of Declan's. I've heard a lot about you."

I smile warmly at him. "Any friend of Declan's is a friend of mine."

"I'll let you two chat." Ethan waves his sword. "I've got scoundrels to catch." He darts after the Jeep, making the boys giggle and squeal.

I glance at Penley. "Declan has mentioned you many times too. Thanks for being there for him."

He smiles. "We single dads gotta stick together. Co-parenting is hard, and I'm one of the lucky ones. I hate that Declan can't be here today."

"Me too. I've been trying to take as many pictures and videos as possible, but I feel so guilty, you know? It's not fair that I get to watch the cuteness unfold when he's home alone. It makes me furious at Darcy."

"I know. I wish she'd ease up on him. Better yet, I wish Declan would fight for what he deserves."

"That makes two of us, Penley."

"I keep telling him happy endings are possible. But he's got to let go of his fear and put in the work. Declan's won so many battles already—I truly believe he'll find the courage to take back his life." He places his hand on his chest. "It'll happen. I feel it in my heart."

In the mood for a trip down memory lane, I climb the wooden staircase to my former bedroom with leaden limbs. I mosey down the hall and push the door open.

Everything is exactly how I left it. My desk, the colorful afghan my Spanish grandmother knitted. Pale yellow curtains. Posters of teenage heartthrobs I lusted after. And my bookshelf. I peruse the titles, tracing my finger along the spines. *Little Women, The Twilight Saga, The Great Gatsby, Pride and Prejudice.* Everything's here. I thumb through one of my middle school yearbooks, shuddering at the reminder of my preteen awkwardness.

I spot my old photo albums and settle, cross-legged on the fluffy carpet. The first picture brings tears to my eyes. It's from our last Christmas as a family of four. Mom looked beautiful in her red pajamas, handing out presents. Dad sat in his chair by the fireplace, a warm smile on his face. Cody lounged on the couch while I played Barbies at his feet. For the life of me, I can't remember who else was there to snap the picture, but I do remember that those were the good old days.

Before I realize it, an hour has passed since I sat down to look at pictures. Since I don't want to be rude, I tuck the photo album under my arm and head downstairs to rejoin the party.

Darcy's leaning against the kitchen counter, talking to someone who has their back to me.

"Oh, there you are," she says, as I enter the room. "We thought you headed out already."

I hold up the photo album. "No, I was just upstairs getting nostalgic. Sorry for being rude."

The man she was talking to spins around, and my heart stops.

SOLANA

MOOD MUSIC: "SEVEN DEVILS" BY FLORENCE + THE MACHINE

An invisible vise squeezes my chest. My skin crawls, and my throat goes dry. Then, the motherfucker has the balls to smile, and it turns my stomach.

Phil points to my costume. "Ah, lemme guess. You're a lumberjack?"

Darcy gestures to him. "Sunny, this is—"

"I know who he is."

Her eyes widen and dart between us. "Wait, you know each other?"

Yeah, he molested me in your basement. Looks like Cody kept that tidbit from his dear wife.

Phil swigs his beer. "We go way back. How's it going, Sunny?"

"What the fuck are you doing here?"

"Same thing as you. Celebrating the little man."

"Phil just stopped by—"

I'm out of the kitchen before Darcy can finish her sentence. I bolt through the living room and out the front door.

I collide with Ethan on the path to the driveway. "Whoa!" He takes one look at my face and grips my shoulders. "What's wrong?"

"I need to get the fuck outta here."

"Sunny, I thought you left." Cody jogs across the lawn. He'd been playing horseshoes with some men out back.

I shake free of Ethan's grip and round on my brother. "You bastard!"

A couple dozen heads turn, and Cody stops in his tracks as if I slapped him. "What's going on?"

"After everything I went through, you bring *him* around?" Angry tears stream down my cheeks. "How could you do that to me?"

"What the hell are you talking about?"

"Fuck you." I make a beeline for my car.

"Sunny, wait." Cody catches up to me and snags my waist. "Tell me what's wrong."

I slap him across the face. "Never speak to me again."

"Solana!" he thunders. "What the fuck is your problem?"

Ignoring him, I jump into the driver's seat and peel out of the driveway like a NASCAR driver.

I speed toward the inn, blinded by tears. I'm so desperate to get home, I barrel past my parents' accident site without a second thought.

Mom and Dad would've believed my story if they were alive when Phil hurt me. But they were dead. Because of me. All because I had to have a stupid birthday party.

How could Cody not protect me? How could my *brother* let that monster anywhere near me? He must truly think I lied about what happened.

So much for having my family back.

DECLAN

I finish up in my workshop and head inside, patting Moira's head as I pass. My cell chimes on the kitchen island. I'd left it in the house while working because the pictures from Liam's party had me feeling blue. I peek at the screen, shocked to discover four missed calls from Ethan.

I dial his number, and he answers on the first ring, "Dude, where the fuck have you been?"

"In the shop. Why? What's up?"

"Is Solana okay?"

I clench the phone. "What do you mean? Isn't she at the party?"

"She left over an hour ago. I've been trying to reach you. I've had a few drinks, or else I would've driven over."

"Why'd she leave?" I glance at my cell. "She hasn't reached out to me."

"Dec, she flipped the fuck out, man. Cursed at Cody and slapped him in the face."

"What happened?"

"She came flying out of the house like she'd seen a ghost.

340

Literally slammed into me. She wouldn't tell me what was wrong. Cody came running over and she screamed at him about bringing someone around. Then she hit him and left."

The hairs on the back of my neck stand on end. "Bringing *who* around?"

"Dunno, but some dude stormed out a few minutes later."

Bile rises in my throat. "What happened after that?"

"Cody and Darcy got in a fight."

"Let me go so I can check on her." I hang up and call Solana. No answer. I try two more times before shooting her a text.

Declan: Call me ASAP.

65

SOLANA

MOOD MUSIC: "PRAYING" BY KESHA

Desperate to cleanse myself of the day's drama, I stay in the shower long after the hot water is gone. My tears have finally stopped, but now I'm numb.

I turn off the faucet and wrap a towel around myself. The material is damp from the room's humidity—nothing like the towels Declan warmed for me at his cabin. My heart clenches at the thought. Maybe I should've driven there, instead, but after he had to endure a day knowing everyone was celebrating Liam's birthday without him, the last thing I wanted was to bring him more stress.

Snatching a second towel for my hair, I give it a quick fluff and step into my slippers. Tonight's plan is to fall asleep while talking on the phone with my man.

I open the bathroom door. The man in my bedroom isn't Declan. A scream rips from my throat.

Before I can move, Phil yanks me toward him. "I'd stop screaming," he slurs, licking his lips. "Nobody's gonna hear you anyway."

"How'd you get in here?" I choke out, trying to wrench myself free and keep my towel in place.

But I'm no match for his strength.

He pins my arms behind me and slams me up against the wall. "Thanks for leaving your door open for me."

"Please leave," I whimper, tears filling my eyes as the towel falls to the floor.

"Nah, baby. I thought we could pick up where we left off." His low whisper at my neck turns my stomach. "I've missed you."

His breath reeks of alcohol just like it did when I was sixteen. I struggle against his hold and manage to elbow his ribs.

"Stop fighting me, bitch," he snarls, grabbing me by the hair. His fist connects with my mouth.

Blood pours down my chin. I let out another bloodcurdling scream and keep battling him. I fight with every ounce of strength and fury I can muster. I fight for the sixteen-year-old girl he assaulted and the twenty-two-year-old woman he's about to rape. I fight for every child, woman, or man, who has ever been in my position.

And when he finally overpowers me, I squeeze my eyes shut and pray. To God. My parents. Anyone who'll listen.

An enraged roar rattles the windows. My eyes fly open as Phil is yanked away from me with a startled shout.

Declan.

"Oh, God." A sob breaks free at the sight of him.

A sickening crunch and spurt of blood follow as Declan's first punch shatters Phil's nose. He staggers backward, covering his face.

Declan's not done.

"You got away with it once," he snarls. "Hell if I let you hurt her again."

"This doesn't concern you, O'Shaughnessy."

"The fuck it doesn't." He grabs Phil by the throat, slamming him against the wall. "You ever go near her again, I'll fuckin' kill you." His voice is unrecognizable, but I've never been so happy to hear him.

"The little slut got what was coming to her." Phil takes a swing.

Declan ducks and tackles him to the floor, fists flying.

Tears of relief stream from my eyes as I crawl toward my phone while they wrestle. I dial 9-1-1 and scream for help.

Phil lands a punch on Declan's jaw.

Declan explodes.

He pummels Phil with a terrifying ferocity. Like an MMA cage fighter on steroids. Phil's body goes slack.

He's unconscious.

"Stop!" I shriek, grabbing Declan's shoulders. "You're gonna kill him!" I trip over Phil's legs and lose my balance, launching myself into my dresser.

Then everything goes black.

DECLAN

MOOD MUSINGS: IT'S NOT WHAT IT LOOKS LIKE.

"Fuck." I release Markle and rush over to Solana. Blood pours from her mouth and a gash on her temple. I gather her in my lap and place pressure on her head wound. "I've got you, honey. It's gonna be all right."

Markle's out cold, lying in a pool of his own blood. I nearly killed him. If Solana hadn't screamed for me to stop, I *would* have killed him with my bare hands. And even though I can hear the approaching sirens, I still want to.

After Solana didn't answer my *third* call, I jumped in my truck and sped over here. Terror gripped me when I saw Markle's truck parked beside her Mustang.

Then I heard her scream.

I don't know how I made it across the lawn and up the stairs as fast as I did—or how my footsteps went undetected—but thank God I made it before he went any further. I release an anguished groan and pull Solana closer. If I'd been even a minute later, he would've raped her.

I hear footsteps on the stairs, so I yank the blanket from her bed to cover her naked body.

A uniformed policeman, who looks to be about seventeen, charges into the room, gun drawn. He takes one look at the scene —two people unconscious and profusely bleeding—then points his gun at me. "Hands on your head."

"Officer, she's hurt."

"Hands on your head!" he barks.

A sick feeling washes over me as I release Solana and hold up my hands. *Jesus Christ, he thinks I hurt them both.* And the only one who can come to my defense is incapacitated. The cop is shaking like a leaf. It's probably the poor bastard's first day on the job and I must look like one hell of a criminal.

"She needs an ambulance," I say, with as much calmness as I can manage. My ears are ringing as waves of nausea slam through me. This is bad.

Really fucking bad.

"They both do. One's on the way." He narrows his eyes on me. "What's your name?"

"Declan O'Shaughnessy."

"On your feet. No sudden movements."

"I swear, this isn't how it looks, Officer." I stand up slowly, careful to keep my hands where he can see them. My eyes and throat burn.

"I hear that a lot."

Outside, another siren draws nearer. The buzzing in my ears grows louder.

The cop approaches, producing a set of cuffs from his belt. "Hands behind your back."

I lower my shaking hands and follow his order. It becomes hard to breathe as the realization of what's about to happen suddenly sinks in.

"Please let me explain," I whisper.

Cold metal encircles my wrists. "Declan O' Shaughnessy, you are under arrest for assault." My knees buckle as he nudges me toward the door. "You have the right to remain silent."

SOLANA

MOOD MUSIC: "MAKE IT RAIN" BY ED SHEERAN

It's too bright.

I lift a hand to cover my eyes, but it's connected to wires and tubes. I lurch upward, the hospital room coming into focus. "Hello?"

A red-haired nurse pops her head into the room. "Hi honey, what can I get for you?"

"Why am I here? Where's Declan?" My voice is hoarse, like I haven't spoken in years. And maybe I haven't. "What day is it?"

"It's Monday morning."

"November first?"

Nodding, she approaches my bedside. "You have quite the head wound, so it makes sense you're confused. How's your pain?"

"I'm fine." *I need Declan.* "Who brought me here?"

"You came by ambulance last night. Now that you're awake, I'll send the doctor in to speak with you." She fixes my pillow and gently touches my shoulder. "I'm afraid you'll also need to answer some questions for the police later on. I'll be right back."

I close my eyes against my throbbing headache and replay

yesterday's events. Anger bubbles in my veins. Fucking Phil Markle. An image of Declan pummeling his face flashes through my head, making my chest tighten. The beep from my heart monitor speeds up.

The nurse returns with a young man in a white coat. "Ms. Delgado, I'm Doctor Flemming. How're you feeling?"

"My head hurts, and my mouth feels like someone went overboard with lip fillers."

"I bet it does. You have fourteen stitches on your temple." He places his stethoscope in his ears. "Let me listen to your heart for a moment." He presses the cold round part to my chest. "Are palpitations common for you?"

"Yup."

"Rate your pain on a scale of one to ten, with ten being the worst."

"Six."

"That's because we only have acetaminophen on board." He glances at his watch. "You can have another dose in an hour."

"Where's my . . . boyfriend?" While we haven't used the label, it's simpler than saying my sister-in-law's ex-husband. Or my step-nephew's father.

"Do you have family we can call?" asks the nurse.

"My only living family member is dead to me, so, no." I sit up a little straighter. "I need my cell phone please."

"You didn't come in with one."

"Shit."

She touches my arm. "Don't worry, we'll let you use our phone soon."

Dr. Flemming studies my face. "All your bloodwork came back normal, but we need your permission to do a rape kit. I know this is hard but—"

"I wasn't raped. My boyfriend arrived just in time to stop it from happening. I need to speak to him." My temple throbs, so I gently probe the bandage. "Actually, can you please give me something a little stronger for the pain? I feel like my brain is gonna explode."

The nurse gives me a small smile. "Sorry, honey, but Tylenol is the safest option during pregnancy."

I blink. "What are you talking about?"

Her eyes widen, and she exchanges a look with the doctor before turning back to me. "You didn't know?"

The realization hits me like a freight train. I clutch at my chest. My breath comes in gasps. The beeping from my heart monitor goes haywire, and my vision gets hazy.

"Oh, God . . . I can't possibly be pregnant. We used protection—"

"With every sexual encounter?" Dr. Flemming touches my arm. "Because even with proper use, condoms are known to fail now and then."

An awareness niggles at my spine. There was definitely *not* a condom involved that time we went at it on his workbench. "Fuck."

It was literally the *only* time we skipped the condom, and here I am, pregnant. I don't even know when my period is due, or how far along I could possibly be.

I'm pregnant.

The words repeat themselves in my head, louder and louder. Drowning out rhyme and reason, wisdom and clarity. A wave of nausea slams into me. My hands twitch and tingle. I try to breathe, but my throat closes, tightening like there's an anaconda around my neck.

I'm twenty-two years old.

I don't have a full-time job or a permanent place to live.

I'm swimming in debt.

How am I going to raise a child when I can't even take care of myself?

"Honey, are you all right?" The nurse's face floats somewhere overhead, her voice a weird echo in my skull.

"I can't be pregnant," I croak, clawing at the sheets as the bed falls out from beneath me.

Then everything fades to black.

The next time I open my eyes, there's a man at my bedside, but not the one I hoped for. Ethan frowns at his phone, a muscle pulsing in his jaw.

"Ethan."

His weary gaze meets mine. "Hey, kiddo. How're you feeling?"

"I'm fine." I lift my head to search the room. "Where's Declan?"

He sighs heavily and takes my hand. "Declan is in jail."

Jail.

"No," I whisper, my eyes filling with tears. "He didn't do anything wrong. He saved—"

"I know. Take a deep breath. He's gonna be all right. The cops are holding him until they get more information. After you tell them what happened, I'm sure they'll release him on bail."

"How much is his bail? I'll pay it."

"Don't worry about that. I already went to the bank."

"Is Phil—"

Please don't tell me he's dead.

He squeezes my hand. "Dec broke the guy's nose and one of his eye sockets, so he's having surgery right now."

"Wait, if Declan's been *arrested* . . ."

Ethan looks down at our joined hands and squeezes mine tighter. He takes a deep breath before speaking, "Per the divorce agreement he signed, he's lost his visitation rights for at least thirty days pending a court date. Given the severity of Markle's injuries—and the legal fallout that's likely to come—probably longer."

The man I love went to jail for protecting me, and now he's lost his son—the one thing he feared most.

And, oh yeah, factor in my accidental pregnancy.

A sob rips from my throat. "I ruined his life."

"No, you didn't." He wipes my tears. "None of this is your fault, Solana. You didn't ask that fucker to attack you. Or for Dec to beat the shit out of him. He acted on instinct to protect you." He cups my face, forcing me to look at him. "Listen to me, he's not angry with you. He's devastated by the situation."

"You talked to him?"

"I was his one phone call, and he sent me to check on you." He releases my face. "I just want you to be prepared," his throat bobs on a swallow, "Dec's going to be in a very dark place for a while. He might even push you away, but please don't take it to heart. He loves you."

Don't factor me into decisions regarding your future. He was pushing me away *before* he lost his son. He'll shove me out of his life when he finds out I'm knocked up.

I open my mouth to tell Ethan, then quickly clamp it shut. I need to come to terms with it first. And as the father of my unborn child, Declan needs to hear the news before anyone else. Even if I lose him forever.

Another sob breaks free. I curl into myself as the room swallows me whole.

Ethan gently rubs my back. He's talking, but I can't hear him over my gasps and the thundering in my head.

I cry until I run out of tears. Until the ache in my chest feels like someone drove a cleaver through my ribcage.

"Just know I'll do everything I can to help him," Ethan whispers, once my breathing finally slows.

"You're not the only person who loves him, Ethan. What about his Dad? Does he know what's going on? If Declan doesn't want *my* support, he should at least know his family has his back."

Scowling, he shakes his head. "He made me promise not to tell his father."

"And you listened?"

Will hands me a glass of water. "Drink up. The doctor said you need to avoid dehydration."

"Yeah, that happens when you cry your guts out."

He settles beside me on his bed. It's Tuesday. We left Montpelier when the hospital discharged me a few hours ago. I'm currently crashing at his place since my room at Maple Haven is still considered a crime scene. I doubt I'll ever be able to sleep there again. Will's solution was for me to stay with him for a while.

Yesterday, I told the police *everything* that happened, starting with when Phil assaulted me at sixteen. During our interview, I learned Phil has a history of sexual assault. Officer Rob Nelligan, a regular at the Bean, thinks my recent tailgater was actually Phil following me home from work, a possibility I hadn't considered.

Rob brought me my phone from Maple Haven. When I saw how many times Declan had tried to contact me before he came to my rescue, I dissolved into a crying mess. Seems that's all I do now.

Ethan left me his number on a scrap of paper when he came to the hospital to visit. As promised, I programmed it into my phone and texted him when they discharged me. That's how I know Declan hasn't been released from jail yet.

Phil's still in the hospital, but I've filed sexual assault charges.

River is leaving Boston after she finishes a test this afternoon. Her parents are on their way home from Nashville. The people finally take a vacation, and it's cut short because of me. What else can I fuck up?

You'll probably fuck up your kid's life too.

Another wave of agony slams me. I've been back in Colebury for less than two months, and I've ruined everything. The one possibility Declan feared most—losing Liam—happened because of his involvement with me. I can't even reach out to him to apologize. And now there's a heartbroken little boy who doesn't get to see his dad.

"Talk to me, Sunny," Will whispers, wrapping his arms around me.

"Coming home was a mistake. I need to move back to New York."

SOLANA

MOOD MUSIC: "MY KIND OF LOVE" BY EMELI SANDÉ

River's dad, Dr. Ernest Washington, is not happy with me. It's Wednesday afternoon, and I'm seated in his home office for an impromptu appointment that's six months overdue. Light from his stained-glass desk lamp illuminates his kind face, which is currently creased with worry. His espresso-colored eyes watch me from beneath a pair of wire-rimmed glasses.

I pick at my nails. "You're being too quiet, Ernie."

"I'm waiting for the rest of your story."

"I . . . uh, I told you everything."

"Sunny, you let me read the hospital report. You're leaving out something pretty damn important."

I bury my face in my hands. "I haven't come to terms with that yet."

"Which is exactly why we need to talk about your pregnancy."

"I wanted Declan to be the first to know."

"I'm your doctor. I don't count as a regular person." He leans back in his chair. "And I'll remind you our conversations are protected by HIPAA."

"I know."

"What's your plan? Are you going through with the pregnancy?"

"Yes. There was never a question in my mind."

"Okay, so what next? How do you think Declan will receive the news?"

"Given that I've fucked up his entire life, probably not well."

"You didn't fuck up his life. His problems existed long before you came onto the scene." He rubs his jaw. "Maybe you did him a favor."

"By making him lose his son?" My voice is shrill, but unlike everyone else, Ernie knows better than to tell me to calm down.

"*You* didn't make him lose his son. His divorce agreement, as you described it to me, sounds like he got royally screwed. Maybe this ordeal will be the catalyst for change."

"I can't do anything about his legal issues with his ex-wife."

"No, but you can approach someone who's extremely influential to her." He leans forward in his chair and rests his elbows on the table. "Cody called me."

I stiffen. "He's a—"

Ernie holds up his hand. "Before you go on a tirade, let me tell you a few things. He didn't invite Phil Markle to Liam's party. In fact, your brother didn't realize Markle was there until *after* you left."

My breath rushes out of me. "Cody didn't invite Phil? Then why did he show up?"

"Darcy invited him."

My blood runs cold. "*What?* Why would she do that?"

"Cody never told her the details of what happened to you back then. Darcy ran into Markle at the grocery store that morning buying last minute supplies for the party. Since the guy works for her father, she told him to stop by. Apparently, she never mentioned it to your brother."

"And now she's letting her ex-husband sit in jail for protecting me?" I shriek, knotting my fingers in my hair. "She's going to keep Liam away from Declan for at least a month because of something *she* started?"

Ernie taps his pen on the desk. "Cody is furious with her—and himself."

"He should be."

"And he's *devastated* you got hurt." Ernie's gaze burns into me. "You need to talk to him, Sunny."

I park beside Cody's truck and glance at my battered face in the rearview mirror. The bruising on my forehead and cheek is intense, and my stitches make me look like Frankenstein. My lip is still fat. I probably should've freshened up a bit, maybe applied a pound of concealer, but I left my appointment with Ernie and drove straight here.

I march up the front path to the farmhouse and ring the bell. Footsteps approach from inside and Cody opens the door.

His jaw drops, eyes widening in horror. "Solana," he whispers. "My God, your face. The doctors wouldn't tell me anything. And you wouldn't let me see you. Are you all right?"

I step around him and walk into the kitchen. He follows a few feet behind me.

"Where's Liam?" I ask. The last thing I want is for him to see me like this or hear the shit I plan to say.

"At his grandmother's."

"Good." I cross my arms over my chest. "To answer your question, no. I am *not* all right. I haven't been all right since Mom and Dad died."

"I'm sorry I didn't believe you when you came to me five years ago."

"You should be. I was a minor, and you were supposed to be my guardian." My voice raises an octave. "Everything I told you that day was the truth. He attacked me in our basement. He made me fucking *bleed*."

Tears roll down my brother's cheeks. "I'm so sorry."

"Then you stayed friends with him."

"Not true. I distanced myself from him after you moved out."

"Bullshit."

"One of the women at work approached Dean about Phil, saying he put his hand up her skirt. Dean blew it off, and the girl quit. I overheard Phil bragging about it to one of the guys. I stopped talking to him because I realized you hadn't lied."

"When was this?"

"Three years ago," he whispers, staring at his feet.

"You found out *three years ago*?" Repressed anger courses through my veins, awakening the warrior inside me. I lift my chin and stand taller. "But you couldn't call and admit you were wrong?"

"I'm sorry."

"Your sorrys don't mean shit right now." I shake my head. "You couldn't even admit to your wife the mistakes you made? Maybe give her a clue, so she'd have the common sense to not invite that bastard over when I was here?"

"I was ashamed."

"Ashamed?" I screech. "Let me tell you something about shame. You made me feel like a filthy slut who deserved what she got."

"Solana, stop." Cody knots his fingers in his hair. "I'm sorry."

"What else are you ashamed of, Cody?" I step closer to him, my body vibrating with rage. "Tell me."

He meets my gaze but doesn't speak.

"Are you ashamed you fucked another man's wife while he was home with their sick baby? How he received news of his mother's passing and drowned his pain in a bottle of whiskey because his *wife* wasn't there to comfort him?"

My brother takes a step back. The color drains from his face.

"He knew she was having an affair for weeks. You were his *friend*." I ball my hands into fists. "I guess you treat your friends as badly as you do your family."

"Sunny, I—"

"Does it ever pull on your conscience how you did *nothing* when she threw him to the wolves for trying to get the child to the hospital?"

"He drove drunk, Sunny."

"To the end of his driveway!" My scream echoes through the kitchen. "He was scared and hurting. He called for help when he realized he couldn't drive. He's nothing like the piece of shit who killed Mom and Dad, and you know it. He got help for his problem. He turned his life around and hasn't had a drop of alcohol in four years. And let me tell you something." I advance on him, my hands shaking with fury. "He's a damn good man and an even better father, but you stood back and let her steamroll him. You watched her take his son away." I shove at my brother's chest. "You let her keep Declan away from the child he loves more than his own life."

"I don't have control over what goes on between them."

"Don't you? Tell me, what would've happened if she'd been home instead of fucking you?" I fist the material of his shirt. "What would've happened if Declan didn't check on me after Ethan called to tell him I left the party upset?"

Cody squeezes his eyes shut. A tear slides from beneath his lashes.

"You weren't there, so I'll fill you in. I came out of the shower to find Phil in my bedroom. He slapped me around, pulled my hair, and hit me in the mouth when I tried to fight him off." Tears stream down my face. "He was *seconds* from raping me, Cody. If Declan hadn't shown up . . ."

I force a swallow and draw a few deep breaths before speaking.

"He did what *you* should've done five years ago. The only reason Phil isn't dead is because I told Declan to stop hitting him when he lost consciousness." I point to my stitches. "Then I tripped and whacked my head on the dresser and knocked myself out. When the cops showed up, they arrested Declan for assaulting *us both*. They thought he hurt me. Not only is he sitting in a jail cell for protecting me, but then he finds out he can't see his kid for at least a month?" I cross my arms over my chest again. "It's unacceptable. And I'll do whatever it takes to help him."

"You two are . . . together?"

"Wake up. I love him, Cody. He's the only man I've ever loved, and the only person I've ever chosen to be intimate with. And not that it's any of your business, but we were involved *before* we knew who we were to each other. We figured it out that day in your living room when he brought Liam home from the hockey game." I wave a finger in his face. "I don't care what you—or Darcy—think about it, either."

"What do you want me to say?"

"Look, I get that you love your wife. I understand you're caught between a rock and a hard place, but I want you to love *me* enough to do what's right. Declan shouldn't have to suffer for protecting me. You say you love Liam? Then, prove it. That beautiful little boy shouldn't have to ache for his Daddy. Declan is a damn good father."

"I know," he whispers.

"I didn't get to have our Dad around, and you were a shitty replacement. I realize you're trying to make up for that with Liam, and I'm proud of you for changing, but don't do it at Declan's expense. Stop enabling your wife's cruelty. Liam is lucky to have a father—and stepfather—who adore him. Why does Darcy want to deprive him of people who love him? Why is she so hellbent on hurting Declan? Is she blind to the damage she's doing to her son? Or is she just that fucking selfish?"

A sob from the kitchen doorway turns our heads. Darcy grips the doorframe with both hands, tears streaming down her reddened cheeks. I don't know how long she's been standing there, and I don't give a flying fuck.

I glare at her. "How long are you going to punish that man for his mistake?"

She opens and closes her mouth, but nothing comes out.

I take a step toward her. "You're just as guilty for what happened that night and you know it. You should've been there for your husband instead of fucking my brother behind his back."

"Solana . . ." Cody warns.

I ignore him and march right up to Darcy. "And how *dare* you badmouth Declan to his little boy. What the hell is wrong with you? Declan makes sure Liam has something to give you for every birthday and holiday and what does he get in return? You break his heart and shit on him every chance you get."

"That's not true," she whispers.

"Then how come Liam announced to Declan that *you* call him an alcoholic? Right in front of Zara at the counter in the Busy Bean."

Cody's jaw drops open. He stares at his wife like she's a stranger.

"No five-year-old needs to hear that about his father. And a man shouldn't have to explain alcoholism to his little boy when he only gets to see the child a few hours a week."

"He did that to himself."

"No, *your* lawyers made that happen. I get it—you were angry that your life didn't go according to plan. Well, guess what?" I screech, standing on my tiptoes to get in her face. "Cody and I didn't plan on losing our parents. I didn't plan to *watch* them die. Plans change, Darcy. Liam has a father who's desperate to be in his life, but you keep him out because you're a vindictive bitch."

"Get out of my house," she whispers, her eyes going wild. "Get the fuck out."

"No problem. I was actually just leaving." I stomp past her and glance over my shoulder at Cody. "How would *our* father handle this?"

69

DECLAN

MOOD MUSINGS: THE ONLY WAY OUT IS THROUGH.

I squint against the sunlight and make my way over to Ethan's Jeep.

"Hi, honey." He hands me a turkey sub and a bottle of iced tea as I slide into the passenger seat.

"Thanks for pickin' me up."

He squeezes my shoulder. "Always."

"How's Solana?" I can't get the image of her bloodied face out of my mind. It's bad enough having to sleep on a cot in a jail cell, but to be tortured by nightmares of what would've happened to her if I hadn't shown up, is the ultimate punishment.

"She's worried about you, Dec. She thinks she ruined your life."

"No, she opened my eyes."

On Sunday night, I hit rock bottom—handcuffed in the back of the police car, sobbing like a bloody fool. The young cop had no idea what to do, so the bastard actually tried to comfort me while carting my arse to jail. By the time I got done telling him what happened, Miranda rights be damned, I think he felt bad for assuming my guilt. Didn't matter though. The blood on my hands was bright red. At least, it *was*, until Solana regained consciousness and came to my defense.

I spoke with the officer who interviewed her, and he told me about her ferocity. It gave me a glimmer of hope.

As expected, Markle pressed charges, but he immediately dropped them when Solana filed sexual assault charges against him. Another spark of hope flared to life inside me. But like with everything else in life, paperwork delayed my release.

I spent three days in jail. Every time I closed my eyes, I saw that picture Solana sent me of her and Liam—the two people on this Earth who I can't live without. While I paced my cell, my pain turned to anger. My fears and frustration gave way to fortitude. The injustice left me battle hungry.

Darcy's lawyers made it clear I can't see my son for at least a month, but this time, I'm not going down without a fight.

I glance at Ethan. "Did you get that list of lawyers from May?"

He points to a folder on the back seat. "Everything's in there. She even set up a meeting for you with one of them."

"For when?"

"Tomorrow. He's some lawyer in Montpelier they call the *King of Custody Battles*. She said he's next to impossible to get an appointment with, but she pulled some strings and called in a few favors."

"She's an angel, that May. I'll have to transfer some money—"

"Don't touch your inheritance. You said you're saving that for Liam's college fund. I'll give you the money." Ethan stares at the road, his jaw tightly clenched. "I won't let you back down from this over a few grand."

My inheritance from my ma resides in the Bank of Ireland so Darcy can't touch it. At least I was smart enough to listen to my father's advice about that. Otherwise, I'm sure she would've taken me for all I'm worth.

I certainly don't expect Ethan to shell out his own money for me. "But Wild River Retreat—"

"Our retreat won't happen without your head in the game, so I need you to get this shit with Darcy ironed out. I don't care how much it costs; we'll make it happen." He stops at a light and meets my gaze, fire flashing in his blue eyes. "If our opening gets postponed for a few years, then so be it. I'm tired of watching people fuck you over, Dec. And I'm fucking sick of you letting it happen."

"I'm done with all that, Eth. I'm ready to fight."

Even if I lose everything.

"Are you going to call Solana today?"

"I'll talk to her after I meet with the lawyer. I need some time to sort through everything."

He presses his lips in a grim line. "I think you should call her sooner. You didn't see her lying in that hospital bed, crying her eyes out, when I told her what happened to you."

I clench my jaw. "I need time."

"Don't wait too long, bro." We stop at another light. "How are the cravings?"

"Worst of my fuckin' life."

"Then maybe you should let her be there for you instead of shutting her out?" His voice is a low growl. "That woman *loves* you, Dec. Don't you dare push her away when you need her most."

DECLAN

I park down the block from the lawyer's office in Montpelier. I'm an hour early, so I stay in my truck listening to music.

Since the assault charges against me were dropped, I'm on track to get my visitation rights restored in twenty-six days. I miss Liam so much, my chest hurts. I yank my phone out of my pocket and unlock the screen. My background image is the picture of Solana and Liam. I stare at their faces for a few minutes, then glance at the manila folder on the passenger seat.

I hope I'm not making a mistake.

What happens if I go after Darcy and fail? Will she retaliate with more venom than when we divorced? Will I lose Liam completely?

The Markle ordeal blew mine and Solana's cover. Cody hasn't tried to kill me yet—or sent anyone to do it for him—but maybe he doesn't know I'm out of jail. I can't help but wonder if Darcy will use the relationship against me in court. Poor Solana doesn't need this drama in her life. I'd give anything to pull her into my arms and never let go.

I climb from the truck and march in the direction of my

appointment. My strides falter when I see the blinking Guinness sign in the window of an Irish pub on the corner. I stop in the middle of the sidewalk.

Just a taste, my addiction whispers. *It'll relax you for your meeting.*

My chest tightens, and my throat starts to burn. I stay rooted to the concrete because I can't guarantee my legs won't carry me into that pub.

Just have a beer. It won't kill you.

My palms sweat. I can almost taste the foamy head against my lips, feel the pint glass in my hand. Better yet, the weight of a crystal tumbler full of whiskey.

Just a taste.

I cross the street to the pub and venture inside, drawing the scent of booze into my lungs.

The bartender greets me with a smile. She's got a Dublin accent, but I have no idea what she's saying. All I can focus on are the bottles behind her. I settle on a stool and grip the edge of the weathered cherry bar.

The bartender speaks again, but I just stare at her. *She's a redhead like Liam. She has freckles too.* I blink a few times. She chews her lower lip, a peculiar expression on her face as she watches me closely. *Solana bites her lip like that. She'd love her yellow bracelet.*

"I'm sorry, what?" I mumble, my tongue thick in my mouth.

She raises an eyebrow like Darcy always does. "I asked if you want somethin' to drink."

My addiction ghosts through my head. *Just a sip to settle you.*

Frozen in place, I watch her face for a few beats. What would Solana think if I ordered a whiskey? It would disappoint the hell out of her. I'd be failing Liam. And myself.

"Hello?" Her impatience morphs into annoyance. She props her hands on her hips. "For feck's sake, do you want a bloody drink or not?" She glances behind me. "Make up yer mind. I got other customers waitin'."

Just a taste . . .

"No," I whisper.

"What?"

"I said, *no*." I slowly rise to my feet. "I don't want a drink."

She points to the door. "Then get the hell outta my pub."

I turn to leave and walk right into May Shipley. "May! What the hell're you doin' here?"

"What are *you* doing here?"

I rub at the back of my neck. "Nearly throwin' away four years of sobriety."

"Well, we don't want that to happen." She hooks her arm in mine. "Let's go."

I let her lead me outside, then stop when we reach the sidewalk. "May, I'm so confused. Why're you here?"

She smiles. "Ethan told me you've been struggling with the cravings, and how stressed you are about Darcy, so I thought I'd lend my support. I figured you might be more comfortable meeting Donovan if you had someone in your corner. I'm happy to sit in on your meeting and take notes. This way, I can explain anything that doesn't make sense afterward."

I wrap her in a hug. "Thank you."

"That's what friends do." May meets my gaze again. "Gotta tell you, it freaked me out when I saw you walk into that bar." She points down the block. "I literally just parked and caught the back of you in the doorway."

"I freaked myself out, May. You don't know how badly I want some whiskey."

"I understand better than you think. I know how it feels when the booze calls your name. And trust me, I was ready to step in if you ordered a drink, but you didn't need me to." She squeezes my shoulder. "I'm really fucking proud of you. And you should be proud of yourself. It takes tremendous strength to walk away from temptation."

"I have something worth fighting for."

May grins. "Glad to finally hear you say that, Declan. Now, let's make some battle plans."

My meeting with Donovan Parker was equal parts overwhelming and encouraging. He's confident I'll come out on top because, according to him, there's no reason I shouldn't have equal custody of Liam.

I'm beyond grateful May was there to ask questions on my behalf and take notes. My nerves had me so shaky, I wouldn't have been able to hold a pencil, let alone write words.

May and I grabbed lunch afterward and she explained the few points I had questions about. Donovan will get everything together, and then he'll serve the papers to Darcy sometime later this month. Overall, I'm feeling better than I have in a long time. One thing's for certain, I have the best friends a man could ever ask for.

I'm seated at my kitchen island, reading through May's notes when there's a knock at my front door. Moira barks and gallops over.

"Just a minute." I tuck my paperwork into a folder and head for the door, yanking it open.

Fuck.

Cody's dark gaze locks on to mine. "You got a minute?"

Moira growls at my side, so I grip her collar. "Depends. Are you here to finish me off?"

"No."

Wordlessly, I hold the door open and motion for him to enter. He settles on a stool in the kitchen and stares at the pictures of Liam I've got plastered on my fridge. I'm sure he notices the ones of Solana too.

I lean against the counter by the sink. Moira sits beside me. She's stopped growling, but her hackles are raised. Makes two of us.

"We need to discuss my sister."

I already planned my response for this type of confrontation while pacing my jail cell. I won't back down from him. I cross my arms over my chest. "What about her?"

"You love her." It's a statement, not a question, and not *at all* what I expected. He's not done, either. "I mean, I *know* you love her."

"Is that gonna be a problem?"

He sighs. "No, it's really not. She needs someone like you."

I blink. "Gotta tell you, Cody, this isn't how I expected this discussion to go."

"I never imagined having the conversation, period. But here we are."

"Here we are," I repeat. This takes the award for strangest encounter of my life. "So . . ."

"Listen, I . . . uh . . . I came here to thank you for protecting her. You did what I should've done five years ago. I was a fucking idiot back then. I still am, apparently."

"I won't disagree with your assessment. And I'd do it again in a heartbeat."

"I'm sorry you landed in jail."

"Well, it was kinda unavoidable. They were both unconscious and bleedin', and I was the last man standin'. But Markle is lucky I didn't slaughter him."

He rubs the back of his neck. "Sun—*Solana* came over and told me what happened. Then tore Darcy and me new assholes."

"Oh, did she, now?" Emotion tightens my throat, making my words little more than a rasp.

"Yeah, she called us out for all the shit we've done to you. Ripped our characters to shreds."

My heart swells. Whereas Darcy turned her back when I crashed and burned, Solana stuck up for me. With the cops. With her brother. And with Darcy.

I release a slow breath. "I'm sure *that* went over well."

"Darcy was pissed, but everything Solana said was true." He brushes some imaginary dirt off his knees, then looks up at me. "I'm a fucking asshole for sleeping with your wife. You and I were friends. It was a fucked-up thing to do, and I'm sorry. I know there's no excuse for my behavior, but my only explanation is that I loved her for *years* before you guys met."

"You can have her, bud. We were never right for each other. I proposed because it was the right thing to do. Won't make that mistake again."

"Darcy's an asshole for stepping out on you with me. For not being there when you found out your mom died. For turning her back when you needed help, instead of supporting you. But most of all, I *hate* how she steamrolled you with Liam." He shakes his head. "I can't apologize for her actions . . ."

"No one's askin' you to. But why does she hate me so much?" The words slipped out on their own, but that's fine—it's something I want answered.

"I really don't know, man. It never made sense to me." He swallows tightly. "But I'm sorry for my part in what she's doing to you and Liam. It's fucking bullshit, and I'm done keeping my mouth shut. You didn't deserve any of it. You're a damn good father, which Darcy knows as well as I do."

"Thanks for sayin' that, Cody. It means a lot."

"Well, it's true." He points to the pictures on my fridge. "I won't apologize for loving your son, though."

"Nor should you. And I won't apologize for lovin' your sister. Solana is the one who made me see how lucky Liam is to have you in his life. I was jealous of your bond. I thought you were tryin' to replace me."

"That was never my goal." He squeezes his eyes shut. "I fucked up with raising Sunny. Then, by the time I was ready for kids, I couldn't have them."

"Darcy castrate you or somethin'?"

He barks out a laugh. "No. I have a low sperm count."

"Fuck. Sorry. Didn't mean to be insensitive."

"It's fine. It's ironic how you spend years trying *not* to get someone pregnant, then when it comes time, you learn you weren't capable in the first place, you know?"

"I'm probably the wrong person to ask."

He snorts. "Right. Anyway, I'm not trying to replace you. I just adore the kid like he's my own."

"I get it. And I realize you're caught in the middle with Darcy—"

"I am, but I'm working on her."

"Workin' on her, how?"

"She needs to open her eyes and see how much she hurts Liam by keeping you away. I stayed out of it for years because it wasn't my business. But now that you've risked everything for my family . . ." He swallows tightly and looks up at me with wet eyes. "The least I can do is make sure my wife knows she's wrong."

Never, in a million years, did I expect to find an ally in Cody Bridges. Nor did I expect to hear his heartfelt apology.

I gesture to the space between us. "All is forgiven between you and me."

"Thank you." He rises and claps my shoulder. "Take care of my sister."

71

SOLANA

Will and I are lounging on his bed, watching a Hallmark movie in our pajamas. Well, *I'm* watching a movie. He's busy playing on his phone—probably flirting with some dude on Grindr.

Suddenly, he sits up. "Be back in a few."

"Okay. Make sure you wash your hands," I tease.

He gives me the middle finger and leaves the room. I chuckle to myself and focus on the screen. A second later, the door opens again.

"That was quick." I lift my eyes to find Declan standing in the doorway. "You're here." It comes out as a reverent whisper, the kind someone would make if the Queen of England stopped by for lunch unannounced.

"Did you miss me, love?" He speaks softly, uncertain as he crosses the room to me.

"Oh, God, I missed you so much," I whisper, jumping into his arms.

His hug is all-encompassing. Soul-soothing. We cling to each other in silence, both too emotional to speak. I thought he'd never want to hug me again, but as he runs his hands up and down my

371

back, like he's trying to make sure I'm real, I know he needs to be held too.

I pull him closer and nuzzle his neck. "I'm sorry for fucking up your life."

He kisses my forehead, the brush of his whiskers tickling my eyebrow. "No, honey, you brought me to life. Please don't apologize."

"But the one thing you feared most happened because of me. It's my fault you can't see Liam."

"It kills me to miss out on even one visit with him, but it's temporary. I'll get through it, and so will he. I just wish I'd been able to give him his birthday present before they locked me up."

"I'm sorry."

My apology earns me an ass pinch. "What did I just say about that?"

Since he doesn't want my apologies, I'll give him gratitude. "Thank you for protecting me."

"I'd do it again in a heartbeat, Solana. Turns out there are things I fear more than losin' my visitation." He tugs me closer, his breath shaky. "When I saw him put his hands on you . . ."

"Thanks for caring enough to check on me."

"Always."

After a few minutes, he pulls back to look at my face, brushing his fingers along my hairline. "When do your stitches come out?"

"Next week, I think."

"I'll go with you to your appointment."

"You will?" I breathe, wishing I could tell him about a different series of appointments I'll need to schedule. My chest tightens with the thought.

His smile's warmth reaches his eyes. "I promised your brother I'd take care of you."

"*What?* When did you talk to Cody?"

"He showed up on my doorstep a couple hours ago."

"Was he looking for a fight?"

"Not at all." He motions for us to settle on Will's bed. "He came to thank me for comin' to your rescue with Markle."

"Oh, so Cody *does* care that I'm alive?" I realize how petty I sound, but I'm still amped up from our confrontation.

"He loves you a lot, Solana." He tips my chin up. "He told me how you blew through the farmhouse like a tornado and ripped him and Darcy to shreds."

"They deserved it."

"Your brother apologized for stealin' my wife. And for doin' nothing when Darcy fucked me over with Liam."

I blink. "Holy shit. He actually listened?"

"He heard every word, and I can't tell you how much his apology meant to me. We cleared the air, and all is forgiven on my end."

"I'm so happy to hear that."

"I want you to make amends with him too. Don't harbor bad feelings because of me. He's your only family."

"I will when I'm ready."

"Fair enough." He strokes my cheek. "The thought of you standin' up to them for me, made me fall in love with you all over again."

"I love you so much, Declan. I'll do whatever it takes to help fix this mess."

"I know you will, honey. Just be patient with me. I'm tryin' to get things sorted out with Darcy. I met with a lawyer today. I'm going to fight for equal custody."

Tears fill my eyes again. "I'm so proud of you for taking that step."

"Thanks, that means a lot." He cups my face. "I should've done it years ago."

"Declan, I . . ." I force a swallow and change course. "I registered for my classes in New York. I'm moving back after Christmas."

His eyes bulge. "The fuck you are! Where the hell's this crazy talk comin' from?"

"I told you from the start I was only staying in Colebury for a semester."

"But you said the online classes were workin' out better for you." His voice is panicked and choppy. "And your focus and grades have improved."

"They have, but—"

He grips my face. "You told me you didn't wanna leave me behind."

"And *you* told me not to factor you into decisions regarding my future." I pin him with my gaze. "You said I'd be a fool to stay in Colebury."

The color drains from his face. "Solana, when I said that—" his voice breaks. "I was tryin' to keep your best interests at heart."

I cross my arms over my chest. "It felt like you were pushing me away. And it was probably for the better. I've complicated everyone's life. Look at what I did to Liam."

"You did nothin' but shower him with kindness."

"No, I made him lose his Daddy. I brought that child pain and ruined his sense of normalcy. I know how much it hurts to ache for your parents. I lost my family. I'll be damned if I destroy his. Me leaving town is the best solution for everyone."

"That's quite enough." Declan grabs my face and covers my lips with his own.

The kiss is possessive. Hungry. He tangles his hands in my hair and pulls me closer with a desperation I've never seen from him. I moan and clutch his shoulders, losing myself in the warm glide of his tongue against mine. A needy groan rumbles in his chest. Every time this man kisses me, he sets my body on fire. Every touch brings me closer to the warmth I've craved my whole life.

Declan pulls back first. "Liam adores you. You're a positive influence in his life and mine. This separation is temporary, and he's the most resilient kid in the world. You said it yourself— online courses are a better fit. You love Vermont. You're tryin' to rekindle your bond with Cody. Please don't leave us all behind, honey.

"I said not to factor me into your future because I was tryin' to protect you. At the time, I didn't think I could give you what you need or deserve because of my situation. Everything's changed now. I can, and *will*, take care of you. I want to be part of your future. Liam needs you in his life too. You aren't a complication, Solana. You're an *enrichment*." He brushes his lips over my ear. "The only thing you've complicated is me decidin' which position I wanna bend you into."

Tell him.

"There's something else we need to discuss. Something that might make you change your mind about asking me to stay."

"We can talk about anything you want, but first, I need to confess to something." He takes a deep breath. "I went to a bar in Montpelier today."

My heart sinks. "Oh, no . . ."

"I was *seconds* from orderin' a drink. But I didn't do it. Do you know what stopped me?" He rests his forehead against mine. "I didn't wanna disappoint you and Liam. You're both worth fightin' for. I can't see him for a while, so I need you more than ever." His words come out on a low growl. "Do you hear me? I love you. I *need* you. Please don't walk out on me, Solana."

I take a deep breath as courage infuses my heart. "Declan, I'm . . . pregnant."

He stills. "Come again?" he rasps, his eyes locking with mine.

"I said, I'm pregnant. The nurse told me when I woke up in the hospital. That's another reason I planned to leave—I don't want to be your burden or tie you down like Darcy did. I'm so sorry."

"Why the hell would you be sorry?" He blinks rapidly, his eyes growing wet. "*I'm* sorry I wasn't there to hold you when you found out."

"Wait, you're not mad?"

"I'm only mad at the idea of you runnin' off to New York

without me." He cups my face. "You're givin' me a gift, love. Now I have three people worth fightin' for."

My relief leaves my lips on a sob.

He kisses my forehead and each of my cheeks. "You're movin' in with me tomorrow." He slides his hand to my lower belly and flattens his palm. His warmth seeps through my pajama pants, into my soul. "How're you feelin'?"

"Really tired." I cup my breasts. "And my boobs hurt."

His lips curve into a wicked grin. "I'll massage them for you."

"I'm sure you will."

"Who else knows you're carrying?"

"River's dad is the only one. I wanted you to be the first to know."

He raises his brows. "You finally had your appointment with him?"

"Yeah, I needed some help coping with everything."

He runs his fingers through my hair. "I'm proud of you."

"Thanks. I'm going to meet with him every week so I can get a handle on my anxiety." I chew my lip. "As you can probably imagine, I'm hella nervous about pregnancy and motherhood in general. I'm only about five or six weeks along."

"It's gonna be all right, honey. I'll take good care of you. We'll figure out everything else along the way."

DECLAN

Thanksgiving Eve

MOOD MUSINGS: THERE IS SO MUCH TO BE THANKFUL FOR.

Solana's been puttering around the cabin all day, cleaning and organizing while Moira follows her from room to room. I've heard about women nesting while pregnant, but I thought that happened later on. The place wasn't messy to begin with, but now it's immaculate.

"You know," I begin, watching her from where I stand at the fridge. "When I agreed to let you help cook Thanksgiving dinner tomorrow, I wasn't expectin' a six-course meal." I point to the turkey defrosting on a platter. "This bird is gonna feed the two of us for weeks."

She laughs. "Maybe I like leftovers? You clearly don't have much experience with American Thanksgiving. There're turkey sandwiches, turkey soup, all kinds of turkey goodness in our future. I'm going to make you a lotta lunches."

My woman, the girl who's terrified of ovens, plans to cook a twenty-pound bird so she can prepare lunches for me. It warms my heart. Having her in my home is one of the best feelings in the world. Knowing she's carrying our child, a baby conceived on my workbench the day she expressed her love in spite of my addiction, is what truly brings me to my knees. Solana is everything I've ever wanted. The hope and solace I prayed for. And I can't wait to watch her belly swell. Parenthood has been my life's greatest gift. Getting to share that treasure with the love of my life, will make it even more meaningful.

After our reunion at Will's house, Ethan and I retrieved Solana's belongings from Maple Haven. I've repurposed my smaller bedroom into her office. She's been hitting the books hard in preparation for her final exams in a couple weeks. She withdrew from classes at her college in New York and registered for online courses instead. She even expressed interest in pursuing her master's degree in math.

I sat her down for a heart-to-heart about her schooling because I wanted to make sure I wasn't holding her back. She swore up and down she hated the idea of moving back to New York all along, and she's much happier with her new path. Once Wild River Retreat opens, she'll serve as our office manager and accountant, so Ethan and I can focus on expansion.

After her bruises faded, she returned to the Busy Bean and plans to work part-time throughout her pregnancy, even though I told her she doesn't need to. She'll take some extended time off once the baby comes in late June.

She still can't believe I'm truly happy about the pregnancy. Unlike when I received that news from Darcy, Solana's announcement filled me with joy and hope. I've always wanted Liam to have a sibling because I never got to experience that bond.

I miss Liam tremendously, but I'm on track to see him in six days. Donovan Parker informed me the paperwork to serve Darcy is all set for when I'm ready to proceed. Since I don't want to jeopardize my reunion, I may wait another week or so before I have it delivered.

"Stop cleanin' and sit, would you?"

Solana waves me off. "I want to get this done before I head into town to run some errands."

"I'll run your errands. What do you need?"

"It's something *I* have to do."

I cross the room and wrap her in my arms. "Once the baby comes, you'll need to let me do some things for you."

She peers up at me with those soul-stealing whiskey eyes. "No guarantees on that one, babe."

***

I'm placing logs in the fireplace when Solana returns a few hours later. She told me she'd be a while, but I wasn't expecting her to vanish for that long. I miss her when she leaves a room, so any absence is unbearable. When did I get so needy?

She texted me thirty minutes ago to let me know to expect a pizza delivery, which makes no sense, given our fridge full of food. But she's the pregnant one, so if the woman craves pizza, I won't stop her.

Moira carries on, barking like a lunatic and running in circles. The dog gets more excited for her than she ever did with me, but I get it. Solana's more fun.

She pops her head in the front door. "Hey, babe, can you do me a favor and stick Moira in the office for a minute?"

That's weird. "Sure." I call the dog over and shut her away in the room down the hall, feeling guilty as hell when she gives me those puppy eyes and whines. "I'll let you out in a bit, girlie."

I head for the door to help Solana carry whatever needs carrying, but she's already inside . . . standing next to my father.

"Dad!" I charge in their direction. "Holy fuck, you're here."

"Declan, me boy. I taught you better'n that. Watch your language in front o' the lady."

Eyes watering, I hug him tightly, questions tumbling from my lips. "How? When?"

He points to Solana. "Was all her doin'. Got a call at the pub a few weeks ago, tellin' me you were goin' through a rough patch, so we put some plans in place. I said it myself, son, planes cross the ocean from both directions. I should've never let all that time pass without comin' to see you."

"It's okay, Dad."

"No, it isn't. But all that's gonna change. I'll be makin' the trip a few times a year, or as often as you'll have me."

"What about Kings of Connacht?"

"Don't worry yourself about the pub. Siobhan can handle runnin' the place for a few days." He grins and rubs his belly. "So, I hear we're gonna eat some turkey tomorrow?"

Solana looks up at me with damp eyes. "I wanted you to have your family around for Thanksgiving, so you know how much you're loved."

"Thank you for doin' this for me," I whisper, blinking rapidly. Apparently, I *am* a crier, after all.

DECLAN

Thanksgiving Day

MOOD MUSINGS: I FINALLY UNDERSTAND.

Dad is stretched out in my recliner, watching the Thanksgiving Day parade on TV. He's never celebrated the holiday, so I want him to get the full effect. We're going to eat until we need to unbutton our pants, then watch the football game in front of a crackling fire. Solana is in the kitchen, chatting on the phone with River.

I can't find the words to adequately express my gratitude. She orchestrated the reunion when I needed it most—during Liam's absence. My home and heart are full, even though a piece is still missing.

Last night, the three of us stayed up talking until midnight. Then, Solana and I snuggled in bed while I made love to her. We did it again in the shower this morning, her back pressed to the tile, legs wrapped around me. It feels so good, having no barriers between us. I love sliding into her warm honeyed depths while whispering sweet nothings in her ear. Pregnancy enhances her libido, but I'm being more careful with her now, trading raw fuckery for decadent lovemaking. Doesn't matter to me—as long as she's in my arms I'm happy.

"Declan, would you please carve the turkey?" Solana calls, setting her phone down. "Everything else is ready."

"Sure thing, honey." I point to the dining room table. "Dad, why don't you have a seat?"

A loud knock sends Moira galloping to the front door. She barks and spins in circles like she's a tiny terrier instead of a wolfhound.

I raise a brow at Solana. "Are we expecting any other long-lost relatives?"

She shakes her head. "I invited Ethan, River, and Will for pie, but that's not until after six."

I tug the door open, sending a blast of frigid air wafting into the cabin.

Well, fuck me arseways.

"Hey, Declan." Darcy shifts her weight and peers up at me. "Can we talk?"

"Right now?" Disbelief colors my voice as I point toward my dining room. "We're just sittin' down to eat, and we've got company."

"I'll be quick." The wind gusts her hair, making her shiver.

I step onto the porch, pulling the door closed behind me. Eyeing her, I cross my arms over my chest. "What's up?"

"I owe you an explanation."

"Can't this wait?" Not only is my food getting cold, but now I am too. "It's Thanksgiving."

"That's why I'm here. You deserve to hear this story. The whole story." She lets out a heavy sigh. "My brother Danny died when I was thirteen."

"I know."

"But you don't know what really happened." She shivers again and rubs her arms. "I've never told anyone this, not even Cody, but I need *you* to understand." Her emerald-colored eyes fill with tears. "It was a Friday night. My mother was working late at the hospital. Dad was supposed to bring me to Kelly's for a sleepover, but he never came home. Instead, he called and told me I had to watch Danny because he had somewhere to be." A tear rolls down her cheek. "Whenever my father said that, it meant he was getting drunk at happy hour with the guys."

She wipes her cheeks. "Anyway, I was sick of making dinner for Danny and missing out on stuff with my friends. Dad drank all the time, so it felt like my sacrifices were a constant. That night, I'd had enough, so I walked to Kelly's without permission." Her voice breaks on a sob. "I left Danny home alone, and he drowned in the pond."

Instinctively, I place a hand on her shoulder. "I had no idea."

"No one does. My family played it off as a freak accident, and none of us talked about it." She holds a hand to her chest. "But I'll never forget that *I* killed my baby brother. He was only seven."

I squeeze her shoulder. "It was an accident, Darce. You can't hold yourself responsible."

I don't know where my compassion is coming from, why I'm standing here consoling the woman who took everything from me. And I really don't understand why she feels it's necessary to confide in me after all these years. Why now? Why show up on my doorstep when I'm supposed to be having Thanksgiving dinner with my family?

She shakes her head. "That night, in the driveway with Liam, the terror and grief came flooding back like I was standing at the edge of the pond while they looked for Danny's body. When I realized you were *drunk*, something snapped inside me. I unleashed all my guilt, and the pent-up rage I felt for my father onto you." She wipes her cheeks again. "But it was never you, Declan. I'm so fucking sorry for how I treated you. I'm sorry for cheating. I'm sorry for everything."

Never, in the length of an eternity, did I expect an apology from her. Nor did I anticipate how deeply I needed one.

"We both made mistakes that night."

"Yeah, but I've perpetuated mine for four years." She looks up at me. "This morning, when we were eating breakfast, Liam told me he didn't want to have Thanksgiving today because he didn't feel thankful. When I asked why, he cried and said he made a wish that didn't come true."

"A wish?"

"He wished to be a better boy so God would fix his family," she explains on a sob. "because he thinks it's *his* fault we got divorced."

My eyes burn, so I clench my jaw. "What did you tell him?"

"I told him you and I would work on fixing his family because he's the best little boy in the world."

I watch her face for a moment before speaking. "Will you let me talk to him if I call later?"

"That's why I'm here. I thought maybe you'd like to have him for the holiday? Do you have room at your table for one more?"

Tears fill my eyes. I can't believe this. All I've ever wanted was to spend a holiday with my son. "You're really gonna let me see him?"

She nods. "He can stay the night if you want. I'll pick him up tomorrow afternoon?"

I resist the impulse to pull her into a hug. "Thank you."

"Cody dropped me off so we could talk. He and Liam are driving around. I'll let him know to head back now." The wind gusts, and she shudders as she taps out a text. "Hopefully, he didn't venture too far."

I open the front door. "Come inside. It's too bloody cold out."

"Declan, wait." She grips my arm, and I spin around to face her. "One more thing. I want us to meet with a lawyer."

"So I can resume my regular visits sooner?"

"No. I want to amend our divorce agreement. Liam needs to see you more. Does fifty-fifty work for you? We could do every-other-weekend and figure out which weekdays work best for our schedules. I know you have meetings on Mondays and Fridays, so we can switch it up if that's better."

I wrap her in a bone-crushing hug. "I can't thank you enough, Darcy. This is all I've ever wanted."

"I know." She hugs me back. "I'm sorry I've been a super

bitch. I'm going to work on that. You're a wonderful father, Declan."

"Thank you. I couldn't ask for a better ma for our son." *Except maybe Solana.* "You're doin' a great job with him, Darce." I hold the door open. "C'mon, there's someone I want you to meet."

"I don't want to interrupt your meal."

I chuckle. "Sure, *now* you say that."

She elbows my ribs. "Solana might throw a knife at me, just so you know."

I flash her a grin. "And you'd deserve it, so make sure you duck."

We step inside, and I lead her into the dining room. Solana's eyes widen, but Dad doesn't react because he has no clue who she is. Or, if he remembers her from old pictures, his poker face is just *that* good.

"Dad, this is my ex-wife, Darcy. She popped by to discuss our son, who will be joining us for dinner."

His face lights up. "I finally get to meet the wee lad?"

"Yes." Darcy walks over to him. "Mr. O'Shaughnessy, I want to apologize for the way I've treated your son and for not letting you see Liam. It's inexcusable, but I'm trying to fix the damage I've inflicted." She gestures to me. "We've agreed to meet with a lawyer to arrange fifty-fifty joint custody."

A knock at the door signals Cody and Liam's arrival. Solana heads over to let them in.

"Daddy!" Liam bursts into the room and collides with my legs. "I missed you so much."

I squat to hug him and kiss his chubby little cheeks. "I missed you more, buddy."

"Mommy said I can sleep over!"

"Yes, she did. Mommy and I are gonna work on fixing our family. We both love you very much and want you to understand you had nothin' to do with why we split up."

"You sure?" he squeaks.

"Yes. You're the best little boy in the world. None of it was your fault. Understand?" He nods, so I take his hand. "C'mon, I want you to meet Pop-Pop." I stand and guide him around the table.

Liam eyes my dad. "Can I give you a hug?"

"I'd love that, me boy." Dad envelops Liam in his arms. "Been waitin' a long time to hug you."

"Darcy and Cody, would you like to stay for dinner?" Solana says warmly. "We've got plenty of food."

SOLANA—MOOD MUSIC: "UTOPIA" BY ALANIS MORISSETTE

I smile across the table at Cody. We make a good team. We banded together to bridge a broken family, making this the best Thanksgiving we've had since before we lost our parents.

Cody returns my smile and tilts his coffee mug in silent acknowledgment. He loops his arm around Darcy's shoulders and feeds her a bite of pumpkin pie while she listens to Will talk about an illustration he's working on.

Will is seated between River and Ethan, who keep casting furtive glances at one another. Ethan just made a comment about taking her for a ride on his motorcycle. River turned him down, but she's not fooling anyone. The matchmaker in me gleefully rolls up her sleeves.

Liam is sitting on Eamon's lap, telling him all about school, his treasure chest, salamander hunting, and all the other things little boys love to do. Eamon is smitten with his grandson, bouncing him on his knee and ruffling his hair.

Seeing Liam happy and smiling, surrounded by people who love him, makes me excited for parenthood. This beautiful, blended family gives me hope.

Beneath the table, I press my hand to my lower belly. *I can't wait to meet you, little one.*

Declan sees me do it and smiles. Then, he interlaces his fingers with mine and lifts my hand, pressing a kiss to each knuckle.

"I love you," I whisper.

"Love you more." He clears his throat. "As we all know, today's the day to celebrate gratitude. Since we're gathered here with our family and closest friends, Solana and I have a little announcement to make."

SOLANA

July 7th

MOOD MUSIC: "SWEETEST DEVOTION" BY ADELE

Declan kisses my forehead for what feels like the hundredth time since we got home from the hospital this morning. He adjusts the nursing pillow beneath my elbow and stares at our three-day-old daughter adoringly. "God, she's perfect." He meets my gaze. "Can I get you anything, honey?"

"I'm good, thanks."

"Does Olivia need her diaper changed?" The man never shies away from the dirty work.

"No, River did it before she and Will left. Ethan should be here with your dad in a couple hours."

We Skyped with Eamon from the hospital on the day Olivia was born, and he can't wait to meet his granddaughter. Since their Thanksgiving reunion, Declan and his father have come to an understanding about their past. They had a heart-to-heart about Declan's alcoholism, settling all unresolved issues between them, which makes my heart happy.

Declan straightens and looks out the window. "Liam's here." He strokes Olivia's cheek. "What do you think, sweetheart? Are you ready to meet your big brother?"

I love Liam like he's my own and can't wait to see him meet his sister.

Declan opens the front door for Liam, Cody, and Darcy, who's carrying a container of food. She turned over a new leaf, and I can honestly say I like her now. I'd even call her a friend.

"Congratulations, man." Cody claps Declan on the back. "Let me see my baby niece."

I snort. "What am I? Chopped liver?"

Darcy laughs. "Don't worry, I've got you covered. I made you guys a lasagna." She winks. "And since you did all the work pushing out that baby, you don't have to share."

"Thank you so much."

Declan holds Liam's shoulders. "Are you ready to meet your baby sister?"

"I can't wait." He jumps up and down, a wondrous expression on his face. "I love her name. Olivia May O'Shaughnessy. It's so pretty. But shouldn't her middle name be July?"

Declan laughs. "She's named for a friend of ours—not the month, silly."

May Shipley was moved to tears when Declan told her we'd chosen Olivia's middle name in her honor. And really, after all she's done for Declan, how could we not show our appreciation?

I motion for Liam to sit beside me. "Do you want to hold her?"

"Yes, please."

I gently place a sleeping Olivia in Liam's arms and look up at Declan. He has tears in his eyes as he snaps a few pictures.

"She's warm and snuggly."

I wrap an arm around Liam and kiss his forehead. "Just like you."

Everyone swoons at Liam's first big brother experience. Darcy and Cody each take a turn holding Olivia, who Liam has already nicknamed "Livi."

Cody is smitten when she grabs onto his thumb. "She's perfect," he whispers. "Look at her tiny little fingernails."

Darcy touches his shoulder. "C'mon, babe. We should get

going. They're both exhausted and Solana needs to eat some lasagna."

Cody reluctantly hands over my daughter, then he and Darcy hug me before leaving.

Declan watches their car bounce down the driveway. "All right. It's just us now." He nudges Liam. "Are you gonna give Solana your note?"

He hands over a card. "I made you something really special because I love you."

"I love you, too, sweetie."

He rubs his hands together. "It's from me and Livi, actually. Daddy helped me with the spelling, but I wrote it."

I open the card and gasp when I read the words:

DEAR SOLANA,
WE LOVE YOU.
WILL YOU MARRY OUR DAD?
LOVE, LIAM AND OLIVIA

"Oh my God. Does this mean—"

"It does." Declan slowly sinks to one knee and holds out a gorgeous ring with a scintillating, canary yellow diamond. "Marry me, Solana. Be my present, my future, my forever family. Be my wife."

"Yes." Tears fill my eyes as a wave of emotion hits me. "Oh, God, yes!"

He kisses me slowly and deeply before sliding the ring on my finger.

"Yay! My wish came true." Liam does a happy dance and hugs us both, settling beside me once more. He looks up at me with his big, gray eyes, just like his father's. "So, when do I get to have a baby brother?"

THE
END

ACKNOWLEDGMENTS

First and foremost, I want to thank **Sarina Bowen** and **Jane Haertel** for taking a chance on a newbie author like me. Yours was the very first "Yes" I've received on my publishing journey, and I will never forget that feeling. Sarina and Jane, THANK YOU for the opportunity to be part of the World of True North with so many incredibly talented authors. I'm truly humbled and grateful for the connections I've made. I wrote Afterglow during the height of the Covid-19 pandemic, when life was a big, murky pool of uncertainty. These characters gave me something to focus on, and quite honestly, helped me keep my sanity.

Dana Fisher and **Jen Liese**: Thank you for supporting me along the way. You're both amazing cheerleaders and I love you.

Kristie Wolf, remember that time you helped me trim *thousands* of words from my behemoth manuscript? Thank you for being the best alpha reader—and author bestie—a woman can have. I adore you.

Becca Hensley Mysoor, thank you for taking me under your wing. Your guidance was invaluable. I appreciate you more than you know.

Michelle O'Brien, thank you for making sure I nailed Declan's

Irishness. Your suggestions were awesome and I appreciate your willingness to help.

To my editor, **Eve Arroyo**, thank you for your eagle eyes. Thank you to **Virginia Tesi Carey** for proofreading.

A special thank you to fellow World of True North author, **Alexa Gregory**, for being an awesome beta reader and friend. I'm so happy our glitchy matrix brains connected. You are a warrior, lady!

To the **Busy Bean Authors**: Thank you for welcoming me aboard so late in the game. Your support has been a gift! I'm honored to share a series with all of you.

Last, but certainly not least, a huge thank you to **Sarina's readers** for letting me share this story with you. I hope you loved Solana, Declan, and company as much as I do.

www.ingramcontent.com/pod-product-compliance
Lightning Source LLC
Chambersburg PA
CBHW050009070726
47598CB00015B/2261